Beneath the Snows of Stalingrad

by

Frank Irgang

DORRANCE PUBLISHING CO., INC.
PITTSBURGH, PENNSYLVANIA 15222

ISBN # 0-8059-5688-9
Printed in the United States of America

First Printing

For information or to order additional books, please write:
Dorrance Publishing Co., Inc.
643 Smithfield Street
Pittsburgh, Pennsylvania 15222
U.S.A.
1-800-788-7654
or visit our web site and on-line catalog at *www.dorrancepublishing.com*

To my cousin, Lieutenant Max Frisch, a reluctant soldier in Hitler's army.

Although his prominent tombstone is located in the family plot in the village of Cham, Bavaria, Germany, his remains rest with hundreds of his comrades in a cemetery far to the east that, long ago, was desecrated, destroyed, and made into a wheatfield.

Contents

Preface

This narrative was written to be neither justification nor condemnation, but merely a witness to one of the greatest man-made tragedies of all time. It is dedicated to a generation of young German people betrayed by Fate and cheated by Time and to countless thousands never born because they were never conceived in love-beds never lain in by the warriors who rest in an eternal sleep in a land far from home, a land bathed in a cold, eerie, blue-white light that shines down from the stars upon the snow-covered steppe southwest of Stalingrad.

February 1943

M aria pulled the door closed behind her and took off her woolen jacket. Looking at the sloping ceiling of the pyramidal tent she shared with Anna, she shook her head and shivered. It was a cold day, and she was tired and her muscles ached. She had been working twelve hours a day, everyday, for four months, and there was no end in sight. The patients were arriving in greater numbers, and their wounds were more severe than when she had first come to Debrecen last summer. The fierceness of the battles had to be intensifying.

Casting a glance at her cot on the far side of the room, she saw a small piece of cardboard propped against the rise made by her pillow. Its gray color nearly matched that of the blanket. She rushed over and picked it up to see if it was hers.

Krankenschwester Maria Juergens
66ᵗʰ Evacuation Hospital
Army Command—Eastern Front

Her heart leaped into her throat. It was from Erich. The writing was less even than his usual firm hand, but she would recognize it anywhere. She turned it over, scanned it quickly, and then, brushing a lock of hair back from her face, sat down on her cot to reread it more slowly.

Stalingrad
January 20, 1943

My Darling Maria,
*   The candle burns so very low*
It may not last the night

But, oh my darling, you must know
How wonderful has been the light
                    Eternally yours,
                    Erich

She let out a gasp and sat down on the cot. Was this his last message? His words sounded so final. He had written in November that they had been surrounded but that there was not real concern. After all, they were an army of 330,000 and could readily break out. And only three weeks ago, the Fuhrer had promised to rescue them. He was bringing several divisions back from the Caucasus to drive in a wedge and rout the Russians.

She tried to reread it again, but the tears blurred her vision.

The door opened, and Anna entered. Snapping her head to fluff her long, blond hair, she tossed her sweater onto her cot. "Damn these Hungarian winters. Too damp and cold!" She looked at Maria for a response and noticed the tear-filled eyes. "What's the matter?" she asked, her voice echoing concern. "You've been crying."

Maria handed her the card.

Anna was four years older than Maria and much less sensitive. Of sturdy peasant stock, her husband had been killed in Poland. She had joined the army partly out of patriotism but primarily to get away from her mother-in-law.

Slowly she read the card and then focused her blue eyes on her friend. Things were going badly at Stalingrad, she knew that. There were rumors the Sixth Army was going to be written off—abandoned. But they were just rumors. Besides, this was not the time to increase Maria's grief. "We've had troops surrounded before and they've broken out," she said. "Think of Staraya Russa." She placed a hand on Maria's shoulder. "He'll be all right. Just wait and see." She paused and then added, "Besides, General Schmidt, the Sixth Army's Chief of Staff said, 'We're surrounded now but in no danger. The Sixth Army will still be in position at Easter.'"

Maria looked up and smiled. "Lord, I hope so." She dabbed her eyes. "Thank you." Although she had heard rumors that the German forces at Stalingrad had already surrendered, Anna's words made her feel better. After all, she reasoned, Anna was much more knowledgeable about the war. She had been involved in it longer and avidly read the news accounts of battle fronts. She was probably right, but there was a gnawing, underlying fear that would not go away.

2

Journey Home

Heat waves radiated upward from the black surface of the macadam ribbon that meandered leisurely through the gently rolling countryside. It was an excellent day for walking—warm sunshine, soft breezes, and a seldom traveled road that permitted the mind to wander instead of thinking about the problems of life.

Erich halted, removed his green Alpine hat, and looked back at the afternoon sun hanging midway in the bright July sky. The knapsack, resting high on his well-built shoulders, was beginning to feel heavy. As he watched a butterfly flit past lazily, he took in a deep breath that filled his nostrils with the scent of wild roses, pine needles, and the decaying residue of the forest. He estimated he had covered twenty-five kilometers. In another hour he should reach Rothenburg, where he could spend the night. Turning on his heels, he started walking again, his gray *lederhosen* scuffing a dull cadence with each resilient step.

At a small, fern-lined brook, he paused and looked at the clear water riffling across its pebble-strewn bottom. It seemed to extend an invitation to cool the sweaty soles of his feet. Sitting down on a rock that protruded over the water, he removed his knapsack and then his shoes and stockings.

The water felt shockingly cold until the briskness became a sedative and he relaxed. He looked at the distortions of his reflection in the rippling water and watched several tadpoles stir the mud in a small eddy pool. Across the stream, a browsing deer was watching in a frozen stance. Suddenly the animal's ears rotated, following the drone of a heavy military aircraft overhead.

After a few minutes, Erich withdrew his feet and placed them on an adjacent rock to dry. Yawning, he leaned back and stared idly skyward, wondering what the future held. He thought of the booming economy, the rising nationalism, the Hitler Youth, and the increasing number of clicking, hobnail jack boots. Perhaps he would be called to serve. At least he had completed two years of medicine at Heidelberg University. If he was allowed to finish, he knew he would be a good physician. Then he could establish a large practice in Munich. His thinking shifted to Holzheim and the soft, white arms of Maria. Suddenly he was anxious to move on, to settle for today and let tomorrow take care of itself.

He topped a slight rise and looked down on a large, green valley. Nestled amid its trees and fields was the town of Rothenburg, a seemingly unbroken cluster of dull red tile roofs tightly confined by a massive yellow wall. As he approached, several children who had been playing along the outer fringes of the moat came out to greet him, and a fuzzy puppy bounding clumsily sniffed his shoes, then galloped playfully alongside.

Crossing the bridge, he passed beneath the spiked bottom of a drop-gate that still hung menacingly between the entrance towers. As he walked slowly along the crooked cobblestone street, the children gradually left him, disappearing down numerous narrow side streets and passages. Looking up, he saw an ornately carved sign: THE GOLDEN KEY.

He pushed open the sluggish oak door and walked over to sit down on the slick bench of a massive plank table. Glancing around the room, he noted two smaller tables occupied by robust older men who were drinking beer from large steins. The heavy air smelled of tobacco smoke, beer, and cabbage. A large, red-faced waiter wearing a white apron that covered him from chin to knees approached.

"Good day, my weary traveler," the waiter began, twisting his handlebar mustache. "Welcome to our inn." He paused to take a short breath. "Would you care for something to drink?"

"Yes. A glass of light beer," Erich replied.

The waiter went behind a polished walnut bar and returned with the beer on a tray.

"What are you serving for supper?" Erich inquired.

"Cabbage and ham hocks."

"Good. Bring me some."

The beer tasted rich and refreshing to Erich, the foam making his upper lip itch as the tiny bubbles burst. When he removed it with his tongue, he tasted the salt from his perspiration. Looking around the room, he saw a line of crests and small shields hanging on the chestnut paneling of one wall. Centered over a large mirror behind the bar was an exquisite rack of stag horns. He glanced again at the older men. They were still sipping beer, preening their foam-soaked mustaches, and vigorously discussing farming and agriculture.

The waiter brought the steaming plate of cabbage and ham hocks and then returned to the bar to refill the stein. Hungry from the long walk, Erich began stuffing the food into his mouth. Suddenly, he stopped and looked across the room. Why, he wondered, was he eating so fast? There was no hurry. He would slow down and relax—just enjoy the evening. When the waiter returned with the beer, he asked, "Would you have a room for the night?"

"Yes, indeed!" the waiter replied huskily. "1 have several upstairs."

After taking the last drink from the stein, Erich pushed the plate away. The warmth of the stuffy room and sated feeling within his viscera made him drowsy. Picking up his knapsack, he slowly climbed the oak staircase, thoughtfully sliding his hand along the rail that had been smoothed to a tacky polish by countless others.

When he pushed the door open, he quickly scanned the room. It was small but had clean towels, an upholstered chair, and a wash basin. A double bed in the far corner was topped by a huge, feather-filled cover.

Opening the window, he looked down on a courtyard. It was a pleasant scene of tables and chairs among chestnut trees. Although it was empty, the scarred bandstand and trampled border flowers indicated it was frequently used. After placing the knapsack in the corner, he rinsed his face, removed his shoes, and dropped down onto the bed.

• • •

Erich was awakened by loud music and gay laughter. A wedding reception was underway in the courtyard. The sun had set and multicolored lights hung from the trees and fence. Although he could not see the bride and groom, people of all ages were dancing and singing. And beer steins, full and empty, were everywhere. A boy with a tray was circulating among the people, gathering up the empty ones. If a stein was not quite empty, the boy picked it up and gulped its contents before placing it on the tray.

Erich bathed, shaved, and brushed his teeth. Before going downstairs, he put on a clean shirt and long trousers. The place was filled with people. They were inside and outside, sitting, standing, and leaning against the bar and walls. There were old people and young people; some dressed in colorful Alpine costumes, others with dark suits, stovepipe hats, and monocles. Looking through the large double doors to the garden, he could see the bride dancing, with a line of waiting men each in turn.

Slowly, he made his way through the crowd to the edge of the dance area.

He watched until the line of men had finished and the groom was again dancing with his bride. She appeared radiant and happy, laughing and chatting with her new husband as they whirled around the dance floor.

Erich took a three-mark note from his pocket, stepped onto the dance floor, and tapped the groom on the shoulder. Taking the bride into his arms, he transferred the note from his hand to hers. "Are you from Rothenburg?" he asked.

"No," she replied, "I'm from Solstein. It's a little village in the foothills." He learned she was twenty-two years old, the daughter of a sheep and cow herder.

Her husband, an apprentice watch repairman, was from Rothenburg.

A tap on the shoulder ended the dance. As he made his way to the sidelines, he picked up a stein of beer from the tray of a passing waiter. Taking a sip, he noticed a young, dark-haired lady beside him. Looking into her blue eyes, he tossed his head in the direction of the newlyweds and asked, "Friends of yours?"

"Yes," she answered with a smile. "Have known her as long as I can remember; him for a number of years." She paused as she looked toward the dance floor and then added, "She seems so very happy."

"Would you like to dance?" Erich asked.

"I'd be delighted," she replied, blushing slightly.

As they danced, Erich discovered that she was light on her feet—nimble and well-coordinated, as individuals were described in medical school. Holding her close so she could follow him, he inhaled the pleasant fragrance she radiated. He thought he could feel the texture of her skin with the tips of his fingers through the sheer crepe dress she wore.

When the music paused, he motioned toward a small table against the far wall. "Shall we sit for a while?" he asked.

Although she would have liked to continue dancing, she nodded consent. This was not a time to disagree, she thought, if she was to carry out her plan.

After seating her, Erich got two glasses of beer and some ham sandwiches from the snack table. "And what's your name?" he asked, taking a sip of beer.

"Rosa," she replied. "Rosa Graebner." She told him she was nineteen and lived in the same village as the bride. "Spent most of my life in school or working around the house."

"This is a nice place to live," Erich said, hoping she would tell him more about herself. "Does your family do any farming?"

A serious look came over her face. "No," she replied. Then she told him about her lonely summer task. With a younger sister, Irma, she tended a herd of cattle and goats high in the mountain meadows. They drove the animals from pasture to pasture, milking them and making butter and cheese.

"Didn't others come past when you were there?" Erich asked.

"Oh, my father came up each month to bring food and pick up the butter and cheese." She shrugged, then added, "Sometimes a climber or wanderer would happen by. But otherwise, there was no one."

Erich's question caused her to recall the lonely, depressing summers she had spent, seeing so few people. And now that she was old enough to be interested, there was the lack of eligible young men. Each successive year she had adjusted her standards to include a wider range of possibilities for marriage. She remembered the visit by the old goat herder from an adjacent range. Irma was away with the cows, leaving her alone in the cabin. He had stood on the porch beside her pointing to a distant landmark, when he placed an arm around her waist. When they stepped off the porch, his hand slid up so it pressed firmly against the underside of her breast. It had felt good in a strange sort of way and had made her pulse quicken. Then she felt the pressure of his fingers on her buttocks and turned to face him. She looked at his sweat-stained hat, food-splattered shirt, and wrinkled, weathered, bewhiskered face. It made her shudder with revulsion. She just couldn't let herself be fondled by him.

When he was about to leave, he brought his hand up to touch her face. She took it firmly in hers and pushed it down. "I prefer you not put your hand on me," she told him matter-of-factly. It saddened her to see the twinkle leave his gray eyes as he walked dejectedly away. But she just couldn't stand it. She needed someone nearer he own age.

Noting a distant look in her eyes, Erich reached for her hand. "Let's dance!" he said, rising to his feet

They danced two dances and sat down again. The festivities were becoming noticeably noisier and more energetic, especially among the older people. He wondered if the crowd had consumed too much beer. Some women had shed their shoes and many of their elaborate hair fashions were hanging limp or had come undone. He looked up through the chains of colored lights at the star-studded sky. The moon, a large golden sphere, was just coming into view. "How about a little stroll around the village?" he asked. "Are you game?"

"I'd love it," Rosa replied, dabbing her forehead with an embroidered handkerchief.

Erich held her hand as they made their way slowly through the narrow, crooked streets. Although the evening air was cool and refreshing, Rosa's pulse was throbbing and she felt warm. Dozens of thoughts were chasing through her mind. Here was the man she was looking for, the one she had dreamed about. Yet, she was troubled.

He was tall, six feet, she judged, because when he held her on the dance floor his slate-blue eyes were about six inches above hers. Looking up, she noted how the street lamp high-lighted his ample lips and gave his blond hair a slight luster. Maybe she had met her future husband; a chill surged through her body, causing her to quiver slightly.

Erich squeezed her hand. "Cold?" he asked, looking at her.

"No," she replied, feeling embarrassed.

"A *pfennig* for your thoughts, then," he said with a smile.

Startled, she hesitated before answering. "Oh—how lovely it all is. The wedding, the people, the evening—all so wonderful." She paused, wondering what else she should say. "How nice to have met you."

He smiled and put an arm around her shoulders.

Thinking it was a good time to learn more about him, Rosa placed her arm around his waist. "Do you have anyone waiting for you in Holzheim—other than your family, I mean?" she had surprised herself and could feel her face redden.

"Yes. She's a young lady I've known all my life. We aren't actually engaged, but we do have an understanding."

"Oh?" Rosa responded, her heart sinking. "What's she like?"

Erich began to describe his lovely brown-eyed blond, but Rosa wasn't listening. She wondered what she should do, all the while being acutely conscious of his warm fingers on her neck. Her inhibitions were rising to the forefront. Perhaps she should go back to the party and forget the purpose she had in mind. Then she thought of returning to the empty hotel room to face another night of lost expectations. It made her shudder.

Shortly after passing beneath the tower and crossing the bridge spanning the moat, they entered the shadow of a large chestnut tree. Erich stopped. Grasping her shoulders, he turned her around. Then, placing his hand beneath her chin, he lifted her face to his. He kissed her lightly on the forehead, nose, and lips. Seeing tears well up in her eyes, he asked, "What's the matter?" His voice echoed concern.

She told him he was the first male, other than her immediate family, who had ever kissed her. "In the mountains, I often dreamed of it happening. I thought it would take my breath away and my lips would be bruised." Tears flowed down her cheeks. "And now you have done it. And it was so light and gentle." She looked up into his face questioningly.

"Since my honor is at stake, I must not disappoint you," he said, taking her into his arms.

As he kissed her, she stood tense and stiff, her eyes shut, her lips and mouth securely closed.

When he finished, she inhaled a deep breath. "I'm sorry to be so awkward," she apologized. "But I must learn everything."

"It will come with time," he assured her, speaking softly.

"But time is passing!" she protested. "For several summers I've been waiting!" She told him how she was determined to find someone at the wedding who would make love to her. She did not mention how she had watched the animals mate, saw their bulging eyes and flared nostrils and listened to their grunts of ecstasy, and afterwards, how she felt when she saw the bull's livid spear still dripping seeds. "I'm afraid you think badly of me, that I'm a terrible person to desire such things. Oh," she paused and shook her head, "sometimes I get so miserable I just want to die."

Erich drew her close to him. "No, I do not think badly of you. Perhaps society is expecting too much."

"What am I to do, then?" she asked, tears welling up in her eyes again. "I want so desperately to try it. For weeks I planned to have it happen tonight. And when you danced with me, I knew you were the one I had dreamed about all those long, lonely weeks in the mountains." She dabbed her eyes with her handkerchief. "I was so sure nothing would sway me from going through with it. But now I don't know. It's so different from what I had imagined."

Erich pressed the side of her head to his chest and then put both arms around her and caressed her back. As he held her, he heard the crickets chirping and saw that dew was forming on the grass. A lone frog in the tall weeds of the moat croaked with a repetitious, deep-throated gurgle.

Erich was concerned and confused. She had stimulated him and he would like to accommodate her, but he was in love with Maria. And Maria had promised him that on their wedding night he would be the first to have touched her. Although he had made no such promise to Maria and had been with two other girls, the developing situation made him uneasy.

Grasping her by the shoulders, he held her at arms length and looked into her inquiring eyes. The light from a street lamp filtering through the trees created a warm glow on her face and gave her dark hair a soft sheen. He drew her near and kissed her. This time her lips were not tense and tight. As he gently plied them apart, she responded by kissing back. Caressing her, he could feel the seams of her undergarments through the sheer dress and sensed the pressure of her breasts and thighs. Her breathing was much faster.

"Will you do it for me?" she asked, her face close to his.

Exhaling a heavy sigh, he took her hand and started for the tower gate. Inside the inn, he pushed through the noisy crowd and led her upstairs. For several minutes they stood at the window in his darkened room looking at the revelers in the courtyard. Then he turned her toward him, and they kissed again.

"Now?" she asked.

"When is your next period?"

She thought a moment. "In about three days."

"All right."

A moment passed. Then she asked, "What do I do?"

"Take off your clothes."

9

They lay side by side, cool skin touching, as he moved his hand across her chest. When he brushed over a protruding nipple, she held her breath momentarily before expelling it with a slight gasp. Slowly, his hand descended to the moss-covered juncture of her legs where his knowledgeable fingers located the sensitive bud of her clitoris. As the spasmodic jerks of her body intensified, Rosa issued audible sighs and spread her thighs.

When he descended upon her, she closed her eyes tightly and clenched her fists. The irritation of his probing suddenly began to burn as he located the proper vestibule. An area numbness had just begun to occur when she felt a sharp, searing pain. She bit her lip but could not keep from crying out. He halted only momentarily and then continued slowly. She felt a fullness, as if there was not enough room within her. Then, suddenly it was over.

Erich waited until her breathing subsided and a series of quivers stopped. Then he kissed her, tasting the beads of perspiration on her upper lip.

Later, as he stared at the faintly lighted ceiling, a surge of guilt swept through his body. But when he looked at the head nestled against his arm and saw she was sleeping contentedly, he felt relieved.

• • •

They were awakened by a crowing rooster just as the sun was clearing the horizon. For several minutes they snuggled together, quietly listening to chirping birds and the shuffling of people along the street. Then, they made love again.

This time Rosa enjoyed it much more than before. Suddenly, she turned to Erich, a frightened expression on her face. "Will I have a baby?" she asked.

"No," Erich replied calmly.

"Are you sure?"

"Yes," he said, looking at her soft, white face wreathed in locks of black hair. "I am sure."

She remained in bed, watching him wash and shave. "If I should visit Holzheim, could I see you?" she asked.

He sat down on the bed and stroked her hair. He had read that women always retain a residual affection for their first lover. But he didn't want to become involved because Maria was meant for him. He would discipline himself to forget Rosa. Kissing her lightly on the lips, he whispered in her ear, "I think it is best we part with fond memories of each other. We must go our separate ways and let fate take care of our future."

She forced a smile, her eyes glistening as she drew him down to her. In a whisper, she asked, "Will you go to the Octoberfest in Munich?"

"I'm not sure." He paused. "Probably."

He kissed her again, inhaling the faint, delicate aroma still issuing from her hair.

"Goodbye, my dearest," she whispered.

After picking up his knapsack, he halted to look back and smile before slipping out the door.

• • •

Squinting into the bright rays of a rising sun as he walked, Erich saw that the fields were alive with peasant workers. The robust women, mostly in their thirties or forties he judged, were dressed in head scarves, long dresses, aprons, and heavy shoes. The men wore hats and rubber boots and had vests beneath their jackets. Some pushed wheelbarrows, and a few rode wagons pulled by horses. Those near the road waved; others more distant merely stared at him for a moment before resuming their work.

As he approached their little settlement, several children halted the game they were playing and, laughing, talking, and jostling, ran toward him. One little girl took his hand and, running to keep up, asked, "What's your name?"

"Erich," he replied.

"Where are you going?"

"Home," Erich answered.

As the girl continued her barrage of questions, others joined them. Soon there were a dozen children and half as many dogs, creating a carnival atmosphere. Since most villagers were farmers who worked the surrounding land, only the very young, the very old, and the merchants remained. A rotund shopkeeper, hearing a commotion on his normally placid street, stepped outside to watch as they passed.

Turning the corner, Erich's sensitive nose detected fresh bread. "Where's the bakery?" he asked, looking down at the little girl.

"There," she replied, pointing up the street.

He bought a freshly baked loaf of black bread and then went next door to a grocery to get a bottle of beer and a Thuringer sausage. When he stepped outside, he found the children had gone.

An hour later on a slight rise along a forested section of the road, he removed his knapsack and sat down, propping himself against the trunk of a large pine. The sun, halfway up its angular path in the sky, had warmed the air sufficiently to absorb the dew. And now insects were hunting food, locating mates, and investigating the disturbance Erich had created by invading their quiet domain. He looked at a large, black beetle walking with a side-stepping gait and smiled. It reminded him of the town drunk he had read about, staggering home after a night of merrymaking.

11

He had just washed down a bite of sausage with a drink of beer when he heard shuffling behind him. Turning his head, he saw a man carrying a small cloth sack approaching.

"Mind if I sit down?" the man asked, pointing to an adjacent tree as he removed his gray felt hat.

"No," Erich replied, noting the squint lines radiating out from the man's eyes. "Take the load off your feet."

"I'm a woodcutter," the man explained, slipping a bottle of wine and a piece of bread from the sack. "Working back up the hill." He motioned with his head. Then he held out two radishes. "Here. They're fresh from my garden."

Erich took a bite from one of the radishes, relishing its flavor. Then he told the man he was on his way home.

"It's a nice time for walking. Every young man should see our beautiful country before he settles down." The man rubbed his leg as he looked off into the distance. "Used to do a lot of walking myself when I was young."

Erich was reassembling his pack when a large truck loaded with tires lumbered up. The driver set the brake and slid across the seat. Sticking his head out the window, he asked, "Is this the road to Nurnberg?"

Erich walked over to the truck so his voice could be heard above the noise of the big diesel engine. "Yes. Continue straight ahead."

The driver looked at the woodcutter, who nodded confirmation. He was about to slide back behind the wheel when he turned again to Erich. "Would you like a ride?"

"Sure would," Erich replied with a smile.

Erich shook hands with the woodcutter, then climbed onto the high seat in the big cab. The engine barked vigorous pulsations of power as the truck moved slowly forward.

"Visiting friends in Nurnberg?" the driver asked, shouting to overcome the roar of the truck.

"No, just passing through on my way home. Been studying at Heidelberg."

"Where is your home?"

"Holzheim." Noting the driver wrinkle his brow, Erich added, "Near Regensburg."

The driver looked at him. "What are you specializing in?"

"Medicine," Erich answered, continuing to look ahead at the winding road.

"Wonderful! Wonderful, if you can do it."

As they talked, Erich learned that the driver, Heinrich Stettler, was born in a village near Nurnberg and had worked at a variety of laboring jobs before becoming a truck driver for the rubber company. "Would still be sweating on a shovel handle if it wasn't for my older brother."

"Oh?" Erich responded, waiting for Heinrich to explain.

"Yes. He's a family man, all settled down. A member of the Nazi party." Heinrich paused and then added, "I joined too, not long ago. Gonna try to work my way up." He moved the lever to shift gears and then turned to Erich. "They're having a rally tonight. How about going with me? I heard the Fuhrer might be there."

Erich thought for a moment. He'd have to spend the night in Nurnberg anyway, and this might be an enlightening experience. "Fine," he answered. "I'd be delighted to go."

Just off Schwabacher Street, Heinrich pulled the truck into a large, fenced yard and rolled to a stop beside a corrugated steel building. A checker emerged, clipboard in hand, and the two of them tallied the load. The checker signed a receipt and handed it to Heinrich.

Heinrich pocketed the receipt and walked over to Erich, who was standing a short distance away. "Come, let's go to my apartment."

Eight blocks away, Heinrich opened a small wooden gate and led Erich along a path beside a large, half-timbered house that contained his two-room apartment. After unlocking the door, he pushed open the windows to dispel the stale air that had absorbed generations of odors from the wood and plaster.

One room had a bed and lavatory. The other, the larger of the two, had a sink, two-burner hotplate, a couch, and a small wooden table with two chairs. "The toilet is through there," he stated, pointing to a wooden door covered with many coats of white enamel. Noting Erich stare at the heavy brass lock, he added, "We share it, so be sure to lock the door on the far side when you enter and unlock it when you leave. A couple months ago, they forgot to unlock mine and I damn near filled my pants before they came home and unlocked it."

They walked to a nearby restaurant where Heinrich pushed open the heavily varnished oak door and stepped inside. "Ah, Mr. Stettler," the rotund proprietor said, wiping his chubby hands on his white apron as he rushed over to shake Heinrich's hand. "Follow me."

To Erich's surprise, they were led to a prominent table with a linen tablecloth. And he wondered why Heinrich was not called by his first name as was the custom in neighborhood taverns.

After they were seated, Heinrich looked up at the blocky man who stood, waiting to take their order. "This is my friend, Erich Stecker."

The proprietor clicked his heels and bowed from the waist. "The pleasure is all mine," he stated with a broad smile.

With the beer, the proprietor brought a slick, cardboard menu that listed the simple fare.

"Nothing fancy about the place," Heinrich stated, fingering the menu as he looked at Erich. "But it's good solid food at a reasonable price." He took a sip from his glass. "The way costs are rising, it's getting harder and harder to get a decent meal at a price you can afford."

Midway through the meal, after noting several instances of special treatment not normally given truck drivers, Erich leaned toward Heinrich. "They're sure good to us here. Do you have an interest in the place?"

Heinrich laid down his knife and fork and then dabbed his mouth with his napkin. "No, not really. You see, I introduced my brother to the owner a short while back. The way the Nazi influence is growing, it's better for businessmen to stay on good terms with them. Although my brother is at a lower level, you never can tell but what tomorrow he might be made district commandant. Then he could make it very good or very bad for business."

It was approaching seven o'clock as the two men made their way toward Frauentor Street. Most people, having eaten, were tending their planters of geraniums or weeding in their backyard gardens. A few, however, had stopped at a tavern after work and, after buying a newspaper and tucking it underarm, were going home. They were the red-faced ones, unsteady on their feet, whom Erich and Heinrich had to sidestep.

When they boarded an eastbound streetcar destined for the edge of the city, Erich noted there was only a sprinkling of paper-reading commuters occupying a few seats. With each stop, however, one or more energetic young adults boarded until, at the end of the run, the car was packed with talkative, enthusiastic people.

Stepping from the car, Erich and Heinrich were suddenly engulfed in a crowd of thousands surging toward the giant Luitpold Arena. As they moved through the north gate with the onrushing crowd, Erich could see through an opening on the far side. Army troops in great numbers were arriving in trucks, buses, and vans.

"Follow me!" Heinrich shouted, leading the way up the steps to a high tier on the north side.

Just as the sun dropped below the tree-studded horizon, the troops marched in. Erich watched intently as they goose-stepped to positions in precisely marked squares and rectangles on the field. Then, with an awe-inspiring suddenness, the floodlights were turned on to reveal hundreds of flags and banners fluttering in a gentle breeze. When the band had finished playing "*Deutschland Uber Alles*," a quiet murmur settled over the crowd.

Erich was amazed at the spectacle unfolding before him. Quickly, he scanned the scene. The east end of the stadium was constructed to provide roomy seating for officials and dignitaries. Each end of its tall, concrete backdrop was topped by a huge, mystically burning firepot. A great sculptured concrete eagle, scrutinizing the procedure with fierce, glaring eyes while perched high atop a Nazi swastika, dominated the center of the wall.

The bank of official seats were filled with uniformed men, all wearing red armbands with a white circle encompassing a black swastika. Their wives were seated on the outer fringe of the group. By their dress, Erich was certain the seating was graduated according to their importance. Those of higher rank wore finely tailored uniforms, heavily adorned with silver and gold braid, and were seated nearest the speaker's platform.

With a suddenness that startled Erich, a heavy black door a few steps above the reviewing platform burst open, and the Fuhrer emerged. Spotlights focused all attention on him. Dressed in a brown uniform, he nimbly descended the steps and stood at the rail of the platform. He was trim and neat, and the spring in his step radiated a quality of agile leadership.

One uniformed man seated nearby sprang to his feet. This seemed to trip a spring beneath everyone present. In an instant, all two hundred thousand rose to their feet. Erich recognized the man as Josef Goebels.

With a repeated upward jab of his outstretched hand, Goebels led the mass of standing people in a tumultuous "Heil, Hitler" five times. The tremendous roar and applause was deafening.

The display of vigor and enthusiasm left Erich awestruck. He felt his pulse surge in his temples and experienced a tingling sensation throughout his body. Then, it was quiet. He looked around and saw that the people were seated. He quickly sat down amid a vacuum of total silence. The troops still stood in formation on the field below and the huge firepots continued to burn, sending their paganistic smoke skyward.

Hitler thanked those present for attending and congratulated them for being part of his movement. Then his voice changed. It became louder and more emphatic.

"Follow me and you will have a much better tomorrow. Only a few more tasks remain. A few more wrongs must be righted. Then we will build an empire that will last a thousand years.

He was interrupted by a great round of applause led by those on the platform. Then he continued. "Twenty years ago Germany was nothing—flotsam of the world. Today, it is a proud, progressive nation with an industrial capacity and spirit of nationalism second to none—truly a power to be reckoned with."

Again, he was interrupted.

"The first step was to place German troops in the Rhineland and kick out those filthy black Senegalese. They were sent there as guards because the French were too damned lazy to do the patrolling themselves. There can never be a complete redemption of the humiliation those black devils forced on our pure German women. The scars of abuse shall remain in their minds forever. But today you will not find a half-breed in existence. The Fuhrer has seen to that!"

Again the air was rent with loud applause and the hoarse shouts of *"Heil, Hitler!"* As he continued to speak, his voice became louder, more terse, more determined. The spectators were spellbound by its electrifying effect. There was an expectation, a feeling of certainty, that he could lead their nation to unparalleled heights of glory.

"There are thousands of German speaking people still within the borders of other countries. Yes, those who were within the borders of Czechoslovakia are now, once again, within the folds of the Fatherland. This was accomplished by merely moving the border to where it was before the manipulations of the stuffed shirts that rigged the Versailles Treaty. The others will be reclaimed in due time!"

He paused for a drink of water, then waited for the applause to die down.

"Now, there is the pressing problem of the Polish corridor. That narrow strip of land, that divider between the two segments of Germany, that barrier requiring Germans to go through Poland to visit relatives in Prussia. It's another abortion of the Versailles Treaty! This was, indeed, the crime of crimes—putting those filthy Poles on German soil. They are a breed of people so stubborn, so ignorant, and so stupid they can be taught nothing! They are the lowest class of pigs and can serve mankind only as beasts of burden. Germany must get the corridor back! We must kick those Slavic slobs out! And then the land will have to be restored before it can be used!"

He spoke about the Polish corridor for another fifteen minutes. Then he said, "Wait for the signal from your Fuhrer! And when it comes, join the frey! The days of waiting are short, for the stars are rapidly approaching the desired positions!"

He whirled about and strode up the stairs toward the black door.

Goebels rose to his feet. Again, the stillness was shattered by the deafening roar of *"Heil, Hitler!"* Then, as the band played, troops on the field lit torches and marched out of the stadium to the waiting trucks and buses.

Erich followed Heinrich down the steps to the ground level. His knees were weak and his body drained by an emotional experience he did not understand. Although aware of enthusiastic conversations going on about him, his brain seemed mesmerized by repetitious passages from the speech he had just heard. As a medical student, he thought he understood the dynamics of hypnotism. But this was greater than anything he had read. Perhaps Heinrich, who had attended such meetings before, was right. The Fuhrer was capable of leading the masses to accomplishments beyond their comprehension.

Early the next morning, after spending a night of fitful sleep on a couch, Erich dressed and packed. As he was shaving, Heinrich awakened.

The truck driver propped himself up on his elbow. "Too bad my route doesn't go east or I could give you another boost today," he said ruefully.

Erich looked at Heinrich's reflection in the mirror. "Oh, that's all right. I enjoy walking. Besides, I can use the exercise after a tedious term of studying at the university."

"Yah, but I know from experience how much better it is to ride. Once the truck broke down, and I had to walk eight miles to a repair shop for help." Heinrich paused for a long moment and then said, "I'm glad you enjoyed the rally last night. Seriously, I think you should join the party. A person with your intelligence and training could really go places. Just think of the power those birds in high places wield. What a life!"

"I'll think about it," Erich replied. "But I want to finish medical school first. I've planned that all my life, you know."

"Oh, sure. But keep it in mind."

"All right," Erich promised, still feeling shock from the frightening experience of last night. Then, shaking Heinrich's hand, he said, "If you get to Holzheim, look me up. It's a very small village, and my parents are well known. They own a general store there."

Erich replenished the food in his knapsack from a nearby market and then boarded a streetcar on Regensburger Street for a ride to the end of the line.

• • •

Rounding the corner, Erich spotted an inviting grassy knoll beside the road. Situated among plots of a carefully tended evergreen farm, it offered a good place to rest for a few minutes. He removed his hat, wiped his forehead on the back of his wrist, and then sat down on the floor of brown needles. Looking around, he noted that each plot had trees of a different size. A short distance up the road, a crew of men were harvesting the larger ones and planting seedlings to replace them.

Looking down the long rows of three-inch saplings near him, he saw that their hanging branches formed ever darkening, arched tunnels that radiated off into three directions from where he sat. He leaned back, exhaled audibly, and looked up at the myriad of shapes formed by the billowy clouds moving slowly across from the west. Squinting, he tried to picture them as animals, buildings, and continents. The warm, rich soil soothed his body, but it seemed to resist his presence by pressing twigs and pebbles against the smooth muscles of his legs and back.

Suddenly, his pleasant dreaming was interrupted by the thought of the rally he had witnessed at Nurenberg. He had been only vaguely aware of Nazi politics, but after attending the massive gathering, he wondered how far they would go. Several times during the morning as he walked along the road, he had mentally relived it to understand its meaning. But its immensity and vigor confused and frightened him.

• • •

Approaching one of the many villages where children ran out to meet him, Erich saw a small boy stumble. The lad got to his feet and, holding a skinned knee as he ran, attempted to keep up with his friends. When he reached Erich, the pain had begun and a trickle of blood was visible.

Erich took the boy's hand and led him to a large rock. "Sit there and don't touch it with your hands," Erich told him.

Slipping the knapsack from his shoulders, Erich reached deep inside and removed a metal box containing medical supplies and a few surgical instruments. With a cotton swab soaked in water from his canteen, he cleaned the dirt from the abrasion. "This may sting a bit," he warned as he applied a clear antiseptic. The boy winced but watched as the wound was covered with a gauze pad and adhesive tape.

When Erich looked up, he saw a little, round face topped by a shock of white hair that was in complete disarray. Although the flow of tears from the bright, blue eyes had abated, they had left telltale dirt streaks on his cheeks. Erich moistened his handkerchief and wiped them away.

"How's that?" Erich inquired, straightening the suspenders that supported the boy's grease-stained *lederhosen*.

"Excellent!" came the enthusiastic reply.

Erich pointed to the badge that bridged the boy's suspenders. "I see you belong to a youth group."

"Yes. It's fun. And they teach you many good things."

The crowd of children who had remained quiet as he administered the first aid, suddenly deluged him with a fusillade of questions.

"Are you a doctor?" one little girl inquired.

"Perhaps, some day," Erich responded with a smile.

"How come you know how to fix people?" another asked

"I'm studying it."

"Where?"

"At Heidelberg University."

As Erich moved on, the barrage of questions continued. And when the children began to melt away, the injured boy sidled up to him. "I want to be a doctor when I grow up," he confided.

"You will make a good one," Erich assured him. "Just study hard."

Approaching the outskirts of Regensburg, Erich was deep in thought as he strode along the tree-lined cobblestone street that had been used by generations of peasants, merchants, and warriors, both Christian and pagan. As a boy, his fifth grade class had been taken on an all-day tour to study the history of a city that no one seemed to know the age. In the museum, he recalled, there was an inscription in stone made when the Roman fortress *Castra Regina* was completed on this site in 179 A.D. And he learned that it was the capitol of Bavaria during the Middle Ages.

The whining staccato of a Messerschnitt factory, straining to fill the requirements of Germany's new air force, caught his attention. He stopped long enough to watch a newly completed fighter plane being towed to a nearby airfield. Above the overall, low-level hum, he could hear a grinding, whining staccato from the factory that spoke a language of urgency and determination.

Near the center of town, the twin towers of massive St. Peter's Cathedral brooded over shop-lined streets that radiated in several directions. The low-hanging sun spread a soft, golden light on the richly carved statuary that adorned its magnificent main portal. Admiring its geranium-filled garden, Erich sat down on one of the wrought-iron benches that had been placed beneath a scattering of chestnut trees. It would take another day to reach Holzheim, so he would rest for a few minutes and then find a place to spend the night.

A bubbling fountain at the base of a statue of St. Peter attracted a half-dozen children who romped at its brim, occasionally flicking water at one another. A mongrel dog trotted up, circumvented the noisy children, and then went directly to the wall of the cathedral. He sniffed the huge cornerstone and then hoisted his leg to its stained surface. Erich smiled, contemplating the generations of canines that had done the same thing.

As his tired body relaxed, Erich tried to picture the tremendous effort needed to build such a structure, to place the heavy blocks of stone at the required heights. Looking at the plots of red and white geraniums, he recalled reading that they honored the spot where King Henry I had his tournaments, where Frederick Barbarossa had assembled his crusaders, and where Napoleon Bonaparte had been wounded the first and only time. And then there was the palace guest house where Charles V had made love to Barbara Blomberg. Sighing, he wished the museum was open so he could see the ancient Medallion Carpet again.

A sudden flash of lightning in a dark cloud to the north caught his eye. He picked up his pack and hurriedly walked off to search for an inn.

The next morning, anxious to reach Holzheim before dark, he rose early. The sun was just breaking above the horizon when he passed through the

Porta Praetoria, the north gateway of the ancient Roman fort. After crossing the medieval Stone Bridge over the smoothly flowing Danube, he headed east again on the narrow macadam road that followed the river.

A few miles down the road a high bluff rose abruptly to his left. Perched at its top in solitary grandeur was a tremendous replica of the Parthenon. The brilliant contrast of its whiteness against the azure sky caught his attention. It was *Valhalla*, the hall of immortality, where the souls of heroes are received. He had visited it once. His teacher had told him it was a sacred place. Looking at his watch, he wondered if he had time to see it again.

A narrow footpath up a steep incline took him to the base of a broad stairway, a flight of steps that seemed to be without end. When he reached the top, he looked up and felt dwarfed by the huge structure before him and the massive Doric columns surrounding it. After waiting to catch his breath, he stepped inside the open door and was greeted by the lone caretaker.

"Welcome, my young man." Although the elderly man whispered, his voice echoed. He handed Erich a printed guide sheet.

Awed by a feeling of hallowed reverence, Erich removed his hat and slowly began walking down one of the rows of busts of musicians, philosophers, statesmen, and historians. He tried to move quietly, but the vast marble complex reverberated with the slightest sound. It seemed so different from the time he was here with his grade school class.

He turned a corner and was surprised by the sight of a woman standing in front of the bust of Johann Sebastian Bach. With her eyes opened wide, she stood with her nose a few inches from the marble head of the composer. Tears were streaming down her cheeks and splashing onto the floor. She seemed to be in a trance. Erich wanted to speak to her, perhaps console her, but he changed his mind and walked past. To show respect he thought he should stay longer, but a feeling of ghostly uneasiness crept over him. He would leave the hallowed shrine for now and return another day, perhaps with Maria.

Outside, the breeze felt cool on his cheeks. He inhaled deeply and then sat down with his back against one of the giant columns and looked at the scenic grandeur spread before him. The blue Danube stretched both left and right, straight for miles except for the bend below that sidestepped the sacred ground of *Vahalla*. Its smooth, shiny surface was being disturbed by a wide wedge of ripples from two barges being pushed upstream. Near the river, a few pockets of amethyst haze remained. Across, on the other side, there was a multicolored checkerboard of fields interspersed with dozens of villages built around onion-domed churches. In the distance, a column of milky smoke climbed lazily skyward from a tall chimney.

Erich smiled. He felt proud. This was Germany, his Germany, a beautiful country. And it was inhabited by a fine, industrious people.

• • •

A narrow, winding road led back into the interior, a route Erich recognized with increasing familiarity. It had holes and cracks in its macadam surface, but the little traffic it served gave it a low priority on the repair crew's schedule. As he walked, he saw a lace-edged stream dash merrily from the brush and ripple mirthfully along the road for a short distance, then quickly dart back into the green undercover. A large crow, cawing to alert its friends, flew lazily past, and a cottontail rabbit hopped slowly across a lush, grassy opening in the forest.

Holzheim was located at the far end of a cultivated valley, nestled snugly against an outcropping of pine-covered hills. The sun hung heavily in the western sky as Erich topped the final rise. Although anxious to get home, he climbed a few yards up a wooded hill and squatted on his haunches to look down on the land that had provided his creation, suckled and nourished him, and now contributed to his support. Below were the flat, cultivated fields that provided life for his family, friends, and neighbors. He could see their bent shapes trudging wearily toward the village where they would complete the evening chores before sitting down to eat their supper. The church steeple with its newly shingled dome dominated the thirty buildings of the little settlement. Occasionally, he could hear the shrill voices of children playing while waiting to be called for the evening meal.

The tinkle of a bell made him stand to see a small herd of milk cows, in single file, coming down the path behind him. They were being returned from their hill pasture to a night of confinement in a barnyard at the edge of town for their evening and morning milking. Behind them was a chunky dark-haired girl carrying a short stick. When she saw Erich, she threw it down and ran toward him. Nearly knocking him over with her momentum, she entwined her arms about his waist and kissed him on both cheeks.

"Inge! Inge Trapp!" Erich gasped, as her tight hold forced him to exhale a portion of his breath. "It's so good to see you."

"Have you been home yet?" she asked, pushing back so she could look at him from head to foot.

"No. But I'm about to go. I was just resting for a few minutes."

"Good!" she responded, grabbing his hand and pulling him to a sitting position beside her. They talked briefly, and then she laid back, using her hand to shield her face from a beam of sunlight. Erich looked first at the braided coil of dark brown hair crowning the top of her head, then into the dark eyes that were located at the vertical center of her full, round face. He could smell an odor of cattle and perspiration.

Admiring her ever rosy cheeks, he realized he had known her for as long as he could remember. As a small boy he and his mother had attended the funeral of Mrs. Trapp, who had died trying to give birth to a fourth child. Led by the hand to drop a flower onto the casket containing the bodies of mother and stillborn child, he experienced a haunting empathy when he looked across the open grave and saw Inge's tear-stained face as she stood beside her father, older sister, and brother.

Never one to be delicate or dainty, Inge, who was two years older than Erich, worked, fought, and played with boys as if she was one of them. She had always possessed a coarseness that he both admired and detested. And she never wore anything beneath her dress.

As he looked down at her parted lips, he recalled that he was only twelve when she seduced him beneath a large pine tree a hundred yards up the trail. After his initial fright, he often enjoyed sessions with her when they explored each other's bodies. But for the past year and a half, since his love for Maria had blossomed, he was reluctant to arouse her passions.

"Now, Erich?" she asked eagerly. "Now?"

He looked down at her heavy work shoes and short wool socks and then unbuttoned the top of her gray dress. It exposed a huge breast with a large, light crimson center. Although he had seen it numerous times before, it still fascinated him to watch the flat, pink areola wrinkle and pucker to form a protruding nipple when Inge closed her eyes and held her breath.

Feeling uneasy, he refastened the buttons and then allowed his hand to descend to the large, soft mound of her abdomen. Beneath the soiled broadcloth he could feel the little mass of wiry hair. She raised her hips, seizing his hand and moving it in a circular motion. Erich stopped the movement and looked down at her flushed face.

Her mouth suddenly closed and her eyes opened. "Let's do it, Erich. Let's do it now!" she pleaded.

"Not right now," he replied, trying to evade the request, hoping not to hurt her feelings. "You catch up to your cows. I'll come along soon."

He pulled her to her feet, and she kissed him again. When she turned to leave, he gave her an affectionate pat on the rump. Although she had grown up without the guidance of a mother, he was pleased she was happy and healthy. Looking down at the ground, he shook his head as he again recalled the vivid picture of the cemetery. Then he remembered he had gone through the same chilling agony of dropping a flower on a coffin when Maria's father was killed two years later. As he started down the path toward the road, the air was still heavy with Inge's lingering odor.

An enthusiastic gathering of noisy children interspersed with several barking dogs followed him into town. The clamor attracted the attention of several adults who, proud to have someone from Holzheim at Heidelberg University, came out to shake his hand. Some merely waved as he passed. When he went by the Trapp barnyard, he saw Inge leaning on a gate watching. She waved and grinned, creating a series of bulging wrinkles beneath a dimpled chin that extended the length of her short neck.

When he entered the Stecker store, his father rushed to shake his hand, and his mother hugged him warmly. Two customers stood back and watched the affectionate greeting. Then, Mrs. Stecker held him at arm's length and scrutinized him carefully with her piercing blue eyes. Erich noticed a tear from each eye trickle down her cheeks and spot the front of her dress.

Mr. Stecker, experiencing a slight embarrassment, introduced him to the two customers. Acquainted with Erich since infancy, they smiled and nodded.

As the father served the customers, Mrs. Stecker led her son into an adjoining family room. "Maria was here less than an hour ago," she said. "She was asking about you. I told her I would let her know when you came."

"Let me clean up a bit," Erich replied. "Then I'll slip over and surprise her."

But in Holzheim, surprises could not wait long. As Erich placed his knapsack in the corner, Maria rushed in.

Tranquil Valley

The coffin, borne on the shoulders of four village officials including the mayor, was being carried to St. Joseph's Church for a funeral Mass. Although the pallbearers tried to keep in step with the mournful dirge played by a small brass band ahead of them, the polished wooden box containing the remains of Albert Juergens rocked and swayed as they made their way along the narrow cobblestone street. A tearful Ilsa Juergens, dressed in somber black and holding the hands of her two small children, followed closely behind Father Kurz at the head of the cortege of villagers.

Albert's body had been prepared for burial in Ritterburg and then placed in the Juergen's small living room for two days. During that time all the residents of Holzheim called to pay their respects and express their sorrow. Their concern had been heightened because Albert and Ilsa had been orphans raised in a church foundling home, and no relatives existed to comfort the family during this time of bereavement.

Ilsa released Maria's hand long enough to dab at her eyes with a wrinkled handkerchief. Not only was she mourning the death of a husband, but she was quietly worrying about how she would support herself and her children. She never expected to earn a living. Her husband was supposed to do that.

Albert had been a woodcutter who had supplied firewood and fenceposts to the inhabitants of Holzheim. Sometimes he stored quantities of these products in a yard beside the family house, but mostly he left them stacked in the woods and made deliveries with his horse and wagon from there. He was a quiet, hardworking man who prided himself in being thorough and efficient. He was admired by his friends for the orderly manner that existed within his family.

Inside the church as Father Kurz explained to the congregation that this calling Albert's soul to the kingdom of heaven was part of God's plan, Ilsa

24

stared blankly at the lone carnation lying on the polished, wooden coffin a few feet ahead of her. She wondered why it had to be Albert. He had much to live for and was needed by his family. And certainly *she* didn't deserve such punishment. She had tried to live a righteous life by being a good wife and mother. She managed an immaculate home and worked hard to grow a productive garden in the backyard each summer. Her children were always well groomed and fed, and she insisted they say their daily prayers. As for charity, since she was adept at reading and writing, she served as go-between for villagers who were illiterate and had difficulty communicating with the outside world. She never charged for this service but had to admit that sometimes she accepted a small sum of money as a gift if the message contained good news.

Albert's death had also stunned the people of Holzheim. They knew him as a man proud of his wife and children who worked hard to give them a good life. Being a devout person, each Sunday as the church bell tolled for ten minutes to summon the faithful, Albert could be seen with his family as they made their way to hear the sermon delivered by Father Kurz. George, in a roomy playsuit, would toddle alongside his father holding on to the strong, callused hand for support, while Maria, wearing a crisp dress, her large brown eyes radiating warmth to everyone she encountered, would walk beside her mother. During the many pleasant Sundays that favored Holzheim, the family frequently took afternoon or evening strolls along the rushing creek that flowed out of the hills and ran beside the town. Sometimes Ilsa brought a basket lunch so they could spend the late afternoon and early evening sitting on the shaded grass watching people pass and feeding bits of bread to the large, white swans. Albert often brought a rubber ball that he rolled back and forth to Maria and George. On occasion when other families with children were present, he organized a game of hide-and-seek. Once he even started a game of soccer, but the resulting roughness made him bring it to a halt.

When word was passed that Albert had been seriously injured, a pall of gloom spread over the village. How could it have happened? He was a careful worker and kept his equipment in excellent condition. That morning, however, he had taken the lunch Ilsa prepared and gone to the woods in his wagon pulled by a faithful old mare he had owned for years. He halted the wagon beside a row of stacked wood and began loading it. Suddenly, the remainder of the stack began to topple. Albert, standing at the foreword edge of the front wheel, was knocked to his knees just behind the mare. The noise, coupled with a piece of wood hitting her on the leg, startled the animal. She snorted and gave one frightful kick to the rear. Her hoof struck Albert on the side of the head, rendering him unconscious.

Two hours later, Franz Schickler, who had been hunting rabbits, found him. Franz loaded him into the wagon and drove him home. The nearest doctor, located five miles away in Ritterburg, was summoned, but he could do little except bandage the three-inch gash beside Albert's ear. Conditions would have been better at the Ritterburg hospital, but Dr. Hartmann did not think Albert could endure the ride.

Albert died that night.

• • •

A month after Albert's funeral, Ilsa took the children by the hand and led them to the cemetery behind the church where he had been laid to rest. The leaves of the aspen and chestnut trees had colored and were lazily spiraling to the ground in the crisp, autumn air. Now that the villagers were no longer offering their condolences, she wanted to be alone with her children near their father. The three of them stood in silence for several minutes at the foot of the grave. Then she said, "Let's kneel down and say the Our Father."

When they had finished and made the sign of the cross, Ilsa remained on her knees studying the upright headstone at the far side of the little plot of newly turned soil. Maria looked up at her and, noting the tears welling up in her mother's eyes, asked, "What does it say, Mother?"

Ilsa looked at her, forced a smile, and then pointed with her finger as she read from the gold lettering on the shiny, black granite slab. "Albert K. Juergens, 18–1–1901, 5–9–1931, May he rest in peace."

Since Maria had practiced writing in school, she understood the words and knew what they meant. But the dates puzzled her. "What do the numbers mean?" she asked.

"Daddy was born January 18, 1901, and died September 5, 1931." Ilsa's voice quivered as she realized his death was exactly two months before her daughter's eighth birthday.

Walking past dozens of weathered headstones on the way out, Maria experienced a profound awareness. Although she was very young and reluctant to believe it, she had to concede that her father was gone and would never return. Suddenly, she felt a deep concern for her mother's newly added responsibilities. She would have to be of more help than she had in the past. When her mother worked in the garden or shopped at Stecker's store, she would watch George instead of playing with her friends. And she would dry the dishes and help with the housework.

Three months after Albert's death, Holzheim's mayor received a directive from the Postmaster of Bavaria in Munich ordering him to establish a branch post office. He was to construct a small building for the purpose and appoint a village postmaster. The villagers were delighted. For years they had pressed for a post office to speed mail handling, but since Ritterburg was a district seat and government center, its arrogant mayor did not wish to relinquish any authority. Although Holzheim's mayor and constable served without pay, they would now have a postmaster who would receive a small salary.

During the four weeks it took to build the little wooden structure, Mr. Stecker, whose opinions were highly respected, let it be known Ilsa Juergens was his choice for postmaster. "She's a smart woman," he repeatedly told his customers, "and she knows how to read and write German very well. Besides, she needs the money to raise her family."

When the villagers were called to a meeting in the school to make the selection, Stecker stood and again reiterated her qualifications. When the vote was taken, Ilsa was the unanimous choice.

Ilsa stood and nodded but was so choked with emotion she could not speak. She knew the salary was small and she would not be entirely without need, but it would provide a living for her and the children. Besides, it would take her off the church charity roll, something she was most pleased to have happen.

As the villagers came to shake her hand, she dabbed her eyes and repeatedly thanked them.

• • •

After completing his second year at the Gymnasium in Regensburg, Erich returned home for the summer recess to find most of the boys away at a Hitler Youth camp in Straubing. Earlier that summer, a state official had appeared at a town meeting and had strongly suggested to the parents that it would be an honor and privilege to have their sons attend the camp. The official promised there would be a similar program for the daughters the following year. Erich's parents did not like the innovation, however, thinking it would be better for him to rest after the strenuous academic term.

The afternoon was warm and quiet, so Erich decided he would spend a refreshing hour at the swimming hole. Many years before, the villagers had constructed a rock dam across the little creek a few hundred yards up the hill to provide a watering place for their animals. As years passed, more wells were dug and catch basins were built so the pond was no longer needed for its intended purpose. It became a summer swimming place for the children. The tall oak and pine trees created ample shade while dense brush that had grown up around the water's edge provided concealment and protection from the wind. A large, flat rock anchoring one end of the dam made an excellent diving platform and a place to dry off before putting on clothing.

As he walked up the narrow, winding path, Erich inhaled deeply, smelling the rich scent of decaying leaves, pine needles, and blackberry blossoms. He smiled as he recalled the pleasant times he had spent at the swimming hole.

The Holzheim swimmers were divided into two groups, those eight to twelve years old, known as the "Sun Worshipers" because they wore no suits, and the older teenagers and young adults. The younger ones came shortly after noon and left at four. The older group, usually at work during the day, went to the pond in late afternoon and early evening to rinse off their bodies. Often they stayed until dark. A few stayed after dark to doff their suits, engaging in horseplay that involved body contact. Inge Trapp was fond of such activity, especially on the weekends when Max Dorten was home.

For several years the two dozen sun worshipers, including Erich, Max, Maria, and Inge, enjoyed playing in the pond during the month of August when school was out. Usually, the members left the group after they had completed the local grammar school. Erich, who had wanted to attend medical school for as long as he could remember, had, over the years, watched the development of the members with considerable interest. The boys became gangly and uncoordinated, developed tufts of hair in the armpits and light, fuzzy showings around their crotches by the last season with the young group. Occasionally, there was a noticeable voice change.

He noted the girls provided more indicators of maturation, but the range of differences was greater. Inge, who was heavy, developed underarm hair and nipple growth when she was ten. By the time she was twelve, her breasts had become pendulous and the lower portion of her abdomen was thoroughly covered with a heavy crop of dark brown hair. In spite of the precocious development, she remained with the group until she was fourteen, enjoying the curious looks of boys as she dropped down on the flat rock to dry. Max, to get a closer look, often stretched out beside her. One day, he made initial body contact when he brushed away a persistent fly from her large round buttocks, resulting in a sequence of pushing, prodding, and fondling. They soon abandoned the Sun Worshipers and joined the older group, where their newly found pleasure was condoned.

By contrast, Kirsten Eckler, who stayed with the young group until she was thirteen, showed no signs of developing. Although she continued to grow in height and appeared healthy and active, her spindle legs, little bony hips, and two small freckles on a flat chest gave no indication of feminine maturation. Erich smiled as he recalled her beautiful, delicate features. She had powder-blue corneas ringed by thin, nearly transparent eyelids that were shaded by long, white eyelashes. Tightly woven flaxen braids that normally extended to her shoulder blades were neatly coiled on top of her head to keep them dry as she swam, a feat she managed with considerable skill. He remembered being nudged as Max snorted and said, "There's a dandy example of human development if ever I saw one."

When she quit swimming with the Sun Worshipers, she enrolled in a parochial school in Regensburg intending to become a nun. Afterwards, she returned to Holzheim for only brief periods, always dressed in a severe, simple manner, never indulging in any form of recreational activity. That was when he found Maria, alone, at the swimming hole drying her lightly tanned body. "Hi, Maria. Nice seeing you again." His heart was racing.

Maria was pleased but didn't want to show her excitement. "Nice to see you again, too."

"Sure quiet here. Where's George?"

"Oh, he's off to camp."

Erich quickly removed his shirt and trousers, revealing the trim blue swimming trunks he wore. After neatly stacking his clothing on a nearby log, he dove into the pond. He made several vigorous turns around its perimeter and then climbed back onto the rock to lie down beside Maria. Dropping down to his elbows, he paused to look at her softly curved hips, long, slender waist, and head of damp, wavy hair. As the front of his moist chest made contact with the warm stone surface, he saw Maria turn her head to rest her cheek on her flattened forearms so she could look into his face with her clear brown eyes.

"How's school?" he asked, noting a golden tuft of hair extending from her armpit just above a bulge of flesh caused by the pressure of her supple breast.

"Oh, fine," she replied. "Did very well on the middle school entrance exam."

Erich smiled and nodded. Both had spent eight years at the same elementary school, he two years ahead of her, so he knew she would do well. However, since he wished to enter the university, he had to go to the Gymnasium, but Maria wanted to be a nurse. She had to complete four years at the middle school before entering the two-year curriculum at St. Joseph's Hospital. "That's right," he responded, as if he had forgotten. "Then, you'll be going to Ritterburg in the fall?"

"Yes. Father Kurz arranged for me to stay with the sisters up there. I report the last week in September."

"Sure you want to be a nurse?"

"More than ever." Her eyes showed determination as she examined the dark eyebrows that arched over his piercing blue eyes. "I spent last month as a volunteer in the Ritterburg Hospital. Makes me feel good to help people who are sick." She paused, smiled, and then added, "By the way, Dr. Hartmann said he'd like to see you if you ever get to Ritterburg."

"What's he want?"

"I don't know," Maria stated matter-of-factly. "I suppose he wants to talk to you about being a doctor."

Maria got to her feet and shook her head. Her blond hair had sufficient body and texture and just enough natural curl, so it readily fell into place. A few strokes of a brush when she got home would give it a delicate sheen and make it lay in a neat series of soft waves. As she slipped into her clothing, she saw Erich watching. For the first time, the exposure of her body made her feel a tinge of embarrassment.

That evening while preparing for bed, she experienced a burning sensation in her nipples. This time it was stronger than in the past. Upon closer examination in the mirror, she found they were larger than she had remembered and slightly darker in color. And the delicate white skin of her chest was being stretched to a glistening tautness by the egg-sized breasts. Then, she found a telltale spot in her panties. She knew her days of swimming without a suit had come to an end.

• • •

August Stecker beamed with pride as he watched his son wait on customers. He was amazed at Erich's ability to carry on an interesting conversation over a wide range of subjects and at a variety of communication levels. The boy could discuss work or politics with a laborer of minimum education and then turn to wait on the mayor, who prided himself with an extensive vocabulary and used terms not understandable to most residents of Holzheim.

But it bothered him when Inge Trapp brought in the two cases of strawberries he had ordered and stayed for a long time talking with Erich. His son was approaching fourteen, and, based on what he had heard over the years, he thought of her as a blocky, sex-oriented individual. When she was a roly-poly little girl, he remembered her laughs and squeals of delight as she was bounced and tossed by friends and relatives. Once Dr. Hartmann had to remove an apple seed from her ear and a piece of crayon from her vagina. And long after she should have behaved like a young lady, she was wrestling with the boys, who tore her clothing and bruised her developing body. Lately, he had heard she was pleasuring Max Dorten whenever he was in town. It would be best for Erich if he did not get too friendly with her. But when Erich accepted her invitation to pick wild strawberries on the hilltop pasture, he did not intercede.

Late that day, Erich was walking slowly down the dry, dusty lane toward the farmhouse, inhaling the pleasant scent of newly mown hay, when Inge saw him. Dropping her hoe in the cabbage patch where she was working, she rushed to intercept him. "Come to pick strawberries?" she asked, smiling as she tried to catch her breath.

"Yes," he replied. "Should be a nice day for it."

Inge was delighted. Erich Stecker was giving her some attention. "Let me put on some shoes," she said, looking down at the mud-caked boots she was wearing.

Hurrying to the house, she said, "Come on upstairs to my room. The others are out in the fields."

It was a large, plastered room with two beds, a dresser, and a bare wooden floor. Several dresses hung from hooks on the back of the door. Feeling uneasy, Erich looked out the lone window as Inge pulled the shoes from under the bed.

Inge paused, dropped the shoes, and said, "Think I'll change my dress, too."

As Erich watched, she pulled her dress over her head and tossed it onto the bed. When he saw she wore nothing beneath it, his face reddened and he turned away. "Would you come over here?" she asked. "I want to show you something."

Reluctant to comply, he turned to face her. She beckoned and smiled, and he walked over to her.

"Just feel this," she commanded, placing his hand on the bulge of fat beneath her navel. "It's always so cold. All the rest of me is warm. What is wrong?"

"I don't know," he replied, hoping she would put on her dress so they could go.

Dropping down onto the bed, she grasped his hand and lay back. "Well, if you're going to be a doctor, you're going to have to find out about these things. Feel how warm the rest of me is."

Erich looked down at her large, sagging breasts and wondered if he should leave.

"Come on. It won't hurt anything." She placed his hand on her chest and moved it in a circular motion.

A nervous chill enveloped his fingers, making her skin feel hot to his touch. When he moved the breasts, she closed her eyes and her breathing quickened. Suddenly, it felt good to him, so he slid his hand over more of her body. Although he felt a throbbing sensation in his loins, he avoided the dark, curly hair on her lower abdomen.

She opened her eyes. "Did you ever look at a woman—close, I mean?"

"No."

"Would you like to?"

Erich felt uncomfortable. "Not right now," he replied. "Let's get started for the berries."

Feeling she had pressed as far as she could, Inge rose from the bed and walked over to the door. She selected an open dress with buttons down the front and then slipped into her shoes. "Now, anytime you want to learn something, just let me know. I'll let you check me anytime."

The strawberry season was near an end, so there were only a few berries on the hill to be picked. Inge had known this, but she had accomplished her goal of an outing with Erich Stecker. On the way down the hill, she paused in the rutted cowpath and pointed to a large pine tree a short distance away. "Let's rest over there for a few minutes," she suggested.

They sat on a cushion of pine needles and ate some of the berries. "It's nice here," Inge said. "I like it." She paused and then added, "Just lay back and listen. The trees seem to be whispering."

They lay for some time, listening to the undulating wind in the trees. Erich could hear the tinkle of a distant cowbell, the volume of which appeared to vary with the direction and velocity of the breeze. Suddenly, Inge broke the silence. "Would you do me a favor?" she asked.

"Sure. What?"

"Would you rub my stomach?"

Erich sat up and looked at the bulk spread out beside him. Inge's eyes were closed and her body motionless. Slowly, he passed his hands in a circular motion over the green cloth. With a suddenness that surprised him, she unbuttoned the dress from top to bottom. Seizing his hand, she directed it to the mossy juncture of her thighs. "Here," she said with a sigh, "rub my jelly roll."

Reluctant at first, Erich sensed a strange but pleasant feeling surge through his body as he complied. And when he was pulled down upon her, he removed his trousers and clumsily made love for the first time.

As he lay beside her trying to sort out the confusion of thoughts racing through his mind, he felt her squeeze his hand as she whispered, "Did you like it?"

"It was all right," he replied, not certain of what he should say. Then he wrinkled his brow and looked at her. "You've done this before with Max, haven't you?"

"Yes. And a few times with others. It doesn't hurt anything, and it's so much fun." There was a moment of silence and then she confided, "Every once in a while I use my sister's candle."

• • •

Erich sat at the desk in his dormitory room searching his mind for the right words to convey his feelings. He had been back in Heidelberg less than a month into his second year of medical school when he realized how he much he missed Maria. For a week he had agonized over many facets of his dilemma. He reflected on her clear, uncluttered mind, her calm, even temperament, and the vocation she had selected. And he smiled when he thought of the uncanny ability she possessed to sense the thoughts that were going through his mind.

While he was completing his final year at the Gymnasium in Regensburg, he had found his interest in her growing rapidly. During that time he had taken her to two parties and one dance, but thought the academic road ahead far too strenuous for a serious relationship. It was there, however, that he encountered a striking parallel in the way the two of them thought and responded. But as he thought of it, this remarkable phenomenon had been occurring for years. There was the time when as children, they were walking by the stream and he wanted to rest. He was about to suggest they sit beneath a large tree for a few minutes when she pointed to it and said, "Let's sit down over there." And there were those times when he was sitting in the living room at the back of the store thinking he would like to go to her house for a visit when the door would open and she would enter, stating she had been thinking about him and had decided to drop by. Then there was the remarkable time when he was in Regensburg and she was in Ritterburg. Neither had planned to come home for the weekend, but both experienced a persistent premonition that something was seriously wrong with a person close to them. When it wouldn't go away, each rode a bicycle home on Friday afternoon. Maria's brother had suffered a severe foot laceration from a broken bottle while hunting frogs in the little stream. They removed the first aid compress Mrs. Juergens had applied and swabbed the wound with a solution of hydrogen peroxide. After applying a fresh bandage, they borrowed a rubber-tired wagon from Mr. Trapp and took George to Dr. Hartmann.

Erich looked down at the blank piece of stationery, still wondering if he should write. There were three years of medical school ahead, and Maria would be at the middle school for two more years before entering the two-year nursing program. Sighing heavily, he grasped the pen and began writing furiously. When he finished, he had written five pages expressing his love and admiration. He closed with a terse statement: "I realize we cannot get married for some time, but my love is deep and sincere. Will you save yourself for me?" He sent it to the middle school in Ritterburg so she would receive it as quickly as possible.

Six days later he received a three-page reply. She promised to wait for him until he had finished his studies and set up a practice. "I will see you at Christmas," she concluded, "and until we are wed, you will be with me in my dreams."

When Mrs. Stecker learned of the informal engagement, she quietly told some of her close friends. The news spread rapidly through the village. By December, when Erich and Maria returned, the people were eagerly waiting to congratulate them. From then on, the citizens of Holzheim would be able to tolerate an outward showing of affection between the two without having it debase the couple's reputation.

After Christmas, just before he left for Regensburg to catch the Heidelberg train, Erich took Maria into the family room at the rear of the store. Making certain his parents were busy with customers, he placed his arms around her shoulders and kissed her warmly. Then he took a small, heart-shaped locket from his pocket and gently fastened the chain around her neck. "Open it," he said, pointing to a wall mirror. "See what's inside."

She walked to the mirror and opened the catch. "It's a picture of you!" she said, her eyes sparkling as she turned to face him. She kissed him and then removed the gold cross that had hung from her neck for years. "Now, you wait right here!" she ordered. "I'll be back in a moment."

Returning a few minutes later, she handed him a package.

"It's heavy," he said, weighing it in his hands. He removed the paper and read aloud the title of the large book, A *Dictionary of Medical Terminology*. Inside the cover, his eyes scanned what she had written: "With all my love until the end of time—December, 1937—Maria."

She pressed her face into his shoulder as they embraced. When she looked up, he saw her eyes were filled with tears.

• • •

When summer came, Erich was glad to go home. After the long, tedious sessions in science laboratories at Heidelberg, he was anxious to spend time enjoying the quiet life of Holzheim. Besides, he would be near Maria.

Two days after he arrived, however, while Erich sat at the dining table watching his mother make potato pancakes, Maria came through the door. "Maria!" he gasped, rising to meet her. She was not supposed to come home for another two weeks, but her smile told him nothing was gravely wrong.

She kissed him and nodded to Mrs. Stecker. "Here's a note from Dr. Hartmann," she said, handing him a folded piece of paper. "He wants you to come in Monday and spend a week at the hospital."

On several occasions Erich had spent one or two days with the sharp-tongued doctor. It was always interesting and rewarding. He was pleased to have been asked but wished he could have rested a while longer. He looked up from the note and asked, "When are you going back?"

"I have to be back tomorrow," Maria replied with a shrug.

Erich looked disappointed. "Tell him I'll be there then," he said.

Monday was clear and unusually hot when Erich mounted his bicycle for the hour ride to Ritterburg. There had been no dew and sullen air lay heavy over the valley. As the sun climbed the eastern sky, heat rose to smother the fields and tree-covered hills. The oppressive humidity suggested a shower, but no clouds appeared.

He was bathed in perspiration when he walked through the admissions door at the hospital. A passing nurse carrying a tray of food looked at him questioningly as she hurried by. "Be right back," she said over her shoulder.

She reappeared. "What can I do for you?"

"I'm Erich Stecker, here at Dr. Hartmann's request."

"Oh yes, Maria's friend. I'll get him." Again, she hurried away.

A few minutes later he saw Dr. Hartmann walking slowly toward him.

The elderly doctor had been in Ritterburg as long as most people could remember. The hospital was an outgrowth of a clinic he had started in a room of his modest home many years ago. His wife, a nurse, had assisted him initially but now preferred the simpler life of homemaker and women's civic leader. Although the doctor had always been interested in helping anyone studying medicine for a career, Erich and Maria had so impressed him that he considered them his personal project.

"Erich, my boy. How nice to have you back," Dr. Hartmann began, showing a rare smile.

Erich looked first at the doctor's slate-blue eyes and then at the creased forehead that separated a heavy shock of white hair from a set of bushy eyebrows. "I'm pleased to be back," Erich replied, feeling the coolness of his drying shirt.

Dr. Hartmann squinted as he scrutinized Erich before speaking. "Let's go into my office," he said, starting for an open doorway down the hall. Inside, he pointed to a large leather chair. "Sit down," he ordered, walking around the cluttered desk to a wicker rocker. "The reason I sent for you is I've scheduled some minor operations I think you should observe." He paused to take a deep breath. "One is a tonsillectomy, which should be fairly routine. But the other involves removal of a toe."

Erich was thrilled but thought he should maintain the pose of a dignified medical practitioner as he had been taught at Heidelberg. He smiled and nodded, noting a twinkle appear in the elderly doctor's eyes. "What happened to the toe?" he asked.

"A woodcutter had it frozen last winter. Thought I could save it, but I think the time has come. Hell, he won't need it anyway." Dr. Hartmann rose to his feet. "See the nurse. She'll give you a room to sleep."

• • •

The morning sun was streaming through a window at the far end of the hall as Erich waited near the operating room. He thought of Maria. She was probably getting ready for her first class in the dormitory just a few blocks away. He would like to see her but had agreed not to leave the hospital. And she could not leave the school compound except on weekends. Maybe he could arrange to have her eat supper with him in the hospital kitchen on Saturday night.

His thoughts were interrupted when a door opened a short distance away and a nurse emerged trundling a loaded gurney toward him. He looked at his watch. It was seven o'clock. Right on time, he thought. As the nurse approached, Dr. Hartmann joined her. Erich held the operating room door open.

Erich could feel a nervous sweat breaking out on his forehead. During the two days he had been at the hospital, he had remained at the elbow of the kindly doctor, carefully observing the bedside manner and listening to the sequence of questions asked to obtain vital information. And there had been times when he was asked to assist with an examination or dispense medication. But this was altogether different. He knew he would be asked to participate in the tonsillectomy on the young boy. Although he did not feel tired, he had slept very little. Throughout the night he had tossed and turned while going over the procedure again and again as he had studied it in Heidelberg. There could be no mistake or hesitation if he was to impress Dr. Hartmann.

Dr. Hartmann turned to the nurse. "You can go now. Dr. Stecker will assist me." He looked at Erich and smiled. Then the smile disappeared and his voice grew stern. "Now, doctor, administer the anesthetic," he ordered.

Startled, Erich quickly placed the gauze-covered mask over the lad's nose and mouth and began to drip ether on it. When the patient's wrist became limp, Dr. Hartmann adjusted the overhead lamp and slipped a snare over a pair of forceps. "Hold the jaw open and man the suction," he said.

In less than five minutes, Dr. Hartmann had finished. "Take care of the bleeding," he said, stepping back.

Erich seized a cotton swab with forceps, dipped it into a dish of calcium, and dabbed the bleeding areas.

As the boy began to moan and cry, Dr. Hartmann pried open an eyelid. "He's all right," he said, turning to Erich. "Stay with him for half an hour. If he vomits, watch he doesn't choke." He started for the door. "A nurse will take over after that.

• • •

It was early morning when Erich was awakened by a sharp knock on his bedroom door and a voice calling, "Erich! Wake up!" Rising to his elbows, he looked at the clock. He had been home two days and was still tired from working in the hospital. A rooster crowed in the distance. The voice was that of his mother. "Tillie is here. She says she needs you right away."

Tillie was an aging midwife who had delivered most of the young people of Holzheim. Lately, Maria had been helping whenever she could because of Tillie's waning strength. She was home. He wondered why she was not helping now. He pulled on his clothes and went downstairs to the store. Tillie, wearing a headscarf and full apron, was wringing her hands. "What's wrong, Tillie?" he asked, rubbing the sleep from his eyes.

"It's Mrs. Kant," Tillie explained. "Her baby will come soon, and it's twisted."

Erich sighed. He hoped he knew what to do. "Let's go," he said, starting for the door. "Can you get Maria, too?"

"I told her," Tillie replied, puffing as she struggled to keep with him. "She's probably there already."

He knew Maria usually visited the expectant mother a month before delivery to inform her about ample hot water, a clean, well-lighted room, and clothing and bedding for the newborn. She also instructed her to loosely stitch together an absorption pad of alternate layers of old blanket material and newspaper.

When Erich entered the bedroom of the small half-timbered house, he saw Maria standing at the head of the bed applying a moist cloth to Mrs. Kant's forehead. "How is she?" he asked.

The expression on Maria's face brightened. "Uncomfortable," she replied. "But contractions haven't started yet. I think she's frightened more than anything else. Baby's not positioned right, and she knows it."

Taking the woman's wrist, Erich studied her eyes. "Just relax," he said calmly. "We'll take care of you."

He pulled the blanket toward the foot of the bed and gently raised her nightgown to expose the bulging abdomen. She winced as he palpated the huge mound. When he stood erect again, he turned to Maria. "Hold her," he said soberly.

Maria handed Mrs. Kant a knotted cloth. "Bite on this," she ordered. Then she pressed against the perspiring woman's forehead.

Using his strong fingers, Erich repositioned the infant. Satisfied with what he had done, he stood up and gave a great sigh. "Now its head is aimed in the right direction," he said, wiping the sweat from his face and neck with a towel.

Two hours later, as he stood by, Tillie delivered Mrs. Kant's healthy boy. He waited for Maria to clean the infant and burn the soiled pad, and then the two of them walked back to the store.

Three days later, Mr. Trapp, while making his weekly delivery of frying chickens to the store, saw Erich sweeping in a back room. Leaning against the door frame, he said, "Hear you fixed Mrs. Kant up with a new little boy."

Erich looked up. "I helped Tillie," he said. "She did most of the work."

"Mrs. Kant says she's sure grateful to you and Maria." Trapp paused, but Erich did not respond. Then he continued. "Wish somebody could do something for my prize rooster."

Erich looked at him questioningly.

"Can't figure it out. Don't seem to have any of the usual sicknesses." Mr. Trapp shook his head. "Got plenty of feed but it's just starving to death."

Although it was a rooster, the thought of something sick interested Erich. Mr. Trapp detected a look of curiosity in the young man's eyes. "Want to look at him?" he asked.

"Sure. Let's go." Erich replied eagerly.

In its weakened state, Mr. Trapp readily caught the rooster and handed it to Erich. Erich looked it over, noting the bright red comb and wattles and healthy covering of gray feathers. Then he felt its shrunken body and bulging crop. "Must be a blockage in the gullet above the gizzard," he said. "What do you think?"

"Well, we get that every once in a while. I just rough up the crop and it clears right out." Trapp shook his head. "With this fellow though, I've done it every day for a week. Don't do any good."

Erich looked up at the grizzled face of the farmer. "I just don't know, Mr. Trapp." His voice was that of resignation. He had always been concerned about the health of people, but since attending medical school and working with Dr. Hartmann, he had developed a strong reverence for all life.

"Tell you what," Trapp said with a shrug. "If he dies, you can cut him open and see what's wrong."

Erich looked into the frightened eyes of the rooster. *It certainly doesn't want to die,* he thought. Maybe there was something that could be done. "Why not do it now and see if we can save him?" he said in a subdued voice.

"Sure. Why not? Take him with you."

"Let me check a few things first, and I'll pick him up later."

After supper Erich went back to the Trapp farm and obtained a complete chicken alimentary canal. Then, with Maria's assistance, he carefully dissected it on an old wooden table in a shed behind her house. As he worked, Mrs. Juergens watched from a distance. Afterwards, while Maria washed the table, he buried the remains in a flower bed. "Have the operating room ready for surgery in the morning," he said, kissing her on the cheek before stepping out the door.

Mrs. Juergens shook her head.

The following morning, Maria put a pot of water on the stove. When she saw Erich coming with the rooster under his arm, she dropped two razor blades, tweezers, scissors, and a coil of white sewing thread into the boiling liquid.

Erich clipped and shaved the rooster's breast while Maria held the unwilling patient. "Now, Nurse, the instruments!" he ordered.

Maria detected confidence in his voice. She retrieved the instruments from the pot, wrapped them in a towel she had sterilized in the oven, and placed them on the table.

Using a razor blade, Erich made a small incision in the gullet just below the crop. Plying the tissue apart, he saw something green. The excitement he felt, coupled with the odor of opened flesh, made him break out in a nervous sweat. He picked up the tweezers and, probing the opening, seized the green object. "There's the culprit," he said, withdrawing a folded blade of grass.

Using a medicine dropper, he forced a bubble of air through the canal into the gizzard. There was a muted gurgle as the bubble returned. "It's open now," he said with a sigh. "Let's close him up!"

He returned the rooster to a crate placed off the ground in the Trapp barn. After staying with the bird for a while, he and Maria decided to leave. "Seems to be in fine shape," he told Mr. Trapp.

"We'll see," Trapp replied doubtfully.

"Look in on him every once in a while. If he picks at the thread, let me know." Erich smiled. "We don't want him to fall apart."

When Erich returned to the barn in early afternoon, he saw the rooster eating. He knew the operation was successful.

News of the operation spread rapidly through the village and the curious came to the Trapp barn to see the rooster. Each evening parents brought their children, and children brought their parents, to view the unusual bird. A week later Mr. Trapp returned the rooster to the flock, and still the people came. If they could not find the rooster, they asked Inge or her father to find it for them. "Had to put it back in a crate and set it on the porch," Mr. Trapp complained to Mrs. Stecker one day when he was in the store. "Couldn't get anything done anymore. Somebody was always poking around trying to find that fool rooster."

Mrs. Stecker beamed with pride.

• • •

Erich sat, holding Maria's hand, at the top of the three wooden steps leading up to the front porch of the Juergen's home. It was one of the long, warm evenings that gave him time to be with her. He liked that.

He looked down at the three weathered treads. They were as familiar as the pages of his anatomy books. He and Maria had spent hours staring at them as they discussed the facets of their lives and plans for the future. He could close his eyes and visualize every gray sliver, black crack, dent, warp and nick they possessed. And he could immediately recognize any new scratches or cuts when they appeared.

Both he and Maria had learned the characteristics of the three steps so thoroughly that whenever they came home after her mother and brother had gone to bed, they always stepped on the outer edges over the support members.

In that way, their shoes made a short click rather than a hollow thud when they came in contact with the wood. He was certain that even if Mrs. Juergens was in bed, she was awake, waiting for her daughter to come in. Besides, George made his bed on a couch in the living room of the small house, and on warm evenings the screen door was the only separation between him and the porch. And they avoided the middle step altogether since it squeaked when their weight was removed from it,

His chain of thought was broken when Maria asked, "Would you have supper with us tomorrow?"

He looked at her and smiled. "Sure," he said. "What can I bring?" It didn't seem right to him for Mrs. Juergens to serve him food she had purchased from the Stecker store when she had to work so hard for a meager salary to support herself and her two children. And he knew she would have to budget even more carefully to send Maria to nursing school.

Maria shook her head. "You always bring something. Why don't you just let us feed you?"

"I can't do that," Erich insisted. "I'll bring a ham and some rolls."

• • •

Erich sat at the edge of the bed rubbing the sleep from his eyes as he slid his feet into his slippers. Standing, he stretched and then walked to the window and pushed open the shutters. The sun, a large, orange ball, had climbed above the horizon and was lifting a moist haze that blanketed the area. A wren that had been flitting among the green apples in a tree below stopped to watch his movements before flying off.

He inhaled a deep breath of the cool air and smiled. It felt good to be home again. He had just finished another two weeks with Dr. Hartmann at the hospital and was pleased with the way he had performed. Because he had completed his second year at Heidelberg, the doctor gave him considerable latitude, often accepting his diagnoses and recommendations with a minimum of checking. And here in Holzheim, the villagers were calling him "Dr. Stecker." It embarrassed him, but he had reached a point where he felt confident to treat their colds, suture their cuts, and set simple fractures.

His thoughts turned to Maria. She was home for the weekend, and he was looking forward to the afternoon walk in the forest they had planned. But nursing school had no summer vacation, so she would have to return to Ritterburg Sunday afternoon.

Then there was his mother's brother Johann and wife Ellen in Straubing. His mother had mentioned they wanted him to spend some time with them. It was true that as a small boy he had visited them one summer, but he hadn't seen them but once since. He was certain his mother had boasted that he was in medical school, and they now wanted to see the little Erich they had supervised for two weeks and claim credit for his accomplishments. He pursed his lips and shook his head. There would be no visit to Straubing this summer if he could avoid it.

A sudden knock on the door made him turn around. "Erich!" It was his mother. "Are you up?"

"Yes," Erich replied, his face showing concern.

"Maria is here. Wants to see you right away."

He slipped into his clothes and bounded down the stairs, wondering why Maria was here so early. She was waiting in the store near the bakery counter. "What's the matter?" he asked, wrinkling his brow.

"Mrs. Geier would like to see you," Maria stated matter-of-factly.

"Is she sick?"

"No. It's Morna."

He knew Morna. At fifteen, she was the youngest of three Geier girls. Her older sisters had married and moved away, leaving her to help her mother and father work the fields of their farm near the edge of town. "What's the problem?" he asked.

"She's having severe abdominal pains," Maria replied. "I didn't look at her. Just came after you when Mrs. Geier asked me to."

Mr. Geier, waiting at the front door of the small farmhouse, shook Erich's hand and pointed toward a bedroom door. The solemn look on the man's wrinkled face mirrored his concern. Mrs. Geier was sitting beside Morna's bed. Erich placed his medical bag on a table and looked down at the small, light-complexioned face whose tight lips revealed the tension her body was experiencing.

"I understand you have a stomach ache," he said calmly.

"Yes," she replied. Her voice was barely above a whisper.

He turned to Mrs. Geier. "We would like to see her alone."

The middle-aged woman rose to her feet and looked down at her daughter. Then she turned to Erich and Maria, nodded approval, and left the room.

Erich pulled down the light blanket that covered his patient and then turned to Maria. "You take her temperature while I check a few things."

He brushed his hand across her forehead, looked into each of her eyes, and felt her cheeks and throat. Then he took her pulse rate and listened to her heartbeat.

Maria removed the thermometer. "Normal," she said.

He looked down at Morna and smiled. "That's good."

Morna's eyes followed his, but she said nothing.

"Have you had an ache like this before?" he asked.

"I get them every month. They've been getting worse lately."

"Does it come at the same time as your period?"

"I haven't started having periods yet."

"Never?"

"Never."

Erich thought for a moment and then unbuttoned the top of her night-gown and pulled it down from her shoulders. As he applied gentle pressure around her well-developed breasts, he noted an abundant crop of underarm hair. "Hurt?" he asked.

"No," came the reply. "It tickles."

Erich carefully refastened the buttons and then raised the gown above her waist. Her lower abdomen appeared slightly distended. When he applied a gentle pressure, she inhaled sharply and winced noticeably.

He looked up at Maria. "Give me a hand," he ordered.

With Maria's assistance, Morna doubled back her knees and spread her thighs. Erich, placing a forefinger of each hand at the sides of the vaginal vestibule, carefully pulled downward and outward. "There's the problem," he declared, nodding for Maria to look. "It's an imperforate hymen."

Erich readjusted Morna's nightgown, and Maria pulled the blanket up to the girl's shoulders. Then he sat on the edge of the bed. "It's nothing serious," he told Morna. "A small operation will fix it."

Sitting down at the large table with Mr. and Mrs. Geier, he told them their daughter was normal except for a thin membrane blocking her menstrual flow. "You should go to Dr. Hartmann and have it done as soon as possible."

"Can you do it?" Mrs. Geier asked.

"I have seen it done, but Dr. Hartmann is better qualified than I am. Just see him."

As Erich and Maria walked away from the Geier's house, they looked back and saw the couple still standing in the doorway. They waved, and the Geiers returned their wave.

Erich ate a late breakfast and then went to his room to play the piano. The piano had a soothing way of making him relax so he could think more clearly. He had been playing only a few minutes when he heard the voice of his mother calling. Descending to the family room, he found Mr. and Mrs. Geier waiting.

"We want you to fix Morna," Mrs. Geier stated, clasping her hands together.

"It would be better if Dr. Hartmann did it," Erich countered.

"Don't you know how?" Mrs. Geier asked with raised eyebrows.

"Yes. But I've never done it before."

"Please. We trust you."

"What does Morna think?" Erich asked.

"She wants you to do it."

Erich stood silent, looking about the room. He had practiced medicine among the villagers in a small way, opening boils and disinfecting abrasions. And there was the Trapp rooster, still crowing each morning from the barnyard fence. He turned to face the Geiers. "Are you sure?" He looked into their eyes as he spoke.

"Absolutely!" they chorused.

"Let's see if Maria will help," Erich said, motioning toward the door.

They hurried down the cobblestone street and knocked on the Juergens' door. The door opened, and Maria, wearing an apron, looked at them and smiled. "Well hello, Erich." She nodded to the Geiers. "I was fixing our basket lunch, and I had a strong feeling you'd be coming early." She paused and then said, "But I didn't know why."

"The Geiers want me to take care of Morna. Will you help?"

"Of course," she replied, pleased to be asked.

"Tomorrow morning?"

She nodded.

Erich turned to the Geiers. "We'll be over at eight tomorrow morning."

Mrs. Geier grasped his hand with both of hers. "Thank you. Thank you, *very* much."

As the Geiers turned to leave, Erich said, "Give her an aspirin to help her sleep tonight."

• • •

The sun felt warm on their backs as Erich and Maria walked slowly down the street toward the edge of town. They stopped momentarily on a little footbridge to look at some ducks floating in a small eddy pool at a curve in little stream that danced and sparkled as it bubbled past. At the Trapp farm, they saw the rooster they had saved the previous summer herding his harem of hens. "Seems all right, now," Maria observed.

"At least the operation hasn't diminished his stamina," Erich chuckled. "And Mr. Trapp says he's meaner than most."

As they passed beneath a chestnut tree at the beginning of a winding footpath leading up the hill, a cool gust of wind rustled its leaves. A fox squirrel, frightened by the sudden noise, scurried to the tip of a limb and scolded noisily. And a blue jay hopped from branch to branch ahead of them, its warning calls interspersed with the staccato of a distant woodpecker. Erich took a deep breath. It filled his nostrils with a mixed scent of pine and the fragrant wild flowers that grew in the moist, decaying forest residue.

He selected a shaded spot on a thick carpet of needles beneath a large pine to spread the blanket Maria had brought. As he helped her to a sitting position, he glanced at a cluster of birches a short distance away. They appeared like stark sentinels placed there to guard against an invasion of privacy.

Lying on his back, he grasped Maria by the hand and pulled her down beside him. They remained quiet for several minutes, holding hands and looking at patches of blue showing through the lacework of branches overhead. Then, Maria broke the silence. "What are you thinking about?" she asked, looking into his eyes.

"A million things," he answered, continuing to gaze upward. "I just can't believe how lucky I am. The older I get, the more amazed I am about the puzzling mysteries around us." He raised up on an elbow and turned to face her. "Here we are, two healthy, intelligent human beings. Just imagine the odds against being born at all." He shook his head as he looked into her face. "And once born, living to reach maturity." He looked off into the distance. "And we were born in this wonderful country of ours, not Siberia, or China, or Africa. We are white, not black or yellow. How did all of this come about? How was it arranged?"

He put his arms around her. "And here I am in this lovely forest on this beautiful day, with the finest young woman this country has produced." He kissed her. "Oh, how very much I love you." Then, slipping his hand inside her blouse, he caressed her breast. She closed her eyes, her lips parted, and her breath came in little gasps. And when he moved his hand to her abdomen, she raised her hips.

Suddenly, he withdrew his had and sat upright. "We cannot go on like this," he stammered.

Surprised, Maria looked at him questioningly. She was experiencing sensations she had not felt before, sensations so pleasant and so strong they overwhelmed her sense of judgment.

Erich looked into her eyes and brushed his fingers across her rosy cheeks. "I don't want to cheapen our love and respect for each other. Nor do I want to circumvent the wonderful plans we have made. We must do it right—like we are expected to do." He was scolding her as well as himself. "We will wait until we are married in a church. And you will wear a white gown. And that gown will not be worn falsely to make a mockery of what we are doing." He paused and emitted an audible sigh. "We must show respect for ourselves and our families. We must make rules for ourselves!"

Maria sat up and straightened her hair. She knew he was right. Their families and the people of Holzheim held them in high esteem, and it would be a disgrace to let them down. "Let's eat," she said, "and we'll talk about it."

The sun was below the horizon when they strolled back into Holzheim. Holding Maria's hand, Erich helped her avoid the middle step of the Juergens' porch. Then, standing beside the door, he grasped her by the waist and kissed her. She quivered. "I'll see you in the morning," he said, quietly.

• • •

Erich looked toward the wood-burning stove at the far side of the room then back at Mrs. Geier. "Well, I see you have the hot water I asked for."

"Yes," the woman replied nervously. "If you need anything else, let me know. Anything at all."

Erich nodded.... "Now you and your husband can go out on the porch. If you are needed, we'll let you know."

Maria helped Morna onto the padded dining table. "Double up your knees," she ordered, slipping the girl's nightgown above her hips. Then she gently washed and shaved the pubic area.

Erich removed his scalpel and an enameled cup from the boiling water and put them on a towel Maria had placed on the table. When he took a small, pressurized can of ether from his bag, Maria wrinkled her brow and looked at him. "Something new," he explained. "Dr. Hartmann gave me this sample. It makes a small area very cold." Pulling up a chair, he sat down and swabbed the site with a mild iodine solution.

"Now, Morna," he said, in a calm, understanding voice, "this will hurt a bit, but only for an instant. In a few minutes it will be all over. Just hold as still as you can."

"I will, Erich," Morna replied.

Maria placed the upper portion of her body over Morna's abdomen and wrapped her arms about the patient's upright thighs. Erich gave the bulging hymen the momentary numbing spray, then made a quick incision eliciting a slight jerk from Morna. As the dark, red liquid issued from the new opening, he pressed the enameled cup in position to receive it.

"It's over and everything's fine," he said, trying to relax the tense patient.

"Now, that wasn't bad, was it?" Maria said, looking into Morna's face as she wiped the perspiration from the girl's forehead.

A few minutes later, Erich replaced the cup with a pad. Then, with Maria's help, he guided Morna to her bed.

"You can come in now!" he called out to the parents as Maria cleared the table.

When he was ready to leave, Erich returned to the bedroom. Looking into Mrs. Geier's tear-filled eyes, he said, "I'll be back this afternoon to see her again."

Forcing a smile, she replied, "We are so grateful to you and Maria."

The next morning when he went to the Geier's house, he found Morna at the table writing a letter. She looked up and smiled. "I want to tell my friend, Lydia, about it," she said.

"How do you feel?" he asked.

"Very good." Her voice was that of a happy person. "It itches where Maria shaved me, though."

"You'll probably go through that again in your lifetime," he teased. Looking around the room, he asked, "Where are your parents?"

"Working in the fields."

When he examined her, he was pleased. Pulling down her gown, he said, "You don't need the pad anymore."

He took a glass rod and small bottle of alcohol from his bag. "I want you to push this rod through the opening two or three times a day for the next three days," he told her. "Clean it with alcohol each time."

Looking at him soberly, she nodded.

"We don't want it to heal shut again," he said.

"Oh," she replied.

• • •

Erich was awakened by a mild shaking. Opening his eyes, he could make out the dim outline of the night duty nurse in the darkness. "Dr. Hartmann wants you in his office right away," she said. Her voice sounded muted to him.

He turned on the light and sat up on the edge of the bed. As the door closed behind the nurse, he looked at his watch. Four-thirty. *It must be a dire emergency*, he thought as he struggled toward the basin to rinse his face. He wondered if he had done the right thing by volunteering to spend a few days at the Ritterburg Hospital so near the end of his vacation.

"Got something real interesting for you," Dr. Hartmann said as Erich entered the office.

"Good, What is it?" Erich asked, stifling a yawn.

"A postmortem."

"This time of the day?"

"Absolutely," Hartmann stated. "The best ones are done within thirty minutes after the heart stops." As he started for the door, he added, "Liver turns mushy after only a few hours."

In a stark white basement room, Erich could make out the outline of a human form lying beneath a sheet on an enameled table. Another table along one wall held a series of jars, surgical instruments, and a note pad and pencil.

"We have to wear these," Dr. Hartmann said, handing Erich a gown, mask, and rubber gloves. Switching on the exhaust fan, he directed Erich to pick up the pad and pencil. Then he walked over and removed the sheet from the body.

Erich noted the top sheet on the pad had been filled in with the man's name and address. It listed his age as fifty-seven, gave his height and weight, and stated that he had been admitted to the hospital two days before. Looking up, he saw Dr. Hartmann pry open each eye and then slip his gloved fingers between the lips and deep into the cheeks. "Blue eyes, upper dentures, no other obvious scars or marks." Erich wrote it on the form.

Hartmann stood erect. "Put down the pad and come over here." As Erich approached, he continued, "See the way the blood settles." He pointed to the deepening reds and purples that had formed along the portions of the body nearest table. "See how different it is from the waxy white of the higher parts. And how very noticeable it is at the ears, jaws, calves, and heels." He turned to face Erich. "It isn't too important here, but if murder was suspected, it could determine if he died at the spot or had been moved after death."

At Dr. Hartmann's direction, Erich placed specimens of tissue and lung calcium deposits in the jars of formaldehyde. Then the doctor pointed to the black and purple deposits in the sliced lung sections on the drain board. "Cigarette smoking," he said prosaically.

He removed the heart, placed it on the drain board and sliced nearly through it in eighth inch segments. Fanning it like pages of a book, he said, "Look, Erich. See how the blood vessels are so loaded with deposits that they nearly close in some places? He was headed for a coronary attack within the next few years."

After the remainder of the viscera had been removed from the abdominal cavity, Erich looked down at the emptied body. It looked like that of an animal hanging in a meat market. Having worked on cadavers at Heidelberg, he thought he possessed a professional indifference to human corpses. But he did not. This man had been alive and breathing a few hours before. Here on the postmortem table, however, not a trace of human dignity remained. He could do such a thing to a person on a professional basis, he was sure, but he would never permit an autopsy to be done on any member of his family.

Dr. Hartmann had removed the brain. He pointed to a small oval object in the depression of the sphenoid bone. "What's that?"

"The pituitary gland," Erich quickly answered.

"You know your anatomy."

"Thank you."

Hartmann carefully plied the brain segments apart. "There it is!" he exclaimed, pointing to a large clotted area. More probing exposed the ruptured vessel. "Good Lord! He really blew!"

The two of them stuffed the distended organs into the body cavities and sutured the incisions. As they removed their protective clothing, Hartmann said, "Call the scrub nurse to clean the room." He scanned what Erich had written on the form, picked up the pen, and wrote, "Massive cerebral hemorrhage." Then he signed his name.

When he looked up, he said, "Come over to the house for breakfast when you get ready."

"Fine," Erich replied, pleased to be invited.

• • •

Mrs. Hartmann placed a tray of rolls and coffee on a round, metal table in her beautifully landscaped garden and then returned to the kitchen. As Erich poured the coffee, Dr. Hartmann reached over and turned on his portable radio. "Like to listen to classical music when I eat," he explained. "Makes the gastric juices flow much more smoothly." He chuckled.

Erich broke open a crisp roll and smeared it with strawberry jam. He took a bite and then a sip of coffee. Looking down at the flowers, he thought the color of the red and white geraniums seemed extra bright this morning. It was a pleasant morning, and the music lulled his senses.

Suddenly, the music stopped. In a sober voice, an announcer made a terse statement, "At four forty-five this morning, troops of the German Reich crossed the frontier into Poland and are advancing toward Warsaw and Krakow."

Decision

The air resounded with a roar when Max Dorten rode his new BMW motorcycle through town. Inge, her jowls and abdomen shaking noticeably as the machine vibrated across the rough cobblestones, sat on the buddy seat with her arms around his waist. A group of children on their way home from Sunday Mass stopped to watch the noisy machine speed past. When Inge dismounted, the children ran up and surrounded the motorcycle.

"Can I have a ride?" an oldest boy asked.

"Sure," Max replied with a wide grin. Turning to Inge, he said, "Help him on."

As the motorcycle headed for the church again, Inge listened to the awed comments of the remaining children. Her face beamed with pride. Max was the first Holzheimer to own a motorized vehicle. And he was her man.

Several men who had stopped at the Holzheimer Tavern on the way home from church to discuss the war news and exchange gossip heard the commotion and came out onto the street. "He might be a sensation in Inge's eye," one of them snorted, "but that damned machine's going to scare hell out of our horses and oxen."

"Noise like that will lower milk and egg production too," another averred with a snap of his head.

Inge continued to smile, pretending she didn't hear them. Seeing that some of the children were staring at something behind her, she turned to see what it was. Erich had parted the curtains and was watching them from the store window. She beckoned for him to come out.

Erich had known that Max Dorten would someday own a motorcycle. As a boy, Max had often run about the streets and playground, holding a stick between his outstretched hands and making noises with his mouth as he pretended to be driving in a race. And now, with a steady job at the Messerschmitt factory, Max didn't surprise Erich when he drove up and down the streets of Holzheim. Erich unlocked the door and stepped outside just as Max pulled up.

Max assisted the boy to the ground and then turned to face Erich. Running a hand through his windblown hair to smooth it, he said, "How do you like it?" His face wore a broad smile and was flushed with pride.

"It's a beauty!" Erich replied.

"Came to see if you want me to take you to the station. Inge says you have to leave today. Can hang your bags right over there." He patted the rear fender.

Erich planned to ride his bicycle to Regensburg to catch the evening train to Heidelberg. With a ride from Max, however, it would be much easier and he wouldn't have to leave until late afternoon. "Sure," he answered. "That'll be great!"

After lunch he walked to Maria's house. Since he had the time and probably would not return until Christmas, he wanted to be with her before his family and friends gathered to see him off. It would provide a few private moments that could be remembered and cherished during his long absence. When he knocked, Maria came to the door. "Come in," she said in a subdued voice as she pushed open the screen door.

Erich noted the solemn look on her face. She had always greeted him with a broad smile and sparkling eyes, but this time her mood was somber. "Let's sit on the step," he said, taking her by the hand.

After helping her to a sitting position, he lowered himself beside her. "Now," he said, "what's the matter?"

Grasping his arm, she studied his eyes for a moment and then stared off into the distance. "I'm afraid," she said soberly. "Afraid of this war."

Erich hadn't realized she was *this* concerned about it. He knew that the people of Holzheim, though far removed from the fighting, were interested and concerned as the German divisions smashed their way through Poland. Two families had sons in the army, but they were stationed along the Siegfried Line on the French border. However, with transportation as rapid as it was, the mothers called on Mrs. Juergens at the post office twice a day hoping for a letter to assure them.

Since not all families had radios, small groups gathered at the barber shop, the Holzheimer Tavern, and his parents' store to listen to the four official newscasts each day. Although great victories were proclaimed, he had noted little evidence of joy or jubilation since many local citizens still held vivid memories of the slaughter and famine of the previous war. And, of course, due to its agrarian isolation and independence, Holzheim did not breed a people who thirsted for additional territory or excessive political ambitions. They were grateful for the opportunity to put forth an honest day's work in the fields in exchange for sufficient food and an adequate roof over their heads. And most sympathized with the Polish people who were now suffering the brutal misery of war.

It'll soon be over in Poland," he said, trying to console her. "And that should be the end of it."

"But now France and England have declared war on us," she countered. "It will be like the last one—go on and on, killing our young men. In the end, we will lose." She held on to his arm and looked into his face. "It has been hard enough without a father. And now I don't want to lose you." Tears welled up in her warm brown eyes.

"I probably won't be called," he said. "Even if I am, I'll more than likely work in a hospital far from the fighting."

Just then George came in from the street and bounded up the steps and into the house. "Hello, Erich," he said as he passed.

Maria forced a smile as she watched him. "And I don't want anything to happen to him, either."

"He's only a boy," Erich replied with a frown. "Everything will be over by the time he's old enough."

Maria did not respond.

After discussing the situation for some time, Erich got her to agree to an optimistic approach. They would assume the Polish conquest would end the fighting and then peace would be negotiated with England and France. In the meantime, they would continue to pursue the goals they had set for themselves.

Rising to their feet, Erich took her soft, warm hands in his and kissed her moist lips fervently. "I love you, my dear," he declared, trying to assure her. "And things will work out all right for us." He knew she was still troubled, but her mood was better.

She stood watching until he disappeared up the street then dashed into the house. In a short time she would go to the store to bid him farewell. Before then, however, she wanted to bathe, change into her satin dress, and place a dab of Chantilly perfume behind each ear and between her breasts. She would be certain all of his senses had been imprinted before he left.

• • •

While waiting with Erich at the Regensburg station, Max expressed concern about the war. "Don't worry," Erich said, trying to assure his friend. "Things will get straightened out soon, and everything will settle back to normal." He paused as Max wrinkled his brow and shook his head. "And Max," he continued, "you're learning a fine trade. Just stick with it, and you'll really have something."

"I don't know, Erich," Max said soberly. "I think we're in over our head, and they're going to need every bit of help they can get."

"But you are helping! You're building fighter planes."

"I know," Max replied. "But other people, older people and cripples, can do that. I think I could be of more help at an air base with the *Luftwaffe*."

In Heidelberg a light mist was falling as Erich left the station to make his way up the street to his lodging house. It gave the cobblestones a dull luster in the reflected glow from the dimly lit streetlamps. Already, he missed the coziness of Holzheim. And he was concerned about Max wanting to enlist rather than wait until he was called up. Much of the uneasiness he felt was caused by an overwhelming enthusiasm for the invasion of Poland he had noticed among the train passengers. Their discussions held nothing but praise for Hitler's actions, stating that the country was being led to its rightful position of world prestige and power.

The stillness of the evening was suddenly rent by the howling shriek of a large cat that leaped from the black shadows of a darkened alley and dashed across the street just ahead of him. Momentarily startled, Erich stopped and inhaled a deep breath, filling his nostrils with the pungent odor of urine. But the smell did not surprise him. Like most alleys in Heidelberg, this one had been used for decades to relieve the overburdened bladders of men on their way home after a night of drinking in a nearby tavern. The rain just made the odor stronger.

• • •

By mid-morning, Erich had completed registration confirming a schedule of primary medical and surgical practice in the hospital. Upon returning to the lodging house, he found his roommate, Heinz Jager, energetically packing a small traveling bag. Heinz, a tall, wiry young man from a wealthy Dusseldorf family, was impetuous as well as innovative.

"Quitting before you start, Heinz?" Erich asked, jokingly.

"No. Since classes don't start until next week, I'm going to make a run to Munich. Just like to see what the *Oktoberfest* is all about." He paused to look up at his friend. "How about coming along?"

The *Oktoberfest*, as Erich understood it, was a harvest festival that over the years had developed into a gigantic beer drinking celebration lasting six weeks. He wanted to go someday but hadn't planned to go this year. "That's some distance. How are you going?" he asked, not sure he should even pursue the thought.

"By bus, I guess."

"When does it leave?"

"I don't know. Let's just go down to the depot and find out."

Hurrying to the bus depot, they were informed the Munich bus would leave in forty-five minutes. "When's the next one?" Erich asked, pulling some money from his pocket.

"Not for five hours," the agent replied stoically as he took the money and handed Erich a ticket.

"Will the first bus wait a few minutes if we're not here when the time comes?" Heinz inquired. "We've got to run back and get our bags."

The agent looked as if he had been insulted. "Not a chance! These buses leave precisely on time!"

Hurrying all the way, they managed to get back and climb aboard just as the agent signaled the driver it was time to depart.

It was after dark when the heavily burdened bus entered Munich. And it took another hour for it to reach the central depot through the milling throngs of people who flooded the side-walks and spilled over into the streets. Erich and Heinz tried several hotels and inns in the vicinity but were informed by each that all rooms had been reserved for the next three weeks. "Let's go in and have a beer," Heinz suggested, pointing to a noisy tavern across the street that had its doors open.

Heinz pushed through the exuberant crowd, leading Erich to the bar. "Two small glasses of beer!" he shouted, trying to be heard above the noise.

After forcing their way to a corner, Erich, feeling the stress of a long, arduous day, propped himself against the wall. He took a sip from the glass and sighed. "What are we going to do for a place to stay?" he asked.

Heinz smiled. "Oh, hell," he replied. "We'll find a place. Got to get inside, though." He squinted to see across the room. "Getting too cold to sleep in the park with these light clothes," he concluded, tugging at the lapel of his jacket.

Erich shrugged and then looked out over the crowd. He knew the *Oktoberfest* was a wild celebration, but how could people be this uninhibited? The heavy air, reeking of beer and perspiration, was so filled with smoke he could not see the far wall. Nudging Heinz, he said. "My history teacher once said we take in seven molecules of Caesar's last breath each time we inhale. I bet he never counted on anything like this."

For several minutes they sipped from their glasses and watched people in various states of inebriation, engaged in friendly discussions, arguments, or song while gulping beer from large steins. One man stood, held his stein high, and toasted those around his large table. When he finished, they all lifted their huge stems, nodded to each other, and then drank their steins empty. In an attempt to outdo them, a woman climbed upon an adjacent table and, waving her stein wildly, tried to lead those around her in singing *"Rosa*

Munde." A short distance away. Erich saw a man sitting in a loose-jointed chair kissing a henna-haired woman while trying to get his hand beneath her tight skirt.

Heinz, noting Erich's awed expression, leaned toward him and chuckled. "Hell, I bet her thighs have felt many a hairy hand!"

Erich smiled and shook his head.

Heinz emptied his glass. "Let's find a place to stay," he said, starting toward the door. As he threaded his way through the crowd, Erich followed close behind. "I bet if we wanted to," he said loud enough so Erich could hear, "we could get one of these women to take us in."

"That's not for me," Erich replied, shaking his head.

After trying three rooming houses and receiving the same negative replies from grumpy, tired-eyed managers, they came upon a marketplace. Several stalls were being used to bed a dozen blocky horses. Heinz approached a lone attendant dozing in a chair propped against a cabinet. "Nice horses," he said, trying to rouse the man as gently as possible.

The startled man opened his eyes and pushed forward so the chair rested on four legs. "Just horses," he said, eying the two intruders suspiciously. "Going to be in the parade tomorrow."

"Mind if we took some straw and made a bed in one of the empty stalls?" Heinz asked.

The attendant seemed relieved. He shrugged his shoulders. "Help yourselves," he said, motioning toward one of the stalls. Then he pushed his chair back and closed his eyes again.

• • •

The shuffle of numerous feet and babble of many voices woke Erich from a deep sleep. He rolled over, rubbed his eyes, and raised up on one elbow to look around. Dozens of vendors were setting up displays of fruit, vegetables, and souvenirs. Looking out beyond the overhang, he could see the sky was just changing from a deep purple to a light gray.

Since it was useless to try to sleep, he rose slowly to his feet, yanked a towel from his pack, and went to a nearby water tap to wash his face. When he returned, Heinz was sitting up brushing straw from his clothes and hair. "Short night?" Erich asked with a wry smile.

Heinz looked up and shook his head. "What the hell," he snorted, rising to his knees. "This is the *Oktoberfest!*" Once on his feet, he sniffed the air. "Smells like coffee."

Erich nodded. "There's a stall down there selling rolls and coffee. We can get some when you're ready."

Later in the morning they watched a long parade of bands, dancers, clowns, and beer wagons. Erich remembered Rosa Graebner's promise and wondered if she would be here. Then he thought of Maria. Perhaps it would be better not to see Rosa. Besides, she probably didn't mean what she said anyway.

As the hour approached eleven, his curiosity mounted. He turned to Heinz. "Let's go to *Marienplaz*," he said.

Heinz shrugged. "Go ahead and I'll follow. It's only about three blocks."

Erich forced his way through the crowd to the edge of the cordoned off square. After searching the vast sea of faces for ten minutes, he decided it would take a bolder approach to locate Rosa if she was here. He would create a disturbance by charging through the police lines. But the timing must be right. If he did it when the mechanical figures were in action, she would be watching them instead of the square.

Three minutes before eleven he leaped over the rope. With two policemen in pursuit, he made a brief run around the square and then returned to his place beside Heinz. Standing erect, he smiled broadly at the staring crowd of stunned people.

Heinz looked at him in disbelief "What in hell hit you?" he asked, yelling at his friend. "You want to be picked up for being crazy? Don't you know what Himmler does with mental defectives?" He paused as he caught his breath. "Off to Dachau!" he said, pointing his finger as his arm shot out before him.

Just then, one of the pursuing policemen trotted up. "You are an ass!" he puffed, shaking his finger a few inches from Erich's nose. "Who do you think you are disrupting our celebration? Where is your sense of pride, your discipline? It's outside assholes like you that give the *Oktoberfest* a bad name!" He looked at Heinz, then back at Erich. "I ought to run you in to teach you a lesson!"

The girl running beside the rope caught the awestruck crowd's attention. When she reached the policeman, she pushed in front of him, wrapped her arms around Erich's neck, and smothered him with kisses. It was Rosa.

The crowd, realizing what the commotion was about, applauded and cheered. As the livid-faced policeman threw up his arms and stamped away, the clock figures began to move.

Erich waited until the clock had finished ringing before introducing Heinz. Then, Rosa, who had brought her seventeen-year-old sister, Irma, with her, motioned for the girl to join them. As she approached, she appeared as beautiful as her older sister. And when she was introduced to Heinz, Erich thought he detected a warm sparkle in her eyes.

The crowd drifted away, and they strolled a short distance to a sidewalk cafe and sat down at a wire-legged table. Heinz ordered a platter of sliced sausage, a loaf of bread, and a bottle of *Liebfraumilch*. "Don't eat too much here," he warned. "Save room for the Hofbrau House."

Erich looked at him questioningly.

"Why, certainly!" Heinz exclaimed enthusiastically, nudging Irma "You must spend an evening at the Hofbrau House to get the flavor and feeling of the *Oktoberfest!*"

Irma, looking for a response, turned to her older sister.

Rosa's mind was occupied with thoughts of Erich. She studied his face and looked longingly into his eyes. *Yes,* she thought, *they are still as clear and warm as she remembered them.* If only they could be alone for a while. When Heinz's words registered, she looked at Irma and nodded. Then she turned to Erich and asked, "Where are you staying?"

Erich shook his head. "Came in last night and couldn't find a room. Spent the night in a straw pile at the market." He paused and then added, "Would be nice to find some warm water to bathe."

Rosa nodded knowingly. "We made our reservations several weeks back. Got a place about eight blocks from here." She looked into his eyes and her pulse quickened. "Why not come up to our room and freshen up."

Erich's face brightened. "Maybe Heinz and I can get a room there."

"We can try," Rosa said. "But rooms are very scarce."

Before mounting the stairs to the girl's third floor room, they inquired at the reception desk. A short, balding man looked over his spectacles and shook his head. "Booked for weeks," he said tersely in an exasperated voice.

It was a small room with a double bed and lavatory. Wallpaper was peeling from the ceiling and the wardrobe doors were hanging precariously from loose hinges. As Erich walked to the window, Heinz grabbed his pack and said, "I'm going to the bathroom down the hall and clean up."

The girls sat on the bed, maintaining an attentive interest as Erich stripped to the waist and poured some water into a basin on a little wooden stand. Since they had no brothers and had never seen their father with his undershirt off, this aroused a curiosity they wanted to satisfy. Irma, however, experienced an embarrassment she tried to disguise by chattering to her sister and occasionally looking away. But Rosa, recalling the night in Rothenburg, felt a throbbing inside she found difficult to conceal. She could almost feel the ripple of his back muscles as she watched him work the razor across his face. And when he approached the bed to retrieve his undershirt, a heavy sigh escaped her lips.

The door opened, and Heinz came in. "Feel a lot better!" he said, dropping his pack to the floor. "Now, let's find a place to stay. Don't want to sleep outside tonight."

"You know," Rosa began, wanting to find a way to remain close to Erich, "if we can rearrange things, you can stay in here."

Heinz and Erich looked at each other and then at Irma. She shrugged and nodded.

"Fine!" Heinz replied. "When we get back from the Hofbrau House, we'll move the bed against the wall, and Erich and I can sleep on the floor."

• • •

They entered the boisterous Hofbrau House wearing paper hats purchased from a street vendor. After a dinner of bratwurst and potato salad on the second floor, they climbed the crowded stairway to the third-floor dance area. It was the first opportunity for Rosa to talk with Erich beyond earshot of Heinz and Irma. She nestled her head in the hollow of his shoulder and pressed her body against his. Closing her eyes, she tried to shut out the loud music and babble of voices. It felt so good to feel the warmth of his body against hers. "Oh, God," she whispered with a sigh. "You can't imagine how hard I prayed last night to find you here. I doubted you would come. And with these crowds, it looked as if I'd never find you anyway."

He felt her take a deep breath.

"But I am so grateful," she continued. "So very, very grateful!"

"I was hoping to find you too," Erich confessed.

"Do you love me?"

"Yes."

They danced slowly for several minutes, enjoying the closeness. Then Rosa said, "I want you so much. You can't imagine what that night in Rothenburg kindled in me. I only wish we could be alone."

"Have you done it since then?"

"No!" she said, pushing back and shaking her head to emphasize the point. "I'm yours. All yours!"

Fearful she had been heard, she looked around. But the din from hundreds of shuffling feet and prattling voices had insulated her words. A short distance away she saw Heinz with a large stein in one hand patiently teaching Irma how to dance.

When she looked back at Erich, she saw he was watching them, too. "I don't think Irma has danced with a boy before," she said.

"They make a nice couple," Erich observed.

It was after midnight when they decided to leave. Pushing through the crowd on the second floor, they passed a long table seated with boisterous revelers. One of the men pushed full steins into their hands and asked them to join in a song.

At the conclusion of *"Kein Schoner Land"* a short, rotund man in Alpine clothing laboriously climbed onto the table "A toast!" he shouted, his sparkling eyes mere slits above his fat, red cheeks.

Those around the table watched and smiled as he raised the huge stein he held in his chubby hand above his head.

"To the German people!" the little man called loudly.

"To the German people!" the crowd echoed, waving their steins above their heads.

"To the *Oktoberfest!*"

"To the *Oktoberfest!*" came the reply, made louder by voices of others standing and sitting nearby.

"And to the *Blitzkrieg!*"

"And to the *Blitzkrieg!*" roared the crowd.

The little man put his stein to his lips and began to drink. Suddenly, he toppled backwards onto the table. His stein dropped and broke, splattering a woman seated near him with beer. As his green hat rolled into her lap, she threw up her hands and gave a loud gasp.

Erich pushed in beside her and pressed his fingers to the man's throat. Feeling a pulse, he pried open an eye, studied it momentarily, then placed his hand on the man's forehead.

"You a doctor?" the woman asked.

"Almost," Erich replied, feeling someone beside him. It was Heinz.

"They're from Heidelberg University," Rosa explained. Her voice sounded with a ring of authority.

Erich pulled the man's chin downward, exposing an open mouth beneath a graying, foam-coated mustache. The man was breathing in a deep, labored manner.

Heinz unbuttoned the man's vest, observed the chest rise and fall evenly, and then pressed an ear against it. When he stood, he looked at Erich and winked. Erich nodded and then turned to the somber, waiting crowd that had surrounded them. "He's had too much to drink," he said. "He'll be all right. But you had better take him somewhere to sleep it off."

"Just drunk!" Heinz chortled.

The crowd roared with delight and raised their steins again. "To brother Josef!" they chorused.

After walking gingerly up the squeaky stairs, Rosa unlocked the door to the room. They quickly pushed the bed against the wall and placed the mattress on the floor beside it. Then, Rosa turned to Erich. "You and Heinz wait in the hallway while we put on our nightgowns," she whispered.

Erich nodded.

In the darkened room, Erich and Heinz removed their shirts and trousers and then got under a single blanket on the mattress that lay on the floor. In a few minutes, Rosa, on the bed just above Erich, silently let her hand drop in search of his. When their hands met, she squeezed his and slowly raised it until it rested on her stomach. As he began to caress her, he felt the cotton flannel of her nightgown slide slowly upward until his palm rested on the cool, pliant flesh he had explored several weeks before. Quickly reaching a tortuous state of arousal for which there was no hope of gratification, he rose to his knees, kissed her warmly on the lips, and then lay down to try to get some sleep.

• • •

It was after midnight when Rosa quietly turned the key in the door and pushed it open. Without turning on the lights, she walked to the window and opened it wide. A gentle breeze moved the curtains, bringing with it the faint odor of cooking food and distant laughter of happy people. When she turned she heard the door close and saw the shadowy outlines of Heinz and Irma embracing. Erich walked up to her, placed his hands around her waist, and kissed her softly on the lips. Taking him by the hand, she led him to the mattress and pulled him down beside her.

For several minutes they lay quietly, holding hands and resting. It had been a long day—folk dancing in the street, a soccer game, and, as Heinz put it, engaging in "Teutonic dissipation" at several taverns. But when Erich saw the dark forms of Irma and his friend move toward the window, he rose to his elbows and gave Rosa a passionate kiss.

Rosa felt the blood surge through her body and throb in her temples. Silently, she rose to her feet and changed into her nightgown. When she returned to the mattress, she found that Erich had removed his clothing and was lying beneath the blanket. Then she saw the silhouettes of Heinz and Irma changing their clothes. Snuggling close to Erich, she put her lips close to his ear and whispered, "I wasn't sure Irma would go along with this." She kissed him, then added, "But I'm glad she is."

Later, after Erich had made love to her, she told him, "It's day seventeen."

The next day, after lunch in a restaurant, Rosa and Irma went to the restroom. "How did you make out last night?" Heinz asked anxiously.

"Oh, fine," Erich replied, attempting to be vague. "How did it go for you?"

"Good as far as it went. Finally got to the point where I could kiss her and feel her up a bit." Heinz paused and shook his head. "Got her to come once, but she wouldn't let me into her."

"Well," Erich said with a wry smile, "you can't expect to do it with every girl you meet, even if it is the *Oktoberfest!*"

Later, when Heinz and Irma were buying ice cream, Erich asked Rosa how her sister liked being with Heinz. "Oh, she likes him a lot," Rosa replied. "She has a very high regard for him and is enjoying his company." She thought for a moment, then said, "But I don't think she is ready to go all the way yet. She's probably concerned about pregnancy. I could tell her some things, but she just might not be ready for it."

Since they were all leaving the next morning, they returned to the room early in the evening. They exchanged addresses, and then Rosa handed her nightgown to Erich and turned out the light. "Want to help me?" she asked, loud enough for Irma to hear.

When Erich's eyes became accustomed to the dark, he saw Heinz was undressing Irma.

Several times during the night, Erich heard muffled activity in the bed. When he opened his eyes at the first light of morning, he saw Irma's nightgown on the floor. He nudged Rosa and pointed to it.

Rosa nodded. "It's day twenty-six for her," she whispered.

As the Heidelberg bus pulled away from the station, Erich and Heinz pressed against the window and waved until the tear-stained faces of Irma and Rosa disappeared from view. They sat in silence for several minutes while the bus made its way through the crowded streets. Then Heinz turned to Erich and said, "We sure got something going there."

"They're nice girls," Erich replied soberly.

"Well," said Heinz, smiling contentedly as he looked out the window, "that Irma's really taken to me." He paused, then added, "You know, we did it last night." He shook his head. "Then she cried."

When they reached Heidelberg, Erich found a letter from Maria. Suddenly, he felt ashamed of the way he had indulged himself in Munich. He knew he could not tell her about Rosa. As for the trip to Munich, he simply would not mention it.

• • •

Erich stood at the Holzheim turnoff and watched as Maria pedaled back toward Regensburg. She had been at the station to meet him, but being in nurse's training, her ten days of Christmas vacation didn't begin for another week. Although he had to push her bicycle as they walked, he was grateful for two wonderful hours they were able to spend together. He waited until she turned to wave for the second time and then started up the narrow, winding road.

As he descended the hill into Holzheim, large flakes of snow were falling, causing the evergreens to droop ever lower under their fluffy, white burden. Although it had been cold, the ground had not frozen and the Trapp cattle stood ankle deep in the soft, barnyard mud. He looked for Inge as he walked past but saw no one working among the cluster of buildings. Entering the family store, he was warmly greeted by his mother, who rushed from behind the counter to put her arms around him. When she stepped back to wipe a tear from her eye, the half dozen customers extended their hands to welcome him. As he looked into their eyes, he sensed that something was different. There was a somberness unlike the holiday cheerfulness he had encountered before.

His mother, waiting on a customer, turned to him. "Go in and see your father. I'll bring you something to eat when I finish here."

He opened the door to the family room and stepped inside. When August, working at a desk in the corner, saw it was Erich, he jumped to his feet and hurried to throw his arms around his son. "Welcome home!" he shouted in a voice filled with elation.

"What are you doing?" Erich asked as he closed the door.

"Making up an order for supplies," August answered with a heavy sigh. "Beginning to have shortages. Trouble getting chocolate, bananas, and oranges."

"They don't have to come through the blockade, do they?"

"No, but they aren't considered essential and have a low shipping priority. There's a big movement of troops and war materiel going on."

"Well," Erich countered, trying to calm his father, "we can live without it." As his father returned to the desk, he took a seat on the sofa. "Besides, the fighting is over in Poland and everything should return to normal soon."

"Over, hell!" August shouted, turning in his chair to face him. "With the buildup on the western front, something's going to break loose. The saber rattlers in England and France have too much pride to back down. The wags call it a *Sitzkrieg*! I know that. But one of these days our army will be scurrying through the mud, crawling over the bones of those we left over there in the last war!"

Erich decided not to respond to let his father return to his work and calm down. After all, the non-aggression pact with Russia had stabilized the east, and action on the western front consisted of only a few isolated artillery duels with the French. Then he thought of the large number of students in Heidelberg who had volunteered or been conscripted. Perhaps, as many of them had surmised during their discussions in the tavern, if the German army became strong enough, the French and English could be brought to some kind of accord. Just then, the door opened and his mother entered with a tray of sliced sausage, bread, and two bottles of beer.

The next morning Erich went to the post office to visit with Mrs. Juergens and was surprised when she handed him a letter from Maria. "So soon?" he asked with a smile.

"She told me she wanted to have a letter here when you arrived," Mrs. Juergens explained. "And she planned to write everyday until she came home."

The letter created the frustrating feeling of Maria's nearness yet aroused a heightened yearning to have her with him. He tucked it into his pocket and lingered a few minutes to talk with Maria's mother before leaving. When he stepped out the door, Inge was waiting. "Why hello, Inge," he said, surprise showing on his face.

"Heard you were back," she said. "Just wanted to see you." She was as effervescent as ever toward him.

"Oh?" Erich replied. "That's nice of you."

"Thought I'd better tell you. Max enlisted in the army."

Erich sensed the pride she felt that Max was in uniform "My mother mentioned it," he said. "Where is he?"

"He's training in a camp near Hannover. We covered his motorcycle and stored it in our barn." They began walking toward Stecker's store and then she said, "But he'll be home on a furlough in February. Wish you could be here to see him. You were one of his best friends, you know.

"I know," Erich replied. "But I can't leave the university." He halted and looked her in the face. "But you give him my best."

With a solemn look on her face, she said, "I will." Suddenly, her expression changed to a smile. "Would you like to come to the barn and see his motorcycle?"

Erich was certain it was a ploy to spend some time with him. But he was engaged to Maria and didn't want to be seen entering the barn alone with her. "I don't have the time right now," he told her, trying to appear hurried. "I'd better get back."

• • •

A soft snow was falling as the Juergens family made their way slowly up the street to the Stecker store. For the past three years the two families had visited each other's homes and exchanged gifts Christmas eve. Maria, walking between George and her mother, felt happier than she had during any holiday season she could remember. On Friday Erich had pedaled to Regensburg so he could ride back with her. And on Saturday, the two of them had enjoyed a delightful romp in the woods while cutting their Christmas trees.

She placed a hand on George's shoulder. "That certainly was nice of you to make a new tree stand for Mother."

"Yes," Mrs. Juergens said, turning to look at her son. "We needed a new one. And that's a beauty."

George was proud of the stand he had made during the past two months, but the overt attention by the two women embarrassed him. He had made a wooden platform thirty inches square, around which he fastened a miniature rail fence. At the center, he bolted half the hub of a buggy wheel, into which the tree could be wedged.

Maria knocked at the Stecker door. The lock clicked and it was opened wide. "Come in! Come in!" welcomed Mrs. Stecker.

After removing their wraps, the Juergens placed their presents beneath the tree. Then, while Mrs. Juergens went to the kitchen to help, Erich, Maria, and George lit the tree candles.

A pleasant evening was spent before a blazing fireplace drinking wine and eating sliced meats, nuts, cheese, and candy. At ten-thirty, Erich stood and announced, "It's time to visit the Juergens' house!" Taking Maria by the hand, he said, "But first..." as he led her to the piano.

As they played, the others accompanied them in singing "*Stille Nacht*" and "*O Tannenbaum.*" Then, as they put on their coats and hats for the short walk, Mrs. Stecker snuffed the tree candles.

Erich, holding Maria's hand, assisted her onto the porch. By force of habit, they avoided the center step. Going inside behind Mrs. Juergens, he stopped. "Oh!" he exclaimed, inhaling the tangy, spice-filled aroma. "That smells so good!"

"It's a pot of Wassail mother left warming on the stove," Maria smiled as she looked into his eyes. "I'll give you a cup if you help me light the tree."

"It's a deal," Erich replied, taking off his coat.

When the candles had been lit, Maria stood back to admire it. The warm glow of the candles reminded her of the many holidays she had spent in this house with her family. The lighted Christmas tree always made her think of her father. She looked at the small, ceramic figures of the nativity scene standing in the fluffy cotton that covered the stand. They had been used each Christmas for as long as she could remember. If only her father could be here. Tears filled her eyes. But perhaps he was in heaven looking down upon them. She hoped he was proud of how well his family was doing.

The snow had stopped and the sky was clear as they joined others walking up the narrow street to hear midnight Mass. Maria, holding Erich's hand, looked up at the thousands of stars dotting the purple canopy overhead. They appeared as brilliant jewels, shining down upon the rooftops, the trees, and the new snow. She hoped they were shining on her face so that when she smiled, Erich would see her as a beautiful person.

As they walked, Erich looked down into her face and noted the soft, warm sparkle in her eyes. With each breath he inhaled, he found the crisp fragrance of the fresh air was mixed with the tantalizing whiffs of her perfume. Just having her near created a warm glow deep inside.

Approaching the church entrance, Maria grasped his arm and halted him. She looked up at the large wooden doors with their elegantly carved figures. "Tonight," she said, "I'm going to pray very hard that next year we will again walk through this entrance to celebrate midnight Mass."

A barrage of thoughts scurried through his mind. He recalled the talk with his father about the wars and the discussions he had with those at the university. "I will pray very hard, too," he promised.

. . .

Returning to Heidelberg, Erich found that Heinz had arrived two days earlier. "And guess what happened," Heinz said as Erich unpacked some food he had brought from home.

Although Heinz' voice seemed gleeful, Erich simply shrugged as he continued to unpack.

"Rosa and Irma are living in an apartment across the river."

Stunned, Erich stood back and looked questioningly at his roommate.

"Yah!" Heinz continued. "Rosa has a job as file clerk in a little factory, and Irma works as a daytime domestic for a rich merchant." He paused and watched Erich take in a deep breath. "Really a nice setup. I've already made a courtesy call."

"Rosa got a boyfriend?"

"No," Heinz stated with a broad smile. "She's been waiting for you to come back."

Erich placed his backpack in the closet and then sat down to ponder the situation. He was pleased to have done a favor, but the complications it created made him wish he hadn't become involved. Rosa was a fine person, he knew that, and would make an excellent wife and mother of someone's children. But for him, there could be no one but Maria. He thought he had made it very explicit. He shook his head and sighed heavily. It would have to be explained again in a very firm, understanding manner.

That evening, as soon as he entered their apartment with Heinz, Erich was overwhelmed by such a deluge of affection from Rosa that he could feel his carefully laid plans eroding. Although he responded, he remembered the promise he had made to himself and tried to dampen any show of ardor as a prelude to what he must tell her later.

Rosa sensed his coolness but continued to declare her love for him. "It's been so lonely without you. After the *Octoberfest*, I felt terribly empty. The longing became so strong that in desperation I decided to move here."

After drinking a cup of tea, the four of them went for a walk. Strolling slowly, they looked in shop windows for several minutes before entering a tree-lined park. Erich, holding Rosa's hand, lagged back to let Heinz and Irma get some distance ahead. "I'm not very satisfied with myself," he stated, looking down at the leaf-strewn path before his plodding feet.

"Yes," Rosa quickly replied, "I guessed something was wrong and was hoping you would share it with me."

"The main reason I want to share it with you is that it involves you."

"Oh?" Rosa said, suspecting what the problem was.

"You know," Erich began, "I'm in love with Maria and plan to marry her someday."

"Yes, I know." Rosa's voice was calm and understanding.

"Well, our relationship has stirred up such a turmoil within me that I think it would be best for us to stop it."

"Do you still love me?" she asked, turning to him so he faced her.

"Rosa," he said, pushing his hands deeper into his jacket pockets. "There are so many meanings to the word *love*. You love your mother or father; you love your cat and dog. But you wouldn't want to marry them." Looking into her tear-filled eyes, he took in a deep breath. "Yes, I love you. I love you very much. But there is someone else. Not only do I love her, but I am *in love* with her." He paused and then continued. "After I have made love with you—and I do enjoy it very much—I am not very pleased with myself because of the guilt I feel. It bothers me very much. It creates a terrible stress inside. I'm just not at peace with myself."

"I know how you must feel toward Maria, but I find myself in love with you. I don't want to hurt anyone, but I would like to continue being loved by you." After dabbing her eyes with her hand, she said, "Right now, I cannot bring myself to consider anyone else." She paused and again wiped away the tears. "Maybe we can ease out of it gradually."

Rosa's heart was pumping hard. She was desperately in love with him and hoped that somehow he could be hers. His presence made her tremble and tingle. And after three months, her body was craving for him to extinguish the fire and release the tension within.

Erich placed his hands on her shoulders. "Rosa, what I'm trying to say is," he stammered, "let's be friends instead of lovers."

Her heart sank. She turned her head and looked at the ground. "Whatever you say, Erich," she conceded.

Heinz and Irma, who had been sitting on a rock beneath a tree a short distance away, walked up. "We're going to the apartment to fix a snack," Heinz said. "Why don't you two join us in about forty-five minutes."

After they had walked off, Erich said, "Looks like they are hitting it off."

"Oh, yes," Rosa replied. "She's very fond of him. Like most girls, never knew such pleasure existed."

When they entered the apartment, Rosa sniffed and said, "Mmm, smells like fresh coffee."

"Yes, it's cooking," Irma said with a smile. "And if you'll sit down, we've got some cookies to go with it."

Erich, noting the flush of her cheeks, nodded as he removed his jacket.

After consuming the snack, Heinz rose to his feet. "It's after eleven and there's a busy day coming tomorrow," he announced, grabbing Irma's hand and walking briskly to the light switch.

Erich could see by their silhouettes that they were kissing and fondling one another. He stood and drew Rosa close to him. Just putting his arms around her would suffice for now and would reduce involvement and temptation. But Rosa snuggled closer and unbuttoned the top of his shirt. Then she plied his lips apart with hers.

Erich could feel his loins began to throb as her fingers caressed his back.

"My darling, my darling," she whispered. "Please stay longer."

"I must go," he protested.

"Just a little longer?" she pleaded.

"Maybe some other time."

"Can I see you again this week?"

"Yes," he replied.

"How about Wednesday?"

"All right," he sighed, realizing he again was slipping from the promises he had made to himself. The only way to eliminate the temptation was to stop seeing her, he knew that. And that would hurt her, hurt her terribly. But he also knew that if he was to avoid the fateful consequences such an affair would bring, he must.

• • •

Erich rose early, as he had for the past three weeks, to prepare for another long shift in the hospital ward. It was Friday, May 10, an overcast day two weeks before the end of the term. As he shaved, he thought of the aching and dying patients in his ward. Watching their gradually deteriorating condition tore at his soul. He had spent many long hours studying in the library and consulting with instructors to more fully understand their cases. And, on occasion, he brought a small gift just to see a tiny sparkle of light appear in a dying person's eyes. He wondered if he was becoming more personally involved than a professional should.

Leaving the bathroom, he turned on the radio to listen to a few moments of classical music, a daily program that soothed and calmed him before leaving for the hospital. Instead of music, however, he heard the voice of a man: ". . . and *panzer* divisions of the Third Reich are speeding toward Liege and Rotterdam. Additional information will be issued at ten o'clock."

Erich was stunned. He dashed to the bedroom and awakened Heinz. "All hell has broken loose!" he shouted.

Heinz sat up and rubbed his eyes. "Oh, hell. It'll be another little operation just like Poland. Be over in a couple weeks."

"Little operation! Couple of weeks! Do you realize there were eleven thousand soldiers killed in three and a half weeks in Poland? And another seventy thousand maimed?" Erich shook his head in disbelief "And now we're at war with England, France, Belgium, and Holland!"

"And Luxembourg," Heinz added, placing his feet on the floor. "I don't like it, but there's not a hell of a lot I can do about it."

The next morning, Erich left for home to have a serious discussion with his father. When he arrived in Holzheim, he found the trees and grass had turned green again and streams were running full. Frogs were croaking, the ground had firmed after the spring thaw, and the apple blossoms were about to burst into bloom.

Although the town had the same appearance, its temperament had changed. Taxes had increased, rationing was in effect, and several sons were now in uniform. As he sat on the sofa in the living room drinking beer with his father, he asked, "Why must all of this happen to us?"

August Stecker was proud of his son and wanted him to complete his education so he could enjoy the wonderful future they had envisioned. But when he considered the gravity of the national situation and the pressure Erich would face, he knew that a change in their plans was inevitable. He had been thinking about it for months. "It appears," he began, "that regardless of the outcome, nothing can ever be the same again. No matter how much we are opposed to war, there is no way we can rebel against it. Our proud country has passed the point of no return. We are committed. We are over the brink." He paused and turned to face Erich

Erich noted tears welling up in his father's eyes. He wanted to say something but wasn't sure what to say, so he merely nodded.

August shook his head. "Probably the best thing for you to do is to jump in with both feet—enlist and see if we can help to get it over with. If we win the present campaign, God only knows what is next. If we lose, God have mercy on us, for the rest of the world will show us none."

The next morning, Sunday, Maria arrived. She had told Erich when he telephoned as he passed through Regensburg, that she would try to get the day off. After Mass they sat on the top step of her porch where he related the discussion with his father. She slipped her arm through his and pulled him close. "Are you going?" she asked soberly.

"I probably should," he replied, looking off into the distance. He knew he would enlist but didn't want to tell her right now.

"Well," she said, drawing in a deep breath, "I want you to do whatever you wish about it." She knew the decision he would make but didn't want to voice an objection. For several months she had thought about it, realizing it would disrupt their carefully laid plans, cause long periods of separation, and create heartache and worry when he left for the battlefront. Twice she had awakened frightened, seized with such a feeling of anxiety that she thought it would be better to get married now so they could enjoy each other while they could.

When they were going to part, she snuggled against his chest and wondered how long it would be until she saw him again.

Returning to Heidelberg, Erich told Heinz of his decision.

"I'm going with you!" Heinz declared with a broad smile.

But when Rosa and Irma were informed, they were sorely disappointed. "We'll follow you wherever you go," Irma vowed, the tears flowing down her cheeks onto the floor.

"Could we spend the last night at your apartment?" Heinz asked, looking at Erich with a devilish smile.

"Will you?" Rosa asked, holding her breath for an answer.

Heinz looked at Erich and then both nodded. The girls leaped into their arms and smothered them with kisses.

After packing and shipping their belongings, Erich and Heinz started across the old stone bridge. Midway across they stopped and looked back as they had many times before at the sacked castle high on the dominating bluff behind them. What Erich saw as his eyes scanned the ancient structure, puzzled him. It was so different, it made him shudder. Instead of a warm, golden glow in the late afternoon sun, the brown sandstone reflected a dull, blood-red. He wondered if it was an omen.

That evening he and Rosa slept on a mattress they had placed on the living room floor. She had insisted on having a closed door between them and the other two in the bedroom. They talked until nearly midnight before going to sleep. In the morning, after they had made love, she snuggled into his arms.

"How are you this morning, Miss Graebner?" Erich whispered.

"Very contented. Totally sated," she smiled, keeping her eyes closed.

He chuckled. "Most old maids would give their life savings to be able to say that this morning."

When Erich and Heinz stepped off the bus at the Frankfurt Army Induction Center, they were greeted by a middle-aged corporal who was unable to speak with his gravel-throated voice unless he shouted. He led them into a large building where they joined a procession of several hundred other inductees. Each man was handed a large envelope containing a sheaf of papers. Then they were ordered to form a single line in alphabetical order. This separated Erich from Heinz.

Following the line through a doorway into another room, Erich saw that a trail of white footprints had been painted on the floor. He was handed a burlap bag and another corporal shouted, "Put all your clothes in the bag and follow the footprints!"

A short, timid-looking fellow ahead of Erich looked around. He seemed terrified. "You mean take our clothes *off?*" he stammered.

"Doesn't make a damn bit of difference to me!" came the rehearsed reply. "If you can get them all in without taking them off, go ahead!"

The line of naked forms moved slowly ahead, following the white footprints through a series of cubicles. In each, a medical inspector sat lethargically on a stool. To Erich the diversity of shapes, sizes, and physical conditions of the men was both interesting and amusing. Some were extremely embarrassed by such wholesale exposure and tried to cover themselves with their hands and sheaf of papers. Others, oblivious to their nude state, laughed and talked to those around them. And the leathery, reddish-brown necks and arms of the peasant farmers stood out in sharp contrast to the soft, milk-white skin of the city sons of wealthy merchants.

Erich, well versed in the processes of a physical examination, was able to anticipate the requests made of him and found compliance easy. As he moved through the various stations, getting his papers stamped at each stop, he listened to a constant stream of dialogue.

"Got that bottle full yet?" "No, I can't." "Can't hell! Let's do it!"

"Now, this won't hurt at all."

"Skin it back and milk it down." "My God! What a concealed weapon!"

"Turn your head and cough." After a light cough, "Turn your head!"

"Bend over and spread your cheeks." A pause, then an exasperated, "No, for God's sake. Back here!"

Two and a half hours after he had begun following the white footprints, Erich emerged at the same assembly room where he had started. Among the dozens milling about was Heinz. "They want us to get dressed and wait until everyone is finished," he told Erich.

The raspy voiced corporal entered and yelled for them to be quiet. From a paper in his hand, he read a list of twenty-four names. "You sorry specimens are unfit for military service!" he shouted in a voice ringing with disdain. "Go outside and get on the bus that's waiting for you!"

When the last of the rejectees had gone, a captain entered. The corporal snapped to attention and then directed everyone to stand. "Raise your right hand," he ordered.

Erich, following the captain's command, took the oath of allegiance:

> *I, Erich Stecker, do solemnly swear to abide by the regulations of the Army of the German Reich and to fight to victory for the land, the people, and the Fuhrer, against all aggressors, for God is with us.*

As the captain slipped out the door, the corporal suddenly changed to the epitome of military authority. "You're in the army now!" he bellowed. "You will stop thinking for yourselves because somebody else will do all the thinking for you. But you will do what you are told, when your are told, and without question. Within twenty-four hours you will be in uniform, and God pity the poor soul who ever stoops so low as to disgrace it."

He paused to look over the assemblage of awestruck faces. "Now for your first military order. There are six brooms hanging over there in the corner. The six men nearest them, grab them. Line up against that wall and sweep to this wall. The rest of you hold the benches and chairs up out of their way."

Unhappy with the slow response, he raised his harsh voice. "Come on! Show some life!"

Heinz looked at Erich. "Good God!" he exclaimed.

The Forging of a Soldier

Corporal Strausmann sized up the squad of ten recruits standing at attention before him. They appeared to be of higher caliber than the last group
he had trained. Every time the Fuhrer launched another campaign, the corporal had noticed a surge like this. But he couldn't let them know it. He had
only eight weeks to mold them into highly trained infantrymen with a devo-
tion to duty, unquestioning loyalty, and exacting discipline. And Colonel
Hans von Grunwald, the camp commandant, had issued orders to all drill
instructors that he would settle for nothing less.

Strausmann had been in the army four years and had trained six previous
cycles of recruits for Company D. A short, blocky individual of rugged peasant
stock from the Ruhr valley, he had enlisted at the age of twenty-two and liked it
so well he decided to make a career of it. When Poland was invaded, he was
advanced to corporal and assigned to Camp Schwartzenborn for recruit training.

To develop necessary discipline, he felt he had to break a man's charac-
ter through threats and humiliation and then remake him into a regimented
automaton with an unswerving temperament guided by army directives and
regulations. In the process, he would also strengthen their bodies and teach
them how to handle weapons with a high degree of proficiency.

"I don't understand why this company has to be given such a bunch of
misfits!" he bellowed, his florid neck bulging over the tight collar of his tunic.
Seeing the muscles in their jaws tense, he continued, "Must be scraping the
bottom of the barrel!" He then pointed to a stack of folded mattress covers
made of striped ticking. "Now, let's see how fast you can fill one of these with
straw from that pile on the company street and get it on your cot!"

The company street was a fifty-foot strip of barren clay that separated the
two barracks of Company D. Five large, red, wooden barrels, each filled with

water and equipped with two cone-shaped buckets hanging from their sides, were evenly spaced along its center. The street had been policed so often by groups of trainees that not a pebble, blade of grass, nor foreign material of any kind remained.

As Erich stuffed his mattress, he could see other squads being badgered by their drill instructors while marching and running about the area. Although several squads were filling their mattress covers from the same pile, he could hear the voice of Corporal Strausmann above the din. "Let's go! Let's go!" the corporal yelled. "Don't act like a bunch of gossiping old women at a fountain! *This* is the army!"

His mattress filled, Erich stood and looked down at the straw being scattered across the ground by the hurrying men. Heinz, holding his partially filled mattress, sidled up to him. "Can you guess how that's going to be cleaned up?" he asked with a chuckle.

Erich sighed, shook his head, and nodded.

As soon as he placed the mattress on his cot and was about to sit down, Erich heard a whistle blowing. "We've got to line up outside!" someone shouted.

"Come on! Come on! Stop dragging your feet!" Strausmann yelled, impatiently shuffling his feet. "When this whistle blows, you've got sixty seconds to be lined up before me. And it doesn't matter whether you're here, out in the field, or somewhere else!" He paused, slowly looked into the faces of the ten men standing before him and then snapped his heels together. "In case any of you have forgotten, my name is Corporal Strausmann, and I can make or break you. Do what I say, and we'll get along fine. Disobey me, and you'll wish to hell you were never born!"

He paced back and forth and then turned to face them again. "My God! What sorry pieces of misery!" He paced some more, shaking his head in disgust. "Those uniforms you are wearing are the best I've ever seen come out of the Wiesbaden Reception Center. They fitted you well!" He took in a deep breath. "But you can't even put them on right! And your boots are a mess! Don't even know how to stand at attention!" Again he shook his head. "How do they expect me to make something out of nothing?"

He took in another deep breath and set his jaw. "But I'll tell you one thing," he said in a lowered voice. "When you're finished, you're going to be the best damned squad in Company D. And Company D will be the best damned company in Camp Swartzenborn!"

Quickly, he surveyed the men, his eyes settling on Erich, the tallest man in the squad. "Well, let's get started. Stecker, bring your bed out here and I'll show you how to make it. Schumacher, you help him."

After the demonstration, which repeatedly emphasized mitered corners and tautness of the gray, reclaimed-wool blanket, Strausmann again lined up the squad. "Now, go inside and practice making beds until you can do it perfectly in the time between breakfast and when you have to fall out for drill each morning!" he shouted.

Erich turned to Schumacher. "Will you help me carry this in?" he asked, thinking he wouldn't have to make it up inside.

"No you don't!" Strausmann yelled. "Tear it apart and make it up inside!"

The next morning, the whistle blew at five-thirty. After roll call, Strausmann complained bitterly that the squad members had not lined up fast enough when they heard the whistle. Later, when he tried to teach close order drill and found that two men could not remember they were to start with their left foot, he had their left boots painted with whitewash. "Tonight, you will polish that boot to perfection!" he stormed. "And if you still can't remember tomorrow, it'll be painted again!"

The following Saturday the squad received a demerit from a captain during barracks inspection because one of Erich's rolled socks was stacked half an inch out of place on the shelf above his bed. Strausmann was furious. He ordered the squad into the company street.

For fifteen minutes while they stood at attention, Strausmann walked back and forth looking for the slightest movement of a finger or elbow. Seeing a button that was unfastened on Schumacher's tunic pocket, he cut it off with a penknife. "Sew it back on!" he scolded, his nose six inches from Schumacher's.

He marched to the front of the squad and clicked his heels. "You men will learn to pass a perfect inspection," he declared in a lowered voice. "As of now, you are restricted to the barracks for the rest of the day." His eyes flashed as he paused to look them over. "And every hour, on the hour, for the next six hours, you will fall out here for inspection!"

• • •

It was a hot, humid afternoon when the squad returned from the firing range. Schumacher found a mouse in a cheese-baited trap he had set. For several days the mouse had plagued the barracks, eating Schumacher's cookies and nibbling at candy Erich had left on his shelf

"Here's the culprit!" Schumacher said, holding the trap up so the others could see it.

Erich looked into the creature's small, beady eyes. "Poor little fellow," he said.

Schumacher shrugged. "Since this mouse died on a military base, it deserves a military funeral," he quipped.

In a few minutes, several men were making serious plans. While Schumacher located a bugle, others laid the mouse on its back in a partially opened, pocket-size matchbox and placed it in a glass jar. When Schumacher returned, a dozen men from the barracks marched to the drill field. Erich, carrying the mouse, lead the procession.

A small hole was dug, and, as Erich stood at attention holding the jar with the mouse, Schumacher sounded a series of soft notes on the bugle.

Just as Heinz stepped forward with an opened prayer book in his hands, Strausmann came running up. "What's going on here?" he demanded.

Several men put their fingers to their lips to silence him.

Heinz read a brief prayer, and then Schumacher again sounded the bugle as Erich placed the jar in the hole and covered with soil.

Strausmann was livid with rage. "My God! My God!" he bellowed, grasping his head with both hands. "What did I ever do to deserve this?" He surveyed the group surrounding him, then continued. "Has everyone gone crazy?"

"But Corporal Strausmann," Schumacher interrupted. "Somebody said it was a military mouse and was entitled to a military funeral."

Strausmann's face turned beet-red, and the blood vessels in his throat and temple bulged. He stepped over to face Schumacher, placing his nose a few inches from that of the sober-faced recruit. "Somebody? Somebody, hell!" he stormed. "I'll bet you can piss on that somebody right from where you're standing without unbuttoning your pants!" He looked around at the others and clenched his jaw as he pondered what to do. Then, exhaling forcefully, he shook his head and stamped off. Schumacher looked at Erich and snickered.

Erich smiled. He liked Otto Schumacher and admired his ability to confound Straussmann. Besides, the young recruit reminded him of Max Dorten. He was the same height and build as Max, and his active, wiry body, driven by a restless brain, constantly created situations that amazed the squad members. Although Otto had barely completed grammar school, Erich found that his ample intelligence and sharp wit allowed him to be conversant in a wide variety of topics.

Otto's father was a freight train conductor in Hamburg who had tried to get his son to go to work on the railroad. But Otto didn't like the regimented life it required. He did, however, give serious thought to becoming a seaman on an ocean-going vessel, but decided he liked the spirited life of the city and became a stevedore instead. This gave him enough pocket money to live, kept his body in excellent physical condition, and permitted him to spend his evenings near the waterfront. Possessing a talent for music, he learned to play the trumpet in a nightclub during intermission while the band was sitting at the bar.

• • •

It had been six weeks since Erich's squad arrived in Camp Schwarzenborn. They had been well trained in military routine, and Strausmann found it increasingly difficult to find things to complain about. The simple daily task of policing the company street forced him to spend as much time searching for faults as it took the men to line up and do the job. But he was pleased with how well the men were conforming to his ideal of soldiers. The time for calisthenics had been tripled to ninety minutes each day, and hikes were lengthened from five miles to twenty-five miles. The men's bodies had become as hard as nails, and their minds mesmerized to react instantly to his commands.

Strausmann considered himself an expert on the use of the bayonet and derived great pleasure battering the trainees about as he taught them. If they winced or flinched, he exhorted them, declaring, "Be mean! Give it everything you've got! The enemy will show you no mercy!"

When Erich discovered that he, also, possessed talent with a bayonet, Schumacher urged him to practice so he could challenge Strausmann. During the next training exercise, Erich managed to parry the corporal's thrust and rammed a rifle butt into Strausmann's stomach, knocking him to the ground. As Strausmann lay on his back in the mud with Erich's bayonet six inches from his throat, he exclaimed, "Excellent! Excellent, Private Stecker!"

But he was not about to let one of his men humiliate him before others. He immediately marched the squad to the muddy end of the field. For the next hour they were ordered to stand, take five steps forward in attack formation, hit the ground on their stomachs, and commence firing by clicking the rifle trigger once. This was done back and forth across the field while he trotted alongside shouting, complaining, and ridiculing until the men were an exhausted, dripping mass of oozing mud. Then he ordered them to line up and stand at attention. "Now," he shouted, his face displaying a wry grin, "you will go back to the barracks and get yourselves cleaned up!"

The men sighed in unison.

Strausmann was infuriated. "And," he stormed, "I will blow the whistle in one hour! You will stand inspection!"

The next morning Company D was taken to a theater to see a training film on cover and concealment. When they emerged from the front door, the drill corporals were waiting for their squads. "Now, men," Strausmann said to the ten recruits lined up before him, "we're going to practice what you have learned in there." He paused and looked into their faces. "And we'll see if you paid attention!"

Three miles away in a wooded area, Strausmann demonstrated how they should fasten twigs and branches to their helmets and uniforms and take advantage of weeds and shrubs for concealment. "And remember, men," he concluded, "when other forms of cover are not available, be sure to make maximum use of depressions in the ground, even though they may be slight!"

He looked directly at Erich. "Do you understand that, Stecker?" he asked in a loud voice.

Certain Strausmann was still smarting from yesterday's bayonet practice, Erich looked him straight in the eye. "Yes sir, Corporal Strausmann!"

Strausmann paced back and forth, then halted and faced the squad. "Now." he began, his voice low and modulated, "I'm going for a walk down this path. I'll be back in ten minutes. By then you should all be hidden."

When he returned ten minutes later, he readily located eight of the men. Enraged, his face turned a reddish-purple. He had the squad form a semicircle around him and stand at rigid attention. Using Schumacher as a model, he laboriously demonstrated how they hadn't used enough leaves and twigs in their disguise. "Laziness! Just plain laziness!" he bellowed, his nose a few inches from Schumacher's face. "Do you understand that?"

"Yes, sir!" Schumacher replied.

Erich noted a glint of satisfaction in Schumacher's eyes. Suddenly, Strausmann was standing before him. "Only a stupid fool could not see that! Isn't that so, Private Stecker?"

"Yes, sir!" Erich replied, feeling his heartbeat quicken.

"Is there anyone who doesn't understand it?" he asked, scanning their faces, but receiving no response.

Strausmann stepped back two paces. "Now," he said, "I'm going for another ten minute walk. And God pity the man I see when I get back! I'll hamstring him! I'll fricassee him!"

When he returned, he could locate no one. "That's fine, very fine," he announced, his voice showing concern. He had never had a squad who had hidden so well. "Now, come on out!"

After thirty minutes of calling and thrashing about, he had flushed Erich and two others. While continuing to search for an additional half hour, he spoke threateningly of desertion, of being absent without authority, and of appearing before a military tribunal. Although his voice was loud enough so anyone hiding could hear him, no one appeared.

As he led the three trainees back toward the camp, Strausmann remained quiet. Erich, noting rivulets of perspiration running from his temples and creases of worry showing on his face, felt sorry for him. Although he didn't like the corporal's cockiness, he respected him for what he was trying to do with a diverse group of recruits. At the edge of the drill field Strausmann dismissed the men, hoping his superiors hadn't noticed there were only three left.

At four-thirty the next morning Erich saw Schumacher slip into the barracks. He was awake because Strausmann had checked the beds several times during the night. "Where did you go?" he asked in a whisper.

"Well," Schumacher began, quietly undressing in the dark. "I remembered from our map reading lessons that there was a little village out there. So, when Strausmann said he didn't want to find us when he got back, we decided to take him at his word. We went to the village and drank beer and danced." He paused and then continued. "I think they're all back now."

"There's still two missing over there," Erich said, pointing across the aisle. "And Strausmann was talking desertion."

"Oh, hell. They'll show up," Schumacher replied, slipping into bed. "And as for Strausmann, if we meet muster in the morning, he'll be off the hook so he'll keep his mouth shut." Raising up on one elbow, he said, "Met a gal from Cologne. She had come home to visit her parents. Got her address so I can look her up when I get a pass."

The next morning when Strausmann again checked the barracks, he was noticeably relieved. All his men had returned, although one was drunk and sick. He ordered Erich to escort the young man to the aid station so his superiors would not see one of his recruits in such a bad state. At roll call, with the company lined up in front of the barracks, Strausmann set his jaw and strutted back and forth in front of his squad, looking sternly into the eyes of each man. For the remainder of the training period, he would see to it they were held under tight rein with strict discipline. Turning abruptly, he clicked his heels and shouted, "All present or accounted for!"

• • •

The Graebner girls wrote that they were moving to Cologne and would be situated by the time Erich and Heinz got their first weekend pass. This served as a special incentive to avoid the wrath of Strausmann, so the two men acted more eager to perform properly and gain favor. Even when their turn at kitchen scrub duty came, they successfully faked a display of enthusiasm, thus avoiding Strausmann's tirade of threats if he received a bad report from the mess sergeant.

The mess sergeant, however, never made an appearance. Instead, it was a bantam-sized corporal with a tight-fitting tunic and gopher face who stormed around the kitchen giving orders, drinking coffee, and continuously searching for things to complain about. Looking at the roster Strausmann had given him, he pointed to a line of scrub brushes, buckets, and mops. "Jager and Knocke, you two will use that equipment to scrub the floor." He took in a deep breath that stretched the button holes of his tunic. "And if you don't do it right, I'll have you here at midnight doing it with a toothbrush!"

"Stecker and Schumacher, you're on pots and pans," he said, tossing them two white aprons he took from a stack on a nearby table. Then he pointed to a pile of enormous kettles beside a huge sink. "And," he continued, "all I want to see for the next ten hours when I look over here is elbows and assholes and soapsuds flying in all directions!"

Erich looked at Schumacher and shook his head dejectedly.

"Oh, hell," Schumacher said. "Should be done in a couple hours."

However, after five hours with kettles continuing to be brought in, he turned to Erich. "Maybe we'll spend the rest of the war right here!"

• • •

It was a warm humid day, the kind that reminded Erich of those he used to spend at the swimming hole in Holzheim with Maria. Company D was on a field maneuver that required the squads to dig foxholes for a perimeter defense of a small, wooded hill. After digging through a difficult tangle of tree roots, Erich encountered a layer of sandstone. He chipped and picked for several minutes with little progress before asking Corporal Strausmann if it was necessary to go any deeper. Strausmann ordered him out of the hole. "Private Stecker," he bellowed, "you surprise me! A man of your intelligence asking such a stupid question! The regulation hole is two and one-half feet deep! And everybody's hole will be two and one-half feet deep! Is that clear?"

Erich's face reddened. He knew the others were watching. "Yes, sir," he replied.

"Then snap to it!"

As Erich continued to dig, blisters formed on his palms and finger pads. Soon the blisters broke and the water drained from them, causing the skin to tear loose and blood to ooze. He looked at the stinging sores and wanted to quit, but continued to pick and chip at the sandstone until the hole was deep enough. Then he laid back to let the perspiration evaporate from his saturated uniform.

Just then, he detected the heavy tread of marching troops. Rising slowly to his feet, he waited for them to come into view. Suddenly, Schumacher called out, "They're women!"

All of Company D stopped digging to watch the small column from the Women's Corps. Strausmann was enraged but strained to hold his tongue so not to embarrass the sergeant in charge of the women. The sergeant, sensing the tension, ordered his troops to trot to get past the hole-digging men as rapidly as possible.

Schumacher, squatting low in his hole, yelled, "Slow those troops down! I smell hair burning!"

Strausmann, too far away to determine who had called out, turned to face the men behind him. "Who said that?" he questioned, his face turning a bright red.

There was no answer.

"I'll find out!" he screamed. "Line up!"

As they stood at attention, their dirty, sweat-stained clothing clinging to their tired bodies, Strausmann paced back and forth before them. "Which one of you said that?" he demanded.

Still, there was no answer. Although not in his squad, he walked over before Heinz "Who was it, Private Jager?"

"I never heard it, sir," Heinz calmly replied.

"Did you hear it, Private Stecker?" he asked, standing before Erich.

"Yes, sir."

Schumacher cringed.

A sly smile appeared on Strausmann's face. "Who?" he asked.

"I don't know," Erich replied. "I think it must have come from another squad."

Seeing he was getting nowhere with his questions, Strausmann decided it was an opportune time to back away from the situation. "You can thank God it was!" he bellowed. "If it was one of you, I'd have your hide tacked to the guardhouse door!"

• • •

It had been six weeks since Company D had begun training, and they had completed a flawless Saturday barracks inspection. As a reward, the men were granted passes permitting them to be away from camp from Saturday noon until roll call Monday morning. Since most were going to Cologne, a bus was waiting at the gate.

Although Heinz had written Rosa and Irma that a bad morning inspection could eliminate the passes, they were waiting at the station when the bus arrived. Rosa, elated to see Erich, could not hold back the tears. She ran to him, wrapped her arms about his neck, and kissed him warmly. "Oh, Erich," she sobbed. "I can't stand being away from you."

"I missed you, too," Erich assured her as he gently patted her back. Looking to his side, he saw Irma caressing Heinz's face as she kissed him repeatedly. It pleased him that their love was growing.

Schumacher walked up to be introduced. When Erich asked if he had a place to stay, he replied, "Oh, yes. Just phoned the girl I met in the village, and she told me how to get to her apartment."

"Then let's all get together for dinner," Heinz suggested. "Know of any good restaurants, Rosa?"

Rosa shrugged. "We haven't been here that long," she said apologetically.

"My friend's well acquainted with the city," Schumacher stated. "She'll know of one." He looked at Rosa. "We'll be at your place at six." Suddenly, a frown formed on his face. "That is, if she doesn't already have plans."

"We'll expect you, Private Schumacher!" Erich barked.

Schumacher clicked the heels of his highly polished boots, saluted, and then strode off briskly.

While walking to their apartment, Irma and Rosa clung proudly to the arms of their neatly groomed escorts. They recounted their move from Heidelberg and told of their parents' fear for their safety since they had left the farm. "Mother is terribly concerned," said Irma. "She is convinced some harm will come to us."

Rosa looked into Erich's face and smiled. "She doesn't know we have two soldier friends to protect us."

They took a few more steps in silence and then Rosa halted Erich by grasping his biceps with both hands. "Know what?" she asked, her eyes sparkling like jewels.

"No. What?" Erich responded, lifting her chin with his free hand.

"I've got a job!"

"Good! Where?"

"Camp Schwarzenborn!"

Erich looked surprised. "Really?" he asked.

"Yes," Rosa answered with a self-satisfied smile. "I start Monday, working in the office of Colonel Hans von Grunwald."

"Good Lord!" Erich gasped, rolling his eyes upward. "The camp commandant! How did you get that?"

"My boss in Heidelberg is a friend of his and wrote him a letter."

Erich poked Heinz. "Did you hear that?"

"I sure did!" Heinz replied, shaking his head.

As they began walking again, Erich whispered in Rosa's ear, "You didn't do any special favors, did you?"

"No!" came the indignant reply. "I'm yours!"

Located on the fourth floor of a new building just north of the railroad station, the apartment had three compact rooms overlooking the Rhine River. Erich removed his tunic, then stood with his arm around Rosa's shoulder looking down at a heavy barge passing beneath the railroad bridge. To the right beyond the railroad station, the giant cathedral dominated the area. "What a nice apartment," he said with a smile.

Turning to face him, Rosa put both arms around his neck. "I had hoped you'd like it. It's a little more expensive than the one in Heidelberg, but when Irma goes to work, we should be able to manage it."

"Has she found a job yet?"

"No. She's holding out for an office job. It'll pay more and she'll like it better."

When Erich looked back into the room, he saw Heinz and Irma petting on the couch. "Let's go for a walk," he whispered. Picking up his tunic, he started for the door. "Heinz, were going out to buy a city map. Should be back in forty-five minutes."

Walking to the river's edge, they sat down on a thickly painted iron bench beside a path that wound its way among carefully tended beds of red and white geraniums. Rosa took his hand. "I wish we could be together, forever," she said wistfully, looking out across the river. "It would be so nice— Mr. and Mrs. Erich Stecker."

"Yes," Erich replied with a sigh. "But we just can't."

"I know. So let's make the most of it while we can. I'm so in love with you."

"How can you be sure? Maybe it's infatuation."

"At first, it may have been. Your making love to me was everything. Oh yes, I still want it very much. I'm on fire just thinking of Heinz and Irma up there in the apartment." She took a deep breath and continued, "But there's more. I just want you to be with me, close to me, when I'm sitting here on this bench, or when I'm walking down the street. I want to share everything with you—what is good and what is bad."

He leaned over and kissed her. "You sound like a very mature lady."

"I owe a great deal to you. Not only did you teach me many things, but you created a desire in me to walk, talk, and act so you would be proud to be with me." She looked into his blue eyes. "And believe me, I have worked very hard at it. I want so much to please you."

"I am very proud of you," Erich said, hugging her.

When they returned to the apartment they found a note stating Irma and Heinz would be back at five. They quenched their hunger in the bed, and then Rosa cuddled into his arms. "Oh, God!" she sighed, "I want to have your baby."

Surprised, Erich looked at her questioningly. "You must not," he said sternly. "Think of the poor child."

"I know." Rosa replied, closing her eyes and settling back to enjoy the afterglow. "We won't let it happen."

• • •

Answering a knock at the door, Rosa found Schumacher and his date standing stiffly erect and smiling. She invited them inside.

"Rosa, may I present Salli Kohler," Schumacher said, gesturing with his hand.

"The pleasure is mine," Rosa replied. Salli nodded and smiled.

After the others had been introduced, Erich looked at his watch. "When you say six o'clock, you mean six o'clock."

"Corporal Strausmann's indoctrination," came Schumacher's quick reply.

Salli was a platinum blond whose skin showed age beyond her twenty-four years. Having lived in Cologne for some time, she was advancing her career by working as a receptionist through a series of city government offices. During the week, she frequently spent her evenings in the company of middle-aged pot-bellied political hopefuls. On weekends, however, she tried to date more virile young men. When she met Otto, whom she preferred to call "Schumacher," she was intrigued by his stamina. She thought it would be fun to spend some time with him, although she normally dated only officers.

As Erich bent down to pour her a glass of wine, he noticed a dark part in her bleached hair and could see the outline of her nipples showing through a snug, blue satin blouse. He suspected her promotions were due more to ability in the bedroom than skill in an office. "Do you have any suggestions for a place to eat?" he asked.

Salli described several restaurants in the vicinity and enumerated the foods they served. As Erich listened, he feared she would suggest one too expensive. Salli, however, was adept at appraising a man's financial capacity. "Why don't we do this," she said, sensing his concern.

"There's a cafeteria not far from here. The food's good and prices reasonable." Snubbing her cigarette in a saucer Irma had put on the table for an ashtray, she clasped her hands. "Shall we go?" she asked.

"Let's," Schumacher replied.

They walked around the railroad station and past the towering arches of the great cathedral, chatting and joking as they went. At the waterfront, they encountered a throng of people being disgorged from the Dusseldorf ferry. Rosa, following closely behind Salli, who was threading her way through the tangle of passengers and greeters, squeezed Erich's hand. "Isn't this fun?" she remarked.

Erich looked at the radiant face wreathed in the soft, black curls of her hair. Then he pulled her toward him and kissed her on the forehead. "It's wonderful!" he replied.

After they had eaten at a candle-lit table inside, Salli suggested they move to the large, open area at the rear of the restaurant. "We can order a drink and do some dancing," she said, surveying the faces of others.

"Sounds like a good idea," Rosa and Irma chorused.

Between dances with Schumacher, Salli, who did not like beer, drank several glasses of wine. Finally, after waiting for Rosa and Erich to return from the dance floor, she turned to Rosa. "Would you mind terribly if I had a dance with him?" she asked, pointing to Erich.

Rosa looked at Erich and said, "No. You'll find him a good dancer."

Salli rose to her feet and took Erich's hand. "I don't care how they dance," she said, her cheeks glowing from the wine. "I just like being held by a man!"

As they danced, she clung so tightly that Erich could feel the outline of her body pressing against him from his knees to his shoulders. Her hair, nestled against his face, reeked of cigarette smoke. Embarrassed, he looked around to see if others were watching, all the while hoping the music would stop. And when it did and they were walking back to the table, he smiled and wondered if the buttons of his tunic had made a row of mottled spots on her skin that would remain until morning.

At the table she lit another cigarette. "Say, I've got an idea," she said enthusiastically. "There's these friends who usually throw a party on Saturday night. Let's drop in on them."

Rosa wrinkled her forehead. "Are you sure they won't mind?"

"They'd love to have us."

"Let's go!" declared Schumacher, rising to his feet

Salli jumped up. "That's the spirit, Ott! Get a bottle of wine to take along."

Salli knocked twice at a ground floor apartment, but no one answered. Gingerly pushing against the ornate door until it opened, she peered inside. There were six couples in various states of inebriation, dancing to music blaring from a large radio located on a table in the corner. One of the girls looked toward the door and then broke away from her dancing partner. "Hello, Salli!" the girl shouted, smiling broadly as she beckoned them inside. "Nice to have you drop by."

When Salli had completed introductions, the girl responded by saying, "Friends of Salli's are friends of ours!" She pointed to a doorway at the far side of the room. "Go into the kitchen and get something to eat and drink, then join us in here."

When they saw how the men ogled and winked, Rosa and Irma felt uneasy. They would stay, however, as a courtesy to Schumacher's friend, Salli. And as the evening progressed and the drinking continued, the aggressive males insisted on dancing with all the girls. Although Salli and Schumacher appeared to enjoy the situation, Rosa and Irma disliked being with the strangers, especially those who danced with unusual intimacy and whispered repulsive suggestions while caressing the full range of their backs.

On several occasions they had received hushed thanks for coming, indicating that the men were looking forward to playing the game with them at midnight. This puzzled them, and they deduced that whatever kind of game it was, it would not be to their liking. After quietly reporting their suspicions to Erich and Heinz, the four of them decided they would leave rather than participate.

When midnight arrived, one of the men whom Rosa had seen look at his watch anxiously several times during the evening, clapped his hands and shouted, "Twelve o'clock!"

Rosa immediately took Erich by the hand and discreetly led him to a corner of the room. Irma and Heinz saw their move and joined them. Most of the others, however, several taking a last swallow from their glasses, started for a door that led into an adjacent room. Salli, with Schumacher in tow, dashed to the corner where the four had retreated. "Oh, I forgot to tell you," she began, her face flushed from drinking and dancing, "this group takes a little intermission at midnight. They just go into the next room to rest and relax for a little while."

Rosa looked into the dimly lit room through the open door and saw the couples stretching out on the carpeted floor. Alarmed, she took a deep breath and turned to Salli. "Really," she said, squeezing Erich's hand, "we should be going."

"Yes, we have an early commitment," Erich asserted.

"Oh, come," implored Schumacher. "They just play a little game. It doesn't take long, does it Salli?"

"No. Not at all."

"What kind of game?" Erich inquired.

"Something they call *cartwheel*," Salli answered with a shrug.

"Sounds like fun," Erich replied, trying to be courteous. "But we must be going." Salli tried to respond, but he continued, "It's been nice meeting you and your friends, Salli. We wish to thank you for a wonderful evening. We'll look forward to seeing you again." As he herded the others before him, he slapped Schumacher on the shoulder. "Take care of yourself, old boy!"

"Sure thing," Schumacher replied with a wry smile. "See you back at the camp."

Schumacher, piecing together information he had gleaned from others during the evening, assumed the game involved petting or lovemaking. Curious, he was anxious to try it. As he and Salli entered the large, unfurnished room, he saw that the others were lying side by side in a circle, their bodies forming the spokes of a large wheel. "Come on, Salli!" one of the men shouted, patting the floor beside him. "Here's your spot!"

When the light was snapped off, Salli unbuttoned her blouse and whispered to Schumacher, "Take off your clothes and stack them at the edge of the rug."

"Where are your friends?" queried a masculine voice from across the room.

"Couldn't stay," she replied, rubbing Schumacher's naked body.

"Damn! I was looking forward to making their acquaintance."

Just as Schumacher could feel Salli's cool nakedness against him, a phonograph began thundering the slow, rhythmic beat of a drum.

Salli whispered a caution in his ear, "Now remember, control yourself as you make it around the circle. You start with me and I want you to finish when you get back to me.

• • •

Squatting in the predawn darkness, Erich peered nervously at the dim, radium-coated figures on the face of the watch he had been issued. It was the final week and this was to be the culmination of their training. Company D was to cross the Rhine in rubber assault boats, storm up the hill on the other side, and dig in on a crest that overlooked a strategic highway. He had been selected squad leader and Heinz his assistant squad leader, each in charge of a five-man rubber raft.

Although he had been well trained and knew exactly what he was to do, he remained uneasy with the responsibility he had been assigned. Only last week during a special ceremony, the commander had praised Corporal Strausmann for his ability to instruct his men so well in bayonet handling, grenade throwing, and finding cover from artillery and air attacks. He was sure he could handle the assignment and hoped the tension would ease after they got under way.

At precisely three o'clock, he stood and waved his arm for the men to follow. Quietly, they slipped from the cover of shrubs they had hidden among since midnight, inflated the rubber rafts, and silently slid them into the chilly water. Fighting the swift current for five hundred yards was a strenuous ordeal, but with the men in top physical condition, Erich was able to land at the calculated landing spot.

As the men pulled the rafts onto the bank, Strausmann, who had been hiding nearby, trotted up. Erich, following orders given by the company commander to check identification of everyone encountered, ordered him taken prisoner.

"Let's tie him up!" Schumacher said, holding out a hand for Strausmann's identification card.

Erich took the card from Schumacher and handed it back to the corporal. "Let him go," he said. Then he turned to the rest of the squad. "Follow me!" he ordered.

Strausmann was furious. "I'll get your ass back at camp!" he bellowed as the squad charged up the hill behind Erich.

Schumacher, looking back over his shoulder, snapped, "Stay clear of the assault troops!"

The purple sky was changing to a dull orange when Erich halted to consult with Heinz on the objective. They studied the map for several minutes but could not find any recognizable landmarks. Nevertheless, by looking down at the river behind and a village a short distance ahead, he found his position. He gathered his squad around him. "The enemy should be dug in about three-hundred yards ahead," he told them, keeping his voice low. "There are other friendly squads to our right and left. Let's deploy in a vee formation and sneak up on them."

Twice he passed the word to maintain a distance of ten yards between men. Then, suddenly, the opposition forces spotted his point man and opened fire, using blank ammunition. With a precision that surprised him, the squad lobbed smoke grenades and quickly overran the entrenched opposition.

When his squad reached the crest of the hill, he ordered them to dig in. But again, they encountered the shale and sandstone that had plagued them throughout their training. Tired and sweating, a rifleman threw down his shovel, took off his helmet, and dropped down on his haunches. "Let's push on and capture some decent land so we can dig a hole," he said sarcastically.

"Pity the poor bastards that have to bury somebody here," Schumacher added.

"The African Arabs would really have trouble," said Heinz. "They have to bury their dead standing up facing east."

"Hell," snorted Schumacher. "At that rate, most of the people I know are so damned crooked they'd have to be screwed into the ground."

"Get those helmets on!" Erich shouted, remembering the regulations he had read in a field manual. Then, feeling an urgency to complete the task he had been assigned, he added, "And let's get those holes dug before Strausmann and his henchmen get here!"

Erich was eating the last of his combat lunch ration when Strausmann, accompanied by a sergeant, strode into view. He could see by the smile on the corporal's face that the sergeant was making favorable comments about the way the men had been trained. Even so, Strausmann had to further demonstrate he was not about to relax discipline. Walking over to the hole Schumacher was in, he saw a spot of mud on the stock of the young man's rifle. "Don't you realize, Private Schumacher," he began, puffing up his chest and looking down into the soldier's sweat-stained face, "that the rifle is the most important item you possess? It is more important than food, than clothing, than your girlfriend!"

Schumacher smiled. He had heard the lecture twice before. The first time was during the lesson on nomenclature and care of the weapon. It had to be disassembled, the parts identified, cleaned and oiled, and then he had to reassemble it while blindfolded. The second time occurred when he dropped the rifle during an inspection because Strausmann had fooled him by flashing his hand past the weapon without taking it. For that error, Strausmann made him walk at attention around the drill field for three hours.

In addition, he had to tuck the rifle neatly into his bed each night for a week while he slept on the floor.

Using his handkerchief, he wiped the mud from the rifle stock. When he looked up, Strausmann snapped his head with approval and then walked away accompanied by the sergeant.

When nightfall came, Erich issued orders for the men to sleep two hours and stay awake two hours in such a manner that half would be on the alert at any given time. "No loud talking or snoring," he added. "If the opposition attacks, fire your rifles and throw plenty of grenades."

The attack came at dawn. But the well-coordinated defenders of Company D repulsed the attacking forces in less than an hour. When the smoke and dust had cleared, Schumacher crawled over to Erich. He was dragging a cleaned and dressed suckling pig.

Erich was puzzled. "How and where did you get that?" he asked.

"Must have got in the line of fire," Schumacher replied with a smile and shrug.

Noting how well the animal had been cleaned, Erich was sure it had been stolen from a farmer's meat house during the night. He heaved a great sigh and shook his head as he looked into Schumacher's eyes.

"We'll cook it today," declared Schumacher.

Continually amazed at Schumacher's resourcefulness, Erich threw up his hands. "All right," he agreed. "But not too much smoke."

Sitting smugly in staff cars, captains and majors watched from a distance as maneuvers among the rocky, tree-studded hills continued for another day and a half. Satisfied the young men were ready for assignment to combat units, they ordered the company back to the river to be loaded on trucks and returned to camp.

The next morning an inspection was held to be certain the equipment of each man of Company D was complete and in good order. A supply clerk replaced defective items with a new issue.

"Hey, Schumacher," Erich teased as the men were in line that afternoon outside the dispensary. "After inoculations they check you for venereal disease."

"Doesn't worry me," Schumacher replied. "Why should it?"

"Those wild games you play."

Schumacher responded with a grin. "Never think about it," he said. Then, reflecting momentarily, he asked soberly. "Say, Stecker, how can you tell?"

"Oh, they'll discover it," Erich answered, tossing his head toward the dispensary.

"Yes. But how can you tell yourself?"

Heinz had been listening to their bantering. "You'll think you're pissing hot lead!" he chortled.

. . .

Corporal Strausmann stood with his hands on his hips looking down the length of the company street. He couldn't believe his eyes. Beer was served in the canteen, but liquor was forbidden in the camp. Although he had occasionally seen some of his men wobbly on their feet, he assumed they were merely acting while conversing with friends. Besides, he had never smelled anything stronger than beer on their breath, and countless inspections hadn't uncovered anything stronger than brandied cake.

It was Friday morning, the time for the final scrubbing and cleaning to ready the company for the next class. The five large fire barrels in the company street had been emptied so they could be scoured and refilled with fresh water. And all of them had been filled nearly to the top with liquor bottles. The men of Company D had consumed the contents, filled the bottles with water, and dropped them into the fire barrels.

Strausmann, standing with the other noncommissioned officers of the company, was furious. How could he have been fooled? And now, what could be done with the bottles? If they were put in the trash, he could picture reverberations throughout the command when such a large number were picked up from one company. And if a truck was requisitioned so they could haul the bottles away, he was certain the truck driver would leak the news, and the officers would come to investigate.

He walked from one pile of bottles to the next with his hands on his hips. His face became livid as he alternately mumbled and cursed about how well things had gone, but now everyone was in trouble. "Colonel von Grunwald is proud of this training command," he stormed. "He thinks we run a very tight company here. And now look what you idiots have done! We'll all be court-martialed!"

Erich could see that the men were enjoying Strausmann's plight. Suddenly, the company sergeant bellowed an order. "Each squad corporal will select a man to go to the drill field! They will dig a six foot hole to bury this mess! Strausmann, you supervise them!" Then he raised his voice to a higher level. "The rest of the men will scrub the barrels and carry the bottles to the hole!"

Schumacher, selected by Strausmann from Erich's squad, was ordered to join several others assigned the task. After the men had dug for several minutes, Strausmann walked slowly around the edge of the developing hole. As he walked, he remembered Schumacher's snippy response across the river. The stern expression on his face gradually turned to a sly grin. Looking down at the four men in the hole, he yelled, "What are you throwing that dirt up here for?"

"Where should we put it, Corporal?" asked one of the surprised soldiers. Turning, Strausmann pointed to a place on the ground a few feet away. "Private Schumacher! You dig another hole right here to put that dirt in!"

Schumacher, still sweating profusely from taking his turn in the hole, glared at the corporal. In the future, he would probably remember the things Strausmann had done for him. But, he vowed, he would never forget the things Strausmann had done to him.

The next morning Strausmann assembled his squad for the last time. After a quick inspection of their uniforms, he issued individual written travel orders, shook each man's hand, and wished him the best of luck. When he had finished, he stepped back, clicked his heels, and studied the squad momentarily. Then, surprising the men standing rigidly at attention before him, he changed the expression on his face to a pleasant smile. "Men," he began, "Camp Schwarzenborn has trained some of the finest soldiers in the German army. And your squad is among the best. When you join your next unit, I know you'll be a credit to Company D." His face suddenly became icy stern again. "Now!" he shouted. "Board that bus over there. It'll take you to the railroad station in Cologne. Remember, serve your country well!"

When they read their orders, Erich, Heinz, and Schumacher had been directed to report to the Frankfurt District Command Headquarters August 26th for transportation and assignment to the French Occupation Forces. "We have two weeks!" Schumacher shouted with glee.

At the station, Schumacher shook hands with his comrades. "See you in Frankfurt," he assured them, slinging his rifle over his shoulder before picking up his duffle bag.

Erich and Heinz waited until he had purchased his ticket for Hamburg. Then, as they watched, he turned and waved before disappearing into the crowd of boarding passengers.

At Rosa's and Irma's apartment, Heinz explained that he planned to spend a few days in Cologne before going home. As Irma threw her arms around his neck and kissed him, Rosa turned to Erich. "What's your schedule?" she asked. Her eyes were sad and sober.

Erich took her hands in his. "I have to catch the train to Regensburg. It leaves Sunday at noon."

As he sat across the table from Rosa in a small restaurant not far from the apartment, Erich knew she was troubled. Right after Irma and Heinz had left for the theater, he had noted a change in her mood. And now she sat quietly, eating very little and speaking only when he directed a question to her. "Let's go for a walk along the river," he said, thinking it might elevate her spirits. She nodded and rose to leave.

They sat on an iron bench beside a gravel path that meandered through a large planting of blooming geraniums. After several minutes of silence, she lifted his hand into her lap and squeezed it with both of hers. Then, wrinkling her forehead, she began to speak in a subdued voice. "There's something I must tell you," she said.

Erich searched her face, waiting for her to continue. He wondered if she was pregnant.

"Colonel von Grunwald has an adjutant, Major Boehmer. He has taken me to dinner a few times and seems to be getting serious. I don't have any strong feelings for him, but he treats me nice. I'm wondering if I should continue to see him."

Erich took in a deep breath and let it out quietly. "How old is he?" he asked calmly.

"Twenty eight."

"Have you gone very far with him?"

"No. On our second date, he started to slip his hand beneath my blouse. I pushed it away. He said, 'Oh, a lady!' and has treated me with the utmost respect since."

"What does he look like?"

"He's not bad looking—a little overweight. He's well educated and seems considerate."

As they strolled back to the apartment hand in hand, she asked, "Do you mind? About Major Boehmer, I mean?"

Erich did mind but didn't want to tell her. She meant a lot to him. He had grown to love her and it bothered him to think she would be giving her love to another man. But there was Maria, and he knew he wanted her for a wife and the mother of his children. "No. I'll always have a tender place in my heart for you. But most of all, I want you to be happy. I can offer you nothing but a big heartache. However, be sure to check him out so you know he'll treat you right. It would hurt me terribly if you were mistreated."

"I will," she assured him, realizing there was no way to get him to change his mind.

When they made love, she insisted he relieve her twice. Afterwards, they lay in each others arms for some time. Then she quivered and squeezed his body against hers. "Even if I marry Major Boehmer," she whispered, "my true love will always be for you."

"Why would you marry him?" Erich asked, kissing her cheek.

"Only for convenience." Then she pushed back and asked, "Should I tell him about us? Should I let him go all the way? He thinks I'm a real lady."

"Don't let him touch you until you've walked down the aisle," Erich replied sternly. "And tell him nothing about us. If he asks, you don't have to reply. Put him in his place by acting indignant over asking such a question."

"Won't he be able to tell?"

"No. Play the role of a novice. Let him lead you and tell you what to do."

• • •

After attending services in the great cathedral, they descended the stone steps into the warm sunshine. As Irma removed her white straw hat, Heinz took in a deep breath and turned to Erich. "Let's go across the street and have some coffee and cake." His voice rang with enthusiasm.

Erich, squinting in the bright glare, smiled and nodded. "Let's!" he replied.

As Heinz sipped his coffee, he looked up at the majestic spires. "I never knew there were so many steps in the world," he sighed, referring to their climb to the top the week before.

"We had sore muscles for three days afterwards," Rosa said with a chuckle.

"When we got to the stone that had '1870' carved in it, we were ready to go back down," Irma confessed. "But you two coaxed and begged, so we kept going." She paused and then continued, "Just watching those big bells work made it all worth while though."

At the railroad station, Erich kissed both Irma and Rosa and then shook Heinz's hand. With a suddenness that surprised him, Rosa threw her arms around his neck. "Oh, God," she moaned. "I wish I was going with you."

Erich kissed her again, tasting the salt from her tears.

As the train left the station and started across the river, Erich looked down at the gray, swirling waters. He wondered if he would ever see her again.

Operation Atlantik Wall

E rich stepped off the train in Regensburg and looked about the station. The number of men in uniform had increased significantly since he had been away. Some were pacing back and forth on the platform, others were resting on benches, and several were in line at the information and ticket booth. He was sure Maria would have been here if she had known he was coming, but since he didn't know his arrival time, he had written that she should wait in Holzheim. After fastening his gas mask canister to his belt, he shouldered his rifle and picked up the heavy bag containing his clothing and personal items.

As he approached the old stone bridge over the Danube, he looked back and noticed a hunched figure sitting high on a wagon that had emerged from a side street. Although the outline of the driver looked familiar, the distance was such that Erich could not be sure who it was. But when he saw the size and coloring of the horses, he knew it was Mr. Trapp's prize team. He dropped his bag to the street and waited for the wagon to draw near. Then he called out, "Mr. Trapp! Oh, Mr. Trapp!"

Farmer Trapp, squinting into the afternoon sun, did not recognize the tall, young soldier ahead of him. The years had dimmed his sight, and an army uniform made so many young men resemble one another. But when Erich removed his cap, the wrinkled old face beamed a broad grin, and Mr. Trapp brought the wagon to a halt beside the young man he had known for so many years. "Erich Stecker!" he exclaimed, extending a calloused hand. "What are you doing here?"

"Just on my way home," Erich replied. "Got a few days leave before my next assignment."

"Put your bag in and climb up," Mr. Trapp said in a cheerful voice. "Ought to be home before dark if we move along."

After placing his bag on the sand-strewn bottom of the wagon, Erich climbed onto the spring-supported seat. "What brings you to Regensburg?" he inquired.

"Brought in a load of potatoes. All these years, I've been selling them to a vendor who came out with a truck and picked them up. But now with the war on, there's a shortage, and I make more money selling them to the food markets." Trapp cleared his throat and spit before continuing. "Could make more at the farmers market, but can't spare the time." He was silent for a moment, then added, "Probably been a lot better off if I'd had some sons instead of three daughters. At least; I'd have more help on the farm."

Erich shrugged and smiled. "Then the army would take them all, and you'd be in a bigger bind."

"Probably so," Mr. Trapp agreed with a sigh.

"By the way, how's Inge these days?" Erich asked.

"Fine. Just fine. She's engaged to Max now. He was home for a few days a month ago. Don't know when they'll get married though."

As the shadows lengthened, the rubber-tired wagon rolled along silently behind the blocky horses, whose steel shoes made a rhythmic clatter against the hard surface of the roadbed. Conversation, mostly about farming and the war, was interspersed with long periods of silence as the two men became occupied with their private thoughts and stared ahead or gazed off into the distance. When the team suddenly turned onto the narrow macadam road that led up through the dark evergreens to Holzheim, Erich felt their pace quicken. And as his thoughts turned to Maria and his waiting parents, he could feel a rush of blood through his temples.

It was nearly dark when Erich smelled the barnyard odor that signaled their arrival at the Trapp driveway. Expressing his appreciation for the ride, he shook the grizzly farmer's hand and stepped down onto the ground. As he made his way up the street, he saw light shining in several windows and a few dark figures walking in the distance. A cricket chirruping in a flower garden became silent when he approached and then resumed its song when he had passed.

He rang the bell and waited. A light came on in the hallway, a key scraped in a lock, and the door opened enough for the inquisitive face of a middle-aged woman to peer out. When she saw the waiting soldier standing in the shadows, she yanked the door open and quickly pulled him inside. "Erich!" My wonderful boy, Erich!" she shouted, wrapping her arms around him and kissing him on both cheeks.

Hearing the commotion, Erich's father rushed up, shook his hand, and took the bag and rifle from him. August Stecker's face was beaming as he led the way to the living room at the back of the store. Inside, Mrs. Stecker made her son stand so she could scrutinize him.

Erich sighed and shook his head. "Mother," he said. "I'm just fine."

"At least they're feeding you well," she said. "Looks like you've even gained some weight."

"Yes. A little."

"Feel those muscles!" interjected the father as he squeezed Erich's biceps. "That army sure knows how to put a man in shape!" Slapping his son on the back, he added, "Solid! Real solid!"

"Let me fix something to eat," volunteered Mrs. Stecker, heading for the kitchen. "My heavens! You must be hungry."

"While you're doing that, I'll get Maria," said Mr. Stecker as he started for the door.

Erich felt tired, but things were happening so fast he could barely keep track of them. Besides, he doubted he could influence them even if he wanted to. He decided to wash his face and hands.

When he returned to the living room, a bowl of steaming noodle soup and several slices of black bread were on the coffee table. As he sat down to eat, the door burst open and Maria rushed in. He stood to kiss her on the cheek. Then he motioned for her to sit beside him. As Mrs. Stecker poured her a cup of tea, Maria continued to look at Erich, her sparkling brown eyes radiating her love. Running her fingers through his short-cropped blond hair, she looked into his penetrating blue eyes and noted the strong muscles of his jaws when he paused from eating to smile and wink at her. It energized a tingle that surged through her body. She yearned for him to hold her, to love her.

Mr. Stecker pointed to the rifle Erich had leaned against the wall. "Sure looks like a good weapon," he said.

"Bolt action Mauser," Erich replied. "It made me an expert marksman."

"How come they make you bring it home?" his mother asked, concern showing on her face.

"Well, it was issued to me new. I cleaned it and learned with it. I know exactly how it works and how it acts. It's supposed to instill pride and confidence."

Still lacking her son's enthusiasm, Mrs. Stecker wrinkled her forehead. "And the gas mask?"

"Same thing. Used it several times in training. I know it works well."

"Do you think you'll have to use it?" Maria queried soberly.

"I hope not, but who knows?" Erich answered, looking into the grim faces around him. Thinking he should change the subject, he turned to Maria and smiled. "How's the nursing business? Still running around pushing big needles into helpless people?"

"Yes," she answered with a chuckle. "This is my last term coming up."

"And all reports indicate she'll be a fine nurse," chimed in Mrs. Stecker. "A very outstanding student!" She snapped her head to emphasize the point.

"And then what?" Erich asked.

"I'm not sure," Maria replied. "There's a nurse shortage, you know."

They talked for nearly an hour before Maria rose to leave. Erich walked her to the door and kissed her goodnight. "I'll come by at ten tomorrow morning," he said, referring to the basket lunch they planned to eat on the hill overlooking the town.

• • •

Dawn broke bright and sunny the next morning, forecasting a beautiful autumn day. Erich stood at the open window of his bedroom looking down at moss-covered tile roofs, dormant chimneys, and little, backyard garden plots. In the distance a veil of mist was slowly rising above the hilly forests to form a pleasant backdrop. *Holzheim, my Holzheim,* he thought. *What a remote, quaint, wonderful village you are.*

He put on civilian clothes and looked into the mirror. Already it felt strange to be out of uniform. Downstairs, his mother waited to serve him breakfast. "It's a nice day," she said, placing a cup of hot coffee before him. "But there aren't many of the boys left." She sighed and shook her head. "Gone into service."

As he walked up the street, two men with hoes on their shoulders halted long enough to shake his hand and wish him luck before hurrying on. The tailor, seeing them through the shop's open door, beckoned for Erich to come in. "I know you'll only be home a few days," the short, balding man said. "But if you'll bring in your uniform, I'll make it a formfit." There was a twinkle in his eye as he winked and snapped his head. "I do it for all our boys. It'll look a lot better."

"Thanks, Mr. Schneider. I'll have it here this afternoon," Erich promised, shaking the little man's hand.

Thinking he should pay a call on Mrs. Juergens, he went to the post office. When she saw him, she came from behind the counter and threw her arms about him. "I always know a week or so ahead when you're coming home," she said, her voice bubbling with enthusiasm. "Maria brightens up and hustles about getting everything done so she'll have as much free time as possible to spend with you!"

"She's a gem of a girl," Erich said when he was released from her grasp.

Mrs. Juergens nodded. Tears had welled up in her eyes. She was proud of the way her daughter had grown up during such trying circumstances. Erich hugged her and then left for the Juergens' home.

When Maria saw him coming, she locked the door and bounded down the steps. She had a basket in one hand, her sweater in the other. Erich kissed her on the forehead and took the basket from her. She smiled and linked her arm with his as they started up the street toward the hills behind the town.

Yellow leaves from poplar and chestnut trees littered the ground but only in sufficient numbers to provide a carpet that barely covered the dirt in the path. Erich looked down and recalled numerous times in the past when they were ankle deep and felt cool on his feet as he shuffled through them. Looking ahead, he noted that the oak and birch trees still held their leaves, live and green, providing cover for the numerous sparrows and squirrels that watched in silence. High in a nearby spruce a crow cawed loudly, telling the forest creatures that their domain was being invaded.

A short distance from the top of the hill Erich pointed to a secluded spot at the needle-covered base of a large pine tree. "Let's go over there," he said.

While Maria spread the blanket at a place where the sun filtered through, Erich stood and looked down at the village. He studied the church tower momentarily and then scanned the surrounding farmland. Several family groups were harvesting potatoes and sugar beets in the rectangular fields that stretched out from the town. Having lived among them all his life, he knew how hard the work was. The wife and older children grubbed the harvest from the soil with large, curved-tine forks, and the small children and old women gathered it in shallow wicker baskets which they emptied into burlap bags. In one of the fields he could see an older man, a grandfather he surmised, driving a team of horses pulling a wagon. A younger man, probably the old man's son, lifted the heavy sacks aboard the wagon for delivery to the root cellar at the house. The hours were long and the labor hard, but for the citizens of Holzheim, it was the only life they knew.

His thoughts were interrupted when Maria handed him a cup of cider. He smiled and kissed her on the nose.

"You know," she began, "Max Dorten is stationed on the west coast."

"Mr. Trapp told me he was engaged to Inge, but he didn't mention where he was located."

"He's in Holland. Apparently they're building some gun emplacements, and he's a security guard there."

Erich looked off into the distance. "Well, if I get assigned anywhere near there, maybe we can get together."

Maria had prepared fried chicken and sandwiches of cheese and ham. Since Erich was especially fond of the way she prepared chicken, she took great delight in watching him devour it. "That chicken is the best!" he said.

Maria smiled and nodded. He said that each time he ate her chicken. She was so used to it she would be disappointed if he didn't mention it.

After they had finished eating, they stretched out in the slanting rays of the afternoon sun. As he held her hand in his, Maria could feel certain urges and impulses growing within her. They had always come whenever she was alone with Erich and she was certain he was feeling them, too. She wondered if they were becoming noticeably stronger and more intense for him like they were with her. It bothered her so much that she wished he would forget his vows of propriety and take her. But she knew he was more disciplined than ever and was determined she would be a virgin when she walked down the aisle on her wedding day.

Taking a different path down the hill, they came to the old swimming pool. It had a scattering of leaves on its surface and a few mallards swimming about, but the water still ran as clear as ever when it passed over the rocky spillway.

"I remember a beautiful August day a few years ago," said Erich, "when I came up for a swim and found you here alone."

"Yes. We both stretched out on that rock to dry," Maria responded as she pointed. Then, squeezing his hand, she blushed and added, "That was before I wore a suit."

Erich shook his head. "You know, it seems like only yesterday."

"Yes," Maria said, drawing him close to her, "but a lot of water has passed over that spillway since."

• • •

Erich spent much of his time during the next few days in the company of Maria. Sometimes he helped about her mother's house or garden, but what he enjoyed most was strolling hand in hand along the narrow country lanes. As they walked, he inhaled deeply, feeling a great sense of pride in his village when he saw farmers pulling their onions, cutting rows of corn and placing it in shocks, or picking their apples and pears. And when he sauntered through the Holzheim park with her, he placed an arm about her waist as they slowed to watch children dash about searching for chestnuts that had fallen from the trees. But always upon returning to sit for a while with her on the front porch, by force of habit, he stepped over the squeaky middle step.

One evening after supper, he went to the Holzheim Tavern. As soon as he walked through the door, he knew he should not have come. With the young men away, he could see only clusters of older patrons through the smoky haze of the dimly lit room. Although he was welcomed warmly and had several steins of beer placed on the table before him as he sat down with one of the groups, he felt uneasy. After answering a few questions about his training, he merely sat and listened, slowly sipping from one of the steins as each man anxiously waited for a turn to tell of his military exploits during the previous war. Staying as long as he thought necessary to avoid offending them, he excused himself and left. Outside, he strolled the darkened streets for nearly an hour, puzzled by the loneliness he felt. He wondered if he was troubled only by the changes in Holzheim, or because of what he feared for the whole country. Returning to his room, he looked at the piano. In the past he had found that it was a means of absorbing his thoughts and easing the tensions he felt.

When his mother, in the living room below, heard the music of Mozart coming from his room, she knew she should not disturb him. A short while later, she slipped noiselessly into his room and left a silver tray with hot tea, sugar, and lemon on a small table. For several minutes she lingered, watching admiringly, and then quietly slipped out the door. She was proud of her soldier son and silently prayed that God would protect him and return him safely to her.

The next morning he encountered Inge, who was driving a wagon to a field that her father was working at the edge of town. "Hello, Erich," she greeted, a broad smile gracing her robust face. "Want to ride along with me?"

At first Erich was inclined to climb aboard. But things were different now. Although she gave the impression her enthusiasm for him had not diminished, she was engaged to Max. And he didn't want to make it appear that he was eager to become involved with her. "No," he replied. "I have a few things I have to attend to. But thanks, anyway."

A look of disappointment covered her face as she flipped the reins. "Be sure you come to see me before you leave," she said, forcing a smile.

"I will," he replied, waving to her.

• • •

After attending ten o'clock Mass, Erich and Maria stood in front of the church to chat with the parishioners they had known over the years. Erich smiled as he listened to the lively conversation. He knew it was the only time that many families had to exchange greetings and gossip. As the crowd thinned, he saw the Feldmann family approaching.

Mr. Feldmann extended his hand. "You know my wife, of course," he said. Erich nodded to Mrs. Feldmann, who had begun to speak with Maria.

"And this young lady," Feldmann continued, pointing to a woman behind him with a baby in her arms, "is my new daughter-in-law, Lydia. Just had a new baby boy." His face beamed with pride.

"The father hasn't seen it, yet," Mrs. Feldmann interrupted, directing her attention to Erich. "He's stationed in Poland."

"Yes," Maria added. "All four Feldmann boys are in the army."

"Oh?" Erich responded, raising his eyebrows in surprise. "I'll bet you miss them around the farm, especially now at harvest time."

"We just had to cut back and let some of the land lay fallow," said Mr. Feldmann. "The agriculture ministry was upset over it. Ordered me to plant all the fields next year. Told me they'd see to it I got help."

"I wonder how they're going to manage that?"

Feldmann shrugged. "I think they're going to bring in some war prisoners."

"Say, Erich," Mrs. Feldmann said, her voice suddenly serious. "Would you look at the baby? I think he's going to be tongue-tied."

"Why do you think that?"

"Well, when it cries, its tongue doesn't behave like those I've seen before. Here, look!" She took the baby from her daughter-in-law and bounced it about to make it cry. The baby woke up momentarily, then went back to sleep without uttering a sound. She shook the child again, gave a heavy sigh, and handed it back to its mother. "Well, I'm sure there's something wrong."

"Bring it to the house when you're through here, and I'll look at it," Erich suggested.

"Good!" Mrs. Feldmann answered. "We'll only be a few more minutes."

When the Feldman's arrived, Erich placed the baby on the dining room table. As he unfolded the blanket from around the child, it began to cry.

"See!" Mrs. Feldmann said, pointing. "The end of his tongue doesn't come up much at all."

Erich inserted his index finger into the small mouth and raised the tiny tongue, exposing the questionable frenulum. He examined it carefully and then turned to Mrs. Feldmann. "It may be all right, but perhaps we should make sure."

Erich got a small scissors from his medical kit and sterilized it with alcohol. Then, while Maria held the baby, he snipped a small section of the thin membrane beneath the tip of the tongue.

Mrs. Feldmann wrapped the blanket around the squalling infant and handed it to its mother. Turning to Erich, she snapped her head. "There!" she said. "Now his tongue's sticking up where it should be!"

As the Feldmann family departed, Erich lifted the blanket from the face of the now quiet baby. A smile of satisfaction graced Erich's face.

• • •

Maria sat stoically beside Erich on one of the cold, wooden benches in the drab, oak-paneled waiting room of the Regensburg station. They had ridden their bicycles from Holzhein, and Erich had given his to the station agent to keep until Mr. Trapp could pick it up when he brought in another load of produce. She squeezed Erich's hand as she recalled how his mother had cried when they left the house and how his father beamed with pride as friends and neighbors gathered to see them off. Listening to the babble of voices and shuffling of feet occasionally punctuated with amplified announcements, she wondered if there was something she should be saying instead of looking grimly into the distance. But she couldn't think of anything she hadn't already said many times before.

Suddenly, Erich stood, "I'm going to the fountain to get a drink of water. Want to come along?"

"No," she replied. "I'll wait here for you."

She sighed admiringly as she watched him walk away in his highly polished, black leather boots that made a striking contrast with the fitted, gray-green uniform he wore. *He is handsome and manly,* she thought. His blond hair, now at a short trim length with a slight wave, seemed to emphasize his clear, blue eyes. And his broad shoulders filled the tunic well as he strode with a forcible step, demonstrating a powerful but nimble body with exacting coordination and control. Thinking of him as a husband and father of her children, she quivered slightly.

When the train came, her heart sank. She held his hand as they walked slowly outside where he dropped his bag onto the platform and kissed her warmly. Then he got on board. She held back the tears until the wheels began to move and he had waved for the last time. Then they welled up and spilled down her cheeks. The train was nearly out of sight before she turned to get her bicycle.

During the lonely ride back to Holzheim, she thought of the days they had spent together and realized he had changed. Although he still treated her tenderly, he was more sure of himself and firmer in dealings with others. Not only was he more disciplined in body but in mind as well. He seemed to face situations with exceptional precision and direction. She hoped it was for the better, but at the moment she was not sure.

• • •

The Frankfurt District Headquarters placed troops waiting assignment in a row of barracks at the far end of the induction center. Passing through the front section, Erich readily recognized the area. Now jammed to capacity with recruits, the cocky corporals were still shouting at the inductees in the same threatening manner. He entered one of the assigned barracks and found a sergeant, who told him to take any bunk he wished. Surprised at the laxity of the situation, he looked about and then tossed his bag onto one of the beds. "Thanks, Sergeant," he said, hurrying on to look for his friends in the other barracks.

Except for 2 men hospitalized with venereal disease, all of the 480 men being assigned to the northern coastal section of France were present at roll call the next morning. After breakfast they were assembled on a drill field with each man's clothing and equipment neatly arranged in front of him. Erich patiently watched as a team of sergeants and corporals carefully examined everything, replacing any item that was badly worn, damaged, or missing.

Later, directed to a warehouse, steel helmets were issued and hobnails were driven into the soles and heels of each pair of boots. Erich looked at Heinz. "This looks serious," he said with a wry smile.

"You'd better believe it's serious," Heinz snorted. "We're headed for enemy territory!" He stamped his feet. "My God! What a clatter."

"Yes," chimed Schumacher. "They're damned slippery, too. Might just fall and break your regal ass!"

"That doesn't frighten me," Heinz replied. "Dr. Stecker would put it in a sling, and I'd carry on."

In the evening the men were processed through the records section, where there papers were scrutinized for accuracy, identification cards were issued, and inoculations brought up to date. A technician made certain each soldier had an aluminum identification disc hanging from his neck and that the information on it was accurate.

• • •

With a high pitched squeal, the train ground to a jarring halt on a siding at the Cherbourg harbor. Erich, tired from the long ride, peered out of the rain-streaked window at the long, dull-gray breakwater that stretched as far as he could see in the falling drizzle.

When the heavily laden troopers stepped down from the coaches onto the wet pavement, a sergeant directed them to a large, empty warehouse a block away where representatives from several units were waiting for them. Erich, Heinz, and Schumacher were among forty-seven men being assigned to the 222nd Infantry Division.

Climbing aboard one of three canvas-covered trucks of the 222nd, Heinz turned to Erich and smiled. "At least we're still together," he said.

As the trucks labored up a steep, winding road, Erich looked back at the large expanse of black water in the harbor. The entire length of the breakwater was bristling with dozens of guns. Although the presence of German troops made him feel secure, a chill raced up his spine as a sense of uneasiness crept over him. He had never been so far from home. And the realization that he was deep in a foreign land, a land filled with enemies, concerned him.

Just as the truck was picking up speed, he felt a sharp jab in his side. It was Heinz, pointing to a watchtower beside the road with a forty-millimeter gun at its base.

"Looks like we mean to stay," Heinz said, shouting to be heard above the roar of the truck.

Erich nodded. "It sure does," he replied soberly.

As the convoy rolled through numerous villages, Erich could see French citizens, frequently dressed in blue, walking along the wet streets. Others rode bicycles with small, wicker baskets fastened to the handlebars. At one place along the narrow highway, an elderly couple riding on a high, two-wheeled cart drawn by a yoke of oxen caused the trucks to go to the opposite side of the road to pass. Looking at their sad, wrinkled faces, Erich sensed that they were not concerned about politics or war but merely desired to continue to live on their small plot of land in the same simple manner they had for years, ignoring such things as guns and foreign troops.

• • •

The rain had stopped and the sun was struggling to break through a hole in the leaden sky when the men arrived at their new quarters. The company was housed in three wooden buildings recently constructed amid the ruins of a medieval castle on a high bluff overlooking the sea. Although the stone wall surrounding the site was in excellent repair, the ancient buildings had collapsed into heaps of stone and rubble. The new men were assigned beds and then directed to the kitchen to be fed.

"Certainly good food!" said Heinz, swallowing a mouthful of thick stew. "Better than Schwartzenborn."

Erich, sitting across the table from him, nodded. "Maybe it just tastes better after that long ride."

A sudden blast from a whistle silenced the group. It was followed by the booming voice of a robust sergeant. "Men," the sergeant shouted, "your company commander wishes to speak!"

A short, blocky officer with a florid complexion stepped forward. "My name is Captain Georg Steinmetz," he began. His voice was low pitched and mild mannered. "I am pleased to have you join my company. Now it is up to full strength. This makes the rest of the men happy because it will relieve them of the work overload they have been carrying."

The men looked at each other questioningly.

"We're a combat unit, all right," Steinmetz went on. "But we must also guard a number of emplacements that are under construction." He paced back and forth before continuing. "In your association with the French, you should fraternize as little as possible. Along the coast, we try to treat them well to gain their cooperation in the event of an invasion attempt. That is why we live in our own barracks instead of hotels and homes.

He surveyed the young men's faces. Then his voice became louder, his expression more sober. "Should an attack come, we will face the brunt of it," he warned. "But a system of strong fortifications is under construction. And this company will be in a constant state of readiness so we can repulse any invasion attempt made!"

The next day the first sergeant assigned the new men to their positions in the company. Noting that their records showed Erich, Heinz, and Schumacher had trained together in basic training, he assigned them to a new squad. Erich was designated as squad leader, Heinz assistant squad leader, and eight other men, including Schumacher, as the remaining riflemen.

Ordering the squad to line up and stand at attention before him, Steinmetz said. "You men have all completed basic training, so you know how to soldier. I'm appointing Private Stecker as acting corporal and assigning him as squad leader. And you will obey him, or you'll answer to me!" He paused, narrowed his eyes, and looked into each of their faces. "Are there any questions?"

After a moment of silence, he continued, "All right then, go back to your quarters and get your bunks together in one section of the building. Then get organized as an individual unit and as part of your platoon. Tomorrow your squad will be given a field assignment."

It was five o'clock when Erich heard the jangle of the alarm clock he had placed on a table beside his bed. Already awake, he wasn't startled by the sudden noise. He hadn't slept well, having spent much of the night wondering how he would be received by his men as squad leader. With Heinz's help, however, he concluded he would make a determined effort to set a good example and gain their confidence. He reached over and shut off the alarm just as someone snapped a switch, turning on a glaring overhead light. Sitting up, he watched as others stirred, put their feet on the floor, and then began to dress.

He was among the company's squad leaders and assistant squad leaders who slept on single beds in a separate room at one end of the barracks. As his eyes became accustomed to the light and the blood began to circulate through his body more rapidly, he quickly sprang into action. By five-twenty he was fully alert, neatly dressed, and ready to challenge a new day with the others.

At five-thirty the leaders burst through the door that separated them from the rest of the platoon. One squad leader turned on the lights and gave three sharp blasts with his whistle. Most of the men sat upright in their double-deck beds, stretched, and rubbed their eyes. A few moaned, turned over, and then pulled their blankets over their heads to ward off the sudden brightness.

Erich looked at Heinz, then motioned for his assistant squad leader to follow him. Walking swiftly to the far corner where his squad was quartered, he yanked the blankets from the two curled forms lying down. "When lights go on, get your two feet on the floor!" he snapped. His voice rang with authority. "Now, get dressed!"

It was five-forty-five when a blast from the whistle ordered the troopers out into the damp, gray dawn for roll call. Afterwards, all squad leaders were told to report to Company Headquarters to receive their orders for the day.

Erich's squad was assigned the task of stretching coils of concertina wire along the beach and planting antipersonnel mines in the sand. As Erich studied a large map on the wall, Captain Steinmetz walked over to him. "We're on a high bluff," the captain said, placing a finger on the map. "Go down this ravine and start right here. You'll find engineers there who'll get you started"

As Erich led his squad down the steep, narrow cut, mist from the sea spray moistened his skin. Licking his lips, he tasted the salt. A smile stretched across his face. He had seen pictures of the ocean and seashore, but now he was here. A ripple of exhilaration sped through his body.

After walking a short distance along a sandy beach dotted with stacks of mines and coiled wire, they encountered a military truck laboriously making its way through the damp sand toward them. As it neared, they saw it was a captain from the engineers with a load of French workmen.

The truck halted, the officer descended from the cab, and Erich saluted.

The captain was a young man who appeared to be more of a scholar than a soldier. "No need to salute down here," he said. "We've got a job to do."

Erich nodded.

The captain gave Erich and Heinz instructions on placing the wire and mines so high tide would not disturb them. "Just take up where it ends over there," he stated, pointing to the end of a line of stretched wire a short distance away. "If you have any problems, my sergeant will be along shortly." He paused to look into their faces. "Any questions?"

Erich and Heinz looked at each other. Heinz shrugged. Erich turned to the captain. "We'll manage," he said convincingly.

The captain pointed to the truck. "I'm going to take this load of Frenchmen up the line to a barge. We'll be dropping big, steel jackstones in the water to stop landing craft. You'll probably see us out there later on."

As the captain walked away, Erich looked out over the choppy water. "He sounds as if an invasion is coming."

"Well," Heinz replied with a sigh, "we'd better get ready."

After working two hours in the cool, damp air, Erich ordered the squad to rest. While the riflemen found rocks at the base of the cliff to sit on, Heinz looked at the punctures in his leather gloves and the tears in his work clothing. "That wire's vicious!" he exclaimed.

"And the salt and sand makes everything burn," Erich added.

As Erich walked slowly over to the base of the cliff, he heard the voice of one of his men. "At first I thought it was fun to dig in the sand and walk along the beach," the young rifleman complained. "But this is damned hard work."

"Good practice," Erich said with a smile, trying to humor him.

"Well," the young man replied, "I don't mind doing for our company. But for the whole European continent, that's expecting too much."

"Besides, we're combat riflemen," another protested.

An engineer sergeant who had walked up a few minutes before explained that it was being done along the entire coast. "We're using every available man to finish as soon as possible. It's called *Atlantik Wall*, and goes inland for several miles. You'll probably see more of it after you've been here a while."

• • •

Wet and tired, the company was ordered to return to its quarters. Erich was grateful. After working on the beach for a week, his squad had rejoined the company for maneuvers with the entire regiment. They had spent six days staging mock counterattacks against a theoretical enemy force that had gotten ashore. The terrain, composed of small pasture fields and orchards enclosed by curious contrivances called *hedgerows* proved ideally suited for defensive warfare. Made by throwing dirt against rows of small trees and shrubs as they grew, the hedgerows were now earthen banks four-feet high threaded with tree trunks, limbs, and vines. For Erich's squad, they were nearly impenetrable walled barriers every two or three hundred yards in any direction.

But to simulate battle conditions, each man had to sleep on the ground in a tent he carried in his field equipment. Frequently in the morning, a soldier awoke to find that a large black and yellow lizard had crawled in with him. And wet most of the time from rain that saturated the grassy fields nearly every day, he shivered as he ate a chunk of dried bread with a can of cold pork and beans for dinner.

Throughout the long nights, members of Erich's squad had taken turns standing the lonely vigil of guard duty. The silence, however, was frequently broken by squadrons of German bombers flying high overhead. Occasionally, when a night was clear, long fingers of searchlight beams could be seen probing the distant English skies.

When they arrived at their quarters, the kitchen crew had a large quantity of hot beef stew waiting for them. From the squad leaders table, Erich looked across the room at his wet and dirty men. They were talking among themselves while eagerly gulping the hot food. He was proud of the way they had blended into a good fighting unit and assimilated with the company.

The First Sergeant entered the dining area and, in a booming voice, said, "I'd like to have your attention, men!"

The room fell silent.

The sergeant continued. "I want you men to return to your quarters and get yourselves and your equipment cleaned up and dried out." Then he turned to the squad leaders table. "Stecker?" His eyes searched the row of faces until he saw Erich nod. "Captain Steinmetz wants to see you as soon as you've finished eating."

"Yes, Sergeant," Erich replied. His heart leaped to his throat. Puzzled, he left the mess hall immediately and returned to his quarters. As he quickly washed, shaved, and put on a clean uniform, thoughts chased through his mind. Several times he reviewed his actions since joining the company. His squad had worked hard on the wire detail and had performed well while on maneuvers. He could find no reason to be reprimanded.

An orderly held the door so Erich could enter Captain Steinmetz's office and then closed it behind him. Standing rigidly at attention, Erich could feel his pulse throbbing at his temples.

The captain was standing looking out a window at the gray dampness that had blanketed the area. Slowly he turned and studied Erich for a moment. "Private Stecker," he began, his words ringing with a measured cadence of authority, "you look much better than when I saw you coming in with the troops this morning."

"Yes, sir!" Erich replied. He could feel perspiration breaking out on his upper lip.

"I suppose you wonder why I called you in."

"Yes, sir!"

"It is the policy of this company to promote personnel to the rank their job calls for as soon as they prove their proficiency. Otherwise, they will be replaced by someone who can do the task." Steinmetz paused and took in a deep breath. "In view of your excellent performance in the field, effective next Monday you will be promoted to the rank of corporal."

"Thank you, sir," Erich replied.

The captain cleared his throat and then walked back and forth with his hands behind his back. Erich continued to stand at attention, his eyes following the pacing commander.

"And there are times," Steinmetz went on, "when I need a medical advisor, especially when I inspect the quarters of our men stationed out on post. Since you have an appropriate background, I'll have you join me on some of these inspection tours." He paused and then asked, "Any questions?"

"Yes, sir," Erich stammered. "What will become of my squad when I'm away?"

"You will turn it over to Private Jager. By the way, his name will be on the promotions list too. Any further questions?"

"No, sir!"

Erich clicked his heels, saluted smartly, and then exited the door. His heart was still thundering inside his chest. Now, however, it was from elation instead of fear.

Heinz was waiting at their quarters. "Catch hell?" he asked, his face showing concern.

"No," Erich replied coolly. "As a matter of fact, it sounds like a good deal. May have to accompany the captain once in a while when he visits outlying posts."

"Oh?" questioned Heinz, hoping for more information.

As Erich worked to clean his mud-spattered equipment, he gave Heinz more details of the visit with Steinmetz. But he didn't mention the promotions. Suddenly, they were interrupted when the mail clerk delivered several letters to the squad leaders room.

Three of the letters were for Erich. He smiled as he read one from his mother, who repeatedly expressed concern about his living conditions and safety among the enemy French. One from Maria was warm, hopeful, and affectionate. And a hurriedly written note from Max Dorten was bursting with gayety, suggesting Erich try to arrange a visit in two weeks to witness a local Dutch festival.

Heinz received a letter from Irma. It was warm and passionate, expressing a great love for him. In closing, she mentioned that her sister, Rosa, was getting married to Major Boehmer at the Schwarzenborn Post Chapel on November 16. Heinz turned to Erich. "Guess what?" he said with a grin. "Rosa's going to marry that major back at Schwarzenborn."

A flash of jealousy raced through Erich's mind. Although Maria was the only one for him, he still held considerable affection for Rosa. In a few minutes, the twinge subsided. But still, he was bothered by the thought of someone he loved so much giving herself over to another man.

• • •

Erich felt embarrassingly conspicuous sitting beside Captain Steinmetz in the rear seat of a Mercedes command car as it made its way past the gate guard and onto the narrow macadam road. A corporal less than two weeks, he had been requested to accompany the commander on an inspection tour of a squad of men guarding an ammunition dump two miles up the coast. Sitting stiffly erect, he was studying the lush, green countryside when the silence was broken by the captain. "How are your men reacting to your promotion?" he asked.

"They're quite pleased," Erich replied. "It seemed to raise their morale." He thought of Schumacher's elation upon seeing his name on the grenadier first-class list but decided not to mention it.

The command car halted near the entrance of a small, wooden shack. As the driver opened the door for Captain Steinmetz, Erich let himself out and walked around the vehicle to stand beside his commander. Suddenly, the wooden door of the building opened, and a corporal emerged to stand stiffly before them. He jabbed an open hand into the air and shouted, "Heil, Hitler!"

"Heil, Hitler!" Steinmetz replied, raising an outstretched hand in response. When he lowered his hand, he pointed to Erich, "Corporal Stecker."

The young man stepped forward and shook Erich's hand. Then, holding the wooden door open, he said, "After you, gentlemen!"

Erich was not certain how he should respond as he walked across the cleanly scrubbed wooden floor, but he scrutinized the facility carefully. The rough, wooden bunk beds appeared adequate, and lighting and ventilation satisfactory. As he looked at a small coal heater used to heat food, he reminded the guard corporal to be certain that dishes and pans were thoroughly washed and rinsed in very hot water.

Behind the building, he looked at the stacked cases of artillery shells and hand grenades camouflaged with netting and tree branches. He wondered if they would ever be used. After looking at the open trench latrine, he turned to the captain. "Lime should be sprinkled in there every day."

"Corporal," Steinmetz said, facing the guard leader, "I'll make some available for you."

"Yes, sir," the corporal replied. Then he said, "Captain, one of my men has a tooth problem."

"That's why we're here, Corporal," the captain said boastfully. He was pleased to have someone with him to handle medical problems. "Let Corporal Stecker look at him."

Erich looked at the swollen jaw of the troubled young man. And when he applied pressure to the swollen, inflamed gum, an amber fluid oozed from it. "This soldier needs immediate dental attention," he said, speaking loud enough for Captain Steinmetz to hear.

Steinmetz, wanting to impress the guard corporal that he was concerned about the welfare of his troops, responded, "Good! We'll take him back with us and have him transferred to the regimental dental clinic immediately!"

Although he had to practice proper social distance to satisfy the army's military code, Erich became sufficiently well acquainted with Captain Steinmetz to get his assistance in acquiring items for an elaborate medical kit. He had demonstrated his need for such a kit on the inspection tours when he administered to a number of medical ailments such as blisters, infected cuts, and sore throats. And the captain was exceedingly proud when a Frenchman came to the company's headquarters in the middle of the night seeking help for his pregnant wife. The Officer of the Guard aroused Erich, who got Heinz to help. They followed the man to a neighboring village and delivered a baby boy. The next day Captain Steinmetz told Erich he could have the weekend pass he wanted to visit Max Dorten.

• • •

Evidence of a tremendous battle greeted Erich as he stepped from the coach. Stunned by the utter destruction that surrounded him, he stood for a full minute surveying the devastation. There had been some evidence of fighting on the way, but nothing that could approach this. He had caught a ride in an army truck from his camp to Caen, and then took the train to Holland. Along the way he had seen a few shell-scarred buildings and some holes made by rifle and machine gun fire. But here, the station had been blown apart and adjacent buildings had walls and roofs missing. Black smoke stains over window and door frames, coupled with sagging steel beams, gave mute testimony to the intense fire that had consumed them. In the switching yard, a tangled mass of twisted, rusting rails formed grotesque patterns around bomb craters that pock-marked it. Two locomotives, their boilers blown apart and wheels facing skyward, lay a short distance away.

At first he thought of the rail yard in Regensburg, then of the quiet village of Holzheim. What if war came there?

Just then some soldiers approached, diverting his attention from the ruined structures. He asked if they knew the location of Max's unit. Pointing, one of them directed him to a truck. "It'll take you to a village. He's just outside of it."

In a barracks similar to his, Erich found his friend. "Well, I'll be damned!" Max shouted as he pumped Erich's hand and slapped him on the back. "I'm sure glad to see you. Have any trouble finding the place?"

"No. Your directions were pretty good. But your writing could use some upgrading."

"Never could write very good. I'm good at figures, though."

Max introduced Erich to two of his friends who were waxing their belts and then pointed to a bunk a short distance away. "That bed's empty, so you can sleep there. And now, we'll go eat."

"Sure blew hell out of the railroad station in the city," Erich said as he started for the latrine to wash.

"Yes," Max replied soberly. "Blew all the bridges, too. Made a mess out of nearly everything." He paused and then continued. "Didn't touch anything out here, though."

The next day they took a short walk to a neighboring village where the streets had been draped with long ropes of evergreen branches. Booths offering food, trinkets, and a variety of games of chance surrounded the town square. Everywhere there were people dressed in brightly colored costumes, the happy sounds of their voices reverberating with the music of a small band.

Erich and Max strolled about for several minutes and then sat down on a slatted, wooden bench. "Looks like a real blowout!" declared Erich, raising his voice to be heard above the din.

"I was told they do this three times a year. Sort of a mating game."

"A what?" Erich's forehead wrinkled as he searched Max's eyes. He wondered if the right words had been used.

"Mating game," Max reiterated with a smile. "Damnedest thing you ever heard of. Nearly every evening, all year long, they get all dressed up and walk around the square from six to eight o'clock." He shook his head. "They just walk round and round that silly square." His voice became more serious. "Actually, the boys are sizing up the crop of girls. The boys walk together and the girls walk together, but they don't talk to each other—just eye each other up.

Erich wondered if Max was really serious. "How do you know all of this?"

"I've been here quite a few times," Max answered. "Walked around myself." He took in a deep breath. "But with this festival comes the real activity. They're supposed to pick their partners and get engaged."

"Have you seen that, too?"

"No. Just heard about it."

Although the fall evenings were chilly, the warm, slanting rays of an autumn sun created a pleasant afternoon. The leaves had fallen from most of the trees. Those that remained exhibited fading shades of yellow and orange, some spotted with dry, brown blotches that would eventually spread like a cancer over their entire surfaces. Looking about, Erich noted a sprinkling of German soldiers wandering through the congested area. They were walking in pairs as they had been ordered. He pointed to a sidewalk cafe. "Let's get a drink of beer and watch the crowd," he suggested.

"What do you hear from Inge?" Erich asked, taking a sip from his stein.

"Oh, she's fine," Max replied. "She doesn't write any better than I do, so her letters don't tell me much."

"Does she tell you the news of Holzheim?"

"A little. She tells me mostly about the farm. You know, the cow having a calf at midnight and how many chickens her father took to the market. Things like that."

"That's a real hot letter from a fiancée," Erich chided.

Max reddened. "Well, she does tell me how much she misses me."

110

A well-dressed man appeared beside them. "Mind if I sit down?" he asked in German.

"Delighted to have you," Erich answered, reaching for another chair.

"You boys interested in some good *schnapps?*" the robust stranger asked, unbuttoning the jacket of his wool suit as he lowered himself onto the chair.

"I don't think so," Erich replied politely, wondering if the man would introduce himself.

"We're beer drinkers," added Max. "Why don't you have one with us?"

"Thank you. I will." The man sensed the two soldiers were waiting for an introduction. "I'm a broker of scarce items," he began. "In such a business, names are not used." Squinting as he sipped from his stein, the man stated that he had several barrels of choice liquor and was selling it to persons who appreciated quality.

Although there was no mention of price, Erich surmised it was from the black market and was expensive, so he did not pursue the matter. And there was another factor present in the back of his mind. He had been instructed repeatedly to exercise caution because German soldiers in occupied countries were resented by some of the people.

With a wave of his hand, the man ordered another round of beer. He was quiet until they were served and the waiter had walked away. Then he leaned over the table. "Even though I'm Dutch, I want you to know that I have great respect for the German people and believe in their cause."

Erich and Max did not know how to respond to the man's statement. They looked at each other, and then Erich said, "Thank you." Thinking it would be better to change the subject, he asked, "Just what is this celebration?"

"Well, it's unique to this section of Holland," the man answered. He explained that when a boy approaches the age of marriage and has decided on a prospective bride during the evening strolling, he will join the celebration and hope the one he has chosen will also be there. "Later this afternoon," the man continued, "the engagement dance takes place."

Erich looked intently at the man. "And they really don't know each other?"

"Not very well, if at all," the man replied.

"How do they get acquainted?" Max asked.

"Oh, they become very well acquainted," the man assured them with a smile. "There's a small bedroom on the first floor of each house. After the celebration, the engaged girl sleeps there. Each evening the boy approaches the window and whistles a little tune. She opens the window and he climbs in." He paused, then added, "He departs early in the morning."

"How long does this go on?" Erich asked, his curiosity rising.

"Until she becomes pregnant. Then they go to the church for a wedding ceremony."

"Good God!" Max exclaimed, nudging Erich. "See what you and Maria are missing!"

"You and Inge didn't miss much," needled Erich, slapping Max on the back. Then he turned to the man. "Does she have to get pregnant before they marry?"

"Theoretically, yes. But if they really want to get married, she can say she is. Later, if she must, she can make up an excuse such as losing it or having false indications." The man inhaled a deep breath. "You see, if he makes her pregnant, he is obligated to marry her. If, on the other hand, he doesn't and the love wears thin, they can call off the engagement by a simple little act. He doesn't show up some evening, and she finds some trash, such as corn stalks, on the porch in the morning."

Suddenly, the band played a loud flourish and the police cleared the people from the central portion of the square. Since the standing crowd that had gathered blocked the view, the stranger stood and motioned with his stein for Erich and Max to follow him. Maneuvering to a position where they could see the square clearly, they watched as the young participants began to appear.

The girls, dressed in starched white hats and long, full dresses that hid their wooden shoes, appeared shy and remained in small clusters just inside the ring of onlookers. Frilly blouses cut a deep vee down the front of their brightly flowered red and yellow dresses. Each had a large bustle that was topped with a neatly tied, heavily starched white bow. Their freshly scrubbed faces, pink cheeks, and shiny noses gave them the look of vibrant, robust youthfulness.

The embarrassed young men made loud, facetious remarks as they pushed and shoved one another toward the center of the slab-covered square. Dressed alike, they wore black hats and knickers, black leather shoes, gray knee-length stockings, and white shirts with large, floppy ties.

Erich stood next to a gaggle of older maiden ladies who were attired in somber gray dresses. He watched the expressions on their faces as they whispered among themselves. He was sure that they were gossiping about the bevy of young ladies. When one of them glared at him, he looked back at the square.

He noticed several family members, obviously concerned about the prospects for their daughters, call the young ladies back for last minute adjustments to their hats or dresses. Special attention was directed to the white bow on the bustle to be certain it was prominent and loosely tied.

The loud voice of an inebriated, middle-aged man caught Erich's attention. "Tis an absolute shame to waste such good looking young innocents on a batch of incompetent studs such as these!" he shouted. "They ought to be broke in properly by someone with well-developed virility and several years of experience!"

The maiden ladies were aghast. They placed their hands over their mouths, stared at the inebriate, and shook their heads.

As two policemen escorted the man away, the band stopped playing. It remained silent for a full minute while a hush came over the crowd and the girls grasped hands to form a large circle. When the music began again, the girls danced and swayed to the rhythm to make the circle turn.

While the crowd of people gathered more closely around the square, Erich noticed that all the villagers had bright red cheeks. Along the coast he assumed it was caused by the damp, cool sea breezes. But this was far enough inland to rule that out. Perhaps, he thought, it was an example his Heidelberg professor had once expounded upon in a lecture. There were certain areas of Europe where small quantities of arsenic in the drinking water turned faces of the inhabitants a robust pink color.

The young men were not so quick to respond to the call, but after someone in the crowd barked orders at them, they formed a circle that surrounded the girls but moved in the opposite direction.

"There are twenty-seven boys, but only twenty-four girls," Erich whispered to Max.

Max shrugged. "We'll have to wait to see what happens."

After several minutes, with the inner circle of girls rotating in one direction and outer circle of boys in the other, the music stopped. A lone drum began a heavy, rhythmic beat. The girls dropped their hands, closed their eyes, and stood motionless like a group of large china dolls. This initiated a frenzied scramble among the boys as each raced to get to the bustle of the girl of his choice.

Erich observed one girl who had opened her eyes to find that two suitors had reached her bow at the same time. She quickly made a choice by taking the arm of the one she preferred. A sad look came over the face of the eliminated one and he slipped dejectedly into the crowd and disappeared. Several other young men did not reach their desired ladies and they, too, disappeared into the crowd of onlookers. But the saddest sight was that of three young ladies who were not selected by anyone. They continued to wait for several minutes, hopefully looking for a suitor, before dashing off into the consoling arms of their parents.

Erich turned to the man standing beside him. "What will happen to them?" he asked, his voice expressing concern.

"Oh, they'll try again next time," the man answered matter-of-factly as he continued to watch the engaged couples dancing together.

• • •

Walking ramrod straight at the head of his squad, Corporal Stecker watched a droplet of water slowly form along the rim of his helmet and fall onto the front of his knee-length slicker. Leading his squad to their next assignment, he hoped the coastal drizzle would stop and the sun would emerge to dry the saturated land. Ahead, he saw an opening beginning to form in the dark, glowering sky. *Perhaps*, he thought, *three miles inland at the construction sight the sky would be clear.*

Tall Lombardy poplars, barren of leaves and with trunks painted white, lined each side of the narrow macadam road. To Erich, they appeared as giant sentinels looking down on his little band whose voices had been softened and clicking hobnails had been muted by the dampness. Alongside the road, cattle and sheep grazed in small fields surrounded by hedgerows. And from gnarled old trees blue-clad farmers were busy harvesting little green apples they would crush and press to make cider, brandy, and calvados.

As he walked, Erich thought of home and wondered how Maria was doing with her studies. He hoped Holzheim would never have to experience the terrible destruction he had seen in Holland. Then his chain of thought shifted to the letter he had received from Rosa. She had expressed apprehension about marrying Major Boehmer. Stating she didn't love him, she wanted to come to France to talk to the man she really loved.

Although he detested the thought of someone else making love to her, he consoled himself in the knowledge that she would have a much easier life with the major than if she married someone from her village. Besides, it would be better to rid himself of such involvement so he could be true to Maria. He wrote an immediate reply, telling her she was undergoing a last minute panic that girls experience before their wedding. Advising her to go through with the wedding, he assured her he would always consider himself her close friend.

At a point where the road made a slight rise, Erich turned into a narrow lane that was formed by hedgerows and lined with slender Italian cypresses. A few minutes later he emerged into a large, cleared area that was a beehive of construction activity. Halting his men, he ordered them to sit in the shade of a large tree while he found the leader of the squad they were to replace.

The squad leader, a slender, dark-complexioned corporal, led him to a small, wooden shack that served as a construction office. There he was introduced to Sergeant Paul Schickler, one of the engineers in charge of the project. Sergeant Schickler pushed his stool back from a high table covered with several layers of blueprints and extended his right hand. "Pleased to meet you, Stecker," he said. "Duty here is easy, but we have to be on the alert. Just don't want someone carrying a satchel charge to get in and blow something up." He explained that there were two hundred French and Pole laborers working under a contingent of army engineers. They worked twelve hours a day, seven days a week, and appeared satisfied with their lot. The site covered several acres that had been cleared, leveled, and excavated for five

240-millimeter long range guns that would be the heavy artillery complex for this segment of the coast. With the exception of a common mess hall, each gun was to be a self-sufficient unit. At the present time, one gun was in place and its crew on hand making final calibrations and adjustments preparatory to a test firing.

"Don't you have a problem with workers wanting to escape?" Erich asked, thinking they would have to be guarded.

"No," Schickler replied with a sigh. "They are serving time for minor offenses. We feed them well, and they like the open air." He paused, then added, "Every once in a while one will run off. But they catch him at one of the roadblocks and toss his ass back in prison."

Erich conferred with the departing squad leader, who told him to keep his squad's presence known during the day and to maintain an alert perimeter foot patrol at night. He directed his men to the guard bunkhouse and then watched the other squad as they disappeared down the narrow lane. The sudden burden of responsibility made him feel alone. He turned to Heinz. "Let's look around," he suggested, pointing to the completed emplacement.

Dwarfed by a three-floor concrete blockhouse, they looked up at the huge, long-barreled gun protruding from a horizontal slot at the upper level. Although the structure was submerged almost entirely below ground level, the area in front had been excavated, exposing a wall four feet thick that would protect the crew from all except a direct hit. Soil had been replaced over the top, and the entire area was being resodded and landscaped to camouflage it from view.

They descended a stairway to the floor beneath the gun mount. Artillerymen were busy filling it with large shells that had to be lowered individually by crane and wheeled on a cart to the storage position. Beneath them on the bottom floor, they were told, was the living quarters of the fifteen-man crew.

They climbed again to the top floor and stood near the base of the awesome weapon. Looking down, Erich saw three artillerymen struggling to activate a crane used to hoist shells into the tremendous breech. He turned to Heinz. "The size of this monster is too much to comprehend," he said.

"Yes," Heinz agreed. "I've seen pictures of big guns, but I never thought they could be this size." He paused and shook his head. "Wonder what it sounds like when they fire it?"

"I don't know, but we'll be certain when they test fire it in a few days," Erich replied, looking his friend up and down. He sniffed the air. "Did you fart?" he asked, a disgusted expression covering his face.

"Of course," Heinz answered, showing a wry smile. "You don't think I smell like that all the time, do you?"

Erich moved away a couple steps and then snorted, "My God, man! You should keep a tighter rein on your pucker string!"

After three fog-shrouded days, during which Erich had seen the laborers urged to work harder to complete the massive installation, the skies cleared and the sun began evaporating the cold moisture that had penetrated everything. Once again, however, the clear night skies reverberated with the roar of heavily laden planes droning their way across the English Channel. Sleep was difficult for his squad.

The next day, after telling Heinz he would be gone for two hours, Erich asked Schumacher to join him in a walk to a nearby village. He wanted to see what the landscape was like and to find out how occupying German soldiers were received by the natives.

The dozen houses of the little town had been built around a large stone church that had a small plaza in front. The homes were drab gray and tan rock structures with slate roofs. Most had been built adjacent to the cobblestone street. Erich saw three, however, with small front yards surrounded by high stone fences that had been topped with a thin layer of concrete embedded with broken glass. Half a dozen people were walking about. They looked at him and Schumacher, then, unsmiling, continued on their way. They were simply dressed and wore wooden shoes that made more noise than his hobnail boots. Their faces, especially their noses and cheeks, were bright pink. He wondered if it was from the large quantity of wine he had been told they drank.

He and Schumacher entered a small tavern. They looked around the dimly lit room and then walked over to a polished wooden bar. "Two glasses of wine," Erich told the short, moon-faced man standing behind the bar. Then he turned to Schumacher. "This is a chance to use the French I've been studying."

As he sipped at the wine, Erich looked up at the dusty display of decanters on a shelf behind the bartender. "Old?" he asked.

The bartender shrugged. "Some yes, some no," he replied soberly in German. "My patrons brought them in to decorate the place."

Two middle-aged farmers dressed in worn blue jackets and trousers sat at a scarred wooden table in a corner. Black felt berets rested on their knees, and they wore rubber boots that were spattered with mud and manure. As they sipped cognac from small glasses, they talked in low voices. Erich noticed they occasionally stopped talking and looked his way. Feeling uneasy, he turned to Schumacher. "Let's drink up and go," he said quietly.

"Surely not much to do in this town," Schumacher observed as they stepped into the street.

"No," Erich replied solemnly. "We're definitely outsiders here."

As they walked quietly down the road, they came to a thatched roof house where a farmer working a large cider press in his yard waved a friendly greeting. The two soldiers waved back. Smiling, they walked over to the farmer.

After shaking hands, the farmer filled a broken glass from the trickling trough of the press and handed it to Schumacher.

"Quite good," Schumacher said, smiling and nodding to the Frenchman after taking a swallow. He gave the glass to Erich.

As Erich turned the glass to keep the sharp edge of the break from his lips, the farmer gave the press screw a partial turn and then picked up two more clouded glasses from a stool and wiped their edges on his sleeve. He filled them with cider, handed one to Schumacher, and then held his high. "*Amitie!*" he exclaimed, his darkened teeth showing through a pair of parted lips that were partially hidden by a graying stubble of whiskers.

Erich, noting the twinkle in the old man's eyes, held his glass aloft. "Friendship, always!" he exclaimed, hoping to convince the Frenchman he was sincere.

The farmer, sensing their interest in his work, invited them to enter a nearby shed. Erich, ever cautious in this foreign land, peered inside before entering.

The farmer showed them a pile of small, green apples he was feeding through a hand-operated cutting machine. By gestures, he explained that after the apples were cut into small sections, they were placed in the press. Erich was puzzled at seeing that a layer of straw had been placed between layers of apples in the press. Because of the language barrier, however, he was not able to understand the farmer's explanation.

The sweet juice had attracted a large number of bees that were ignored by the spunky Frenchman. But when an old billy goat approached, he was chased off before he could get near the press.

As the two soldiers left the farmer's yard, Erich looked back. The Frenchman, standing beside his cider press, waved his beret. Erich flashed a smile and waved to him. Then he turned to Schumacher. "That goat sure smelled strong," he said.

"Yes. But he doesn't have to," Schumacher replied.

"What would you do, sprinkle him with toilet water?"

"Hell, no! Shave off his beard!"

"Shave off his beard!" exclaimed Erich. "What good would that do?"

"Well," explained Schumacher, "a goat is built so he pees on his beard. That makes him stink. So, shave off his beard and he doesn't stink anymore."

Erich looked at him seriously and then broke into a hilarious laugh. "What a farmer you'd make! Going around shaving billy goats."

"Laugh, by God!" shouted Schumacher. "I've got an uncle who owns a farm and he told me that."

117

"Does he have any goats?"

"No." Schumacher hesitated. "But he knows about them."

At the guard bunkhouse, Erich told Heinz about the cool reception he and Schumacher had experienced in the village. "I think it would be better to restrict our men to this compound," he said. "Steinmetz thinks highly of our squad. I wouldn't want some incident to mess that up."

Heinz looked at Erich and then gazed out the window. He knew the squad members would be disappointed. But he had heard of another area where German soldiers had been beaten, resulting in a nasty investigation. He wanted to avoid that. "Well," he said, "we're only here for a few days. They can stand that."

The next morning an order was issued for everyone to stand by for a test firing. Erich assembled his squad in an open space not far from the big gun. "The gun captain will raise his arm when he's ready to fire," he told them. "When you see that, cover your ears. I don't want some damn fool complaining he can't hear for two days." He looked at them sternly. "Got that?" he barked.

As the gun captain raised his arm, he looked at his men to see if they were ready. Seeing they all wore either communication headsets or earplugs, he dropped his arm with a forceful movement and shouted, "Fire!"

The ground suddenly shuddered and a tremendous tongue of orange flame flashed from the muzzle, pushing before it a huge cloud of black smoke. A vee-shaped swath of grass before it flattened, and nearby trees danced and swayed with the muzzle blast. Erich felt a sudden pressure against his face and chest that subsided as quickly as it came. Then, there was silence, total, complete silence. Erich removed his hands from his ears and stared at the flattened grass and torn leaves for some time. "My God!" he said. "What awesome power!"

"Too bad it's for destruction," Heinz said soberly in a voice that echoed fear.

Twice more during the day everything came to a halt while the colossus belched flame and smoke as it dispatched a projectile out to sea. Afterwards, the artillerymen seemed pleased with the results. They cleaned the monstrous weapon and then finished the task of putting their quarters in shape.

• • •

Early Thursday morning during the last week in November, an orderly located Erich who was eating breakfast in the mess hall. "Telephone call for you at the company office," he said.

"For me?" Erich asked, his face showing disbelief

"For Corporal Erich Stecker," the orderly reiterated. "The First Sergeant seemed to think it was important."

As Erich trotted to the headquarters office, he tried to think of a reason for the call. "Stecker," the sergeant said, raising his eyebrows while holding a hand over the mouthpiece, "it's from the office of Major Leon Boehmer of the Paris District Headquarters. Hope you don't have your ass in a jam!"

"This is Corporal Stecker," Erich said, trying to repress the heavy breathing generated by the excitement.

The call was from Rosa, the sound of her voice calming his fears. Since it was being transmitted through military channels, she spoke formally, asking if he could serve as a consultant to her husband for a few days.

Erich was certain she wanted him to visit her and had conspired through her husband for such a visit. "I'd be pleased to lend whatever assistance I could," Erich replied sedately.

"Good!" Rosa said. "I'll see that arrangements are made." She paused and then added, "And you'll receive a letter from me directly."

Later in the day, he was called back to the company office by Captain Steinmetz. The captain informed him he was to report to the Office of Military Intelligence on December 9."Just who do you know to arrange something like this?" the captain asked with a stern, quizzical look.

"A distant relative," Erich lied.

"Think you'll be transferred?"

"Oh, no," Erich replied hesitantly. "I doubt it very much."

When Rosa's letter arrived, Erich could hardly wait to open it. As he read, each word was a stimulant for the eagerness he felt to make the trip to Paris.

> *My Dearest Darling:*
>
> *This is the first opportunity I've had to write you, and I wanted so very much to tell you how I appreciate your advise. The wedding ceremony was fine, but as for the first night— naturally he tried. But he didn't succeed until the third! He is rather clumsy at it, and thankfully the wiry hair hurt him, so after several minutes he gave up. Thank God for your gentle breaking in! He tries to be nice about it, but he just doesn't understand, and it is rough on me. Sometimes he gets so frustrated—I've learned some non-clinical terms for parts of the anatomy!*
>
> *I'll keep this letter brief and tell you all the news when I see you. About the visit—your orders will direct you to District Headquarters. Instead, come to the apartment. It's not far from the Concorde at 15 Rue Neil. I'll be waiting for you!*

Frank Irgang

If you wish to write, use the French mail and send it to the apartment. I can hardly wait to see you!
All my love,
Your Rosa

Erich, thrilled at the thought of seeing Rosa and visiting Paris, found it difficult to keep his mind on his assignments. He had read about Paris and dreamed of seeing it someday, but when the war erupted, he doubted the opportunity would ever arise. He tried to recall the attractions he wished to see, but could think of only a few. Perhaps Rosa could direct his sightseeing when he got there.

Heinz was pleased for Erich. However, it increased his yearning for Irma. "If only I could see her again," he confided.

"Maybe you should marry her," Erich suggested.

"Believe me," Heinz replied gloomily, "I've been giving it some thought."

Erich decided to change the subject. "Have you noticed that discipline in our squad has been slipping?" he asked.

"Yes," Heinz replied. "Think we should do something about it?"

During the few days before his departure, Erich had the squad engage in vigorous physical exercise. In drills that used hands and arms, he had them drill while holding their rifles. He decided the added seven pounds of the weapon while doing squatting and pushup exercises made the activity much more effective. In addition, he insisted the men keep their uniforms clean and pressed. Although the men grumbled at first, after a few days he found a noticeable difference in their attitude. A definite pride in their unit was emerging. His attitude was also changing. He was gradually acquiring a hard-nosed position on military discipline.

• • •

It was early evening when Erich arrived in Paris, much later than he had expected. He had been driven to the Cherbourg station at the first light of dawn, but the Paris Express had been sidetracked en route several times for high-priority military trains. Seeing a *gendarme* standing not far away, he walked over and asked for directions to Rue Neil.

The *gendarme* took a small book from his breast pocket and fanned through it. "Ah, yes," he said, holding a finger against one of the pages. "Take Metro to Clemenceau. You can walk from there."

Although Erich thanked him, the *gendarme* saw the bewildered look on the young soldier's face. "The underground," he said with a swoop of his hand. "The Metro." He pointed to a sign in the distance.

At the *Place de la Concorde*, Erich stopped to seek direction. The streets were nearly deserted. The tall obelisk, silhouetted against a charcoal sky, was shining dully in the dim moon-light. Air raid precautions had necessitated minimum lighting and operation of few vehicles. The brownout would make it difficult to locate Rue Neil. He would ask the first person he encountered.

Arriving at the correct address, he was hesitant to ring the bell. The darkened, shuttered front made the building appear void of habitation. He rechecked the number and then took in a deep breath and pressed the button.

A maid opened the door a few inches. "Yes?" she asked.

"I'm looking for the residence of Major Boehmer," Erich replied.

The maid opened the door and pointed upstairs. "His apartment is up there," she said quietly.

A chill raced through Erich's body as he stood before the heavily varnished door. He raised his hand to knock but then hesitated. After removing his hat and smoothing his hair, he moved his hand across his waist to be certain his belt buckle was centered. Taking in a deep breath, he rapped lightly on the door.

When Rosa cautiously opened the door, a wedge of light illuminated the front of Erich. She quickly grabbed his hand and, squeezing it, pulled him inside. The happiness she radiated as she shook his hand made her face beam. "Erich!" she said. "My, how very nice to see you!"

"It's nice to see you again, too," Erich replied hesitantly, noting a heavy-set man lounging in a large chair.

"Come over here," she said, leading him by the hand. "I want you to meet my husband."

The man put aside the newspaper he was reading and pushed himself to his feet.

"Erich, this is my husband, Leon. Leon, this is Erich Stecker."

"Pleased to meet you, sir," replied Erich.

"Major Boehmer," the man said, extending a hand. "Rosa told me you were an old friend."

They talked briefly about Erich's train ride and locating the apartment in the dark, and then Rosa excused herself to prepare something to eat. The two men continued to talk about army life and the war. Not certain what Rosa had told the major, Erich avoided giving any information about his relationship with her. As often as possible, he directed the conversation so the major talked about himself and his activities in the military intelligence. Erich got the impression the major thought that military intelligence was extremely essential and he, Boehmer, was one of the most important officers. Although Erich nodded assent, he deemed these noncombatants as mere military eunuchs who consumed choice supplies that could be put to far better use in the hands of the fighting forces.

Leon Boehmer came from a poor but devout Lutheran family who eked out a meager living from the sandy soil of Luneburg Heath. As a boy he was plump, but his mother was certain he would lose his chubbiness in adolescence. However, nature had plotted a path of obesity that he would follow through life. Although he possessed the mental ability to excel in school, initiative was lacking. So after completing grammar school, he worked at a number of menial jobs in the community. Finally, at eighteen, he joined the army.

The rigors of basic training did little to improve his *pyknic*-type body, and it was ascertained that he could serve his country better as a clerk than as a combat-trained field soldier. He was eventually promoted to sergeant because of length of service. When Germany's military commitments required large numbers of men to be drafted into the army, however, his ascent through the ranks was rapid.

Boehmer's first romantic endeavors were limited because he lacked initiative to arrange dates with women. Those he did manage were usually disappointments because the girl became bored with his bland personality and absence of spirit. This dearth of success further dampened his desire to go out with girls, and he did so less frequently.

When he was promoted to captain and then to major, the added money and prestige gave him more confidence. From a woman's standpoint, it also made him more desirable. With a resurgent interest in women, he began to date again. Soon he was fondling those who would permit it. Although he was introduced to a few town tramps who would have permitted him any liberties, he felt it beneath the dignity of a major to associate with them. Therefore, the girls he dated allowed him only sufficient access to their bodies to maintain his interest.

By the time he met Rosa at his office, he had decided it would be better to find a girl who would marry him rather than continue the frustrating chase of dating a variety of girls. Not only was he looking for a bed partner but someone who could cook his meals, wash his socks, and keep his uniform in good condition. He decided Rosa was an acceptable candidate who possessed everything he desired, including good looks and attentiveness. And when he took her out on their first date and she rebuffed him for attempting to slip a hand beneath her blouse, he was certain she was every inch a lady. He quickly proposed marriage.

Rosa liked the major because he was neat, clean, and courteous. But he was so unlike her vision of a husband that she could not fall in love with him. After they had dated several times, she permitted him to kiss her and to hold her close and caress her back, but he generated no passion in her. And when he proposed, she delayed giving an answer until she could consult with Erich. But when Erich told her there was no possibility of him becoming her husband, she consented to accept the major's proposal.

Rosa appeared at the kitchen door. "If you two gentlemen will come in here, I have a little something for you to eat."

Sitting in bowback chairs at a small wooden table that had been heavily coated with white enamel, they made sandwiches of sliced sausage and rye bread. Erich took a bite and chewed it momentarily before washing it down with a drink of beer. "Sure tastes good!" Erich said, looking across the table at Rosa."Just wonderful to have a meal in a home for a change."

Rosa, who had been waiting for Erich's reaction, looked at him and smiled. He could tell by the warm sparkle in her eyes that she was pleased.

"Yes, sir," said Major Boehmer. "There's nothing quite like having a little woman around to look after you. You ought to consider it yourself."

"It sounds like a good idea," Erich agreed. "But I think I'll wait until the war's over."

"Yes, I suppose an enlisted man wouldn't have much to offer a girl, at that," the major said smugly.

This statement gnawed at Erich. He was certain by the way Rosa looked at him that she had noticed the momentary flash in his eyes. But he retained his composure and nodded half-heartedly. She smiled, indicating she was pleased with his response.

Later in the evening, Erich was informed that, officially, he was to report on resistance activity and citizen morale along the Normandy coast. "Unofficially," the major said, "you are to be our guest for three days. It was Rosa's idea. And I wanted to show her I could arrange it."

Erich slept well in the small guest bedroom and was curled up facing the wall when he was gently awakened by someone slipping beneath the blankets behind him. Military training had taught him to remain perfectly still until he had analyzed the situation. However, the fragrance he inhaled identified the intruder as Rosa. He turned his head so he could speak over his shoulder. "What are you doing here?" he whispered in a scolding tone.

"I wanted to get warm," she replied calmly.

He turned over to face her and his hand came in contact with her bare side. He saw her nightgown draped over a nearby chair. "But you shouldn't be here. You're married now!"

"Not to the man I love," she replied with a smile. "Besides, Leon's gone to the office and won't be home until five forty-five. The door is locked, and we're alone." Her voice was full of glee.

"Don't you understand?" Erich asked sternly. "You're married, and you shouldn't do this. Besides, do you have any idea what would happen to me if he found out?"

Rosa's response was to throw her arms around his neck and kiss him.

Initially he resisted, but the pressure of supple breasts against his chest and the pleasant irritation of pubic hair on his hip aroused him. Afterwards, they lay cuddled together with eyes closed for some time. Then Rosa broke the silence. "That's the first good one I've had since the last time with you."

"Doesn't your husband satisfy you?"

"Not very well. He just doesn't go about it right."

Later in the morning, they walked past the *Madeleine*, stopping momentarily to look at the statue on the side of the structure that had been beheaded by German shelling during the last world war. As they began the long walk up the *Champs Elysees* to *Etoile*, Rosa tugged at Erich's hand. "Let's take the Metro," she suggested. "It's much easier."

Erich, deep in thought, looked around. "No," he said slowly. "All through school I read books and saw pictures of the world's greats who traveled up this boulevard. I want to walk it."

Holding Erich's arm, Rosa smiled with rapt admiration as she walked proudly beside him. She talked idly about problems she encountered converting to a housewife. "The first morning in our Schwarzenborn apartment," she said, "the light bulb burned out over the wash stand while Leon was shaving. Like a good wife, I tried to replace it by taking one from the bed lamp. I dropped it on the floor and it broke. He shaved without a light while I swept up the mess."

Erich pretended to listen, but his mind was elsewhere. Although he patted her hand as he admired the broad expanse of the beautiful boulevard, he was feeling a tinge of guilt. Maria should be walking at his side, not Rosa.

They stood in momentary silence at the perpetual flame honoring the unknown soldier and then climbed to the monument's top. "Have you ever been kissed on top of the *Arch de Triomphe?*" he asked with a sly grin.

"No," she replied, turning to face him.

"Would you like to be?" he teased.

"Yes, indeed!"

After lunch at the *Eiffel Tour Restaurant*, they went to the *Place de Invalides*.

Looking down at the rose-colored tomb of Napoleon, Rosa had Erich move a few feet from where he stood. "There," she stated. "You are standing precisely where Hitler stood last summer when he came here."

"And how do you know?" Erich inquired.

"I have a picture of it that Leon brought home."

At precisely five forty-five, Major Boehmer entered the apartment door. Erich was reading the newspaper in the living room and Rosa was pouring drinks of cherry brandy in the kitchen. She always prepared a drink for him when he got home because he liked to sit in his lounge chair and leisurely sip on one before dinner. His systematic promptness allowed her to predict his time of arrival within two or three minutes. This evening they were going out to dinner, and he had invited a member of his staff to join them. The lieutenant was to pick them up in a staff car at seven.

Later, when Rosa heard a soft knock on the door and got to her feet to open it, she came face to face with a short, slender officer dressed in a neat, form-fitting uniform. "Lieutenant Hessel, madam," the young man said, clicking his heels. "Would you please inform Major Boehmer that his car awaits him."

Boehmer looked at his wrist watch and turned to Erich. "Promptness," he said quietly. "That's what I like!" Then he raised his voice and beckoned for the lieutenant to join him. "Come in!" he declared. "Tonight we will not be so formal."

As Erich shook Hessel's hand, he looked at the lieutenant's pointed nose, beady eyes, and close-cropped dark hair, thinking these were supplemental attributes of a shrewd investigator. But the illusion vanished when Boehmer stated that Hessel maintained a portion of the vast filing system at the Office of Military Intelligence.

After drinking another round of brandy, they went downstairs, where Erich held the rear door of the command car for Leon and Rosa. Then he climbed into the front seat beside Lieutenant Hessel. "Where to?" Hessel asked.

"I have reservations at the Club Reynard," Boehmer replied.

When Boehmer entered the club, he was immediately recognized by the head waiter, who escorted him to a table not far from the stage. As the waiter seated Rosa, Erich's awestruck eyes swept the room. *Boehmer may not think it's the most elegant club in Paris,* he thought, *but it is the finest I have ever seen, except for those portrayed in the cinema.* The floor was covered with plush carpet, ornately carved chairs upholstered in bright red mohair were in place around linen-topped tables, and heavy velvet drapes seemed to hang everywhere. Crystal chandeliers suspended from the ceiling, and gold-colored light fixtures protruded from damask-covered walls. Although he saw a few French civilians, most of the clientele were high-ranking German officers and their dates. He sensed that enlisted men were out of their element here, but he would exercise his best etiquette and maintain proper decorum so Rosa and Major Boehmer would be pleased with his conduct.

As the Boehmer party dined on chateaubriand and red wine, they were entertained by a dozen graceful dancers in plumed costumes who gradually shed their clothing until they were nearly nude. Afterwards, a French comedian gave a monologue in halting German that was only half-heartedly received.

While Erich watched, he thought of how this contrasted with the simple peasant life of Holzheim and the Spartan conditions of his company in Normandy. The wine made him even more resentful. He looked at Rosa, then at Boehmer, who was stuffing food into his mouth. In a self-satisfied manner, he smiled. *You may be a major in intelligence,* he thought, *but you are a stupid ass when it comes to knowing your wife.*

He got along well with Lieutenant Hessel. Comments between him and the young officer often resulted in poking fun at military life, especially as it existed in Paris. Hessel had given up his job as a truck driver and joined the army shortly after the invasion of Poland. Because of his brother's influence in the Nazi party, he had been sent to officers training school and then assigned to non-combat duty in Munich. When Paris was occupied, he was transferred. He thought he would remain for some time.

When Rosa excused herself to go to the powder room, the major decided to visit with a colonel who was seated at the front table. "Who's that?" Erich asked, nodding in that direction. "Everyone seems to cater to him."

Hessel inhaled a big sigh. "That, my friend, is Colonel Strottlemeyer. He's very important in Paris circles. Controls rations and supplies."

"Nice looking young lady he's with," Erich observed.

"She's nice looking, but not very young."

"Sure looks young from here," Erich insisted.

"The wine must be going to your head and the smoke getting in your eyes," responded Lieutenant Hessel. "She's old enough to be your mother. But she was the long-time mistress of a renowned plastic surgeon. He wanted her to stay young looking." He paused, then softly chortled, "Word is, she's had her face lifted so many times she has to shave her neck."

By midnight the long day was showing on Major Boehmer. The dark beard stubble that covered his face emphasized his blood-laced eyes and sagging jowls. Erich studied him momentarily and then looked at Hessel. Even though the lieutenant appeared alert, Erich was concerned about his ability to chauffeur the car. Erich himself had consumed enough wine to sour his mouth and stomach, but when looked at Rosa, he smiled with admiration. She had exercised the good judgment to drink little by only occasionally sipping at her drink.

Suddenly, the major rose to his feet. "Let's go," he said, weaving slightly. "Lots to do tomorrow."

The night seemed short to Erich. He was aroused early by Rosa so he could accompany her husband to the office and carry out the official obligation for his trip to Paris. A hasty breakfast was eaten with little enthusiasm, and then the two men walked the four blocks to the large office building the German army had requisitioned. There, Erich was handed a ten-page document that he read and signed.

"This is actually a formality," Major Boehmer explained. "Supposedly, we got this information from you. In reality, we know all about the morale and underground activity in your sector. I had this report written to justify your trip."

Just then, Lieutenant Hessel entered the office. "I could sure use a cup of coffee," he moaned. "Join me?"

"I can't," Boehmer replied. "I've got a conference to attend. How about you, Corporal?"

"Yes, sir," Erich replied. "I'd like that."

"Excellent!" the major declared, grabbing a sheaf of papers as he headed for the door. "I'll see you this evening."

As they sipped coffee in a cafe on the first floor, Hessel stated that his job was very easy. "Any girl could do it," he said, with a snap of his head. "But one must be very careful dealing with all these strong-willed officers."

Erich finished his coffee and then stood and extended a hand to Hessel. "I must be going now," he explained. "It's been nice knowing you. Perhaps we will meet again, sometime."

"Perhaps," Hessel replied, rising to shake Erich's hand.

Rosa was waiting when Erich returned to Rue Neil. She turned the key in the lock and threw her arms around his neck. Although Erich had promised himself he would resist her advances, he soon found himself making love to her.

They ate a sandwich and drank a cup of tea and then left for the *Louvre*. As they passed through the *Jardin des Tuileries*, Erich looked at the barren trees and dormant fountains. "This must be a beautiful place in summer," he said.

"I suppose it is," Rosa agreed. "Do you remember the little park in Heidelberg the four of us walked through and sat in on the benches?"

"And took turns going back to your apartment," Erich added with a smile.

"You know," Rosa said, squeezing his arm, "Irma and Heinz are very serious about each other. As a matter of fact, if they could get together, they would probably get married."

"Heinz often tells me how much he misses her and how he wishes she was near. He never mentioned marriage, but he isn't one to talk too much."

"Well, she can't leave Germany, and he's under control of the army, so they'll have to wait until he gets leave. You know, at one time she thought she was pregnant, but it turned out all right."

It was a drab day, and a thick haze had enveloped the city so there was little they could see from the top of *Montmartre*. Returning to the apartment, Rosa busied herself in the kitchen preparing the evening meal while Erich sat in the living room reading about the massive bombing raids on England. Occasionally he lowered the paper and stared at the wall, reflecting disappointment on his visit to Paris. The overcast sky, barren trees, lifeless parks, and the repression of occupation combined to make it so different from what he had imagined. He half-wished he had not come. He was pleased to see Rosa, of course, mostly because she was so happy to see him. But a pall of guilt hung over him like a wet blanket because of his relationship with her.

Putting his paper aside, he went into the kitchen to watch. She was humming to the music coming over the radio as she flitted about tending steaming pans on the stove. "You seem so very happy," he said when she, holding a large fork in her hand, turned to face him.

"Mostly because I am doing something for you," she replied, throwing her arms about his neck and kissing him.

"I should think you would have a maid to do the work for you," he said, pushing her back from him.

"I could have. But I wanted to show Leon how good a wife I could be. He likes that." She paused, wrinkled her nose, and said, "Besides, it lets me get the things I want from him, such as having you come for a visit."

The next morning, when she slipped into his bed, she whispered, "Make it good, my darling. It may have to last a long time." Two hours later, she tearfully watched him depart from the *Gare du Nord*.

• • •

When Erich arrived at company headquarters in Normandy, the leaden sky was blanketing the area with large, damp snowflakes. He found most soldiers who were not on duty were in the recreation room reading, listening to music, playing cards, or drinking beer while relaxing. A few were decorating a Christmas tree with ornaments that had been sent from home or that they had made. The primary item of conversation, however, was their destination. The company had been alerted for transfer to another area.

"Where do you think we're going?" Erich asked Heinz as they sat on their cots shining their boots.

"Don't really know," Heinz replied. "Rumors are rampant. One says were going to guard Hitler's Eagle's Nest in Berchtesgaden, another that we're going to fight the Polish underground, and another that we're going to parachute into England." He stopped polishing and looked up at Erich. "I really don't give a damn but I'd at least like to spend a few days in Germany so I could see Irma."

On the morning of December 30, Captain Steinmetz assembled his company in the mess hall. "It is both an honor and duty for me to inform you," he began, "that the 222nd is being directed to Italy for further assignment."

The Afrika Korps

The sun was bright and warm as the drab, gray troop train threaded its way through the numerous tunnels that pierced the red sandstone cliffs of the Riviera. There had been only four coaches when the train left Cherbourg, but three more coaches were added when it picked up another infantry company at Limoges. Then at Marseilles, it coupled on a dozen more filled with a large contingent of troops from several branches of the army.

Tired from the long, jerky ride, Erich stared lazily out the coach window. The vast expanse of the gently rolling, glasslike sea mesmerized him. He looked at the water lapping the beach that the train was rolling past. It was so calm, clear, and blue, and the azure sky and warm breeze presented a great contrast to conditions at Normandy. He thought of the complaining sergeant of the company that replaced the 222nd. The veteran soldier was upset because the foul coastal weather and austere living conditions were much more severe than those his company had grown accustomed to in the city of Nancy.

As he continued to look out the window, Erich could sense a strong desire to get out and walk across the pink sand at the water's edge. A sudden outburst of shouting from the front of the coach directed his attention to a bevy of shapely young ladies who, lounging on the beach, had gotten to their feet and were waving. "My God!" Schumacher exclaimed jubilantly. "They're wearing only patches!"

Another soldier sitting nearby, turned to him with a broad grin. "Sometimes they don't wear anything at all on top," he said, moistening his lips.

Schumacher looked at Erich. "Since this is now part of the *Reich*, why don't we make them citizens? Then we could do some serious fraternizing."

A few miles below Naples, the train slowed to a crawl as it entered a guarded gate in a high stone wall surrounding an army camp. Erich thought he smelled the aroma of spaghetti sauce and wondered if it was coming from a home they were passing or a mess hall within the camp. Inside the compound, he could see row upon row of white stucco barracks covered with red tile roofs.

Later he would learn that it was a permanent army camp that had been turned over to the German army. Within a week it was filled with soldiers drawn from a variety of units and locations. And still they came, making it necessary to erect dozens of tents to accommodate those who could not be housed within the buildings.

Initially, the troops spent their time refurbishing equipment and engaging in several hours of calisthenics each day. Many had not exercised sufficiently since basic training, and the workouts caused pain and soreness. Erich's squad, however, was in excellent physical condition and was not bothered by the vigorous exercise.

At the beginning of the second week, Captain Steinmetz had the company line up in front of the barracks. After the First Sergeant had them standing at attention, Steinmetz paced back and forth before them. Looking first at them, then at the ground, he kicked the ground with the heels of his highly polished boots at every step. Erich knew when he did this that the topic was very serious.

"Men," he began soberly, "we are going to prepare for combat. Everyone will have to requalify for all areas of training. Specialists will train you. Do it well and make this company a proud fighting unit." He paced some more and then added, "War is a serious business, so take this training as a serious matter." He paused again and looked reflectively at the rows of men before him, continuing, "When you fight the enemy, be it one man or a legion, you must make every incident a maximum effort. You must go into it with all the fury you possess. Should you underestimate his ability or strength and start with anything less, you might be surprised and overwhelmed before you can initiate *your* greatest effort." Before turning to leave, he jabbed his open hand skyward and shouted, "Heil, Hitler!"

The next day, all combat companies were ordered to begin retraining under supervision of war-seasoned specialists brought in specifically for the purpose. At the rifle range, all men of Captain Steinmetz's 222nd Company had to requalify as marksmen. If someone had difficulty, he had to return to the rifle range until he could ualify. Because of their keen eyes and steady hands, both Erich and Heinz qualified as sharpshooters. Schumacher, selected for special sniper training, had a telescopic sight mounted on a *Gewehr* rifle. His elite group was readily identified within the camp because their right eyes and cheeks were perpetually black and blue from the recoil of the weapon.

Obstacle courses had to be run and run again to the satisfaction of the supervising sergeant. In one exercise in which two men had to fall on wire entanglements to form a human bridge, the troopers on the wire complained bitterly because hobnails in the boots worn by those running over them bruised their backs and buttocks. And in bayonet practice, the men were constantly upbraided for making their thrusts too low. "Aim at the throat!" the instructor repeatedly shouted. "When you parry left or right, you aim at the throat! If you penetrate the chest, the bayonet may get stuck in the ribs! Before you can get it out, somebody will get to you!"

At the straw-filled dummy next to Erich in one of the exercises, Heinz cursed under his breath in defiance. "To hell with that nonsense!" he muttered. "If I get that close, he can have the bayonet, rifle and all!"

Erich grunted as he made a tremendous thrust at his target. Withdrawing his weapon, he said, "I'm with you on that one." Then he looked around, hoping no one had heard him.

Each afternoon numerous platoons were taken on hikes, the distances being increased each time. Erich, leading his men along roads and trails from a map issued to him, went out the camp gate past the mud and lava-covered ruins of ancient Herculaneum, and then inland through a profusion of vineyards planted along the base of Mount Vesuvius. During the ten minute rest the soldiers took each hour, children gathered to listen to their foreign tongue, see the weapons of war they bore, hope for a bit of candy, or merely sit and stare at these strangers in their land. At one point, Erich saw an admiring boy sitting across from him. Although the boy said nothing, Erich could tell from his mimicking expressions that he was pretending to be a member of their warrior force.

The boy studied Erich for a time, who was sitting on a patch of grass beside the narrow, winding macadam road, then walked over and pulled at Erich's sleeve. He pointed to his own eye, then to Schumacher, who was resting on the other side of the road. Erich understood. He rose to his feet, took the boy by the hand, and walked across to Schumacher. "He wants to know about your black eye," he said with a grin.

Schumacher removed the chamois cover from the telescopic sight on his Gewehr rifle and let the lad look through it. Then he held the weapon to his shoulder and, with a jerk, demonstrated how the recoil of the rifle forced the sight against the cheek below the eye.

Heinz, sitting a short distance away with his back propped against a small tree, squinted as he looked at the distant, gray-brown slopes of Mount Vesuvius. "You know," he began, looking up at Erich, "when I was in grade school, I read about Mount Vesuvius and Pompeii. But I never *dreamed* of actually seeing it."

Erich sounded his whistle. The rest period was over.

• • •

Stepping aboard the bus, Erich handed his ticket to the Italian tour guide, a short, slender, middle-aged man whose deeply tanned skin appeared wrinkled beyond his years. Selecting a seat in the middle of the bus, Erich remained standing until Heinz, who was several persons behind him in line, saw where he was saving a seat.

As Heinz sat down, he exhaled loudly. "It's sure good to get out of camp," he said, shaking his head. "The way they've been working us, I was certain they'd have shipped us to the front by now."

Just then Schumacher appeared beside the bus and saw Erich and Heinz. "Where are you going?" he asked, walking up beside their partially opened window.

"The top of Mount Vesuvius," Heinz replied. "Come on. Join us."

"Climb that hill?" Schumacher complained. "Hell, I'd just as soon go right into Naples. To me, it's a lot better than climbing that smoking hill!"

"Tell you what," Erich said, as Heinz listened. "If you'll go with us first, we'll go with you into Naples."

Schumacher sighed. "Oh, all right," he agreed with a frown.

The sweating driver patiently struggled to maneuver his straining bus up the steep, winding incline to the end of the road where a flat notch had been dug three hundred yards below the rim of the crater. Applying the brakes, he ordered the guide and passengers to disembark so he could more safely turn the underpowered vehicle around.

A brisk breeze was blowing as the guide led the trudging column of troopers up the sloping path in the gritty, ankle-deep scoria. As Schumacher watched the glossy shine quickly fade from his polished boots, a gust of wind whisked a blast of the abrasive material into his face, stinging his skin and lodging dirt in his eyes and nostrils. Wishing he had gone directly to Naples, he shook his head and cursed under his breath.

The bottom of the crater was a hundred yards wide and twenty feet below the narrow rim upon which the group stood. Erich looked down at smoke rising from fissures in the bottom of the cup-shaped depression. When he inhaled, an acrid sulfur odor stung his nose and throat. Then he looked out over the surrounding countryside. He was awestruck by the magnificent view.

The guide began his historical explanation of the volcano, but the wind carried his words away so only a few men standing near him could hear. Besides, his poor command of German allowed little to be gleaned from what he said. And there were others, like Schumacher, who showed little interest in history or the volcano. The little Italian quickly realized the problem that confronted him. To redeem himself, he picked up several black, hexagonal quartz crystals that were scattered about the area and handed them to the troopers as souvenirs.

• • •

The sidewalks of Naples were teeming with groups of soldiers, mostly German, and the primary streets were clogged with military traffic traveling toward the waterfront. Standing at an intersection, Erich, Heinz, and Schumacher watched for several minutes as tanks, half-tracks, artillery pieces, and armored personnel carriers rumbled slowly past. "My God!" said Schumacher, scratching his head. "I never knew there was that much military hardware in all the world!"

"And there's something different about these," Heinz said, turning to Erich with a puzzled look. "Notice how the vehicles are painted?"

Erich nodded. The camouflage paint was in light, earthy colors instead of the darker green, brown, and black. And there was no sign of horses, which were used extensively for transport wherever they had been before. "Must not be for the Eastern front," he said with a shrug.

Schumacher looked around impatiently. "Let's find a beer garden and wash down these exhaust fumes," he said, pointing up the street.

"Want to sit at a table on the sidewalk?" the bartender asked in halting German as they walked into a tavern.

Erich shook his head. "No. Too noisy out there."

The bartender nodded that he understood. "Yes," he agreed. "It's been going on for several days now." He paused while they sat down and then added, "Day and night."

Schumacher took a sip of beer from his glass and then looked into the faces of his comrades. "Then you think we might take a boat ride?" he asked soberly.

"Along with 30,000 others," Erich replied.

Heinz decided to change the subject of conversation. Slapping his thighs, he said, "Let's get the waiter over here and order a genuine Italian meal!"

The initial course of spaghetti was so filling Erich was not sure he could eat the plate of fish that followed. He looked at Heinz and shook his head.

Heinz merely smiled. "Looks like he's got a case of measles," he responded, tossing his head toward Schumacher.

"At least I can wash it off," Schumacher snorted. "Your tunic will have to go to the cleaners."

Later, when the waiter delivered the dessert pudding, Erich threw up his hands and exclaimed, "How do they expect a person to eat so much?"

The rotund cook, watching from a distance, chuckled with delight.

• • •

The next morning, after spending the night in a seedy waterfront hotel that had a coating of mildew on the walls of the bathroom and closets, they were standing at the rail of the Capri ferry when it stopped at Sorrento. Heinz sensed a brief moment of inviting eye contact from one of three young ladies who walked up the gangplank. He watched them enter the lounge and then nudged Erich. "I think they're interested," he said quietly, noticing another demure glance.

"Don't just stand there," Schumacher said, slapping his hands together.

Heinz took a deep breath and then strode over to them. "May I introduce myself?" he began, bowing slightly. "I am Corporal Heinz Jager."

To his surprise, one of the young ladies spoke fluent German. She stated her name was Angelina and that she had learned German in a parochial school. "I can interpret for my friends," she said.

"Good!" Heinz replied. "My friends and I would be honored if the three of you would join us for a drink."

After a brief consultation, Angelina turned to face him. "We would be delighted." she said with a smile. Then, her face stiffened. "But we don't drink anything stronger than wine, and that only at dinner time."

Sitting on chairs around a small table Erich and Schumacher had assembled, the group sipped lemonade as they introduced themselves and tried to communicate. Pointing to the baskets her friends carried, Angelina stated that they lived in Sorrento and frequently went to Capri for a Sunday outing. "We would be pleased to have you join us," she said, looking at Erich with a warm smile. Then she looked at her two friends, shrugged, and added, "This lunch may be somewhat short for six people, but we'll manage."

"Can we get more on Capri?" Erich inquired.

"Of course," Angelina replied.

For the soldiers, the Isle of Capri seemed a paradise. The gentle breeze, warm sunshine, and clear, blue water was something they had only read about. And the girls became beautiful guides who accompanied them to the *Blue Grotto*, *Anacapri*, and the ruins of *Villa Jovis*.

Then, in the early afternoon, the young ladies selected a grassy knoll atop a high cliff overlooking *Marina Poecolo* to spread their cloth. Motioning for the three troopers to join them by sitting around the edge of the delicately flowered linen, they served a lunch of bread, cheese, and sausage. Periodically, a bottle of red wine was passed so each could drink from it.

When they had finished eating, Erich took Angelina by the hand and led her a short distance away to the edge of the bluff. They sat crosslegged looking down at little waves lapping a sandy beach far below. Erich had never seen such bright sun and blue seas. A short distance away, a power boat knifed its way through arches that had been formed by centuries of erosive action. The wake in the crystal-like waters created beautiful blends of blues and greens as it splashed against a ridge of offshore rocks. He waved a hand toward the sea. "This is a lovely place," he said, smiling as he looked into Angelina's soft brown eyes. "It is a paradise."

Angelina smiled and nodded.

Drawing in a deep breath, Erich picked a stem of grass and placed it into his mouth. Then he laid back, squinting as he looked into the cloudless, azure sky. He could feel the warm rays of the sun on his clean-shaven face as he inhaled the sweet scent of roses wafting from a nearby flower bed. *If only Maria was at his side to share this lovely place,* he thought.

Just then a shadow came over his face. Angelina, on her hands and knees, was hovering over him. She had become intrigued by his short-cropped, blond hair and smooth, oval face as it appeared wreathed by a patch of tall grass that was gently swaying in the light breeze. She had never been alone with a man, and now that most of the young men of Sorrento were in the army, she wondered if it would ever happen. She raised her hand to caress his cheek, but suddenly withdrew it.

Through his partially opened eyes, Erich watched her movements. Reaching up, he took her hand and held it. She relaxed momentarily and then withdrew. Such activities were not condoned without a chaperone. But, noting the disappointment on his face, she held out her hand. When he took it, she pulled him to a sitting position.

"Do you have a *Senorina?*" she asked.

"Yes. Her name is Maria."

"That is a pretty name."

Erich nodded agreement. He was going to show her a photo of Maria and his family, but changed his mind.

Just then he saw Heinz, stretched out a few yards away, placing his head in the lap of the girl he was with. She gently raised his head with her hand and slid her legs from beneath it.

Angelina, who also saw what was happening, turned to Erich. "Such displays of affection are forbidden unless the girl knows the boy's intentions," she explained. She paused a moment, then added, "And the family must also know his intentions."

On the return trip of the ferry, the young ladies agreed to a meeting the following Sunday in Naples. Angelina gave Erich a warm smile as she squeezed his hand. "And if you like, we can visit Pompeii."

"We would be delighted!" Erich and Heinz replied in unison.

. . .

Late in February, the gates of the camp were slammed shut, isolating the troops from the rest of the world. All communication from the military compound was under strict censorship. Then came the routine task of a final inspection of equipment, records, and inoculations that had been experienced prior to each move. Finally, the troops spent a morning scrubbing down the barracks they had vacated.

It was early evening when Erich heard the heavy diesel engines increase their tempo and felt the vibration of the steel floor beneath his feet intensify. He turned his head toward Heinz, who was lying on the lower bunk across the narrow aisle from him. "Thank God!" he said with a gigantic sigh, grateful the large, gray troop transport was under way.

It had been five long hours since they entered the hot, cramped quarters. Captain Steinmetz, marching at the head of the column, had led the 222nd through the streets of Naples to the crowded dockside. There they boarded the *Valkyrie*, one of nine ships loaded with troops and materiel. The men were directed down three decks into the warm bowels of the ship to a compartment crammed with five-tier bunk beds. "Get yourselves and your equipment into a bed!" bellowed the company First Sergeant. "That'll keep the aisles clear and speed up the loading!" He paused and then looked around at the men struggling to comply. "The sooner we get loaded, the sooner we'll move out!"

Like a giant ghost, the *Valkyrie* sliced through the glassy water, sliding past Capri and into the Gulf of Salerno. Located in the center of a convoy that was following a course parallel to the coast, it was sailing under very strict blackout regulations. Although his company was ordered to remain in their cramped quarters for the night, Captain Steininetz was permitted on an open deck near the cabin he shared with three other officers.

Standing at the rail, he looked across the black water at the outline of another ship that was running several hundred yards off the side of the *Valkyrie*. A chill raced up his spine as he noted how clearly it was silhouetted against the scattering of lights along the shoreline. And there was the phosphorescent wake trailing behind each ship that was impossible to disguise beneath the starry, moonlit sky. He took in a deep breath and looked into the sober faces of two officers standing at his side. He knew they, also, were hoping enemy planes and submarines would be hunting elsewhere this night.

In the early morning hours the convoy slipped smoothly through the Strait of Messina along the Sicilian coast and then nosed bravely into the open waters of the Mediterranean. The five thousand men aboard the

Valkyrie would be fed two meals a day. And during daylight hours, one deck at a time could go topside for a period of one hour. It would provide an opportunity for the troops to see the vastness of the open water and observe the many ships that surrounded them.

A heavy, muffled explosion shook Erich's bed. His first reaction was to sit upright, but he could only rise on one elbow because of limited space. He dropped his arm to the floor and squinted at the luminous dial of his wristwatch in the dim aisle light. It was three-thirty. He hadn't slept well, but now he was wide awake. Looking around, he saw others tossing about, trying to get out of their bunks. Some were struggling with their boots, attempting to put them on. Several men of his squad were staring at him, their puzzled faces silently asking for direction.

He heard the distant whistle of a ship's siren, followed by two more explosions that caused the ship to shudder as if it had run into something. Men began to shout, and he could see arms and legs flailing in the dim light. Suddenly, the speaker system crackled and a deep-throated voice calmly announced, "Remain where you are. A destroyer of the Italian navy has just dropped some depth charges as a precautionary measure." There was a brief pause, and then the message was repeated. The last words were lost in the noisy shuffle and the swearing and complaining of the men as they crawled back into their beds.

Shortly before dawn, the *Valkyrie* glided into the quiet, sheltered waters of Tripoli harbor.

The sudden rumble and vibration of reversing engines followed by the rattle and quiver of dropping anchors alarmed some of the troopers. Erich listened intently, not certain of the sudden noise. Others nearby looked at him questioningly, their eyes opened wide and bodies noticeably tensed.

• • •

Erich sat quietly among his men on the wooden bench seat in the open back of a large truck. The troopers had their coat collars up around their necks as a protection from the early morning chill. They were part of a long column of tanks, half-tracks, and supply vehicles that had departed the tent camp at the edge of the city. Although the sun was still below the horizon, the entire eastern sky was glaring with a bright spectrum of blazing colors. His men seemed deep in thought, hunched over, staring at the truck bed. They knew they were on their way to meet the enemy.

For the first few miles, the convoy moved slowly along a narrow, holefilled macadam highway. Beyond the paved section, however, the road turned to sand and coarse gravel. Soon the mile-long column of vehicles was creating a huge cloud of choking dust that rose high into the air and covered everything with a heavy coating of tan powder. The men looked up momentarily as four Italian fighter planes roared past. "I'm glad we've got air protection," Heinz said as he tried to keep the butt of his rifle from banging against the steel bed of the bouncing truck.

"I'd feel better if it was the *Luftwaffe*," snorted Schumacher.

Erich nodded agreement. The Italian soldiers in Tripoli had showed no concern about the gravity of the situation as the radio and newspapers were reporting a rapid British advance. He was certain Tripoli would be under siege in a few days if the British were not halted.

When the sun had climbed halfway into the morning sky, the air became warm and the men shed their coats. Their perspiration turned the dust into a brown paste that gathered under their arms and in the creases of their necks and foreheads. A few minutes later, the convoy paused so the men could relieve themselves.

When evening approached, the vehicles were dispersed on both sides of the road. Field kitchens were set up, and the troops were ordered to make their beds near their transport. The self-propelled eighty-eight millimeter antiaircraft guns were immediately placed in a state of readiness, their muzzles pointing skyward. And maintenance crews swarmed over the dust-covered tanks and trucks, servicing them with gasoline, oil, and water.

Erich rinsed his face and hands with a small allotment of water doled from a water trailer. Then he got in line behind his squad for a ration of pork and beans that had been prepared by the 222nd field kitchen. Schumacher dropped down cross-legged on the ground beside Erich. He put a spoonful of food into his mouth and began to chew. Suddenly, he spat it out onto the ground. "It's full of sand!" he complained. "Is yours?"

"No," Erich replied calmly. "You didn't wipe your mess kit out before you got in line."

Schumacher shook his head. "I'll be damned!" he exclaimed, setting his jaw.

"Go back and get some more," Erich advised. As Schumacher rose to his feet, Erich added, "And remember, sand is everywhere out here."

As the sun, a huge, orange ball, settled quickly into the western horizon, the air became suddenly chilly. Guards were posted, and the troopers donned sweaters and jackets. A few of the men erected small tents, but most chose to sleep beneath the open sky.

After clearing stones and gravel from a level spot, Erich spread his bed roll and placed his rifle and equipment on top of it. Then he joined a small circle of men from his squad who were sitting on the ground. For several minutes, he listened to them talk. A few complained about the sand and temperature extremes, but most seemed excited about going into battle. Since dawn came early in the desert, he decided to turn in. As a squad leader, however, he must first check the well being of his men. Rising to his feet, he quietly slipped away. Although there was no moon, he had no difficulty finding them. The tan desert floor was well illuminated by the clear, star-studded sky.

Erich did not sleep well. Although he was among several thousand soldiers, he felt alone. The desert seemed like a vast, isolated sea that was hundreds of miles from the land he knew and understood. He was certain others felt the same loneliness, but he was a leader, a noncommissioned officer, and could not let his feelings show. And he knew his unit would be facing the enemy soon. Men would be killed. If he must die, he preferred to do so on German soil, not in such a distant wasteland.

Since the ground made an exceedingly hard bed, he found it difficult to get comfortable. The smallest pebble he thought would be of no consequence felt like a boulder in a few hours. And although he was warm enough, little gusts of wind blew sand into his eyes and nostrils, making it necessary to keep his head and face beneath the blanket. Then he heard footsteps. Thinking that somehow the enemy had invaded the camp, he sat upright, only to discover it was one of the troopers some distance away walking to the latrine. Time and again, he checked the luminous dial of his wristwatch, hardly believing the slowness with which the night passed.

The next day the long convoy moved on across the virtually unbroken vastness. Occasionally, it passed through an isolated village of mud buildings where poorly clad, barefoot residents gaped in awe. At a point where the roadway passed near the sea, the convoy stopped long enough for the soldiers to dash into the water and rinse the grime and sweat from their clothing and bodies. But the hours passed with little to see except sand, rocks, and scrawny shrubs. Once in a while a trooper who had gotten a fleeting glimpse of a scurrying lizard or gopher shouted and pointed. But there was little to break the monotony of squinting into the unrelenting sun and grinding one's teeth on everpresent sand that sifted into everything.

• • •

It was late afternoon when the convoy halted. Units were organized into combat groups and given geographical assignments. Erich's *Panzer* company drove south two miles, then spread out in a line facing east before coming to a halt. After waiting for the men of the 222nd to dismount from the trucks, Captain Steinmetz assembled his squad leaders. "Take your men five hundred yards beyond the tanks and form a skirmish line," he began, looking into the dusty faces of the corporals and sergeants he had trained. "Dig in deep enough to protect yourselves from tracked vehicles." He waited a moment and then asked, "Any questions?"

Erich took in a deep breath, then looked at Heinz with raised eyebrows as he expelled it.

"Then, let's do it!" Steinmetz barked with a snap of his head. He turned on his heels and walked briskly toward a headquarters tent that was being erected a short distance away. Erich selected locations for the row of six holes his squad would dig. "Take turns sleeping," he said. Then, raising his voice to a harsh pitch, he added a stern warning, "There must be someone awake in each hole at all times!" He swept his hand toward the east. "And shoot anything that moves out there! I don't want to find a bunch of slit throats when the sun comes up in the morning!"

Noting that his last statement visibly stirred the men of his squad, Erich thought he would give them another prod. "Now, get those holes dug! And when you're finished with that, check your weapons to be sure they're clean and loaded with full clips! I don't want to have to dream up some damn letter for your mother about how brave you were when you died!"

Erich and Schumacher had just finished digging the hole they would share and were gathering rocks for a parapet when the nearby eighty-eights began firing. The riflemen dove for their holes and tank crews scrambled into their vehicles and started the engines. Erich was pleased to see that his men got quickly into their holes and had their rifles aimed and ready. He noted that some from another squad who had not completed their holes, were lying on their stomachs, frantically scraping to reach the desired depth.

Schumacher, white-faced and nervous, gazed fixedly at Erich. His mouth was closed as if his voice box was out of order. Suddenly, his lips parted. "What's the matter?" he asked with a wide-eyed stare.

Erich, crouched beside him in the hole, was peering at the firing guns trying to ascertain the direction of their target, when suddenly the sky in front blossomed into a mass of black smoke puffs. Then he saw a light observation plane that was barely discernible in the distance. It quickly turned and fled.

The eighty-eights were suddenly silent, leaving a blanket of quiet alertness over a division of nervous troops. The men continued to scan the horizon for activity, but saw only spots of dust puffs where pieces of shrapnel fell to earth.

Later, a squadron of Italian fighter planes roared past at low level. They did several dives and turns and then sped back toward Tripoli. "Where in hell were you half an hour ago?" snapped Heinz disgustedly as they zoomed past.

"Drinking wine in Tripoli!" came a shouted reply from down the line.

His mouth dry and heart still pounding, Erich knew he had an obligation to check the wellbeing of his squad. But he did not wish for them to see that the firing had stirred him. As a squad leader, he must appear calm. Walking in a low crouch, he went from hole to hole asking if they were all right. Although their faces mirrored both fright and concern, each man quietly nodded, indicating he was fine. One pointed to a large wet spot on the trousers of his partner. The embarrassed young soldier, a shy lad named Horst, looked up at Erich and shook his head.

"Don't feel bad," Erich said, attempting to ease the irritation the trooper felt. "It will happen to most of us sometime or another." Then he smiled. "It'll dry fast out here."

• • •

After a sleepless night of no military action, the division headed eastward in two columns. The heavy machines created giant dust plumes that rose high into the air. Erich's squad was carried in an armored personnel carrier near the front of a long line of tanks and other troop-carrying vehicles. Their assigned task was to protect the tanks from enemy infantry. Although fearsome monsters to foot soldiers, tanks become vulnerable if infantry could get beside or on top of them.

Early in the afternoon, just as the troops were feeling drowsy from the afternoon sun, the vehicles suddenly halted. The enemy was attacking. Geysers of sand and rock, accompanied by a loud thumping of explosions, were spouting a short distance ahead. Since the firing was coming from the left front, the tanks and armored vehicles quickly dispersed and formed a line facing that direction.

As the vehicles charged ahead, Erich saw smoke from British guns and dust rising from their lines. Suddenly, the vehicles stopped again. Captain Steinmetz's shouted command was clearly heard above the din of idling engines. "Squad leaders! Get your men on the ground!"

As soon as Erich's squad stepped from the personnel carrier, he split them into two groups. Breathing heavily from fear and excitement, he knew his men were frightened, too. But as a leader, he was to calm and assure them—lead them into battle like a true Teutonic knight. Turning to Heinz, he shouted his first combat order. "Jager!" he yelled, hoping to be heard above the roar of the personnel carriers that were speeding back to the safety of the eighty-eights a mile to the rear. "Get your half of the squad in the track of that *Panther!*" He pointed to a tank that was crawling forward a short distance away. Then he led his half of the squad to the other track being made by the track-laying vehicle.

A few moments later, the tank halted and fired its cannon. He looked back at his men. "Don't bunch up!" he shouted, still breathing heavily. "Keep your interval!" He took in a deep breath, exhaled it, and then took in another. "And stay in those tank tracks if you don't want your balls blown off by a mine!"

Just then the tank lurched forward, speeding up to maintain its place in line. Leaning to the left, he peered around the advancing machine. A short distance ahead he could see eruptions of a massive British artillery barrage. Advancing on a broad front, it was moving rapidly toward them. As he continued walking behind the tank, he searched about nervously for Captain Steinmetz. The captain was a hundred yards behind, gathering his staff together. Erich inhaled another deep breath. His heart was thundering in his chest. "When that barrage gets here," he shouted to Heinz, "get down!"

After the wave of marching fire had passed, Erich rose quickly to his feet and caught up with the tank. Looking back, he saw two of his men were still stretched out on the ground. He trotted back to them. They were not injured, just badly frightened. Grasping each by the underarm, he pulled them to their feet. "Let's go!" he yelled, turning to pursue the tank.

There was a loud splat as a screaming shell hit a tank a few yards to the right. A section of its tread flew high into the air. Only one of the crew emerged from it, rolling off its side and falling onto the ground. Erich saw an agonized expression on the young man's face before it turned crimson from profuse bleeding.

Not knowing what to do, the men following the tank flattened themselves against the ground. The platoon leader, a lieutenant, ran to them. "Get behind another tank!" he ordered, flailing his arms. "And keep moving!"

Several more waves of artillery fire passed over the men of the 222nd, spouting great geysers of rocks and sand. The frightened troopers fell flat against the ground as each wave passed, gripping the warm sand in a desperate attempt to hold on as the earth heaved and shuddered. Erich's squad was unscathed, although hot bits of shiny shrapnel rained down upon them after each explosion. But when they looked around, they saw columns of black smoke rising from burning vehicles. And above the roar of engines and whine of incoming shells, they could hear the screams and moans of wounded men.

Suddenly the shelling stopped and the troopers could walk erect instead of in a crouched position. Ahead, the massive dust clouds of a retreating enemy filled the sky. Then a muffled blast shot out from beneath the *Mark III* they had been following. Dust and sand stung their faces and burned their eyes. A large portion of the explosion, that puffed out the top of the tank turret, heaved the dismembered gunner partially out of the vehicle. His body hung, limp and torn, down the side of the steel monster.

Erich, his heart pounding and his mouth dry, signaled his squad to a prone position. Leaping upon the stalled tank, he peered into the smoke-filled interior. Its white enameled interior was splattered with blood and dirt. And the mangled bodies of the crew were draped over the jagged remnants of the floor. The sight made a surge of nausea grip the pit of his stomach. As he stepped down, Captain Steinmetz dashed up to confront him. "Get your squad moving!" the captain bellowed. "There are others to take care of the casualties!"

Signaling his sweat-stained men to follow, Erich led them around the disabled tank. As the point man of his squad strode off at a cautious pace, he took the position in the center of the column. A moment later, another tank detonated a mine. Captain Steinmetz ordered his men to halt and prepare to hold.

Erich organized his men in a broad arrow formation and ordered them to dig in. Although tired and drenched with perspiration, they chopped at the earth with feverish determination. They had experienced battle and witnessed death at close range. Now life, precious life, held an exceptional meaning for them.

Erich, still breathing heavily, dug a hole to lie in that was shallow enough to see all his men when he sat up. Then he removed his helmet. Thoughts raced through his mind. His nostrils were still filled with the acrid odor of exploding gunpowder, the putrid stench of burning tanks, and the sweet smell of blood. The manuals never described such a desolate place to fight a war. He wondered if he would ever see Holzheim again.

A nervous calm settled over the area when the artillery stopped lobbing shells at the British. Small groups of engineers came forward with mine detectors and began clearing lanes, which they marked with white tapes. Afterwards, the men and machines made their way carefully through the mined area. When they arrived at the enemy positions, they discovered the British had withdrawn. Since the sun was now low in the western sky, the brigade halted for the night. The grimy infantrymen called for the jackets and sweaters they had abandoned in the personnel carriers and then settled into foxholes the British had abandoned.

• • •

At first light, after shelling the British with a tremendous barrage from the eighty-eights and one-hundred-and-fives, the armored brigade launched a final drive to capture the coastal town of El Agheila. Captain Steinmetz's 222nd was assigned to follow the lead tanks that were to enter directly from the south. Another column spearheaded a drive to cut the highway just east of town. Then it was to turn west and link up with the rest of the brigade at the main square.

At the first house on the edge of town, Erich saw an Arab citizen beckon to his squad. Erich turned to Schumacher, "Cover me," he said, crouching low as he cautiously approached the Arab.

The Arab, flipping his hand toward the east, repeatedly sputtered in halting French, "British gone! British gone!"

Erich reported to the lead tank driver and then waved to Captain Steinmetz that his squad was proceeding to the center of town.

As the tanks and infantrymen gathered in the town square, a colonel charged through the crowd flailing his arms wildly. "Get the hell out of here!" he screamed at the tanks and their protecting infantrymen.

The tanks quickly lumbered away down streets radiating from the square to take up positions at strategic points. Meanwhile, the infantry set up a defensive perimeter around the town. Shortly afterwards, a report was received on a headquarters radio from a reconnaissance patrol that had gone a mile to the east. The decoded message informed the brigade they could not establish any contact with the British.

• • •

Before setting up his defensive positions, Erich watched as his squad dipped water from a community well to shave and to rinse the grime from their upper torsos. A few minutes later Schumacher returned to the low, mud wall on the eastern outskirts of town where they were to dig their defensive positions. Making sure Erich saw him, he halted, raised his right leg, and let roar a mighty fart. Then he turned to Erich with a contented look on his face. "That, my dear comrade," he said, "is known around the world as the pause that refreshes!"

Erich shook his head with a wry smile. "I think you should go down that street over there and dive into the sea, clothes and all."

There was a flurry of activity as vehicles were serviced and repaired and ammunition was distributed. Erich went to each man in his squad to be certain they were situated to create a field of crossfire to thwart any surprise attack from the enemy. He conferred with the crew of a tank parked in a shed behind him so they knew where his men were. Then he ordered half of his squad to go to the town square where the kitchen crew was serving hot beef stew to the men of the 222nd. Above the din of activity, he listened intently to hear the strains of "Lili Marlene" being played on an accordion.

Erich's squad spent a sleepless, chilly night before being fed a breakfast of hot coffee, hard rolls, and jam and then being loaded aboard trucks and personnel carriers. They covered twenty miles when they came under British artillery fire. The vehicles spread out, dropped off the infantry, and, after an intense artillery duel, the tanks began moving forward. Erich led his squad very closely behind one of the lead tanks, often crouching against it as it moved ahead haltingly in convulsive jerks while firing its cannon.

The British did not give way until several of their tanks had been destroyed and their infantry positions overrun. Erich's squad, leaping into the

British trenches, became involved in a wild melee of shooting and hand-to-hand fighting. When it was over, the area was littered with dead and wounded, and two hundred British prisoners, primarily Australians, had been taken.

Two men from Erich's squad had been killed. He knelt by each of their bodies for a moment, straightened their contorted limbs, and closed their clouded eyes. Then he returned to the rest of his squad.

"My God!" Heinz declared, looking at a trickle of blood running down the side of Erich's neck. "The lobe of your ear is missing!"

"How in hell did that happen?" Erich asked, feeling stunned as he tried to determine the extent of his injury.

'Keep your dirty hands off it," Heinz ordered. "Let the medic take care of it."

"You take care of it," Erich pleaded. "He's so busy now, it'll take forever to get help from him." He paused, then said, "Besides, I trust your competence."

"Well, all right. But have him look at it later on."

Heinz got some supplies from the busy medic and cleaned and bandaged the wound.

After the company had dug in that evening, Captain Steinmetz called the platoon and squad leaders to his tent for a briefing on the next day's action. When he had finished, he asked Erich to remain for a few minutes. "That was some fight your squad put up today," he began.

"Thank you, sir," replied Erich. "The squad was quite enthusiastic."

"Yes. But it looked to me like it came from your example and leadership."

"Thank you, sir."

"I do believe, however," Captain Steinmetz went on, "that you'll live longer if you make better use of grenades."

"How do you mean, Sir?"

"Have your men toss a grenade or two into the holes and trenches before charging them. Do you understand?"

"Yes sir!"

During the following days, a series of sharp encounters occurred as the *Afrika Korps* blazed a swath thirty miles wide along the coast. In each incident, the superior German Mark III tanks and high-velocity eighty-eights made the German army victors. Also, there was speculation among the troops that the many nationalities in the British army created problems of commanding men with such diverse backgrounds and training.

The Germans encountered problems as well when they asked the Italian army to lead some of the attacks. The confusion and lack of enthusiasm so infuriated the highly organized German commanders that they decided to relegate the Italians to mop up operations.

• • •

As the *Afrika Korps* aimed its thrust toward the seaport of Benghazi, they were met with considerable stiffening of resistance, especially after they captured Soluk with its little airfield and railroad terminus—a route leading directly to the coastal city. Captain Steinmetz found his 222nd frequently fighting the enemy at very close range. In these situations, Erich liked to work with Schumacher. Schumacher seemed to sense where to be and what to do at the right time. While Heinz and several others kept the British riflemen in their trenches by firing low over their heads, Erich and Schumacher crawled within grenade-tossing range of the perimeter that protected the enemy positions. In one such situation involving three British machine guns and two mortars, Erich, lying low in a slight depression, handed two of his grenades to Schumacher. Erich unscrewed the cap from the handle of the remaining one, pulled its string, and heaved it forward. When he reached for the second, Schumacher had the cap off and the white wooden ball on the end of the string hanging free, ready to be pulled. Erich, who could toss a grenade a great distance with accuracy, learned to work with Schumacher like a well-lubricated machine. He found that without looking back, he could reach for a grenade from Schumacher and have the handle placed in the palm of his outstretched hand, ready to be activated and thrown.

Pieces of soil, flesh, and equipment had not finished falling from six rapid grenade explosions when Erich and Schumacher charged over the British parapet, rifles firing, to seize the position. When Heinz saw what was happening, he stood, waved his arm forward and shouted, "Let's go!" Leading the little band of men forward, they surged ahead to wrest the remaining trenches from the stunned enemy.

● ● ●

On a warm day in early April, armored columns of the *Afrika Korps* rumbled through the streets of Benghazi which were lined with cheering people who appeared exceedingly happy to see them. White flags flew from windows and sheets hung down the fronts of buildings. But Captain Steinmetz shouted to his troops, "Don't trust the bastards! Keep alert and watch every rooftop, window, and doorway."

Erich saw a civilian fire a shot from a window of a building a short distance ahead. A squad quickly alighted from a halted personnel carrier and entered the building. After a few muffled shots, the soldiers emerged to again climb aboard their waiting vehicle. As the carrier drove off, curious natives entered the building. A few minutes later they emerged with the bloody body of the sniper. It was dropped onto the sidewalk for others to see.

. . .

Although vast quantities of supplies and numerous vehicles were captured in Benghazi, the main British units had successfully retreated to the east. This was a dilemma for the German officers who had hoped to eliminate the British as an effective fighting force. Now they would have to continue the running battle with tired troops in reduced strength and over-extended supply lines. Perhaps, they hoped, supplies and troop replacements would arrive soon at the newly captured seaport.

Civilians living in houses around the edge of town were told to leave and stay with friends. German troops, who could guard from upper floor windows and rooftops, then moved in.

"How nice it is to sit on a toilet again!" exclaimed Heinz as he returned to the kitchen where Erich was shaving.

"Yes," added Schumacher. "Seems almost as good as sleeping with a woman."

Without looking up, another rifleman cleaning his rifle while sitting on the floor nearby snorted, "The heat really *has* baked your brain!"

The 222nd had hoped for a rest since the grueling pace of the past weeks had exhausted them. But the Brigade Commander informed his company leaders they would push on the next day. He had enough gasoline and supplies for another fifty miles, so they would push on and hope the supply ships just offshore could resupply them. "If we're going to capture Tobruk and Alexandria, we have to keep going!"

When Erich heard of the plans, he went outside, sat on a low, mud wall and looked up at the clear sky. The sun was just going below the horizon and the bright blue overhead canopy was becoming a deep purple. Brilliant, diamond-like stars were beginning to emerge. He had lost six men from his twelve-man squad: two had been killed and four wounded. Yet his men were expected to carry the burden of a full squad. Only the adrenalin surging through their veins from the stimulus of battle energized them enough to carry on. He thought of their bloodshot, red-rimmed eyes caused by lack of sleep, the glaring sun, and the constant irritation of dust and sand. Their bodies had been bruised by rocks, scratched by thorns of scrawny shrubs, and bitten repeatedly by an assortment of insects. Uniforms, so neat at the beginning, were now faded, dirty, and torn. And their supplemental clothing of jackets and sweaters had been abandoned or lost.

He sat, puzzled at the thought of capturing Tobruk and Alexandria. *My God! Why does little Germany have to conquer all this land—this useless desert?* They were going to meet their comrades on the eastern front somewhere in

Palistine. *Why? Why?* He shook his head as he continued to ask himself a myriad of questions.

• • •

After launching a spearhead to the east, the brigade found that the British had fled, leaving only a small rear guard detachment, which they easily overran. Then they dug in to permit communication and supply lines to catch up. Two days later a large convoy arrived with food, clothing, gasoline, and replacements. Erich's squad was issued new uniforms and two new men to replace those who had been lost. "More replacements may arrive in a few days," Captain Steinmetz told him, "but that's all we can get now."

At ten o'clock the next morning, an honor guard was assembled on a flat, barren area at the south end of the encampment. A small band played "*Horst Wessel*" and "*Deutschland uber Alles*" in the glaring brightness of the hot desert sun while medals were pinned on the chests of forty-one members of the 78th Brigade of the *Afrika Korps* who had distinguished themselves on the field of battle. Erich stood at attention in a new, tan desert uniform that still possessed its packing wrinkles as Captain Steinmetz faced him. He could feel a throbbing sensation in the ear that had been partially shot away as the captain read an order from a paper he held in his hand. "For displaying conspicuous bravery in action while leading his men in a charge against a well-defended enemy machine gun and mortar emplacement, Corporal Erich Stecker is awarded the Iron Cross First Class." He then had Erich remove his helmet as he placed the ribbon with its medal over his head.

"In addition," he added, "I hereby promote you to the rank of sergeant." Erich saluted and clicked his heels. "Thank you, Sir," he said quietly.

• • •

Although the British were in full retreat toward the Egyptian border with Marshal Erwin Rommel's *Panzer* units in close pursuit, the troops decided to hold Tobruk. Captain Steinmetz's 222nd was one of several companies ordered to surround, contain, and capture the city. Although the city was surrounded on three sides, it soon became clear the British had no trouble supplying it from the sea.

Initially, through a series of short, probing attacks, the ring about the city was tightened. However, by the time the outline of the city could be seen on the hot, quivering horizon, resistance had stiffened sufficiently so additional ground could be gained only with a maximum effort before being lost again in a few hours or days. Occasionally, a *Mark III* tank rumbled up and maneuvered about, trailed by a great plume of dust, only to be chased back again by intense fire from British big guns.

"Tanks are like women," Schumacher philosophized. "You can't live with them and you can't live without them."

"How's that?" Erich inquired.

"Well, they're nice to have around for their fire power, but did you notice how they draw the artillery?"

The troopers discovered that night on the desert was a splendor to behold. There was a canopy of deep purple aglow with a million blue-white jewels glittering, twinkling, and gleaming overhead in such a mesmerizing manner that the men experienced lapses of time in which wars did not exist and everything became reality merely by thinking of it. Stars that one could see only in the moistureless air shone clearly and brightly and were shot through with tracers of meteors that seemed to signal the end of some unknown world. The desert was a place where the moon lighted the heavens long before its blotchy face appeared on the horizon, before it glided silently toward zenith, bathing the beige, barren landscape in iridescent light. The scene appeared little different from daylight.

Almost nightly Erich was called upon to lead a three- or five-man patrol into no-man's-land to string barbed wire, observe enemy activity, or capture a prisoner for interrogation. Sometimes they had to rescue a wounded man left behind after a fire-fight or to retrieve a body so it could be properly buried.

The static front made for light casualties. But it was artillery, that damnable artillery, that caused the casualties and created a fear men of the 222nd would never forget. It came in barrages, churning the earth and filling the air with dirt and shiny, hot steel that ripped through everything in the area. Even the rocks kicked up were as lethal as the shrapnel itself. The sound of the first incoming shell caused experienced men to dive into little wind-formed depressions behind ugly camel thorn bushes that dotted the area.

During one of the barrages, Erich noticed that the two newer men in his squad were so terrorized they could not locate a depression unless it was more than a foot deep. Erich grabbed one of them and pulled him down. The two of them lay, pressing their bodies against the hot sand, breathing heavily and perspiring profusely, as the ground reared and convulsed. Erich slipped the leather helmet strap from beneath the young man's chin so a close blast would not snap his neck. He then crawled over and tried to do the same with the second replacement, but was greeted with a wild-eyed stare and an arm-thrust pushing his hand away. Erich slapped his hand and glared at him with cold, blue eyes. "Unhook that strap, soldier!" he bellowed between explosions, his voice turning hard.

The replacement slid the strap up under his nose and then placed both hands over the top of his helmet and buried his face in the sand.

When the shelling stopped, Erich raised his head to peer out over a landscape shimmering with heat waves. Heads popped up all around him. He slapped the replacement on the back and said, "Let's go!"

"I can't," the young man said meekly.

"Why not?"

"I've filled my pants," came the embarrassed reply.

"Well, take care of yourself then!" Erich ordered.

A few feet away, Erich noticed the sprawled body of the other replacement. Propping him up, he saw a thin steam of blood trickle down his tunic to make a little stain on the ground. It was not much blood, just a small spot that the first good wind would cover over. But it was the life flow of this soldier, and it was pouring out onto the desert floor.

Erich called for the medic, but it was over in just a few minutes. Another member of his squad, a twenty-year-old who had just begun to experience life, would not be around to witness the next sunrise over this barren wasteland he was attempting to capture.

"Let's move out!" Erich ordered, getting his seven man squad under way to continue the patrol, leaving the dead man to be returned by others.

In his continuing battle with fleas and spiders, Schumacher had located a folding cot that he erected beside the hole he was sharing with another rifleman. He reasoned that by getting up off the ground, the insects wouldn't be able to get at him, especially those that fell into his hole as a natural trap. But the persistent pests had no trouble getting to him. Then he placed the legs of the cot in little ration cans that he filled with water, but this merely delayed them. He continued to sleep on the cot, however, because it was more comfortable than the ground, even though he occasionally had to leave it in a hurry to seek the safety of the hole.

• • •

Captain Steinmetz was informed that a unit a mile away on the right flank had made a two mile thrust forward. He was ordered to send a reconnaissance team to make immediate contact with their lead patrol to test the feasibility of a possible linkup. Erich and Schumacher were selected for the team and issued a motorcycle with sidecar.

Schumacher was an excellent driver, so Erich felt secure as they picked their way through the rocks and shrubs with remarkable speed. They had gone less than halfway, however, when the front wheel detonated a cleverly hidden land mine. Most of its force hit Schumacher. Large pieces of the mine as well as broken bits of the motorcycle tore through his abdomen, penetrating far into his chest cavity. His body was tossed ten feet through the air, landing in a grotesque heap on a gnarled camel thorn bush.

Erich still sat in the sidecar. Being momentarily stunned, blinded, and choked by the explosion, he had slumped forward so his helmet fell to the floor between his legs. When his senses cleared sufficiently so he could raise his head, he felt a searing pain on the left side of his face and in his left arm. With great effort, he got out of the wrecked vehicle and made his way toward Schumacher. He stumbled over a beavertail cactus and then crawled the rest of the way. When he rose to a standing position, he was certain Schumacher was dead. He pulled him from the bush and sat, cradling him in his arms. For a full minute he sat, staring down at a column of ants making their way across the sand before him, as he shooed flies from the battered body he held.

"Damn the war! Damn Libya!" he protested. "It isn't worth it!"

After stretching Schumacher out on the ground, he took inventory of himself. Blood was oozing from a gash on his cheek and the left sleeve of his tunic was torn and wet. He removed his tunic and discovered puncture wounds in the biceps and several lacerations on the side of his chest. Taking a compress from his first aid packet, he placed it under his arm and then propped himself against the wreckage to rest. He closed his eyes against the searing heat of the burning sun, which bore down lemon yellow as it parched the land and pinpointed its rays on his sweating, bloodstained face. He thought of Maria, the soft, white arms of his darling Maria, and he wondered if he would ever again enjoy the wonderful smell of Holzheim's flowers and trees after a warm summer rain.

Captain Steimnetz, who had been watching the plume of dust through binoculars as it made its way across the arid terrain, knew immediately what had happened when he saw the giant black and yellow puff. He quickly dispatched another team to complete the mission and then sent a patrol to investigate the fate of Erich and Schumacher.

• • •

The hospital in Benghazi was a whitewashed adobe building with walls two-feet thick that provided insulation from the broiling heat of the merciless sun. The primary salvation, however, was the cooling breeze that blew through the open windows and down the dimly lighted corridors. The hospital was staffed with male German military personnel and a quiet, subdued contingent of Arab maintenance people of light-footed men and women.

Erich was assigned to a narrow, metal cot that showed its age by the amount of white enamel that had been chipped from its scratched and worn surfaces. Although crowded, the sixty-bed second floor was considerably better than the tent wards of a field hospital.

After four days of allowing his body to catch up on sleep and regenerate the fluids it had lost, Erich slowly made his way to a balcony that overlooked a lush, neatly groomed courtyard. The balcony, its floor covered with yellow ceramic tile, was surrounded by a bright red wrought-iron railing. Although the slight temperature he was running made his lips dry and burned his eyes and made his muscles to ache, he breathed in the sweet, cool air and looked out over the clean white stucco houses topped with orange tile roofs. He admired the green and yellow awnings that hung over the windows and the strings of colored beads in doorways. But, most of all, he was away from the sight, sound, and smell of battle. He went down a flight of steps and strolled among other pajama-clad, convalescing patients. And there was grass, flowers, and birds—the simple things he now revered.

During the next few days, the fever subsided. He read magazines, played scat with fellow ward members, and wrote letters. He informed Maria and his mother he had received a minor wound and would probably rejoin his company in a week or two. In addition he wrote Max Dorten in Holland, telling him not to be anxious to leave occupation duty, explaining that regardless of how poor conditions were, they were considerably better than combat. Finally, in a letter to Rosa, he told her he hadn't written for a time because he had been on the move but would try to do better in the future. He didn't mention his wounds. He wanted her to remember him as he had been.

After the bandages and sutures had been removed from the lacerations on his cheek and chest, he was sent to the quartermaster for a new uniform. He liked being back in uniform, even though the tunic had to be of a large size to accommodate his heavily bandaged left arm that was still in a sling. The ribbon denoting his Iron Cross had even been sewed on.

After three weeks, the surgeon still would not release him. "You need more time to be sure the underarm will not reopen," the doctor told him. "We want you combat ready when you leave."

Erich played more cards, read magazines, and helped other wounded about the hospital. *Yes,* he thought, *it would be dangerous to return to the front, but that's where my friends are, what I trained for, where I belong.* Besides, he was a combat-tested sergeant of the *Afrika Korps,* a much more disciplined aggressor than he had been before.

He strolled the streets of Benghazi, got his uniform tailored to fit, and mingled among the conglomeration of military and civilian personnel working at the busy wharf. It was there he noted a curious group of animal figures painted on the floor beside the gearshift levers of trucks driven by black men in Italian uniforms. He strode up to a German sergeant supervising the operation. "What in the world are those animals for?" he asked.

"Oh, that." The sergeant replied with a smile. "We're short of truck drivers. These are Ethiopians we were given by the Italians." He gave a heavy sigh. "They can't read, can't speak our language, and don't understand our trucks. Hell, they don't even wear shoes! By painting these pictures where they're supposed to push the lever, they caught on fast."

They walked over to a parked truck and the sergeant continued, "You see, the elephant is for first gear, ox is second, horse is third, and the gazelle is fourth."

"And the crab is reverse," added Erich. "What an idea!"

"Our job is to get this stuff to the front," explained the sergeant with a degree of pride. "And, come what may, we'll get it there."

As they walked away, he added in a lower tone, "But, just between us, if the engine stalls or a part falls off, they don't know what to do. I've seen them get out and kick all the tires. If one happens to be flat, they'd change it, then jump in and expect it to start."

• • •

Erich was sitting on his cot playing solitaire when he looked up to see Heinz striding down the aisle, a broad grin on his face. He jumped up, scattering the cards, and grabbed Heinz's out-stretched hand. "Man, am I glad to see you!" he half shouted. Suddenly realizing he had spoken too loudly, he continued in a lower tone, "Just glad to see somebody from the outfit."

He stepped back and looked at Heinz from head to foot. "How come you're here?" he asked, his voice becoming serious.

"Just a three-day leave," Heinz assured him. "The line is stationary enough so they're granting a few leaves. I managed to get the first one in our company." He looked at the long row of cots occupied by the casualties of war. "Rather nice hospital," he said with a nod.

"Oh, yes," Erich agreed. "Staffed with doctors and orderlies though—no nurses." Then his facial expression changed to an expectant smile. "Did you take Tobruk yet?" he asked.

"Hell, no. They'll never take it until the *Luftwaffe* shuts off their supplies from the sea."

"How's things at the Company?" Erich inquired.

"Fine. Haven't moved far since you left. The squad is still understrength, and I'm the new squad leader." He pointed to the sergeant's emblem on his epaulet. "Captain Steinmetz is trying as hard as ever to get more supplies and men, but most of it is going to the units farther ahead."

That evening after wandering through the narrow streets near the hospital that were teeming with people, many of them military, they entered a dingy, smoke-filled bar. It was crowded with soldiers, sailors, and the flotsam from the backwash of war. A belly dancer was performing to the high-pitched rhythm emanating from a musician sitting cross-legged in the corner.

After they had consumed a bottle of sour red wine, Erich, his speech slightly slurred, explained how he'd fill Captain Steinmetz's shoes. "You know," he said, narrowing his eyes, "if I was him, I'd get those supplies, by God!"

"How?" Heinz asked with a crooked smile.

"You know that supply line for the east front that runs a few miles behind our lines? The one that runs day and night? Well, I'd form a combat patrol and hijack a couple dozen trucks."

"You'd be strung up by the thumbs when they caught up with you," Heinz replied with a snap of his head.

"Maybe so, but they'd have to come and get me first. Most of those strategists wouldn't know what happened, anyway. Wouldn't even miss the stuff!"

"Then what would you do?"

"Get an armored company to go in with us, and we'd take Tobruk! Don't roll up and stop! Just keep going. Go like hell. That way we'd always be ahead of their artillery and mortars. We'd go in so fast and get so close they couldn't touch us. Run right over them. That's the way to do it!"

Heinz shook his head

• • •

The next day, after Heinz had spent the night on a cot in the quartermaster room of the hospital basement, the two men went to the wharf, where Erich showed Heinz the animal pictures the Ethiopians used for truck driving. Nearby two rusty Italian freighters were disgorging tons of supplies that were being hauled away in an endless line of trucks. A thin film of oil made the milky harbor water surrounding the ships glisten in the bright sunshine. Later, when they walked over the cracked planking bristling with slivers, their noses smarted from the dense, pungent odor of creosote mixed with diesel exhaust that hung heavy over the area.

They found a sidewalk stand that sold a bun sandwich of roast lamb that had been sliced from a vertical spit rotating slowly over hot coals.

"That lamb is very tasty," Erich said, smacking his lips.

An impish smile grew across Heinz' face. "I thought you said all fires here were made of camel dung," he needled.

At the beach, they sat on the soft sand and let it sift slowly through their fingers as they squinted into the glare coming off the clear, green water. The sand was not sharp and abrasive like the beige desert sand they fought in, but light pink and had been rounded and gentled by a million waves that had rolled it back and forth. And it was washed to a glistening cleanliness, its dirt and dust having been carried away and deposited in the quiet depths of the sea.

The stillness of the area was broken only by soft splashing of the surf and an occasional cry of a gull. Spindle-legged birds ran along the water's edge, poking their long beaks at tender morsels exposed by a retreating wave, only to be chased away again as it returned.

Heinz broke the silence. "That's quite a scar," he said, looking at the narrow pink line on Erich's cheek.

"Yes. Luckily, however, it didn't break anything."

"You look like one of those Heidelberg duelists," Heinz teased. He paused and then asked, "What's the story on your arm?"

"Oh, they removed some pieces of metal, but it seems to be all right. Scar tissue keeps me from raising it over my head. It'll be all right when I can exercise it more. They want to be sure it's well healed before stretching the skin too much."

Just then they heard a large, noisy crowd walking down the street behind them. Standing, they saw the boisterous group was following a sedan chair being borne on the shoulders of several brightly clad young men. "Let's see what it's all about," Heinz suggested.

The procession came to a halt in front of a hotel a short distance away. "Newlyweds," smiled an elderly Italian standing beside them who spoke German haltingly.

The groom and his heavily veiled bride quickly disappeared into the building. After several minutes, the throng began chanting, singing, and hurling phrases toward a second floor balcony. Erich, Heinz, and the Italian walked nearer to the building.

Suddenly, the French doors were flung open and the groom emerged to drape a sheet bearing a large red spot, over the iron railing. The crowd gave forth a great roar, broke into a five minute dance, and then dispersed.

The elderly Italian turned to the two soldiers and smiled. "This is a ritual whereby the groom assures all his friends he married a virgin."

"All that blood?" Erich asked with a surprised look.

"Well," said the Italian with a sly grin, "they always have a couple of chickens hidden in a closet whose neck they can wring, just in case."

"Oh, my!" chuckled Heinz, shaking his head.

Before Heinz left to return to the front, Erich persuaded the hospital supply sergeant to exchange Heinz's uniform for a new one. With heavy hearts, the two men parted. Heinz missed the comradeship and well-disciplined leadership Erich gave the squad, and Erich feared for Heinz's safety. "I'll be with you in a week or two," Erich assured the dear friend he had known since long before they had joined the army.

. . .

Early one morning Erich was awakened and told to prepare for evacuation. At first he thought it was merely his turn to return to his unit, but when he saw a panic-like urgency in the orderly's face, he knew there was a serious problem. "The British have broken through and are on their way!" the orderly exclaimed as he rushed about. "We're going back to El Agheila!"

Quickly and quietly, the nonambulatory patients were loaded aboard ambulances for the one-hundred mile ride. After two days of round the clock evacuation, the remainder of the patients, as well as the hospital staff were loaded into trucks and departed.

The road was choked with trucks, tractors, trailers, horses, motorcycles, and bicycles. There were soldiers from quartermaster, engineering, communications, medical units, and ordnance. Although not fleeing in terror, they knew they must keep moving to stay ahead of the retreating combat units that were fighting a delaying rear guard action.

There had been the loss of thousands of combat troops, primarily Italian soldiers who had been captured, and a tremendous loss of equipment. However, the *Afrika Korps* threw up a defensive line outside of El Agheila that halted the onrushing British. The infantry and artillery had dug in and could not be dislodged.

After a two-day search, Erich located the 222nd. Captain Steinmetz and Heinz, along with the men of his squad, were delighted. "You know, of course," Captain Steinmetz informed him, "Sergeant Jager has his own squad now."

"I'm pleased," Erich replied, shaking the captain's hand.

It was there outside of El Agheila that the *Afrika Korps* would stay for the next several months, waiting. Waiting to get organized and reinforced; waiting to see if the British were going to launch another attack; waiting for mail to arrive from home; waiting for artillery barrages that shattered the stillness of the night; waiting for occasional passes to go to El Agheila for three days; and waiting for "Lili Marlene" to be played again.

. . .

At midnight, late in January 1942, Erich was checking his men in their fortified foxholes when suddenly the eighty-eights and one-hundred-fives to the rear opened up with a thunderous roar. As the shells hissed and whispered overhead, he shivered, not only from the chill of the desert night, but from the fear of what lay ahead. All along the northern horizon he could see the curtain of lightning-like flashes and hear the constant rumble of the crashing shells.

The men of the *Afrika Korps* were psychologically ready. They were tired of waiting—they had trained with an iron-fisted discipline to peak efficiency. And they were ready militarily. Replacements had brought all units up to maximum strength, vast quantities of shells and gasoline had been stockpiled; and additional combat units had arrived, some with the heavier, more powerful *Mark IV* tanks. In addition, the *Luftwaffe* brought in several squadrons of *Stuka* dive bombers that carried heavy bombs designed with holes in the fins. They made a frightful, screaming whistle when they were dropped.

It took three days to root the British out of their trenches and work through the vast mine fields they had planted. This time, General Erwin Rommel, the Desert Fox, decided to head directly east across the sand-blown, rock-hard wasteland toward Tobruk instead of taking the well-defended coastal route around the big bulge of land through Benghazi.

This new approach developed some quick learning by the men of Erich's armored division. There was no cover and few landmarks on which to take bearings. They had to navigate like sailors reckoning the featureless landscape by speedometer, compass, and stars. But their success was phenomenal. Lying in their wake was a trail strewn with burned-out British vehicles, thousands of corralled prisoners, plus a multitude of dead and dying. And the countless tracks left by the treads of numerous vehicles, zigzagging in all directions, looked as if a migration of giant beetles had traversed the area.

The British put up a stubborn defense at Tobruk in a furious, week-long battle. Swarms of *Stukas* and *Messerschmitts* in desert camouflage colors strafed and bombed British defenses and fought agile *Spitfires* and *Hurricanes* in dozens of dogfights. Infantry squads rallied behind superior *Mark IV* tanks as they lumbered through carefully prepared fortifications. And the eighty-eights, using armor-piercing shells, shot completely through the heavy armor of British *Matilda* tanks. Then the *Afrika Korps* raced for Egypt, not stopping until they could see the lights of Alexandria in the clear night sky. Once again they had run low on gasoline and artillery shells. They had to wait for the over-extended supply lines to catch up.

Erich's squad had been reduced to eight, having had two killed and two seriously wounded. He looked at the extremely tired young men with empathetic concern. Their clothing was torn, water was rationed, and the choking dust had made their eyes very red and teeth very white. Now, however, they could dig in and rest.

• • •

Erich received several letters from his mother and Maria. After reading one from Maria for the third time, he sat back in his foxhole with a contented smile on his face. Just then Captain Steinmetz's orderly walked up. "Sergeant Stecker," he began. "Captain Steinmetz wants you and Sergeant Jager to report to his headquarters in thirty minutes."

"Tell the Captain we'll be there," Erich replied.

"Yes sir."

Upon arriving at the tent, the orderly escorted them inside and left them standing before a small table that served as a desk for Captain Steimnetz. They clicked their heels and saluted smartly. The captain, still seated, returned the salute.

"How are you feeling, Sergeant Stecker?" he inquired.

"Just fine, Sir," Erich replied.

"Is your arm all right?"

"Yes, sir."

"And how are things with you, Sergeant Jager?" he asked, looking at Heinz.

"Excellent," Heinz replied.

Captain Steinmetz rose to his feet, placed his hands behind his back, and then began pacing the slatted wooden floor. He always paced back and forth when he had something to tell his men. His head and neck were red from the heat and sun, but his face was clean-shaven, his hair closely cropped, and his khaki uniform freshly laundered and neatly pressed.

"You men," he began, "have been selected for Special Forces training."

They noticed his florid face was now much more red than it was back in Normandy.

"Your orders state that you are to report to the Special Forces Training Camp at Augsburg. There you will be given six weeks of intensive training and then transferred to the *Shutzstaffel*." After a moment's pause, he added, "Are there any questions?"

"Yes, sir," stated Erich. "Is that the political or the fighting *Shutzstaffel*?"

"The fighting *Shutzstaffel*! The *Waffen SS*!" Captain Steinmetz snapped brusquely. "Anything else?"

"No, sir!" the two men replied in unison.

The captain walked over to them and shook their hands. "Good luck. You're good men. I'll miss you."

"Thank you, sir," they replied.

As they walked back to the squad area, Erich confided to Heinz, "I'm sure glad it's the fighting SS. I don't want to have any part of those political bastards."

The Waffen SS

The citizens of Holzeim were becoming weary of war. In a few months it would be three years old, and, although many great victories had been won and vast areas of land captured, the conservative village people had always been less than enthusiastic about it. In their remote status, these hard working agrarian people were content with the simple way of life. They would prefer to be left to themselves so they could continue doing the same things in the same manner as the generations that preceded them. Afraid to voice their concern to a government official, however, they complained to one another in such places as the Stecker store, the Holzheim Tavern, and in front of the church after Sunday Mass.

But the long arm of the federal government had been extended and the inflow and outflow of the community was carefully regulated. Decrees were issued dictating the hours they must work, harvest quotas expected to be met, and prices they would be paid. A wide variety of commodities they consumed were rationed, and the most precious of all possessions, their sons and husbands, were being taken from them and killed or maimed on distant battlefields. Initially, the end could be seen after a few quick military triumphs and the recapturing of territories lost during the First Great War, but now the people of the village were beginning to fear the awesome truth that was emerging. It was obvious to them that the little vest-pocket war had been stretched, expanded, and overextended until hundreds of thousands of troops were needed to control and retain the lands occupied in the west and in Africa. And now the vast open steppes of Russia was swallowing up millions of soldiers and thousands of machines with no foreseeable end in sight. Although not in zealous agreement with the turn of the war, they continued to give it a very somber maximum support, not just because they had no alternative, but because of the tremendous investment in local lives that were scattered across the various battlefronts.

• • •

Maria had been working with Doctor Hartmann at the Ritterburg Hospital for over a year when she concluded it would be best to volunteer as an army nurse. Upon finishing her training at St. Joseph's Hospital in Regensburg, she had gone to work in Ritterburg with the expectation that the war would last only a few more months. Then Erich would return to Heidelberg University, and they could get married. Prior to the war, he had planned to complete his medical degree before marrying her. Because of the interruption, however, she felt he would consent to get married, and then she could work in Heidelberg to support them. Then came the involvement in Africa, followed by the invasion of Russia, which taxed every resource to the limit. And now German cities were being subjected to night bombing raids by the British that were increasing in intensity. Although Hitler had promised to unveil some secret weapons that would quickly and decisively end the war, she wondered if he was really sincere. And, if so, would they materialize in time to bring Erich back safely to her?

On a weekend late in the spring, Maria returned to Holzheim to discuss the situation with her mother.

"I don't think it's a very good idea," Mrs. Juergens told her. "Enough young people have gone to war from Holzheim. You could work at a hospital in Regensburg or Ritterburg." She paused for a moment and then added, "Besides, the people around here would feel better with someone like you nearby."

Maria nodded assent, but inside she knew she must join the war effort.

Although Mrs. Juergens was not very happy with the idea, she knew her daughter was exceedingly level-headed and had arrived at such a conclusion only after giving it very careful thought. Maria's brother, George, considered the decision to be a great one and expressed his hope that the next two years would pass quickly so he would be old enough to volunteer.

Now that she had declared her intention to those close to her, she would reconsider it again to assure herself she was doing the right thing. That afternoon she left the house, intentionally stepping on the squeaky middle step of the old porch, to take a leisurely stroll through town along the narrow cobblestone streets she had trod since childhood. Occasionally she stopped to look at the budding trees, a newly planted garden, or a window box of carefully tended geraniums. She encountered Mrs. Feldmann, who was still very depressed about her son who had been killed in Russia two months before.

"He's buried in some lonely field out there," she sobbed. "They'll never bring him home."

"How are the other three?" Maria asked.

"They're on the Eastern front," Mrs. Feldmann replied, wiping a tear from the corner of her eye. "Their letters tell me not to worry. They are well and unharmed. But, of course, it takes two weeks for a letter to get here."

"By the way, how's that little grandchild?" Maria asked, changing the subject.

Mrs. Feldmann beamed. "He's growing so fast," she stated with a smile as she wiped another tear from her cheek. "Really keeps his mother busy." She reflected a moment and then added, "Just wish his father would come home before something happens." She shook her head, then turned and walked slowly away. Tears were again welling up in her eyes.

When Maria came to the church, she took a kerchief from her purse and placed it over her head, climbed the stone steps, and entered through the heavy wooden door that thudded as it closed behind her. Tiptoeing up the center aisle of the dimly lighted interior, she went directly to the communion rail and knelt in silent solitude. She looked up at the gold cross faintly shining on the altar, closed her eyes, and said an Our Father and Hail Mary. Then bowed her head in a gesture of humble humility.

It was very still and she was alone, but she felt peaceful and secure. The odor of burning wax from candles that had been lighted for the departed dead filled her nostrils, and a reflection of the flickering red sanctuary light danced in her clear, brown eyes as she prayed for guidance and help.

Shafts of pale, colored light streamed through the stained glass windows, illuminating fine dust particles that remained suspended in the air. The only break in the silence was an occasional creak of the rafters and the rubbing of her stockinged legs as she shifted her weight from one knee to the other. She recalled her childhood, her family, Erich, her father, and the Feldmann boys. She thought of her training, of Dr. Hartmann, of the farmers of Holzheim, and of the plight of her country. Her decision to join the army was right; she was sure now. Silently, she thanked God for his help, made the sign of the cross, and then left. Outside, the air was clear and fresh, and the sun made her squint. She felt better, much better, than when she had entered.

She hiked up the path leading to the wooded hill she and Erich had climbed when they ate a picnic lunch beneath the big evergreen trees. On the way, she watched a pair of young cottontail rabbits frolicking in the barren, gray shrubs. The new crop of grass had sprouted, just showing green through the brown mat remaining from last year. And tender, young buds on branch tips proclaimed that mother nature's faucets had again been opened, delivering the juices of life that forced them to awake from a long winter sleep. The soil under foot was soft and spongy, having not had time to absorb the mois-ture of the melted winter snow, and it smelled sour with the processes of decay and fermentation. She paused beneath a large pine tree and looked out over the countryside. On several occasions, Erich had stood there beside her. But that was long ago, ever so long ago. Although she had not seen him for more than a year and a half, she felt a certain flush of warmth and nearness as she looked at the carpet of dead brown needles and speculated that some of them had been there long enough to have felt the crush of his weight when he was home on his last furlough.

Letters had arrived regularly from Normandy, but when Erich transferred to Africa, they came less frequently, sometimes having long gaps of time between them. Maria also felt he had changed, although she was not sure it was due to the war or just a matter of maturation. It was evident, however, the war had placed a strain on him, for the quality of his penmanship varied from time to time, and the content of his letters often reflected his moods. Those from Normandy were well written, but when Erich reached Africa, several weeks often passed between letters and held little news. He had writ-ten about the weather, the native population, and the insects. Often, he expressed concern about conditions at home. Even though her letters stated that everyone and everything was fine, he wanted to be reassured that the people were safe and that there was ample food. The last two letters had been composed at a time when the *Afrika Korps* was engaged in fierce battles and had to be written in haste. They were short and confused and created a deep concern within her.

The following day she rode her bicycle to the city hall of Regensburg and enlisted. She was granted a week to put her affairs in order and return. She worked five more days at the hospital in Ritterburg, experienced a tearful farewell with her mother and George, and was taken to Regensburg in a buggy by Mr. Trapp. A government ticket to Munich was issued at the Regensburg depot. While awaiting the train, she was again engrossed by the thought of Erich as she sat on the same oak bench, looked at the same dark walls, and smelled the same odors she had shared with him. She knew he would be disappointed when he discovered she had enlisted, but hoped he would understand when he learned of her rationale.

• • •

Camp Klosterfeld was a medical training camp located southwest of Munich designed to train medical hospital and field personnel. Situated on a gentle slope overlooking a peaceful valley of small farms, its mood and atmosphere was of a gentle nature rather than the vigor and aggressiveness of camps housing combat troops. It consisted primarily of two-story barracks and a large number of classrooms to teach trainees medical techniques for use in support of combat operations. Even though many of the troops were to be hospital orderlies or surgical technicians, they still had to learn the art of soldiering such as hiking, close-order drill, and military discipline. There was also a contingent who were being trained as corpsmen to accompany troops in battle. Their schedule was considerably more rigorous.

Nurses were housed in a separate section of the camp. Nestled in a grove of old oak trees, there was an abundance of shade, small wild animals, and cool breezes. According to the camp commandant, Colonel Blutfeld, it was designed to create a pleasant surrounding for the "Ladies of Mercy," as he called them.

When Maria stepped down from the command car that delivered her to the area, she stood for a full minute watching the black Hungarian fox squirrels scurrying about the trees, chattering as they went, often flying through space while leaping from one tree to the next. The sad cooing of a mourning dove reminded her of early morning in Holzheim.

After being directed to a bed on a second floor to deposit her luggage, she reported to the orderly room. There she was given a training schedule that her group was to follow during the fourteen-week training cycle. It consisted primarily of classroom instruction on military nursing interspersed with sessions of calisthenics, marching, and field problems. The following day, she reported to the quartermaster clothing warehouse, where she was issued a smart brown dress uniform, two sets of green trousered fatigue suits, and six pin-striped poplin nurse uniforms.

• • •

The pilot eased the throttle levers slowly forward, and the ungainly *Condor*, its four mighty engines throbbing with power as the propellers sliced through the thin desert air, began to roll down the bumpy, concrete runway of the Tobruk Airport. It had unloaded a cargo of supplies and now, sitting on the hard, drop-down benches along the sides of its corrugated fuselage, fifty select, battle-hardened veterans of the *Afrika Korps* sat nervously wondering how much louder and rougher the ride might become. They had been away from Germany for more than a year and were anxious to set foot on their homeland again. Before boarding, each had gotten a haircut and had his uniform laundered and pressed as ordered. They were to become part of an elite force where slovenliness would not be tolerated. It was their first plane ride, and beads of nervous perspiration were showing on their faces and foreheads. Two sitting across from Erich and Heinz had soaked through the underarms of their tan cotton tunics. Once airborne, however, the tension eased as the rhythmic vibration and roar of engines lulled their senses.

It was a smooth flight across the brilliant, blue Mediterranean, and then the engines labored again to reach necessary altitude for crossing the Alps. Finally, the throttles were eased as they entered the glide path to Munich. Once on the ground, the troopers were quickly loaded aboard trucks for a ride on the *Autobahn* to Augsburg.

• • •

Colonel Helmut Newmeyer, the tall, wiry, sharp-nosed commandant, climbed the steps of a platform overlooking the drill field where several hundred soldiers stood at rigid attention. He took a few steps and paused, standing ramrod straight in his trim black uniform to scan the sea of eager faces with his piercing steel-gray eyes. Then he walked briskly to the podium and firmly grasped the sides of its slanted top. "I want to welcome you men to Camp Reichstein," he began. "We are assembling the finest warriors in the army to create an elite fighting force that will serve as a world example of superiority and pride. You men are part of that group. You will receive six weeks of intensive, no-nonsense training using the best weapons in the world." He paused and then continued. "Those who successfully complete it will be transferred to the *Schutzstaffel*, promoted, and given a leave. Those who are eliminated will be returned to their former units." He looked them over once again and then concluded, "So, we'll be seeing a lot of one another. Good luck!" He stabbed his right hand into the air. "Heil, Hitler!" he shouted.

"Heil, Hitler," a mass of voices responded in unison.

The next day the assemblage of men, representing dozens of different units, turned in their uniforms for the standard green *Wehrmacht* tunic, trousers, and jack boots. They were then separated into two groups: commissioned officer candidates and noncommissioned officer candidates. Erich and Heinz were placed in the commissioned officer group, which was promptly marched to the camp theater for an orientation meeting.

"You will notice that your uniforms have neither insignia nor rank," stated a highly decorated lieutenant standing on the stage before them. "Your pay will be the same as you have been getting, but there is no rank consideration here. Here, you are all trainees. The word of the camp staff is first and paramount. Those eliminated will be returned, without delay, to their former unit. Those who finish the cycle will be granted a leave before their next assignment." He paused as if to let his words register and then asked, "Any questions?"

One of the men stood and meekly asked, "Any weekend passes?"

"They will be issued only on a limited basis," came the reply. "And travel is restricted to a maximum of fifty miles."

"Well, so much for that idea," Heinz whispered to Erich. "But maybe we can get someone to visit us here."

That evening Erich wrote letters to Maria and his mother. Not knowing Maria had enlisted, he sent both to Holzheim.

• • •

The day began early for the Special Forces group with a bugle call at five-thirty in the morning. At six they stood in formation for roll call, went to breakfast, and then returned to the formation area again at seven-thirty for inspection. The inspection was both critical and thorough, having one team of instructors checking the ranks for appropriate posture, neatness of dress, and closeness of shave and haircut. Another team checked the barracks for neatness, cleanliness, and orderliness. A verbal reprimand was given for the first infraction, the second resulted in considerable extra duty, and the third was grounds for elimination. Exactness and precision were emphasized every minute of the day, including mealtime. The men had to sit at attention while eating and feed themselves by lifting the fork or spoon vertically from the plate or bowl until it was level with their mouths before bringing it horizontally to their lips.

The trainees also had to jog in step between various classrooms and drill fields where instruction was held. Since the sessions lasted fifty minutes and it took between five and ten minutes to jog to the next location, there was little time for rest or relaxation during duty hours.

Basic skills were tested and upgraded, and a special emphasis was placed on handling automatic weapons, using explosive devices, and operating the newer machines of war. "You are superior, both mentally and physically, to any enemy forces you will encounter!" an instructor stated forcefully. "Be proud! Walk with your chest out and your chin held high! With this training and the high order of new weapons you will have, you will be invincible! When you leave here, you will have the strength and appetite to quickly overwhelm your opposition! You must believe it!"

The rifles they used were of a semi-automatic, gas-operated, ten-round variety. They had to learn to fire the *Luger* and *Walther* pistols as well as machine pistols from many different positions. Classes in boxing, wrestling, and the disabling tactics of martial arts were taught and practiced. The instructors repeatedly emphasized the necessity of making a maximum effort in every encounter because if, by underestimation, the enemy is permitted to get the upper hand, there might not be the opportunity to correct the mistake and gain the upper hand. "If you tangle with one of those Cossacks in the Russian army, you might come back carrying your head under your arm," one instructor warned wryly.

• • •

When Erich's letters to his mother and Maria arrived at the Holzheim post office, Ilsa Juergens took one look at the return address and became so excited she could not finish sorting the mail. Father Kurz, who was mailing a package, noted her plight and volunteered to help in order to take care of those waiting for their mail. She sat down for a moment but could not calm herself, so she put the two letters in her pocket and went directly to the Stecker store.

Mrs. Stecker tore open the letter and scanned it quickly, all the time fearing the worst, but then happily announced to all present that Erich was safe and sound. He had merely been transferred to a camp near Augsburg. Her first reaction was to go there immediately and visit him. Then, as rationality returned, she spoke in terms of calling him on the telephone. Since there was no phone in Holzheim, Mrs. Juergens suggested she write a letter to see if she could visit or call him.

"I've got a letter he wrote to Maria, too," Mrs. Juergens stated, removing it from her pocket and displaying it. "I'm going to forward it right away, and maybe they can get together too."

Mrs. Juergens waited while Erich's mother penned a brief note to her son. In the excitement of opening his letter, Mrs. Stecker had partially destroyed the return address so she had to get the remainder of it from Maria's mother. She then made an additional copy for herself.

As Mrs. Juergens scurried back to the post office, Mrs. Stecker reread the letter. Bubbling with joy, she went behind the counter to aid her husband while the two of them announced the good news to each customer.

• • •

At Camp Reichstein, the day for the officer candidates had been particularly strenuous. It was the middle of the second week of the training cycle and they jogged and hiked five miles into hilly country, practiced scaling high cliffs by using rocket-propelled rope ladders, and crossed canyons by sliding along stretched cables. Drenched in perspiration and covered with dust and dirt, they were repeatedly harangued and berated by the instructors.

"Soldier! Why did it take so long to get up that ladder?"

"No excuse, sir!"

"Then let's get with it!"

"Yes, sir!"

At three o'clock they were given a short break before starting back. Erich stretched out on the ground beside Heinz, his camouflaged helmet over his face to shield it from the warm sun. He liked it here. It was peaceful and quiet, and the sounds and smell of the land were tranquilizing to mind and body. Others would occasionally complain about the harsh discipline and the rigorous training, but he had been with the *Afrika Korps* and knew how precious the gift of life was. He was much more aware of the pleasure of walking in the shade of green trees, of hearing birds sing, of drinking cool, clear water, and of sleeping in a secure, comfortable shelter. He knew he could never complain about conditions here and realized the discipline instilled may someday make the difference between living or dying. In Africa he had witnessed what the concerted, well-disciplined action of a few was able to accomplish. And here it was being developed to a much higher degree of perfection.

"Sure wish I'd hear from Irma," interrupted Heinz.

Erich moved his helmet away from his mouth. "Did you write her?"

"Twice already."

"She'll answer," Erich assured him.

"I hope so," replied Heinz. Then he added, "I sure think a lot of that little lady."

The whistle blew sharply signaling the end of the break. "Let's get in formation," ordered the instructor. "We've got some distance to cover."

As they jogged along, it was evident some trainees had not properly assembled their equipment or pack harness. It squeaked or rattled. During the next break they were required to correct the errors under the watchful eye of the instructors.

"Why is it," snarled one of the instructors, "there's never time to do it right but always time to do it over?"

After reaching the barracks area, they were assembled on the drill field before being dismissed. When Erich's platoon had been released, the instructor heard him mention to Heinz that he was so tired he had wondered if he was going to be able to run the last half mile.

"Soldier!" he shouted, halting Erich. "What was that you said?"

"I just told my friend I was tired," explained Erich.

"I heard what you said. That's a negative attitude!" he bellowed. "Here we think only in the positive. Nobody at Camp Reichstein gets tired! Nobody!"

"Yes, sir!" replied Erich.

"Now, to prove to yourself you're not tired, run three laps around this field! Get going!"

Since Erich was in top physical condition, it was easy for him to comply. Each time he came past the waiting instructor, however, the instructor trotted alongside for a few yards. "Now that's not very difficult, is it soldier?"

"No, sir!"

"You're not tired now, are you, soldier?"

"No, sir!"

After finishing the third lap, Erich clicked his heels and stood at attention ramrod straight, his shoulders squared, and two creases of wrinkles beneath his chin. The instructor, his nose six inches from Erich's, lectured him on always thinking positive. When released, Erich walked slowly to the barracks, his sweat-drenched clothing adhering to his body.

At the barracks he found a letter lying on his bunk. It was from his mother. Dropping his equipment to the floor, he hurriedly opened it. Because of its briefness, the hurried penmanship, and lack of continuity, he could sense her excitement. Her mention of Maria being stationed near Munich surprised him, but he was disappointed she did not include an address. Enjoying a surge of elation he had not felt for a long time, he grabbed a towel and, smiling, headed for the bathroom to wash.

That evening at the canteen, he joined Heinz at a small table to drink a glass of beer. As soon as he sat down, he told Heinz of the letter from his mother. Heinz smiled and said, "I got one from Irma, too. She's thinking of moving to Augsburg."

"Doesn't she realize you'll only be here another month?"

"I told her that," Heinz explained. "But you know women. She's determined we should get married."

"Good Lord! You *are* in trouble."

Heinz took a sip of beer, licked the foam from his upper lip, and then wrinkled his forehead as he thoughtfully looked down into the glass. "Not really. I wouldn't mind marrying her. It's the times, though. A man in our business shouldn't get married."

"I agree."

"By the way," prodded Heinz with a sparkle in his eye. "Are you still tired?"

"Hell no!" smiled Erich. "I'll not make that mistake again." He paused a moment, then added, "One thing for sure though—they'll make a fighting machine out of you, or break you trying."

When they returned to the barracks, Erich found a note on his bed indicating a long distance call was waiting for him. He hurried to a booth in the recreation room and contacted the Munich operator, who connected him with Maria at Camp Klosterfeld. For a short moment Maria broke down and sobbed. But after listening to Erich's calm, reassuring voice, she regained her composure. "I prayed every night for your safe return," she said between sniffles.

"But I'm here—safe and sound," he assured her.

After comparing duty hours, she suggested they meet in Augsburg on Saturday. "Fine. I'll meet you by the *Denkmal* in the central plaza at one o'clock," he promised her.

"I'll be there," she vowed.

"I love you with all my being," he wooed in a soft, warm voice.

"I love you, too," she answered.

"Goodbye, my darling."

"Goodbye."

Erich had trouble sleeping that night. In his mind he reread his mother's letter several times, and the echo of Maria's voice continued to ring in his ears. He was deeply touched by her sobs and tears. It revealed the sensitivity he knew she possessed but what the long separation had made him nearly forget. The next two and a half days passed very slowly.

• • •

As soon as they were dismissed on Saturday, Erich and Heinz gathered together a few toilet articles and caught the camp bus for Augsburg. They quickly walked the three blocks to the town square, scarcely noticing the carefully tended plots of geraniums and roses that grew in a great profusion of color. They scanned the benches filled with elderly couples basking and dozing in the warm sunshine and noted dozens of people walking briskly along its many paths who were using it as a shortcut to their destination. Erich stood before the large statue with its bubbling fountain and quickly looked around at all the people, but he did not see Maria until she rose from a nearby bench and started toward him. She was dressed in a trim brown uniform, the skirt falling just below the knees, accenting her shapely calves and ankles.

He tossed his satchel of toilet articles to Heinz, rushed over, and as they met, threw his powerful arms around her, nearly sweeping her off her feet. He kissed her on each cheek and tasted the salt from tears that had begun to flow. For a moment she held her face against his chest to allow time to regain her composure, then, pushing back, looked up into his face where, for the first time, she saw the long pink scar on his left cheek.

"Africa?" she asked, touching it gently.

"Yes."

Heinz walked up and Erich retrieved his satchel.

"Maria, I'd like for you to meet my friend, Heinz Jager." Then, turning to Heinz and nodding toward Maria, "Maria Juergens."

"I'm very pleased to meet you," said Maria.

"The pleasure is all mine," stated Heinz, clicking his heels.

"Heinz and I were classmates at Heidelberg," added Erich. "We enlisted at the same time and have been stationed together ever since."

"Oh, how nice," answered Maria, noticing the missing tip of Erich's ear.

"Must you go back today?" Erich asked. "Or can you stay overnight?"

"I can stay overnight," she stated before walking back to the bench to pick up a small suitcase.

"Good! We'd better get a room while it's early. They're scarce, you know."

They checked into the Hotel Baumhofer, which fronted on the square. Maria and Erich got second floor rooms adjacent to each other. Heinz left them in the lobby, stating he would look over the town and then return to camp in the evening.

Once in his room, Erich stepped through a pair of French doors that opened onto a balcony. He watched the busy square below for a moment and then leaned out to look around a partition to see if Maria was out on her balcony. She was not, so he went back inside and knocked on her door.

"Come in," came the soft reply.

He stepped inside and closed the door.

"I was hoping you would come," she said, turning to him.

She had removed her brown tunic and was standing in her stockinged feet. The crisp white blouse she wore accented the soft pink flesh of her cheeks and neck. He put his arms around her and drew her to him. "You can't imagine how long I've waited and dreamed of this moment," he whispered.

"Me too."

He kissed her several times and caressed her back and then wrapped his arms about her. He could feel the pressure of her breasts and thighs against his body. A fire ignited within him and was being fanned by the increased pace of her breathing and the soft white arms that clung about his neck. With a feeling of guilt, he gave an audible sigh. "Let's step out on the balcony," he whispered.

"All right," she answered reluctantly.

Erich tugged to open the stuck doors, and they stepped out, putting their arms about each other's waist as they looked down on the square below. The benches were still filled with the elderly while others continued to hurry along the many walks that crossed the sqaure. But now there were multitudes of soldiers loitering about.

"Have you eaten?" Erich inquired.

"I had a sandwich just before I met you," she replied.

"Why don't we go for a walk and get something?"

"All right."

They followed the dimly lighted, creaking stairway down to the stuffy lobby, where they turned in their keys. It was warm and balmy as they threaded their way through the crowds of Saturday afternoon shoppers, workers, and soldiers while trying to hold hands on the busy sidewalk. In an attempt to get away from the mass of people, they entered a small confectionary store and ordered coffee and cheesecake.

Maria watched with interest as Erich tasted first the coffee, then the cake. Fortunately, he had gained ten of the fifteen pounds he had lost in Africa, but creases and shadows had developed in his face, indicating to her he had aged beyond his twenty-one years. She also noted he spoke less frequently, but when he did, it was not of the inconsequential minutia they used to banter about a few years back. He appeared to be concerned about significant items from a more sophisticated viewpoint. She looked at his deep-blue eyes and scarred face, and wished she could take him somewhere that was free of world problems and conflict—where they might live together in the peace and harmony of which they once had dreamed.

"The coffee is not so good," he stated, looking at her quizzically.

"It's *ersatz*," she informed him. "There is no more real coffee to be had."

"Well, the cheesecake is sure good, though," he said with a smile. "It's been a long time since I tasted that."

They talked on, mostly about Holzheim and conditions on the home front. She told him not much had changed except for tighter rationing, more regulations, and the lack of young men in the area. "Some farmers have been given prisoner-of-war workers to help with their work," she stated matter-of-factly.

"Really? How do they work out?"

"All right, I guess. Mr. Trapp has several helping him. Mostly French and Russians."

When they returned to the hotel, he kissed her at her door and told her he would knock for her at five-thirty to go to dinner. Since the hotel served only continental breakfasts and meals to those in their rooms, he thought additional time would be needed to locate a restaurant.

In his room, he kicked off his boots, shed his uniform, and stretched out on the bed to take a short nap. However, sleep evaded him. A myriad of events raced through his mind so fast they seemed to be chasing one another. What a fast, wild, bewildering series of episodes he had lived through during the last few years, each appearing more complex, more dynamic, and more involved than the previous one. Where would it all end? What did the future hold?

He arose, bathed with pine-scented soap, and dressed carefully. At five-thirty he rapped at Maria's door. It opened instantly, giving him the impression she had been standing there waiting for him to knock. He stood back for a moment, looking at her. She remained very still, waiting for him to do or say something. Then, grasping her by the shoulders, he kissed her on both cheeks. "Oh Lord! I'm so proud of you," he muttered with a low sigh.

"I'm glad," she whispered.

At a restaurant two blocks from the hotel, they ate a dinner of noodle soup, roast pork, and boiled potatoes. Erich drank a glass of wine with his meal, but Maria preferred the bitter *ersatz* coffee. "Food isn't as good as it used to be," she complained, wrinkling her nose.

"Oh, I don't know. It sure tastes good to me," Erich replied.

"The food in your camp must not be very good."

"It's fine. I just think I appreciate being able to sit at a table and order what I want. You know, you don't really appreciate something until you've been without it for a while."

"That's a true statement," she concluded.

When they left the restaurant, they walked leisurely along the no longer crowded sidewalk. Maria held his arm tightly as they sauntered slowly from one store to the next, often stopping to comment about the items on display. Since the war had intensified, metals had become very scarce, so there was noticeably less in the way of domestic items available for purchase, and those that could be bought were often made partially or wholly of substitute materials such as wood, Bakelite, or cloth. When they came to a bridal shop, Maria brightened and tugged at Erich's sleeve.

"This is exactly the wedding dress I want to be married in!" she exclaimed, smiling as she watched the expression on Erich's face. "What do you think of it?"

Not being well versed about bridal gowns, he replied, "Yes, yes. It looks great." Then he questioned, "How did you determine this?"

"Oh I saw it in a magazine a year or so ago. See the tag?" She pointed to a silver card hanging from the bosom. "Designed by Schwayder," she read.

They walked a bit farther, and then she stopped and turned to face him. "I've decided on the place I'd like to get married, too. I hope you'll agree."

"Oh?" he responded, wrinkling his forehead. "Where?"

"Ulm."

"Ulm?" he questioned. "Have you ever been there?"

"No. But Father Kurz loaned me a book on cathedrals, and I read all about them. I just fell in love with the one at Ulm. It's very large, second only to the one in Cologne."

Erich winced a bit, remembering the time he had spent in and around the one at Cologne.

"And," she added, "it has the tallest spire of any in the world. It's very beautiful."

They walked a few more steps, and then meekly she asked, "Well, what do you think of the idea?"

He considered it for a long moment. "You apparently have given it a lot of thought. It's perfectly all right with me. I haven't thought too much about marriage lately. Just been too busy with the war. Sure, I'll marry you, wherever you wish. We'd better get the war over before we plan too much though."

Back at the hotel they went to her room and, without turning on the light, stepped out onto the balcony. They stood for some time, arms about each other's waist, watching the twinkling stars in the purple canopy above. Below, a few people still strolled the streets, some window shopping, others walking a variety of breeds and mixtures of dogs. Erich kissed her on the forehead and she quivered slightly. Then, taking her by the hand, he led her back inside. They sat on the edge of the bed as he removed his boots, she her shoes. Then they laid back, and he, rolling over on his elbows, plied her soft, warms lips apart with his.

"Let's take off our uniforms so we don't mess them up," he suggested.

Without answering, she stood and removed her blouse, skirt, and hose. He took off his tunic, shirt, and trousers. They lay beside each other, Maria resting her head in the hollow of his shoulder. He smelled the sweet fragrance of her hair and felt the warmth from her body seep into his. She broke the silence. "So you're a member of the Special Forces."

"Hope to be in another four weeks."

"We have heard about them over the radio. Supposed to be made up of the finest German men there are." She hesitated a moment. "They have been urging the girls to let them father a child."

"Without being married?" Erich asked skeptically.

"Yes. They say this will improve the race."

She waited a full minute for him to reply, but he did not. "Would you like that?" she asked.

"It doesn't appeal to me. Does it to you?"

"No!" came her emphatic reply.

"*You* bring out the animal in me," he teased as he caressed and kissed her.

He rubbed her stomach and she responded by lifting her hips so he could raise her slip and touch the flesh above her panties.

"Do you want me to take it off?" she asked.

"Yes," he answered.

As she sat up and pulled the slip over her head, he removed his undershirt. Afterwards she hesitated, wondering if she was to remove more. He pushed her down. "That's all," he ordered.

He lay over the top portion of her and kissed her nose, chin, and lips, brushing the hair from her forehead and lightly stroking her neck and cheeks. She placed her arms about his bare shoulders and, by gently rubbing, came in contact with the fibrous strips of scar tissue on the side of his chest. He could feel her muscles tighten and breathing stop as her fingers carefully explored the area. "My God!" she whispered forcefully. "What have they done to you?"

"It was a land mine in Africa," he explained.

She was showing considerable concern. "Your face, your ear, and now this. Is there anything else?"

"No," he assured her

"May I look at it?" she asked sympathetically.

"If you wish."

He closed his eyes as she turned on the bed lamp and examined him carefully. She snapped off the lamp and threw herself on him as she began to sob. "Oh my darling, how they have hurt you!"

"Actually it's just some lacerations—nothing very serious," he declared, trying to ease her concern by cuddling her in his arms.

This discovery led to a serious conversation about their future. When Erich first enlisted, they had hoped the war would be over by now so they could return to their peaceful pursuits and the plans they had so carefully laid. But it had developed into an all consuming quagmire that seemed to have no end. They discussed the possibility of getting married now, but Erich was very much opposed to the idea. He wanted their marriage to have a firmer foundation and a secure future. Inwardly, he recognized the possibility of getting killed in action. And he didn't want her to be left a widow, especially since her young life had not been an easy one. After several minutes of silence, he asked, "Do you want me to stay here with you tonight?"

"I'd like that," she whispered.

He turned her on her side facing away from him, then, cuddling up behind her, drew the sheet up over them.

"Is it all right if I don't put on my nightgown?" she asked, feeling his arm about her.

"Yes."

The next morning he woke early, kissed her gently, and then slipped out of bed and dressed. After going to his room where he bathed and shaved, he returned to find her still sleeping. As he opened the French doors to admit some light and air, they broke free with a rattle. Looking back, he saw her stirring beneath the sheet. He walked over and sat on the edge of the bed and, bending down, kissed her on the forehead. She smiled contentedly.

"How did you sleep?" he asked.

"Better than I have in a long time," she replied, putting her arms about his neck.

He returned to his room, rumpled the bed, then went downstairs and requested that two breakfasts be sent to his room. The desk clerk raised his eyebrows, so Erich explained that the young lady in the next room had agreed to have breakfast with him.

The clerk nodded. "Oh, good!" Then he asked, "When do you wish it?"

"In thirty minutes."

Forty-five minutes later, Maria entered his room. She looked neat and crisp and radiated a lovely fresh fragrance. They sat at a small table and ate hard rolls and black bread spread with butter and jam. The coffee, although sufficient in quantity, was not to Erich's liking.

"We are fortunate to have butter," stated Maria with a smile.

"Oh?" questioned Erich.

"Yes. It is becoming quite scarce."

When they checked out, they inquired if they could leave their bags until later in the afternoon. The desk clerk assured them it would be all right.

Walking slowly toward the church to attend nine o'clock Mass, they went past the bridal shop. Maria paused to gaze again at the wedding gown. "Oh, how I would like to own that," she uttered in a tone so low Erich barely heard her.

"I wish you could, too," he murmured.

When the Mass was over, they walked out into a warm sunshine filtering through large chestnut trees that grew along the street. As the crowd drifted away from the front of the church, they strolled hand in hand up a narrow side street leading into a quiet residential district. Erich squeezed her hand and swung it back and forth. "Such a nice day. Such a nice place. Germany is beautiful."

"Oh, I think so, too," Maria added. "I'm proud of our land."

They walked a short distance, then Maria broke in again. "You know, when I was kneeling in church, I thought about us and what we did last night—you know, sleep together. It didn't seem to bother me."

"What do you mean?" Erich queried.

"Well, I used to think that if I ever did anything like that my conscience would eat me alive."

"We didn't do anything wrong," he hastened to assure her. "We merely laid beside each other."

"I know. But it seemed so natural, so right. I couldn't possibly do it with anyone else."

"And I plan to keep your conscience clear, too," he stated firmly.

When they came to the *Fugger Haus*, they stopped.

Maria, noting Erich's reluctance to proceed, turned to him. "I want to go in," she said.

"What is it?" Erich asked.

"Dr. Hartmann told me about it. A long time ago, in the sixteenth century, Jacob Fugger, a wealthy merchant, set aside this plot of land where he then built many homes and apartments for Augsburg's elderly citizens—a place where they could live a simple, quiet life without taxes or rent."

Erich shrugged. "Let's go," he said, pulling her by the hand.

Slowly, they wandered through the maze of yellow stucco buildings, frequently stopping to talk with the residents who had brought chairs outside to sit in the sunshine. Erich sensed they were very hungry for conversation. While talking with them, he learned they had concluded the world was one of rapid change, designed only for the young. They felt shunted off to the side, out of the mainstream of life where they would not impede progress. They were so pleased that two young people were willing to spend time with them. And they took great pride showing items of various hobbies, explaining in considerable detail the processes involved. To show their appreciation, they offered Erich and Maria bits of jewelry, small flowers made of human hair, and an occasional hand-worked handkerchief. Both the men and women seemed very impressed with the uniforms Erich and Maria wore. Several brought forth photographs of relatives currently in the war or of themselves when they had been in service.

As Erich and Maria left the *Fugger Haus* compound, she grasped his arm and pressed her cheek against his sleeve. "You know," she said with a contented smile, "I feel good about visiting those elderly people. They are so nice."

"And lonely," Erich added.

"I'll tell Dr. Hartmann about it the next time I see him."

After retrieving their bags from the hotel, they went directly to Augsburg's *Hauptbahnhof* so Maria could catch the two o'clock train to Munich. Erich bought two ham and cheese sandwiches from a snack stand. While they ate them at a small, stand-up table, he told her, "I'll call you Thursday evening to see if we can get together next weekend."

When her train was called, he kissed her warmly, then watched her disappear into the crowd that was threading its way through the turnstile.

• • •

The third week of training proved no less energetic than the previous two. Required to make three low-level parachute jumps, the trainees prepared by grasping a strap with both hands and gliding down an inclined cable. When fifteen feet above the ground, they had to drop and tumble in such a manner as to avoid injury.

On Wednesday morning trucks conveyed the troopers to Munich, where they were loaded aboard Junkers transport planes. Flown to a designated area, they jumped from an altitude of eight hundred feet. In the afternoon they jumped again from five hundred feet. "And Thursday, you'll jump from four hundred feet," an instructor told them.

"What in hell are they trying to do, kill us?" Heinz moaned.

"Oh, they figure eventually you'll be able to do it from ground level without a plane," chuckled Erich. "Just keep practicing."

The next day as the transport soared low over an open field, the instructor slid open the door and ordered the men to jump. When Erich moved up along the line of men disappearing in the rush of air that sped past, he swallowed hard because he could see the grassy hillocks moving at tremendous speed below. An instant of fear flashed through him, but his iron-hard discipline returned, along with the confidence he had acquired in the army's ability to provide a safety factor. He thrust himself forward, was caught in a mighty blast of air, felt the light tug of his static line, and then the violent jerk of his opened parachute. He had very little time to orient himself when he saw the ground just below his feet moving swiftly past and coming up at a very rapid rate. Landing on his heels, his knees buckled and he tumbled forward. As quickly as possible he scrambled to an upright position and spilled the air from the parachute. A few minutes later, as they assembled in small clusters to be picked up by trucks, he noticed several of the men were limping, some quite badly.

When they returned to camp, Erich goaded Heinz. "Well, I see you have attained the status of a paratrooper."

"Oh, yes," spouted Heinz. "I feel like the shortest one in the country though."

"How's that?"

"I think my asshole is located squarely between my shoulders."

"They just don't want the enemy to draw a bead on you."

"He may not have to if I land any harder," came the sour reply.

• • •

Saturday, shortly after noon when the camp buses began arriving at the Augsburg *Hauptbahnhof*, both Maria and Irma were waiting, each alone, not aware they would soon become acquainted. Maria had arrived by train, but Irma had moved to Augsburg earlier in the week. They had been sitting on benches facing one another, but when the first camp bus squeaked to a halt they stood, nodded, and smiled as they acknowledged awaiting the same thing. Then they became engrossed in the process of watching the flow of green uniforms dismounting from the seemingly endless stream of buses. When Erich and Heinz stepped down together from the same bus, the girls rushed forward to meet them. After the initial greeting, Maria, surprised to see Erich and Irma engage in a brief hug, looked at him questioningly. Smiling, he said, "Maria, I'd like you to meet Irma. She's a friend of Heinz."

Relieved, she smiled and offered Irma her hand. "I'm pleased to meet you," she said.

Heinz suggested they go to a cafe where they could sit down and talk, but Maria reminded Erich they were going to Ulm and thought they should get under way in order to find lodging.

Erich nodded affirmation to Heinz

Irma looked at Heinz. "I have a room in a private home. Maybe we should go there and see if we can get a room there for you, too."

"A good idea," Heinz agreed.

• • •

Ulm was a quiet little city with minimum traffic and only an occasional serviceman. Not far from the railroad station, they obtained a room in the ancient, half-timbered *Gasthaus Taube*.

"And where can we have dinner?" Erich inquired of the desk clerk.

The clerk pointed down a hallway. "In the dining room beginning at six."

After putting their bags in the room, Maria said, "First off, I want to visit the cathedral. Why don't we go there now and see it?"

"Fine," Erich agreed.

Holding hands as they approached the steps leading to the massive doors, they paused to look up at the tremendous spire silhouetted against a billowy white cloud. Then, passing through the vestibule where Erich removed his cap, the two of them stood, looking up the dimly lighted center aisle at the distant altar. Erich took her by the elbow and slowly, very slowly, walked her between the two rows of pews, looking first right and then left at the large, stained-glass windows that filtered and colored dozens of beams of light, which illuminated the shadowy passageway ahead. Upon reaching the communion rail, they knelt, offered a silent prayer, and then slowly retraced their steps to the doorway, looking up at the massive rose window before them. As they walked down the steps, a large choir of young boys dressed in black robes topped with lacy white mantels was entering.

They walked a short distance into the square and then turned around to survey the masterpiece of gothic architecture. The sun had settled low in the sky, its reflected rays casting a dull, golden glow on the gray stone face of the gigantic structure. It created a rich luminescence about the statuary located in various niches that adorned the facade, making warm, colorful highlights on the ashen faces and along the folds of the cold, stone robes. Higher up, the white cloud had turned to a delicate pink that peeked through the ornamental structure of the belfry located near the top of the great spire. Just then, soft strains from the choir welled up and drifted over the square.

"Oh, Erich," Maria sighed as she squeezed his arm. "This is the place. It's even more beautiful than I had imagined."

After dinner they went for a stroll through the business section before returning to their room. Erich, sitting in a worn, plush-covered chair, paged through a magazine he had purchased that had an article telling of the progress the German forces were making on several fronts. Of special interest to him were the photos and captions about Rommel's successful campaign with his *Afrika Korps*.

Maria, having washed her hands and face, returned and sat on the bed near him. He rose from the chair and sat beside her. "Here," he said, pointing to the article in the magazine. "This is where I was."

As she scanned it, he gave a heavy sigh. "Sometimes I wonder why we are there though."

When they prepared for bed, Erich snapped off the light and stripped to his underpants, the only sleeping attire he had worn since being in the army. Maria put on a flannel nightgown and climbed onto the bed, stretching out beside him. Placing his arms about her, he brushed her forehead with a kiss.

"You took off your brassiere," he scolded in a whisper.

"With this nightgown, I didn't think you'd care," she countered meekly.

"And underpants?"

"Left them on."

"Good."

As the evening wore on, they became more passionately involved. In spite of Erich's determination to leave her untouched until they were married, he unfastened the top buttons of her nightgown. Slipping his hand inside, he gently caressed her firm left breast. When he touched its sensitive, protruding nipple, she struggled to contain an audible gasp. He slipped his hand beneath her gown and lightly rubbed her abdomen, eliciting an audible sigh as she thrust her hips upward. But when his hand came in contact with her silky pubic hair, it shocked him. He suddenly suspended his actions and refastened the buttons at the top of the gown.

He wrapped his arms about her in a warm display of love and respect. "We cannot continue like this," he whispered.

"Please, Erich. Please do it to me," she begged, tears coming to her eyes.

"Let's discuss it at a time when we're more rational," he insisted, kissing her again.

The next morning they attended Mass at the cathedral. The number of those in attendance seemed small for such a huge house of worship. The voice of the priest echoed and reverberated throughout its vastness. When services had concluded and the choir was singing the recessional hymn, Maria and Erich walked around the interior perimeter observing the priceless paintings, the tombs of the church's greats, and the relics and remains of its martyrs. Later they circled its exterior, noting the magnificent flying buttresses and observing how carefully the huge stone blocks had been fitted together. The base stone at each corner they turned was covered with a yellow-green moss revealing a legacy left by centuries of passing dogs.

As they made their way back to the hotel, Erich halted and looked up and down the streets. "What a pleasant, beautiful city this is."

"Yes," Maria agreed. "It's so different from the rush and drive one feels in Munich."

"Or even Augsburg," added Erich as he took her hand and began walking again.

In Augsburg they stopped at a sidewalk cafe for a bite to eat before Maria had to catch the Munich train. As they were discussing Erich's next leave that was due in another three weeks, they were suddenly joined by Heinz and Irma.

"Guess what?" blurted Heinz in a great show of enthusiasm. "We've decided to get married!"

"Wonderful!" congratulated Erich, shaking both their hands.

"Yes," added Irma, nodding her head and beaming with a broad smile. "In two weeks."

"Have you decided where?" asked Erich, a bit surprised.

"Yes," Heinz answered. "In Irma's hometown, Hesselhaus. Their church is in Dinkelsbuhl. She'll make all the arrangements this week." He paused briefly. "There's one other detail. Will you be my best man?"

Erich thought a moment. "I'd be honored," he said with a broad smile.

Then Heinz turned to Maria. "Do you think you can get away so you can come with Erich?"

"I don't know, but I think so," answered Maria, feeling completely overwhelmed by the tide of enthusiasm.

"I'd be pleased if you could," said Irma, grasping her hand.

A short while later, Heinz took Irma by the hand and walked toward her room, the two of them talking energetically. Erich took Maria to the depot and kissed her goodbye. "Phone you Thursday," he called out after she had gone through the turnstile. She nodded.

· · ·

The next week, Erich's company studied *panzer* vehicles and *panzer* tactics. They were taught identification of enemy tanks from all angles, especially by silhouette. And they learned about their strengths and weaknesses.

"The *Panther* and *Tiger* are a match for any two enemy tanks," boasted the instructor. "The eighty-eight will outshoot and out-penetrate any others, and the protective armor exceeds them all, even on the underbelly."

They drove the tanks in flat, open fields and then along paths through wooded areas. They also learned how to operate the weapons they possessed. The task Erich liked best was that of directing the tank by standing with the upper portion of his body protruding through the steel hatch while wearing a set of headphones to keep in radio contact with his driver as well as those in nearby tanks.

The trainees were happier with armored force training than with the infantry tactics they had been practicing during the first three weeks. In addition to the appeal of working with machines, they also found that the amount of running and jogging had been reduced. However, the sternness, the badgering, and the discipline had not been relaxed by the camp personnel, and the instructors appeared even more distant and more demanding. Perfection was required in everything, and there was no toleration for anything less.

On Thursday evening, after Erich had confirmed with Maria that she would meet him in town on Saturday, he and Heinz went to the canteen. Sitting at a table sipping beer, their conversation turned to the upcoming wedding.

"I realized Irma is a very fine person," Erich began. "But why did you decide to do it now?"

"Why not?" argued Heinz. "We have known each other long enough; she feels she can support herself, she wanted to very much; and besides, I'm very much in love with her."

He took another gulp from the glass and looked off in the distance. Without turning to face Erich, he continued, "It was like a dream seeing her again last Saturday. Just heavenly holding her, smelling her, loving her." His eyes were still transfixed out across the smoke-filled room. "And when I made love to her—oh God, it felt like a startled bevy of quail had just taken off from my inner soul."

"And how are plans progressing?" Erich asked.

"Fine, I guess. She went to her parents' home Sunday night to make the arrangements. Should be back tomorrow, and we'll know for sure. I made a formal request to the Commandant for permission to be released from duty Saturday so we can have the wedding in the early afternoon.

The next day he was notified that both he and Erich were excused from duty as of eight Saturday morning. That evening he called Irma. She stated plans were complete, and her sister, Rosa, was going to be Matron of Honor.

"How can she?" asked a surprised Heinz.

"Well, she has connections," Irma told him. "Besides, they're being transferred to Berlin shortly, so she'll just leave a little earlier than she had planned."

The following week passed quickly for Heinz and Erich. Their units were driving and commanding a squadron of heavy tanks over rough terrain at high speed. They charged across streams and wooded areas and over ditches and gullies. Once, while crossing, a small bridge collapsed beneath them. "It's better to ford such a stream than take a chance of landing upside down while tumbling off a sagging bridge," warned the instructor.

• • •

Saturday morning Erich and Heinz boarded a camp bus, and in a few minutes were in Augsburg. They purchased tickets for Dinkelsbuhl, passed through the turnstile, and stood waiting on the platform. Maria arrived from Munich and they boarded the northbound express.

They were met in Dinkelsbuhl by one of Irma's relatives, who was driving a newly painted carriage drawn by a pair of neatly groomed plow horses adorned with brightly colored ribbons, crepe paper, and flowers. Driven directly to the church, Maria was shown to the front entrance while Erich and Heinz were guided to a side door. Inside, the two troopers were introduced to the priest, who appeared relieved they had arrived.

When Maria entered the small, darkened church, she noted that a few persons had already arrived and were seated near the front. She went halfway up the center aisle, selected a pew, and knelt to pray. When she sat back, the lights were turned on. Looking around, she was awestruck by the sight she saw. It was the most magnificently adorned places of worship she had ever seen. The delicately carved rococo interior had been painted a gleaming white and possessed a rich, ornamental trim that glistened under a heavy coating of gilt. The many columns located throughout were exquisitely tinted and striped to make them appear as marble. And on the ceiling an elegant painting gave the triumphant illusion of a heavenly host swirling about. Heavy oak pews resting on a floor of polished gray granite had been stained a rich brown and varnished to a high luster. She wondered how the village of Dinkelsbuhl, only slightly larger than Holzheim, could afford such an ornate place of worship.

As the organ played, the priest began the nuptial Mass and then beckoned to Erich and Heinz. The two young troopers emerged from a side door and took their places before him. When Erich looked out over the people gathered to witness this occasion, he thought he recognized some who were present at the reception in Rothenburg. Then again, that seemed so long ago. Perhaps he was confusing them with other people he had encountered at some other time. He had met so many people in the last two years that sometimes faces became indistinct and blended into one another.

When the vestibule door of the church opened revealing Irma and her sister, Rosa, Erich's heart leaped into his throat. It had been nearly two years since he had seen Rosa. He was certain others had noticed his reaction. And, he thought, his heartbeat could be heard by Heinz. As the girls made their way slowly up the aisle, he and Heinz stood rigidly at attention. Heinz was watching his graceful Irma, and Erich was staring, transfixed, at the blue eyes of Rosa. Her gaze had locked onto his the moment she appeared at the rear of the church. As if casting a spell upon herself as well as him, she walked unblinkingly before her sister.

When she approached the front of the church, Erich saw that her softly curled black hair was as lovely as ever. However, life in Paris had not been so kind to her face. Her eyes had lost some of their sparkle, and lines and creases were developing in a skin that used to be so soft and smooth that it intrigued him to touch it. He also detected a certain puffiness about her eyes and beneath her chin.

After the brief service had concluded and the newlyweds were marching down the aisle, Rosa grasped Erich's arm so they could follow. She held it very tightly and very closely. Erich detected an odor of stale cigarette smoke that had replaced the wonderful fragrance that used to emanate from her head of beautiful hair. As they walked past the pew where Maria was standing, Erich winked at Maria, and she smiled back. Rosa squeezed his arm.

Heinz and Irma were taken by carriage to the reception at the Graebner home, a small, one-story building a short distance from the church. Outside the church, Erich introduced Rosa to Maria, and then they began the walk to the reception. Rosa, stating it was difficult for her to walk in a long dress and high heels on the cobblestone street, held onto Erich's arm. Erich, however, held Maria's hand as well.

Tables, benches, and chairs had been placed on the lawn and were tended by neighbors and relatives. Erich, Maria, and Rosa went directly to the bride and groom to wish them luck and happiness, afterwards sitting at a table where they were served beer and sandwiches.

"Well, how's your husband these days?" inquired Erich, looking at Rosa.

"Oh, he's fine," Rosa replied, lighting a cigarette. "Working as hard as ever at the same job." She paused to take a puff from the cigarette. "Being transferred though."

"Really?" Erich gave a surprised look, not wanting to reveal he already knew. "Where to?"

"Berlin."

"You'll probably like Berlin as well as Paris," Erich opined.

"Oh, I suppose," she said with a flick of the wrist, dropping cigarette ash onto the table. "Just as long as they have champagne." She smiled.

Life in Paris had changed Rosa, and Erich was not pleased with what he saw. She had been attending parties and nightclubs like so many officer's wives do that live in the big cities. This was considered appropriate, especially in occupied territory where activities were limited for reasons of safety.

As Erich danced with Rosa, she inquired about the scar on his face. When he explained he had been wounded in Africa, she seemed surprised. "It *is* more hazardous than occupation duty, I suppose," she stated matter-of-factly.

"Would it be all right if I came to Augsburg?" she inquired.

"I'm restricted to camp," he informed her, hoping she would drop the idea of trying to see him. "I get off only on weekends and am seeing a lot of Maria lately.

"Is she the one you used to tell me about?"

"Yes."

When they finished the dance, Rosa gave a big sigh. "Well," she said with a shrug, "the Special Forces does sound exciting."

The party lasted late into the night. Near the end, Irma and Heinz waved as they left to retire to a guest cabin on her uncle's nearby plot of land. Erich, along with several other men, slept in the parent's hay-filled barn while Rosa and Maria were invited to share a bedroom inside the Graebner house.

The next morning after attending an eight o'clock Mass, Irma, Heinz, Maria, and Erich were taken to the railroad station. In the process of saying farewell to the Graebner family, Erich was warmly hugged and ardently kissed by Rosa, much to the dismay of Maria. On the train back to Augsburg, he held Maria's hand all the way. He was very grateful to her for what she was. And he felt so sad and disenchanted with what had become of Rosa.

• • •

The final week of training at Camp Reichstein consisted of four days of strenuous, head-battering *panzer* task force maneuvers and a fifth day, Friday, of cleaning and packing equipment.

Each man was issued a black specially tailored, form-fitting uniform trimmed with red piping. Since the tunic was an open-lapel type, they were given light brown shirts and black neckties. There was a skull and crossbones emblem on their caps as well as on a silver ring each received. The phrase on the new belt buckle read, "My Honor is Loyalty."

Erich was pleasantly surprised to find his Iron Cross emblem had been sewn on his tunic. Later the company commander informed the men that these clothes were to be worn for the graduation ceremony scheduled for Saturday morning. "And from then on as long as you are in dress uniform," he added.

• • •

The graduation ceremony was a brief ritual as the men stood at stiff attention on the large, open drill field. First, Colonel Neumeyer stood on the platform and made them take the Waffen SS oath of allegiance by raising their right hands and repeating it in unison after him:

I swear to you, Adolph Hitler, as Fuhrer and Reich Chancellor, loyalty and bravery. I vow to you, and those you have named to command me, obedience unto death. So help me God.

He ordered them to stand at ease. "You are to be congratulated for the perseverance and determination you have shown in completing this rigorous training that has eliminated 15 percent of your initial number. Now you will be assigned to lead the best-equipped, toughest trained, most efficient fighting forces that exist in the world. Later, when you attach the rank insignia to each other's shoulders, look about you. You will note the caliber of men in your midst. It will make you proud, very proud. Germany is proud of you and expects you to bring her great victories."

He turned, and as he walked down the steps to leave the field, a major called the troops to attention. "One last thing before you are dismissed. As you know, you will be going on leave today. In nine days you will report to Army District Headquarters in Vienna, where you'll be assigned to your next unit. Since you are the elite, the finest of the finest of German manhood, you are expected to leave your seeds with high quality German women for them to nurture before you leave for the front. But be selective. You are to chose young women of highest quality—of strong, Aryan stock. And now, goodbye and good luck!"

As Heinz fastened the epaulets on Erich's shoulders, he observed, "You know, this is an outstanding looking group of men."

"Like Neumeyer said," added Erich. "Standing here they're a fine looking bunch of gentlemen, but what a rough group to turn loose on someone. It really is a shame that they have to be a group of specialists in killing."

"And a bunch of studs," Heinz chuckled.

Before leaving, they shook hands with the many friends they had made as well as with the instructors, who suddenly had become friendly and jovial.

• • •

When Erich got off the train in Munich, he found Maria waiting for him, her intense brown eyes sparkling with pride. It was eleven-thirty, and she had met every train from the west since nine. "How sharp you look, Lieutenant," she said as he kissed her. "But because of duty, I cannot accompany you this weekend."

Erich frowned questioningly.

"But I have arranged to get next weekend off." She took in a deep breath and exhaled. "So I'll meet you at six next Friday evening in Regensburg."

"Oh, good!" he replied.

He took her into his arms and kissed her warmly and then climbed aboard the waiting train. The locomotive, smoking and hissing, slowly began to move.

It was early afternoon in Regensburg when Erich dismounted at the station. This time he carried no weapon except, attached to his belt, a small chrome dagger with a black bone handle that had a silver skull and crossbones imbedded in it. His bag of clothing and other articles was light, so he picked it up and started for Holzheim at a rapid pace. After the strenuous exercise at Camp Reichstein, he felt light on his feet and considered the walk a minor inconvenience.

As he crossed the old stone bridge over the Danube, he heard the roar and whine behind him of a Regensburg that seemed to be working harder and bustling louder than when he was here before. He nodded his head. It was apparent that the magnitude of the war was having a dramatic effect on the entire nation.

A truck stopped and offered him a ride. The truck was returning to a small factory down river after having delivered a load of parts to the Messerschmitt plant in Regensburg. The driver, an older man, was very pleased to give him a lift and was impressed by his uniform. Then he asked about the scar on Erich's face.

"Wounded in Africa," Erich stated with a smile.

"Rommel's *Afrika Korps?*" the driver asked, raising his eyebrows.

"Yes."

Feeling it his patriotic duty to deliver the warrior to his home even if it meant violating the rules of his employer, the driver turned up the narrow, winding road that led north to Holzheim.

The truck stopped in front of the Stecker store, and Erich thanked the driver and hopped out. He went directly inside, where his mother and father were busy assisting a half dozen customers. His presence caused immediate bedlam that lasted for several emotionally filled minutes. Finally, Mrs. Stecker led him by the hand to a rear room while Mr. Stecker began waiting on customers again.

She gave him another hug and then made him sit while she, dabbing her eyes, began scurrying about setting the table and preparing something to eat.

He protested mildly, indicating he wasn't hungry. "Anyone would be hungry after such a long trip," she stated, continuing to bustle about. "Besides, it's time you were served a decent meal anyway."

Occasionally she stopped and looked back at him, wrung her hands, and muttered about how he had been abused. Then, in a slightly disorganized manner, she continued to set the table.

She walked over and looked at him again. "My handsome boy. They've scarred you for life, haven't they?" she complained, still dabbing at her eyes.

"Not really, Mother. It's hardly more than a scratch," he said, trying to comfort her.

To the Volga

The first few days in Holzheim were busy and interesting to Erich and passed rapidly. Toward the end of the week, however, he began counting the days and hours until Maria would arrive. The first evening home after his parents had closed the store, the three of them retired to the living room, where Erich was expected to tell them everything that had happened to him since the last time he was home. It was then they discovered he was no longer Mrs. Stecker's boy, Erich, but a mature man who found it difficult to feel enthusiastic about discussing his role in the war.

"Did you kill anyone?" his father asked eagerly.

"Yes," he replied hesitantly. Then he added, "Sometimes I wonder about it though."

In Holzheim, where things were peaceful and quiet, it was difficult to rationalize his reasons for killing anyone. When he reflected upon such things, it bothered him. But he knew that once back with his unit, all such inhibitions would vanish as he played the game of kill or be killed. His parents pumped some more, so he told them about Paris, Vesuvius, and Capri. Then he countered by asking about Holzheim and the people of the community.

The next morning, by force of habit, he awakened early. The day was breaking and the eastern sky was streaked with a rainbow-hued ribbon that blazed and flamed like the torch of a marathon runner. Standing at the window, he looked out over the moss-covered tile roofs that were still wet with dew. Misty shafts of light created by a sun were struggling to penetrate the thick forest of trees on a hillside that jutted upward a short distance away. After a while he laid back on the bed again, stared at the eggshell-colored ceiling, and vicariously relived some of the treasured times he had spent with

Maria. The tolling of the church bell at seven o'clock woke him again to the realities of life. He would get up and get dressed.

Attending the ten-thirty Mass with his mother and father, he saw by the expressions on their faces that they were exceedingly proud of their soldier son. His trim, black uniform enhanced his handsome physique. And there was the admiring approval of members of the congregation as he walked down the aisle, tall and straight, between his parents. At the conclusion of the services, the worshipers kneeled and joined the priest in prayer for an end to the war and the safe return of their sons, brothers, and fathers. Erich bowed his head, closed his eyes, and prayed with sincere compassion, for he had experienced the bitter taste of battle and knew the dangers these men were facing.

During the week, when he strolled through town, he frequently stopped to talk with people he knew, people who had not seen him for the many months he had been away. Most inquired about the scar on his cheek, asking whether it had occurred in Africa. When told it had, they informed him they had known he was with the *Afrika Korps* and were proud of its accomplishments. They said they clearly remembered when his mother was notified he had been wounded. "We thank God you have returned," most concluded.

When he stopped to visit the village tailor, Mr. Schneider, he was told how well his uniform had been fitted. "Whoever did that was an expert," the little man stated, stroking the sleeve and back.

"It feels good too," Erich replied.

"So, you're an officer in the SS."

"Yes."

The little tailor looked down at the floor. "Some of them don't have a very good reputation, you know," he stated meekly.

"That's the political arm," countered Erich. "I'm with the fighting branch."

The tailor looked up and smiled. "Oh?" Then he added, "They're a fine bunch. Good fighters!"

"Yes," Erich went on. "I'm being assigned to a *panzer* unit when I go back."

When he visited the Trapp farm, he found Mr. Trapp in the barnyard filling a fertilizer tank wagon at the manure pile. He was being assisted by one of the four prisoner-of-war laborers assigned to help with the farm work.

"Yes," stated Mr. Trapp. "Got two Poles and two Frenchmen."

"How are they?" asked Erich.

"Oh, all right. But they don't strain themselves. I can get the Poles to work hard if I press them. But those Frenchmen." He waved his hands as a sign of hopelessness. "They're a lazy bunch."

As Erich looked about, he noted that the premises had the same state of untidiness it possessed as long as he could remember. "Where's Inge?" he asked.

"Oh, she's in the barn tending the calves."

Carefully picking his way through the manure and mud, he made his way to the barn. Upon entering, he halted to permit his eyes to become accustomed to the dark interior. Hearing noises in another section of the structure, he proceeded down a straw-littered aisle way. As he peered into the area that contained the calf pens, he saw Inge in the passionate embrace of a stocky, dark-complexioned man. Her chin was resting on his shoulder, her eyes closed, and her face glowing with the rapt and tranquil joy of an ecstasy trance. The man was nibbling at her neck and vigorously caressing her fat buttocks. Erich quickly retreated a few steps, coughed, and then strolled casually forward again. This time Inge was ladling scoops of grain into metal feeders and the man was distributing fresh straw to the pens.

"Hello, Inge," he began.

"Oh, Erich!" she called. "I heard you were home. So nice of you to come by."

Erich walked over and shook her hand. Other than gaining a bit of weight, she had not changed much. She was wearing rubber boots and had on a well-worn cotton dress that was badly soiled, especially in the areas where her breasts and stomach protruded. The odors she emitted recalled the encounters he had had with her in the past.

"Erich, this is Maurice. He is from France."

The man stepped forward and shook Erich's hand. He said nothing but his face displayed a warm smile. As Inge continued their conversation, Maurice returned to his task of forking straw.

"What do you hear from Max?" Erich asked.

"Oh, he's fine," she replied, putting down the pail and scoop she was holding. "Got a letter from him last week."

"Where is he now?"

"In Russia—by Smolensk." She paused a moment and then added, "He was home on leave last winter."

They talked a few minutes, Erich telling her that Maria would be home Friday night. As he left, she asked if he would come by again before he left.

"Probably," he lied. "Anyway, give my regards to Max when you write him."

"I will," she promised.

It was Friday when Erich got his bicycle out of the back room and checked it over for the trip to Regensburg. After dusting it, applying some oil, and inflating the tires, he rode over to the Juergens' home, where he and Maria's brother, George, prepared her bicycle for the trip. They stopped at the Stecker store, picked up a satchel of sandwiches and cookies Mrs. Stecker had prepared, and then pedaled down the road toward Regensburg.

When Maria stepped off the train, Erich walked briskly over to her, put his arms around her waist, and gave her a brief but affectionate kiss. She then turned to George, who appeared embarrassed as she kissed him on the cheek.

"How's Mother?" she asked, showing some concern.

"Fine. Just fine," George replied.

After tying Maria's small bag onto the rear of her bicycle, they rode off, George sitting on the crossbar of Erich's bicycle. The sun was still shining brightly as they pedaled over the bridge to the north side of the Danube. A short time later, they stopped at a grassy place on the edge of the river to eat the sandwiches and cookies. Looking up the hill high above them, they saw the great structure of *Valhalla*, its facade and columns glowing a rich golden color in the slanting rays of the sun.

"Erich goes to Austria when his leave is up," George told Maria enthusiastically. "Going to ride in a tank."

"Yes, I know," Maria said calmly.

"Are you going someplace else when you go back?"

"No, I've got a few more weeks of training to finish before I'm reassigned."

"Oh," George responded, somewhat disappointed.

They talked for a few more minutes and then started for Holzheim. To Maria it was obvious George was proud to be in the company of two members of the armed forces and pleased to converse with them the way he did. They made two more rest stops as they ascended the hills along the narrow road. Instead of sitting down to rest, however, they stood beside their bicycles, talking and watching the big, red sun slowly lower itself to the horizon. The air was filled with a pungent odor from blooming wild carrots and the oozing resins of pines, and the tree frogs and crickets chirruped a continuous melody.

At the Stecker store, both Mr. and Mrs. Stecker hugged Maria.

"My, how trim you look in uniform," Mrs. Stecker remarked, stepping back to admire it

"We have rolls and coffee ready," Mr. Stecker bubbled. "How about having some with us?"

"No, thanks," Maria smiled. "Mother's waiting and I must get home to her."

Erich escorted her and George to the door.

"Goodbye," Maria called back over her shoulder. "We'll see you tomorrow."

Erich kissed her and watched as she and George walked up the street toward the Juergens' home.

The next morning Maria returned to the store for some groceries. Erich volunteered to carry them back to the house for her. The laundry she had done was hanging on a clothesline in the backyard where George was pulling weeds in the garden. The first task, Maria decided, was to get some stew meat on the stove to cook while she continued to clean the house.

"I don't know about Mother," Maria stated, displaying a degree of concern. "She just doesn't do the job of housekeeping she used to."

Erich moved the furniture about as she swept and dust mopped. "What seems to be the trouble?" he asked, raising his eyebrows.

"Well, I don't know. She just isn't as thorough as she used to be. George says he helps when he can, but she just seems to be so tired."

"You know," Erich replied, "she's approaching an age where people begin to slow down.

"Well, maybe," Maria sighed. "But she has never been one to compromise on neatness."

When they had finished, Maria fixed some tea and they went out on the front porch. Before sitting down on the top step, Erich bounced his foot a couple times on the warped center step. "Still squeaks as loud as ever," he said with a grin.

"Yes, I test it myself every once in a while. It reminds me of you," she said, leaning her head against his shoulder.

"We'll have to remember it tonight when I bring you home."

She squeezed his arm.

Several people walking past stopped to chat. They told Erich how well he looked in his uniform and asked Maria where hers was. "In the closet while I'm doing the housework," she answered. One couple asked to see it. When she brought it out, they looked it over carefully, feeling the fabric as they scrutinized it.

At noon Mrs. Juergens came home for lunch. Erich kissed Maria as he left, promising her he would return at two so they could go for a walk.

That evening the Juergens were dinner guests at the Steckers. When they finished eating, they sat around the table for a time talking about Holzheim and how the war was affecting the residents. Suddenly, during a brief lull in the conversation, Mrs. Juergens stated that it was time she return home. "I've had a strenuous week at the post office," she said. "Besides, I must get up early to go to eight o'clock Mass with Maria so she can get back to her camp on time." As she rose to her feet, she turned to her son. "Come, George, we'll go now."

Maria said nothing, but noted how unusually tired her mother appeared.

During the evening, friends of the family dropped in to exchange greetings with Maria and Erich. Most stayed but a few minutes, making a sandwich with the sliced sausage and bread Mrs. Stecker had set out. Some drank beer or wine. Everyone wished the young couple health, happiness, and a safe return.

At ten-thirty Erich escorted Maria down the narrow street to her home. Thousands of stars glittered in the clear sky above and a full, blue-white moon, almost directly overhead, made short shadows that bounced along and chased them over the irregular surface of the cobblestones. At the Juergens home they went up onto the porch, taking care to step over the squeaky middle step. Erich held her close as he kissed her, all the time wondering when the next opportunity would occur to hold her like this. After a moment, he made a whispered suggestion, "Let's sit down for a few minutes."

When they were seated on the top step, he took her hand. "You know, it may be a long time before we do this again."

"I know," she answered dejectedly.

They sat for nearly an hour, saying little while looking out over the empty street and listening to the songs of crickets and frogs. Once in a while they heard a faint burst of laughter that escaped from the Holzheim Tavern two blocks away. And each time Erich drew her over to him and kissed her on the nose or cheek, Maria smiled. It made her feel safe, warm, and contented.

• • •

The Steckers rose early, had breakfast, and dressed carefully. They were proud of their son and wanted him to be proud of them on the beautiful Sunday that found the family together again. Erich wore his complete uniform, including the gleaming dress dagger and silver ring. And he had shined his boots to a high gloss. As they made their way slowly down the street, greeting and chatting with friends they encountered, the Juergens joined them. At the church door they were welcomed by Father Kurz, who shook their hands and stated that Holzheim could be justly proud of its contribution to the war effort.

Once inside, the two families filed into a pew in such a way that Erich and Maria sat side by side. They made an impressive pair as they stood or kneeled at various times during the services. Afterwards, they lingered in front of the church as the aroma of hot wax and burning palm leaves drifted out past the large, open oak doors. As they chatted with the many people who had come to know them through the years, Erich looked around. It was evident the war had taken away a goodly portion of the male population. This concerned him. He knew the struggle was far from over and that many more young men would be taken in the future.

• • •

It was a sad and tearful event when Erich and Maria mounted their bicycles. Mrs. Stecker, fighting to hold back the tears, clung to Erich. She did not want to see him leave again. The last absence had been so long, and when he returned scarred, she knew he had suffered from his wounds. He finally steeled himself with a discipline the army had instilled in him and stated simply and sternly, "Mother, we must go."

It was a beautiful Sunday morning and the crooked macadam road offered a pleasant ride to Regensburg. The countryside was quiet, the dew had lifted, and an occasional deer or squirrel watched as Erich and Maria glided past. Occasionally, they heard the faint ringing of a church bell from a distant village or saw a lazy curl of smoke climbing skyward from the chimney of a far-off house. They listened to the birds singing, larks taking flight, and the noisy warning of crows and jays. The scene was like an idyll, an island of tranquility, where all the agitation of a violent world was suspended. Inhaling the cool, clear air with deep breaths, they felt a flood of exhilaration.

The train ride to Munich was uneventful. However, while passing through the marshaling yards as they approached the depot, they saw for the first time the bomb damage that had been inflicted upon their homeland. Crews were removing twisted rails, filling craters, and repairing the roadbed.

"How did this happen?" Maria asked, wrinkling her forehead.

"Probably some British bombers—raiders that slipped through our defenses at night," Erich replied in a calm but serious voice.

She stayed at his side until the Salzburg Express arrived.

"I'll write to you as soon as I get another permanent address," Erich promised.

"I'll look for your letter everyday," she vowed.

Just before passing through the turnstile, he grabbed her in a warm embrace. "Be good, my darling," he whispered. "I love you very much."

"I love you with all my heart," she assured him, choking up as she spoke. "And always will."

He looked down into her moist, brown eyes. "Take care of yourself, and don't visit Munich at night. I don't want a stray bomb to hurt you."

"I won't."

When he looked up, he saw dozens of servicemen, some in black uniforms, bidding friends, relatives, and sweethearts farewell. Turning his attention to Maria, he saw that she was crying. He kissed her again, tasting the salt from her tears, and then turned and walked briskly through the turnstile.

• • •

It was late when he stepped off the train at the gray stone *Westbahnhof in* Vienna. After trying several hotels in the vicinity, he finally located a room in a shabby inn. The room was neat and clean but had a musty odor associated with buildings that had not been refurbished for many years. He went to the bathroom down the hall and then climbed into an old brass bed with clean, white sheets and a feather-filled comforter.

At first the sheets felt cool, however, in a few minutes the comforter made him too warm, so he pushed it away. Stimulated by the activities of the past few days and the uncertainty of the future, he did not sleep well. He arose early, had a quick breakfast, and then boarded a streetcar on *Mariahilfer Strasse*.

At District Headquarters, located in a converted classroom on *Shillerplatz*, he checked in and was told a camp bus would depart from the front at eleven o'clock. That was nearly two hours away, so he walked to the opera house and slowly circled its exterior before peering inside the front doors. As he gazed at the delicate chandeliers that graced the red-carpeted lobby, he heard the voice of an elderly Vienna citizen behind him. "Beautiful, isn't it?"

"Very," Erich replied, turning to face the man.

"Perhaps you would enjoy visiting the burial crypt of the Hapsburgs," the man suggested, pointing down the street. "It's located beneath the Kapuzine Church just a couple blocks away."

"I'd like that," Erich replied, thanking the man for the suggestion.

When he entered the dimly lighted structure, he saw nothing indicating a crypt, but a few people were kneeling among the pews, beaded rosaries hanging from their clasped hands. As he turned to leave, he encountered a rotund, middle-aged woman. When he asked about the crypt, she replied, "Oh, yes. Go into the side door just around the corner."

"Thank you," he said, replacing his cap.

Inside, he was met by an elderly, soft-spoken gentleman who took tiny steps and breathed noisily. After leading Erich through a long corridor, the old man turned on the crypt lights and pointed down the stairs. As Erich descended into the dimly lighted complex of rooms, he was aware of an odor that seemed present wherever bodies were stored. It reminded him of post-mortem classes at Heidelberg University. He made his way slowly among many bronze vaults containing the remains of past rulers, reading the inscriptions as he went. Among the coffins of several children, he found those of an assassination victim and a royal person who had committed suicide.

When he emerged, the old man was waiting for him. "You must see the heart crypt too," he wheezed.

"Oh? What's that?" Erich asked.

"Well, when they embalm a body, they must remove the inside organs."

Erich, his curiosity aroused, nodded assent.

"So, they have the hearts of these people in the crypt at the St. Augustine Church."

"Oh?" questioned Erich, arching his eyebrows.

"And their intestines are in St. Stephen's Cathedral."

"They *are* scattered around, aren't they?" Erich said, shaking the old gentleman's hand before departing.

When he arrived back at *Schillerplatz*, he found a gathering of soldiers in black uniforms. Seeing Heinz, he went directly to him.

"Erich! Erich, my friend!" Heinz shouted happily.

"You look as if the leave did you some good," Erich replied.

"Living with a girl like Irma would be good for anybody."

"You really enjoyed yourself?"

"Oh, it was wonderful!" confirmed Heinz.

The convoy of camp buses drove to the other side of town, crossed the Danube Canal, and headed east past an amusement park. Erich and Heinz, sitting together, halted their conversation to listen to someone a few seats behind explain that the gigantic Ferris wheel that dominated the park was the largest in the world.

"Maybe we can take a ride on it," suggested Heinz.

"Fine," agreed Erich. Then he added, "If we can get loose."

"Just wish Irma was here to go with me," sighed Heinz.

They crossed the Danube River, and the buses turned into a fenced compound. When an armed Wehrmacht sentry came aboard the bus Erich and Heinz were in, he walked the length of the aisle, scrutinizing the passengers. Then he returned to the front of the bus, telling the driver to proceed as he stepped back onto the ground.

Upon reaching the central part of the camp where several rows of barracks were located, they dismounted. A captain in a green uniform directed their attention to the mess hall. "When you have finished eating, come back here. You will find rosters posted on this bulletin board that will give you your barracks assignments."

• • •

Erich stood facing the platoon he been assigned to lead. He wore a semi-gloss black helmet with white runic SS letters stenciled on each side. In a black leather holster on his hip was a newly issued *Luger* pistol. He had introduced himself to the twenty men who stood waiting four abreast in a sea of black uniforms that covered the large drill field. When he looked around, he noticed Heinz standing in front of a platoon a short distance away. A colonel, standing tall and slender, appeared on a platform before the assemblage. "Commanders!" he shouted, using a speaker microphone. "Bring your men to attention!"

"Greetings, men! I salute you!" the colonel began as he scrutinized the field of young men before him. "My name is Colonel Stauffer. Your brigade, The Death Head Brigade, has three regiments—the Black Hawk Regiment, the Black Cobra Regiment, and the Black Dragon Regiment. Each regiment has 165 tanks and a large number of support troops." He paused to look out over the sea of young men facing him. Then he said, "I am your regimental commander, and it is my proud duty to inform you that you have been assigned to the Black Hawk Regiment of this SS Death Head Brigade, the best unit in the German army. As of now, people don't know we exist. But in six months, I assure you, the entire world will be well aware of our presence."

The soldiers continued to stand at attention in the warm sun, the black uniforms absorbing its heat until perspiration was showing on their upper lips and foreheads.

"We will leave tomorrow for the Eastern Front. You men represent the rolling tank crews—drivers, gunners, and commanders. The rest of the men as well as all of our equipment awaits us in the east. Tomorrow we will leave to meet them."

The colonel paused for a moment, trying to think if he had forgotten anything. Satisfied he had not, he continued. "Now, you have the rest of the day to pack, check your equipment, and become acquainted. See you tomorrow!"

Erich marched his platoon to the shade of a nearby tree and had them sit down. Many clusters of men were scattered about the area, some beneath other trees, some sitting on bleachers across the way, and many standing in groups on the field. As he looked at the young men before him, some already decorated from previous action, he asked if they felt well and were ready for action.

"Yes, sir!" the troopers answered with a resounding reply.

Then he asked about their clothing and equipment. Sergeant Kohlmann informed him they had ample clothing and more was waiting in the east. "Each driver has been issued a *Walther P-38* pistol," Kohlmann added. "And each gunner a *Schmeisser* machine pistol."

"Have they been able to test fire them, yet?" Erich asked.

"Not yet," Kohlmann informed him. "But I plan to take care of that this afternoon."

It was fortunate for Erich he had been assigned the rugged, ten-year veteran, Sergeant Kohlmann, as his platoon sergeant. Albert Kohlmann, tall and slender with piercing blue eyes, the bastard son of a Hamburg prostitute, had spent much of his childhood on the back streets of that wild city. At the age of eighteen, he had enlisted in the army and found it to be the first real family he had ever known. Although he had little education, he had learned to understand the ways and wiles of human beings much better than most. And he had been in combat on the Eastern Front much of the past year with the 94th Infantry Division.

"Any questions?" Erich asked the platoon.

None were asked. He smiled and then in a firm voice commanded Sergeant Kohlmann to get the men into formation. Kohlmann quickly formed the platoon, turned around to face Erich, and then clicked his heels and saluted.

Erich returned the salute. "See you tomorrow morning," he snapped.

· · ·

Early the next morning they were loaded aboard a train that had been brought to the far end of the camp. The officers were assigned to compartmentalized coaches and the enlisted men loaded into boxcars that had a layer of straw scattered on the floor. Before boarding, Erich checked to see that his men were properly situated. Since each boxcar held thirty men, his platoon was located in two adjacent cars.

"Apparently the Transportation Corps doesn't recognize any special privileges for the elite," Heinz remarked as he and Erich returned to their coach.

"No," agreed Erich. "This is an ordinary troop train."

The marshaling yard in Vienna was a beehive of activity. Empty trains were arriving from the east and loaded ones coming from the west. The man in charge, the *bahnhofmeister*, used switch engines to shuffle, regroup, and organize trains according to military requisitions before dispatching them to various fronts.

Thirty minutes after arriving at the yards, the Black Hawk train was placed on the main line for departure. Initially, it sped over rails that had been laid across the flat land of the fertile Danube valley. At Pressburg, however, the electric engine was traded for a steam locomotive to accommodate the abrupt change in landscape to wooded hills and steep river valleys. The speed was noticeably slower as the train wound its way around numerous curves and over dozens of trestles. By nightfall the engine, blowing its squeaky whistle heartily, was struggling to haul its human cargo up the narrow Laborec River Gorge toward Lupkow Pass.

Late in the night, the train reached the summit and was shunted onto a siding so the men could eat. The officers ate in a dining car with table linens. The enlisted men walked through a line at a temporary outside kitchen that had been erected to take care of the numerous troop trains coming through.

Seated at a table in the dining car, Erich looked out at the enlisted men gathered at tables and benches beneath a scattering of glaring light bulbs. Then he looked at his friend, Heinz, sitting across the table from him. He wondered how many had preceded his friend, sitting at this table on that chair, and where they might be at this moment. Suddenly, he was startled by a voice stating the train would depart in ten minutes.

For a brief moment before boarding their coach, he and Heinz looked over the vast panorama of multicolored shadows interspersed with small clusters of twinkling lights that were spread over the valley before them.

"Sure looks like a long way down there," ventured Erich.

"We'll soon find out when this rattler gets underway," chuckled Heinz.

The next morning the train stopped at the rail yard in Lvov to change the mountain climbing engine for a faster, flatland locomotive. The yard was bustling with trains loaded with troops, equipment, and ammunition. While there, the men were fed breakfast and had time to wash and shave. During their brief stay, the Black Hawk men saw a heavily laden hospital train receive westbound priority to pass swiftly through the yard. As it passed, they observed through the open doors that the sick and wounded were lying in rows of multitiered beds. Bandages, splints, and casts were numerous and prominent.

Hills covered with birch, aspen, and scrub oak trees gradually gave way to a flat land of rich, black soil planted in wheat—a vast steppe of featureless terrain with a seemingly endless horizon. Erich had read that on a overcast day such terrain caused one to lose all sense of direction. Great stretches of the wheat fields, however, had been burned to an ugly black, either ignited by the flames of battle or deliberately fired by the retreating Russians as part of their scorched earth policy. Although the distance to Kiev was not great, it took twice the normal time to get there. The troop train had to stop numerous times to give right-of-way to higher priority gasoline, ammunition, and hospital trains. Each time it was sidetracked, the men got out and walked about, requiring the platoon sergeants to make a head count before moving on.

After passing through Kiev, the rail traffic was no longer heavy, and signs of recent battle were everywhere. Frequently, the train had to slow when traversing a segment of new roadbed or a reconstructed bridge. Looking out the window, Erich noted that the nearby fields were laced with vehicle tracks. *Similar to North Africa,* he thought, *except the camel's thorn bush and sand had been replaced by lush grain rooted deep in moist, black soil.*

Fifty miles short of Karkov the train pulled onto a siding. It was an open air supply depot where many men and vast quantities of equipment lined both sides of the tracks for a considerable distance. As the Black Hawk men disembarked, the locomotive was turned around and attached to the other end of the train. It started back before the men had time to assemble.

Each platoon leader was given a list of five tanks he was to command. Erich marched his men down one of the rows of vehicles until he came to the numbered vehicles on his list. They were new, seventy-two ton *Tiger* tanks that had been painted a dull black. White numbers had been stenciled on the side of each gun turret, and an attacking black hawk had been painted on a rectangular red field across the rear of the vehicles. They were battle-ready, filled with gasoline and ammunition, and fully prepared and tested by the brigade's ordnance personnel.

As the crews swarmed over the tanks, an ordnance sergeant walked up to Erich and saluted.

"Very good-looking equipment," Erich complimented.

"They're ready for action," stated the sergeant. "Can go seventy miles before you have to fill them with gasoline again." He cleared his throat and then added, "Of course, that's on a good road."

"How far is the front?" Erich asked.

"About a hundred miles from here."

"How long have you been here, Sergeant?"

"Two weeks, sir. We came with the tanks and half-tracks. Got them ready to go. I guess they thought they might be needed to drive the Russians out of Karkov."

"Yes, I heard there was quite a battle there," shouted Erich, trying to be heard above the roar of engines the crews had started.

Erich climbed aboard the tank driven by Sergeant Kohlman. Placing his headphones in position, he talked to each of the crews in turn. When confirmed that all was working properly, he had them drive forward a few feet and then back again into position. He felt pleased and confident with his new command.

That evening, as the platoon sat around a small fire made of packing crates and listened to Sergeant Kohlmann play his accordion, Erich walked over to check on them. He waited for Kohlmann to finish playing "Lili Marlene" before he spoke.

"I'm pleased to see you are becoming well acquainted," he began.

"The train ride did most of it," responded Kohlmann.

Erich grinned. "Tomorrow we enter the battle zone. I know several of you have been in combat already, but Sergeant Kohlmann was in this area before. I'd like to have him inform you about fighting the Russians here. Can you do that, Sergeant?"

Kohlmann nodded and was about to rise to his feet as Erich walked off

"Well," he began, setting his accordion aside. "These Russians are a tough lot. And you shouldn't trust any of them. Never go anywhere alone, and always have a backup."

He paused, looked around to see that Erich was gone, and then continued. "And another thing. Their standards of sanitation is very primitive. For example, if you use one of their toilets, piss in spurts. That'll keep the bugs from swimming upstream."

He was waiting for a reaction when one of the troopers asked, "How about the women?"

"You won't find any beauties here. They're all in the army or working for the government. The ones you'll see are sturdy *hausfrau* peasants, either farmers or factory workers. They take a bath and change their clothes once at the beginning of each season." He looked around again and then, in a lower voice, said, "If you get involved with one of them, it'll be so bad you'll have to crawl off over her head."

The members of the platoon slapped their thighs and roared with laughter.

"That's enough of that!" Kohlmann concluded. "Now, go to your tent and get some rest!"

The next morning, as the long convoy of the Black Hawk Regiment rolled along on the broken macadam road toward Karkov, Erich, standing in the lead tank of his platoon, felt certain his men were ready for battle. Most were combat veterans, their equipment was the best in the world, their tanks were loaded with fuel and ammunition, and each carried a case of canned pork and beans to sustain them for several days.

Captain Hofmiller, the company commander, had given each of his four platoon leaders a map and showed them the route they were to follow. "We will be given ample air cover," he had told them. "But beyond Karkov, we may run into artillery fire."

The convoy reminded Erich of those he had seen in Africa. This force appeared much more formidable, however, with its greater concentration of trooper-laden half-tracks and heavy *Tiger* tanks. There were fewer self-propelled eighty-eights since each of the tanks was equipped with one, although it could not point skyward to ward off an air attack. He had been told that the greater speed and mobility of this brigade plus the overwhelming strength of the German Air Force in this area made them less susceptible to attack from the air.

● ● ●

The city of Karkov was a great mass of ruins. The boulevard down which they were directed by military police was wide enough, so the fallen buildings along either side did not present an obstacle. But the side streets were completely blocked by great heaps of rubble—twisted steel beams, bricks, mortar, and broken concrete. And the odor of the smoke-stained debris combined with the putrid stench of decaying corpses buried in it made for a sickening mixture to breathe.

Erich, standing in his command hatchway, could not see any remaining structure with a roof. He had seen destruction in Africa but nothing on such a massive scale involving a modern industrial city. A number of citizens appeared, seemingly from nowhere. They stood and watched with awe as the impressive column of Black Hawks rumbled along the boulevard. Occasionally, a battered building crumbled and fell in a great puff of yellow dust as vibration created by the heavy track-laying vehicles completed what bombs and fires had started.

On the outskirts of the city, the column halted so the vehicles could be refueled. As the men dismounted to relieve themselves in the ditch beside the road, they could hear the distant rumble of artillery fire.

Heinz walked over to Erich. "Do you hear what I hear?"

"Yes," replied Erich. "And we will hear it without letup until we are pulled back for a rest."

"Or killed," added Heinz solemnly.

"Or killed," Erich agreed, as others gathered to listen.

At that moment, a squadron of planes appeared on the horizon behind them. The crews of the anti-aircraft eighty-eights prepared for action, but relaxed again as the planes were identified as Heinkel bombers. When they had passed, Captain Hofmiller gathered his lieutenants around his command car and unfolded a battle map on the hood of the vehicle. "We meet up with the rest of the brigade here," he said, pointing with his finger. "Then our regiment will cross the Donets River here and clear the north side of the valley. The other two regiments will stay on this side and push along parallel with us."

He looked up to note any reaction. Then he asked, "Is everything working all right yet?"

The four lieutenants looked at one another and then back at him. They nodded in the affirmative.

"Fine! Mount up and stay alert!"

The four clicked their heels and saluted.

In a few minutes they came to an area where progress was slow. The road was nearly obliterated, and the fields on either side had been churned into a sea of water-filled craters. It was testimony of the writhing agony this sector had suffered during three months of seesaw fighting. Smashed tanks, trucks, and guns stretched as far as the men could see. Rifles, helmets, gas masks, and mess kits littered the area. And yellow tape with white signs identifying mine fields were everywhere.

Nearing the Donets, the Black Hawk men found batteries of German artillery covered with camouflage nets firing from ravines. As swarms of *Messerschmitts* and *Focke-Wulfs* prowled the skies overhead, convoys of supply trucks bounced along as fast as the rough terrain would permit. An occasional shell burst spouted a geyser of water near the pontoon bridge spanning the river.

Near the bridge, the vehicles paused for a final refueling before crossing. With the engines silent, the men could clearly hear the roar of a tremendous battle being fought. Dead animals, their skins taut with the bloat of decay, lay among the wrecked machines of war, reminding Erich that armies on both sides relied heavily upon animals for transport. A pall of acrid cordite smoke hung over the area, stinging the nostrils of those who were forced to breathe it.

Sergeant Kohlmann walked a short distance and picked up a scuffed, mud-spattered jack boot. Noting something rattling inside, he tipped it up by the heel. A remnant of green uniform, several small bones, and an amount of liquefied flesh poured from it. He shook his head and tossed it into a water-filled crater.

• • •

Slowly, the heavy *Tiger* tanks of Colonel Stauffer's Black Hawk Regiment were coaxed across the flexing pontoon bridge. Once on the other side, they sped into a formation of two battle columns supported by infantry in armored half-tracks and personnel carriers. Several members of the Engineer Battalion remained on the bridge to dislodge floating debris along with a number of bodies that had become wedged against the pontoons. The first half of the regiment, including Captain Hofmiller's company, took an inland road that paralleled the river. The other half drove along a trail near the riverbank.

After traveling two miles, Captain Hofmiller ordered his men off the road and into a deep ravine. They were ordered to space themselves in battle formation facing the front and then told to cover their tanks and half-tracks with camouflage nets.

That evening all officers in Colonel Stauffer's command were ordered to report to his headquarters tent to learn of the next day's battle plan. While waiting for them to get seated on folding chairs, he, tall, slender, and erect, paced slowly back and forth. The lapels of his neatly pressed black uniform were decorated with the skull and crossbones emblems, and a *Luger* pistol and black dagger were strapped to his waist. When satisfied they were ready, he turned to face them. "This is going to be a test of your ability to fight the enemy," he began, shouting to be heard above the overhead hiss, whine, and sizzle of German artillery shells being fired at the Russian lines. "German troops are dug in a short distance ahead. This very ground was taken early last winter, but cold weather immobilized our machines and transport, so we were driven back to the outskirts of Karkov. We didn't get winter oil for our equipment, and the machines simply wouldn't work. Even the hydraulic fluid in our howitzers congealed." He cleared his throat and continued. "The Russians have rounded up more troops, got better equipment, and have been putting up quite a fight. As you have noticed, the *Wehrmacht* has recaptured nearly all the ground that was lost—but at a big price. They buried sixty thousand of their troops to do it. And now they are weary and their equipment is badly worn. They lack the zest and initiative for a needed lightning thrust. That's where we come in."

Using a pointer, he turned to a map on a board behind him. "Here's the plan. We'll have two columns that will rip through their lines and link up afterward. Then we'll go after that damnable artillery. I want you to capture as much equipment as you can."

He turned back to face them. "Your equipment will be fully serviced tonight. And guards will be posted." He snapped his head. "Now let's show the world what we can do!"

The men all rose and saluted. The colonel returned the salute, jabbed his hand into the air and shouted, "Heil, Hitler!"

"Heil, Hitler!" came the resounding reply.

Before dawn, several companies were ordered to mount their vehicles. When the engines were started, they created a dense pall of black smoke that covered the area and made several troopers cough and gag. As some the tanks moved slowly forward into position, Erich was certain all troops in the vicinity had been alerted by the low roar of the powerful diesel engines coupled with the clanking, grinding, and squeaking of the track-laying machines. By the time they reached the entrenched *Wehrmacht* line, artillery fire from both sides had intensified. Some of it was falling among them.

Erich stood in his *Tiger*, listening intently for the order to move forward. The shells were falling dangerously close, and he knew his platoon must move out or they most certainly would be hit. Standing motionless in the gray morning dimness, he watched the fog lift as the infantry moved forward to protect engineers searching for mines. When a thin streak of red penciled the eastern sky, the *Stuka* dive bombers appeared and began to dive bomb the enemy lines. His mouth was dry, and he tried to breathe his heaviness out upon the morning, but it wouldn't leave him.

When the order finally came, the engines of his tanks were started, and they lurched forward, leaving wide tracks across the trenches, ditches, and barbed wire that jutted out in all directions across a no-man's-land of churned soil. Erich was in the center tank of the five he commanded. Heinz's platoon was to his left. Artillery shells were raining down, but he saw no evidence of any tanks being hit. Suddenly they were stopped at the brink of a tank trap, a very deep ditch with a sloped surface on their side but a vertical wall on the opposite side.

The tanks opened fire with their machine guns and eighty-eights to furnish covering fire as the engineers and infantry worked with shovels to cut several sloped surfaces in the opposite wall. In a few minutes their work was completed, and Erich ordered Sergeant Kohlmann to try it. The heavy *Tiger* sank deeply into the loose soil, but soon pulled itself up to the flat area on the other side. He then ordered the remaining four tanks under his command to follow. In a few minutes, Heinz's platoon came along. Then a gush of armor flooded the field, machine-gunning and crushing all that stood in its way.

Erich was ordered to charge straight ahead while others fanned out to trap a large force of bewildered enemy, most of whom cowered in their holes and trenches as the great wave of machines rolled over them. Those who did not readily surrender were quickly disposed of by eager infantrymen who were jubilant with the flush of success. The Black Hawk Regiment had knifed through the enemy defenses and was determined to drive a deep wedge into their line by nightfall.

Erich's heart sank as he saw one of his tanks take a direct hit from a large caliber Russian artillery shell. The tank was enveloped in a cloud of smoke and showered with hot fragments. Fortunately, the shell was of the explosive type rather than of solid, armor-piercing steel. Since the crew was locked inside, neither they nor the tank was harmed. But Erich knew the crew would have impaired hearing for several hours.

With a suddenness that startled Erich, a sharp voice began barking over his headphone. "All tank commanders! All tank commanders!" It was from Colonel Stauffer's headquarters. "You are to proceed forward—roll forward with all possible speed. Roll forward to silence enemy artillery! Roll forward to get out from under the rain of hell that is chewing up Black Hawk infantry!"

As the clanking *panzer* line bolted ahead, some infantrymen clambered aboard the tanks. Most, however, got into half-tracks that roared up from behind. The platoon leaders stood in their command hatches, the upper portion of their bodies exposed, as they guided the tanks and urged other troops forward. Overhead, supporting *Messerschmits* and *Stukas* were seeking out the enemy artillery positions.

After traveling half of the three miles to the artillery positions, the troublesome shelling ceased. When they arrived at the site, the Russian artillery units had withdrawn, taking the field pieces with them. They had left a few dazed women huddling in an earth-covered shelter as well as the bodies of four dead artillerymen.

"They sure left in a hurry," observed Sergeant Kohlmann, looking out over the vast sea of waving grain before them.

"What in hell are the women doing here?" asked one of Erich's gunners standing on top of the *Tiger* watching the Black Hawk infantry search the area.

"Some Russians bring their wives," Kohlmann answered. "They cook, mend their clothes, and even dig trenches for them."

"My God!" sighed the gunner. Then he asked, "How do you know this?"

"I fought the Russians in Poland before, and right here last year," came the reply.

Erich dismounted and watched as a group of Black Hawk infantry rounded up surrendering Russian soldiers. Other infantry units were waiting in their half-tracks for further orders. He holstered his pistol and turned to go back to his tank when he heard Heinz shout, "An observation plane spotted the artillery being set up in a ravine just ahead."

"Let's go!" he shouted, climbing into his command hatch. "We'll catch them before they can park their caissons!"

But before he could slip his headphones over his black hat, he heard a muffled rumble of twelve distinct explosions. He knew the Russians were already dug in well enough to commence firing.

"Move!" he yelled into the microphone. "Move forward fast!"

Squatting low in his hatch as the shells came in, he counted them—ten, eleven, twelve. Standing up, he saw a loaded half track on his right side get hit, scattering pieces of the machine and parts of bodies over a large area. Some remnants of flesh had hit his *Tiger,* and some splatters of blood were on his hat. He thought of Schumacher and how he had been splattered with his young friend's blood in Africa. The accuracy of the Russian's first salvo amazed him. Usually, one gun fires three shots before the rest zero in.

The *panzer* unit moved quickly forward to a dirt road forming two columns, one breaking to the left, the other to the right. More shells came in but landed harmlessly behind them. The two armored columns got on parallel roads nearly a mile apart that led to the east. Then, keeping abreast of each other, they sped forward. Any suspicious building or arrangement of farm machinery was raked with fire as it came into view. Some confused peasants set fire to their buildings and crops while others attempted to put out the fires set by the retreating Russian army.

When the two columns were ordered to leave the roads and link up, they found they were behind the Russian artillery. A dazed and tired enemy quickly capitulated. The Black Hawk Regiment had captured a dozen one-hundred-millimeter guns and their crews plus more than a thousand infantry soldiers. As Erich stood and watched the Black Hawk infantry disarm the perspiring Russians, Heinz came over to him. "Are you all right, Erich?" he asked.

"Oh, yes. Fine. How about you?"

"Lost one of my tanks back there."

"What happened to the crew?" Erich asked.

"I don't know." replied Heinz. "The last I saw of them, they were scrambling out of it."

"We'll probably find out when we stop for the night."

They walked over to inspect the captured artillery pieces. After noting the well-dug pits housing the weapons, Erich looked up and said, "You know, it must have taken a full day to dig these."

"I've been thinking the same thing," observed Heinz. "They probably have some more a few miles farther on."

"I'm glad we got the guns, anyway."

• • •

The Black Hawk Regiment charged down the fertile Donets Basin day after day, over-whelming all resistance with its tremendous firepower, great mobility, and enthusiastic troops of superior quality. It could have advanced at twice the speed if the supply lines could have kept up with it. Its rapid firing weapons used considerable quantities of ammunition in each engagement, and the heavy *Tiger* tanks consumed dreadful amounts of fuel. The troops were told that it was the results that counted, however, and they were achieving the desired results that permitted the generals to move the pins on their maps everyday.

Yet there was a developing problem of great concern to Colonel Stauffer. Each day the regiment lost some men and machines, and each day he requested replacements to fill the growing gaps in his command. But none arrived. One afternoon as he stood with Captain Hofmiller looking out over a vast field of waist-high grain at the ever present glow of battle on the somber, endless horizon, he voiced his concern. "The Black Hawks can beat any military force on earth. And we advance mile after mile but seemingly get nowhere. For every village we capture, there is another within sight. For every river we cross, there flows another just ahead. We are merely swallowed up by the immensity of the land."

"Perhaps the Russians will capitulate," suggested Captain Hofmiller.

"Perhaps," Stauffer replied, shaking his head. Then he gazed into the distance. "But by God, give me the tanks and gasoline and the Black Hawk Regiment will meet the Japanese in Vladivostok!" He snapped his head to emphasize the point.

• • •

It was a sweltering August day as Colonel Stauffer sat at the portable desk in his headquarters tent poring over the sparsely detailed maps he had been issued while his regiment was halted to resupply and regroup for the next push. Most of the information on the maps had been gleaned from aerial photographs obtained from the *Luftwaffe*. He knew the only paved roads across the vast Ukranian steppe lay between major cities. But most of the country he had been traversing was serviced only by deeply rutted dirt trails that were either extremely dusty or impassably slippery with mud, depending on the weather. Much of the time he found it easier operate his machines across the smoother grain fields.

He heard a motorcycle stop out front and then his aide stepped inside carrying a slender mail pouch. "A courier just delivered this, sir," the aide reported. "Said he was instructed to wait for an answer."

Stauffer undid the straps of the pouch and withdrew a brown envelope. When he opened it, he found a directive from the brigade headquarter:

HEADQUARTERS
WAFFEN SS DEATHHEAD BRIGADE
To: Colonel Siegfried Stauffer, Commander, Black Hawk Regiment
From: General Manfred von Bludhardt, Commanding

The Black Hawk Regiment is to leave the Donets Basin and take the most direct route to the Volga River. It is to reach the Volga River in the shortest possible time.

Your requisitions for personnel, equipment, and supplies are being filled immediately.

Need immediate response.

Four maps with much greater detail than those he had been using were included.

Stauffer penned a response note on Black Hawk stationery, stating the Black Hawk Regiment will proceed with all possible haste and that it should be ready to leave the next morning. He slid the note into the pouch and handed it to the aide. When he heard the messenger's motorcycle leave, he smiled, rose from the table, and put on his hat. At last his troops were getting the attention they deserved.

As the regiment made its way in a more easterly direction, it met very little resistance from the enemy. However, the ascent out of the valley was marked by a great change in both topography and vegetation. The rich, black soil of the river basin gave way to undulating hills of light-colored sandy loam used for pasture and hay. Then it gradually changed to yellow clay covered with slender birch and aspen trees struggling to keep their roots hidden beneath the uneven, rock-strewn surface.

The armored columns stayed on primitive roads most of the time but on occasion; found it necessary to follow a woodcutter's trail to pursue snipers or hidden pockets of resistance. For the *Tiger* tanks and half-tracks, it was an easy task to shear a path through the thin, slender foliage.

When they reached the summit of the road on their gentle upward climb, they found a deep cut with vertical walls that had been made through the solid, gray granite. Adjacent to it was a railroad tunnel with shiny steel rails that had been bored through. Midway through the cut, the Russians had erected a well-fortified obstacle made of several rows of heavy timbers standing on end and wedged deeply into trenches dug across the road. Captain Hofmiller's company, the lead company, came under intense fire. In addition, he saw evidence that mines had been planted about the roadblock.

After trying for several minutes to silence the enemy guns, Captain Hofmiller ordered Erich to probe the tunnel with his platoon. Erich knew tunnels were very risky, but if it could be used to circumvent the roadblock and get behind it, the rest of the brigade could use the road. Erich consulted his drivers momentarily and then lined up his five *Tigers* so he was in the second one.

As they slowly approached the tunnel behind a squad of infantry and engineers searching for mines, each stayed in the tracks of the previous vehicle to avoid triggering a mine that had been overlooked by the search crew. Upon entering the tunnel, they turned on their lights and continued moving without opposition. Erich swallowed hard and licked his dry lips as he began thinking of all sorts of possible problems. Could they seal both ends of the tunnel and trap his platoon? Since the rails were shiny, what would happen if a locomotive ran head-on into a *Tiger* tank? Just then a sudden explosion triggered a rock avalanche, sealing the entrance behind them.

"What in hell was the rest of the company doing to let that happen?" bellowed Sergeant Kohlmann.

"God only knows," replied Erich, dismounting to urge the mine-detecting crew to hurry.

Dust from the explosion and exhaust from the tanks combined to make breathing difficult, but he urged the men on until they reached the exit. Ordering the tanks to stay back a few feet in the safety of the tunnel, Erich cautiously peered out. Seeing nothing, he asked the infantry squad to follow him on a reconnaissance of the area just beyond the tunnel. They were immediately fired upon by a machine gun. He exposed himself briefly again, drawing more fire. But he had located the troublesome machine gun nest in a hillside niche.

He jumped into the front hatch of the lead tank, informed the eighty-eight gunner of the approximate location of the machine gun, and told him he would pinpoint it with the tank's machine gun. "Then you blast the hell out of it!" he ordered.

Using the radio, he told the other tanks to follow him out at one-hundred-foot intervals, firing as they came. As the *Tiger* crawled forward, he began spraying the area before him with the machine gun and then, upon emerging from the tunnel, zeroed in on the nest. The eighty-eight fired, the tank shuddered, and the machine gun nest disintegrated in an explosion of fire, smoke, and rock fragments. At that same instant, the *Tiger* was hit from the side by a weapon powerful enough to dislodge one of its treads.

It continued forward until it ran off the tread and then pivoted and began a slow turn. The driver, sensing what had happened, halted it. Fearing another hit, the men opened the escape hatch on the under side, but being astride the railroad tracks, it would not open far enough. They clambered out an upper hatch, rolled down the side of the disabled *Tiger*, and scurried back into the tunnel.

"We've got to get out of here," declared Sergeant Kohlman. "They're apt to seal us in."

Erich nodded. "I'm sure they're waiting for the next tank."

"Then we'll have to go out and get them."

"They aren't firing at the tank any more, so I'll go back in it and see what I can see," Erich volunteered.

His heart was thundering in his chest as he crawled slowly back to the tank. Believing he was shielded from the enemy by the massive gun turret, he cautiously climbed atop its good tread and slid carefully into the open hatch. Scanning the surrounding area through the tank's periscopes, he saw no sign of the enemy. He tried the radio, hoping the tank was far enough out of the tunnel. Captain Hofmiller responded immediately.

"Glad to hear you're not trapped in the tunnel," stated the relieved captain. "Do you want me to call in air support?"

"No," answered Erich, breathing heavily. "The bombs might seal the tunnel. Besides, the enemy is quite well protected." He paused to catch his breath and then suggested, "Give me an hour. I think we can work it out from this end."

"I want a report in thirty minutes," Hofmiller ordered sternly.

"All right."

Wiping the perspiration from his forehead, Erich again looked into the periscope. There was a faint sign of movement in another cave-like niche.

"It's worth a try," he muttered and fired the machine gun at it.

It was a machine gun. It returned the fire immediately. He loaded the eighty-eight, and, as the electric motor labored to slowly rotate the heavy turret, another shell slammed against the side of the *Tiger*. The gun left a telltale puff of smoke. Carefully, he aimed and fired, destroying the weapon and scattering the crew. Then he relocated the machine gun niche and again fired the deadly eighty-eight.

He cautiously climbed out of the tank, rolled to the ground, and dashed back into the tunnel. After obtaining a machine pistol and two hand grenades, he ordered the crew to return to the crippled *Tiger* so they could furnish protective fire for the infantry squad he was going to lead on a cleanup operation. "And get your tanks ready to roll!" he shouted at the four crews standing beside their vehicles in the tunnel.

He turned to the infantry squad. "Go out, turn right twenty-five yards to the boulders, and form a skirmish line." With a disciplined firmness, he looked each man in the eye. "Follow me!" he shouted and then dashed out with the riflemen close on his heels.

Russian riflemen managed to cut down two Black Hawk men before they could reach the boulders, but the remainder successfully located isolated rocks and depressions in the ground. Erich charged ahead in a zigzag path and managed to reach the ditch on the near side of the road. Then, using hand signals, he ordered the tank crew to fire at the Russians with their machine gun as he waved his infantrymen to join him in the ditch. They came in a low crouch, firing their semi-automatic rifles from the hip as they ran.

"Make those Russians keep their heads down!" he bellowed.

While the infantrymen fired a volley, he sprinted across the road, bullets scattering the gravel around his feet as he ran. After firing a burst from his machine pistol, he ordered his men to follow. They came, one by one, as the bullets hissed and popped about them.

The *Tiger's* machine gun chattered again, tearing up the ground around the Russians, but they were well concealed and merely waited for it to stop. Again, they were firing at Erich and his infantrymen. Then the eighty-eight fired, momentarily stunning the Russians. Erich seized the opportunity for his final assault.

"Let's go!" he shouted, charging part way up the incline where the Russians were located. He squatted, waved a hand grenade to his men, pulled its cord, and tossed it. After several more grenades had exploded among the Russians, the Black Hawk men charged their positions, methodically shooting or disarming each of the Russian occupants. When finished, they fired a round through the trigger mechanism of each Russian's weapon so it could not be used again.

Erich now had an unobstructed view down the road to the roadblock. He could see considerable activity, indicating his men would soon be under fire again. After ordering them to dig in on each side of the road, he ran back to the tunnel and asked the engineers to check for mines while he tended the two wounded men. As soon as the engineers signaled there were no mines, he climbed aboard his command tank. "Follow me around that disabled *Tiger*," he snapped. "And begin shooting when I give the order!"

The four tanks roared forward, climbed upon the road, and, with Erich waving for the infantry to come along, led the column on a gun-blazing run back toward the roadblock. Feeling certain there would be no mines on this side of the roadblock, he had the men concentrate on entrenched enemy soldiers and gun emplacements. In addition, he established radio contact with Captain Hofmiller. "We're giving them hell from this side," Hofmiller assured him. "But we won't fire beyond the roadblock."

In a few minutes the fighting was over. Erich walked up to the roadblock and looked around it as his men disarmed and searched the prisoners. As soon as Captain Hofmiller saw him, the captain raised his arms and cheered. Mine removal squads went into action, and soon half-tracks, using steel cables, were ripping an opening through the logs.

Colonel Stauffer inspected the area with Erich. "We were concerned about you after the explosion closed the tunnel," he stated as he walked past the Russian prisoners.

"Our greatest fear was they'd seal the other end also," Erich replied.

He showed the colonel the disabled *Tiger* and the Russian entrenchments, many with enemy dead still in them. "I'm glad they didn't have anything larger than fifty millimeter," he confided.

When they returned to mount up, Colonel Stauffer slapped Erich on the back. "When I heard all hell break loose, I knew the Black Hawks were in action and would soon have the situation in hand."

"Thank you, sir," Erich replied, a glow of pride showing on his face.

• • •

It was late at night as Colonel Stauffer sat at his desk in the headquarters tent looking at maps, requisition forms, and troop strength reports. The lantern, sitting on one corner of the desk, cast a yellow glow across his face and created long shadows stretching out from his cot and other chairs in the sparsely furnished shelter. The Black Hawk Regiment, along with other units of the Death Head Brigade, had been surging ahead at great speed. But he was continually haunted by the specter of supply shortages, the most serious being fuel for his thirsty tanks. Although he had received some replacements for the men and machines lost, they could never surpass more than three-fourths of their original strength. And he was receiving lighter *Panther* tanks to replace the *Tigers* that broke down or were destroyed. The best he could do was assure his men that once they reached the Volga, they would be given a rest and the entire brigade would be equipped and outfitted to maximum capacity again.

The next day the regiment rolled forward over the rich wheat land of the Don River basin. There had been a gradual increase in Russian troop resistance, but the peasant population was more friendly. Often the Black Hawk men were given flowers or food—even invited to spend the night in a house or barn rather on the ground. These people exhibited a desire to escape from the tyranny of a dictatorship they despised. Although welcomed as liberators, the German army, especially the Death Head Brigade, was so occupied with fighting on a swiftly moving front that little time or energy could be devoted to fraternization. Perhaps the rear echelon troops, due to arrive in a few days to govern the newly captured area, would grant these friendly peasants the consideration they longed for.

While waiting for the engineers to complete a pontoon bridge across the Don River, the regiment established positions along its west bank. *Messerschmitts* provided air cover and the self-propelled eighty-eights gave artillery support designed to minimize enemy harassment by determined Russian troops. For the past two weeks, the Black Hawk troopers had encountered an increasing number of one-hundred millimeter field guns and the new *T-34* tanks, either of which was a cause for concern. And on occasion they had been strafed by American-built *P-40 Warhawk* fighter planes the Russians were receiving in substantial numbers.

Regardless of how rapidly they advanced, the horizon before them continued to glow with the continual fires of the scorched earth policy. But since the wheat had been harvested, the smoke was now white from straw and stubble rather then than black from burning grain.

At long last, the mail arrived and was distributed. With an opened letter in his hand, Heinz dashed over to Erich. His whole body radiated excitement. "I'm going to be a father!" he yelled.

"Wonderful!" congratulated Erich, throwing his arm around him.

"I hope it's a boy," said Heinz, looking at the letter again.

"Oh, sure. Then he can join the Black Hawk Regiment when his father retires."

"That's a thought."

Just then there was a loud explosion. Captain Hofmiller, while walking along the river bank, had detonated an antipersonnel mine. It shattered his legs, tore up the front of his body, and mutilated his face beyond recognition. Erich and Heinz dashed to his side as he wilted into a blood-spattered, crumpled heap. A medical aid man came over and checked him carefully.

"There's no hope," he said flatly. "He will just suffer for an hour or so and then die."

Both Erich and Heinz nodded agreement.

The medical aid man took a small caliber pistol from his kit, turned Captain Hofmiller's head to the side, and then shot him behind the right ear. The captain stiffened, exhaled heavily with a low, rasping sound, and then relaxed. Erich ordered a detail of men to wrap his body in a gray blanket and place it beside the road so the burial detail would find it.

Colonel Stauffer walked up, looked down at the covered body, and shook his head. Then he turned to face Erich. "Lieutenant Stecker, you are now company commander."

"Yes, sir!" Erich responded with a salute.

Stauffer returned the salute and then walked briskly away.

The brigade crossed the deep, black waters of the Don, fanned out, and then lunged forward in several *panzer* columns on a twenty-five mile front. Now considerably under strength, with enemy resistance stiffening, it became increasing difficult to maintain the swift pace they had enjoyed in previous weeks. To the men, it was becoming clear that for each mile they advanced into Russia, food, fuel, and ammunition was much more difficult to deliver. And the opposite was true for the enemy. The spirit and initiative of the men, however, never diminished. Frequently, they charged enthusiastically into an engagement as the cry, "To the Volga!" resounded over the radio and loud speakers. Sometimes it was mixed with strains from "Lili Marlene." They were counting on Colonel Stauffer's promise of rest and replacements when they reached the Volga.

• • •

On the evening of Saturday, August 22, the Black Hawk Regiment halted on the outskirts of Dubovka. Erich had his company of tanks take cover in a ravine that ran parallel to a narrow belt of trees. Since the trees provided cover and concealment, the infantry dug their holes and trenches beneath them.

Erich walked among his men and tanks on a routine check. He stopped to talk with Sergeant Kohlmann. "The Volga is just on the other side of town," he said, noting several troopers waiting to hear what he had to say. He raised his voice. "Are you ready?" he called out. "*Jawohl!*" the men shouted in unison.

"We're a bit low on fuel," Kohlmann warned. "But we should make it if we don't get into a prolonged fight."

Erich nodded that he understood.

He walked over to where Heinz was busy writing a letter on his knee. "Another letter to Irma?" he asked.

"Yes," replied Heinz, shaking his head as he looked up. "I just wish I could be with her."

"Well, that would be nice," stated Erich reflectively. "But you know, she's a very capable girl."

"I know, but I have a vested interest in her condition."

"Maybe you can get a leave when she's due," Erich said, trying to ease his concern. "Besides, she can probably get along just fine without you."

He slapped Heinz on the back and walked off.

The next morning, as the darkness faded and gave way to an opalescent dawn, the wall of birches and quaking aspens took shape, their white trunks appearing ghostly in the half light. Beneath them, Erich could make out the forms of infantrymen adjusting their clothing and equipment in anticipation of the order to move forward—an order they had heard often and knew was forthcoming.

A thin mist arose from the land, giving a strange and weird appearance to the area. Erich was concerned. Intelligence reports indicated a strong, well-equipped enemy force was waiting in the city that he knew they were backed against the river and would either have to be killed or captured.

When the order to advance came, Erich's company was directed to spearhead a drive through the center of the city. Two other columns were to drive through on either side. Out of an original complement of twenty-five tanks, only fourteen remained. He lined them up on the roadway and, with Black Hawk infantry walking on either side, began advancing toward the first buildings. Soon mortar rounds began to drop among them. Erich increased the speed, and some self-propelled eighty-eights at the rear began firing overhead. Then the tanks began firing their weapons as they advanced block by block.

Erich, commanding from the lead *Tiger* tank, approached the main town intersection. There he saw a barrier of automobiles. He ordered Sergeant Kohlmann to reduce the speed of the *Tiger* to a slow crawl and then had the gunner fire two rounds from the eighty-eight at it. The explosions shifted the automobiles enough to expose a waiting Russian *T-34* tank that began firing at him.

He contacted Heinz on the radio. "Take your platoon down the next street over. See if you can get a side shot at the *T-34*."

Although the Russian marksmanship was poor, the *T-34* scored two glancing hits off the front of Erich's tank but caused no damage. To disable it, a tread would have to be blasted off. But he also knew that soon heavier guns from the Russian rear would be firing at him. With this in mind, he had the *Tiger* move upon the sidewalk close to a large building. He hoped other tanks behind him as well as supporting infantry; would protect him from the sides and above.

Heinz, knowing Erich was in difficulty, raced over to the next street; then proceeded parallel to Erich's path. He stopped to check each intersection he crossed, and then, peering around a corner, he saw the barricade and the *T-34*. His *Tiger* rolled ahead a few feet as his gunner carefully aimed the eighty-eight. There was a deafening explosion, and the armor piercing shell tore the tread and drive wheel off the *T-34*.

Erich saw the tread fly. He knew Heinz had accomplished the task he had been assigned. He waited for the crew to abandon the disabled *T-34*, then, urging the infantry to proceed with him, rolled rapidly toward the roadblock.

Heinz called Erich on the radio. "I think I see the river another block farther on. Should I continue on this street?"

"Yes," replied Erich. "Keep me informed on your progress."

"I will."

Heinz lead his platoon cautiously but without opposition to the bank of the somber, wide Volga. "I'm looking at the Volga," he happily reported.

"Good!" replied Erich. "We have a few snipers to take care of but should be with you soon."

Heinz could hear some machine-gun chatter and an occasional whomp-whomp of the eighty-eight.

Sergeant Kohlmann drove Erich's *Tiger* to the river's edge. Looking up the street that ran along the river, Erich saw Heinz standing in his tank. He waved and then asked over the radio, "How does it feel to be the first Black Hawk trooper to see the Volga?"

"Wonderful! Just wonderful!" came the joyful reply.

Erich directed Kohlmann to drive his tank up the narrow street toward Heinz. They had gone but a few yards when a tremendous explosion ripped through Heinz's *Tiger*. Erich saw Heinz, who was standing in his hatch smiling, rise a few inches and then drop back to hang by his armpits. His head, still wearing the headphones over his black hat, sagged to one side.

Erich assumed he had been hit by cannon fire from down the river. He had Kohlmann halt his tank. He leaped down, *Luger* in hand, and ran toward Heinz. He was halted by rifle and machine gun fire coming from a concrete warehouse just beyond Heinz's still smoking *Tiger*. He turned to Kohlmann. "Get a combat patrol organized immediately!"

Kohlmann quickly assembled a twelve-man patrol of Black Hawk infantrymen, armed them with automatic weapons, and led them through a series of buildings to within a hundred feet of the warehouse. They fired a few rounds and were immediately fired upon.

While other Black Hawk men kept up the fire, Erich and Kohlmann ran in a zigzag crouch across an open area to a steel door of the warehouse. Although bullets they fired penetrated it, it remained securely locked. Erich yelled for a satchel charge. In a few minutes, another trooper was at his side with a canvas bag filled with small bricks of high explosive. Erich lit the fuse, and the three of them took cover around the corner of the building.

The tremendous explosion blew the heavy steel door nearly through the opposite side of the building. In an instant Black Hawk troopers, led by Erich, were inside spraying the dust-filled interior with their machine pistols. They killed every man of the Russian unit and then blasted the breech of the lethal one hundred fifty-two millimeter artillery piece.

"That gun will kill no more," stated a stern-faced Erich, who was breathing heavily as he looked across the devastated interior of the building.

He walked over to Heinz's *Tiger*, noting the four inch hole in its side. It still emitted small amounts of smoke from burning electrical insulation.

Looking down into the hatch behind Heinz's dangling torso, he saw there was nothing left below his waist. He removed the headphones, gently lifted the bowed head, and carefully pinched the eyelids closed to hide the cloudy stare of death.

He stood for a long time in dry-eyed sorrow, looking out over the sluggish Volga, holding and caressing Heinz's cold, waxy hand. Small gusts of wind swung the dead trooper's identification disk to and fro, creating a muted tinkling sound as it came in contact with a control lever inside the tank.

Lieutenant Heinz Jager, he thought, an elite Black Hawk trooper in the Waffen SS Death Head Panzer Brigade, the first member of the brigade ground forces to reach the Volga River, and first to die on its banks. Here he hangs by his armpits, more than a thousand miles from the expectant wife he loves so dearly, killed in one of the countless series of battles in a war that appears to have no end.

He felt a hand on his shoulder. He turned to see Sergeant Kohlmann with some blankets to wrap the bodies.

"Lieutenant, if you wish, I'll remove the bodies," volunteered Kohlmann.

Without speaking, Erich took one of the gray, woolen blankets and spread it on the ground. Then he carefully lifted Heinz out of the hatch and gently placed him on it. Kohlmann quickly folded the bottom of the blanket up to Heinz's chin. Erich kneeled and drew the sides of the blanket up around his friend's body, leaving the head exposed.

Kohlmann climbed onto the tank and peered inside for signs of the other three crewmen. Warm air wafting up from the open hatch exuded a sweet smell of blood mixed with the scorched odor of burned steel. When he looked inside, he found nothing he could identify as part of a human body. The entire white, enameled inside was coated with a mixture of flesh and blood. He dropped back onto the ground and watched as Erich said a final farewell to Heinz.

Erich touched Heinz's eyes again to be sure they were shut and then pushed upward on his chin to close the mouth tightly. "I'll visit Irma for you, Heinz," he murmured. "I'll tell her how proud and happy you were that she is going to have your baby."

Then he closed the blanket folds over his friend's head.

Maelstrom of Agony

When Maria saw Erich go through the turnstile at the Munich depot and watched his trim black uniform disappear into a surging sea of people rushing to board the Salzburg Express, she felt terribly depressed and very much alone—so all, all alone. She remained long enough to watch the train depart, all the while biting her lip in an attempt to hold back tears that welled up in her warm brown eyes and flowed down her smooth, pink cheeks onto her blouse. Deep inside, she had a premonition it would be a long time before she would see him again. And she feared for his safety because of the special training he had received and the type of unit he undoubtedly would join. She also knew he was no slouch. Whatever task he undertook would receive his total endeavor and maximum effort.

That week at Camp Klosterfeld seemed slow and drab. She expected no letters from anyone, had no news about which to write home, and no address for Erich. In addition to her mental attitude, there were three dreary days of intermittent rain that restricted activities to only those that could be accommodated inside. She did some washing, ironing, and mending and then spent time studying classroom notes and medical administrative forms she would be using in the field.

"I don't see why they make so many copies of everything," said the nurse who occupied the bed next to hers as she shuffled and reshuffled the samples given to them in the classes.

"Don't worry about it," Maria advised her. "Before long you'll be assigned to a medical unit, and the forms won't be so important anymore."

When Saturday morning arrived, warm and sunny, Maria decided to break the spell of gloom that had prevailed over her for the past week—she took the camp bus to Munich. Upon seeing the number of men in uniform at the bus depot, she experienced a tremendous yearning for Erich. She walked directly to the rail depot and boarded the train for Augsburg.

She was thrilled when she encountered numerous soldiers at the Augsburg square without insignia of rank or unit. She knew they were from Camp Reichstein. Slowly she circled the fountain and then sat on the same bench she had occupied the first time she met Erich there. Her thoughts strayed to the Hotel Baumhofer, the little confectionary, and the bridal shop. After sitting on the bench for some time absorbing the pleasant warmth of the sun, looking at clusters of soldiers in green uniforms standing about wondering what to do with their free time, and watching the elderly citizens dozing or idly conversing on other benches, she rose and made her way to the sidewalk that passed in front of the Hotel Baumhofer. She peered through the glass of the door into the dimly lighted lobby and saw the same room clerk on duty that had been there when she and Erich checked in. A light, tingling surge raced through her body, causing her to shiver slightly.

She walked to the bridal shop and was disappointed to discover the window display had been changed and that the wedding gown she so dearly desired was no longer there for her to admire. Pretending to be interested in the articles now exhibited, she looked through the windows into the store. There was no sign of it inside. Glumly, she made her way back to the confectionary, sat at the same table she and Erich had occupied, and ordered cheese cake and *ersatz* coffee.

It was a lovely day, so she tried to think pleasant thoughts to raise her spirits. But she couldn't get the idea of not having that wedding dress out of her mind. The coffee was bitter, the cheese cake dry, and her appetite for food had disappeared. Oh, how she wished she had gotten it when they were here before. Then she would have been certain of having it whenever the two of them decided the time was right to marry. Perhaps the store could order another. But with the war on, the prospects of getting it would be extremely poor. But maybe she should at least inquire.

She quickly retraced her steps to the bridal shop and entered, causing a little bell attached to the door to jingle. An overly painted, middle-aged woman; with a long, sharp nose and taffy-colored hair in a braid coiled on top of her head; emerged from a small back room.

"Yes?" the lady asked.

"I am interested in a bridal gown," Maria stated nervously.

"Oh, yes, I have several right over here," the woman replied, leading the way toward the back of the shop.

Maria looked over eight that were displayed on an elongated rack. To the woman, it was obvious she was disappointed.

"What did you have in mind?" The woman asked curtly.

"You had one in the window a few weeks ago," Maria answered. "A Schwayder."

"Oh, yes," the woman responded, brightening.

She went into the back room and brought it out. Noticing the smile appear on Maria's face and the sparkle in her eye, she immediately sensed the strong desire Maria had for the dress. "I think it's your size too."

Maria scrutinized it carefully. "Yes, this is it."

"Would you like to try it on?"

"Oh, yes! May I?"

As the woman assisted Maria with it, she explained that a local housewife had been in earlier that day looking at it. She was to bring her daughter back within an hour, but it had been more than two hours and she had not returned.

"It's a perfect fit," she stated, turning Maria to the mirror.

Maria, elated beyond words, beamed. "It's beautiful," she sighed.

"Would you like it?"

"Yes! Yes, indeed."

The shopkeeper boxed the dress, being careful to fold it at the proper places, and packed it with tissue paper to prevent wrinkles.

As Maria was leaving, the housewife and her daughter entered. Maria did not hesitate but made her way back to the square where, before heading for the depot, she stood for several minutes looking at the fountain, the people, and the balconies of the rooms she and Erich had occupied at the Hotel Baumhofer. Once back at Camp Klosterfeld, she carefully packed the gown in the bottom of her footlocker.

During the remaining three weeks of training, letters began arriving from Erich on a regular basis. Prior to this she had not saved his letters, but now she tied them in a bundle with a blue ribbon and kept them in her footlocker. As each arrived, she read it two or three times, answered it promptly, and then patiently awaited for the next one. Sometimes in the evening, she took them from the footlocker and reread all of them in an attempt to feel a greater closeness to him.

When the training cycle ended, the nurses were ordered to put the barracks in order, pack everything in their footlockers except those items they wished to take on leave, and then stencil their names on the tops and ends of the lockers. The stenciled footlockers were then trucked to a warehouse to be stored until the nurses returned. The young ladies of mercy were then issued leave papers and told to report back for reassignment in nine days. Despite the fact they were all returning in little more than a week, tears were shed as they bid one another farewell.

At home Maria found life to be more dull and depressing than it appeared a few months back. The young men were gone and the young women were either away working or married and attempting to manage without the stabilizing influence of husbands. She tried to keep herself busy around her mother's house and garden, but after the first few days the loneliness she felt within its confines, coupled with her constant thoughts and fears about Erich, overtook her. She decided to assist her mother in the post office. At first she merely helped with sorting the mail but soon decided to dust, sweep, and mop the little wooden structure. After looking at the dotted Swiss curtains her mother had made for the windows, she concluded she should take them home and launder them.

As the remainder of the week dragged by, Mrs. Stecker received a letter from Erich, which she shared with Maria. In it he indicated all was going well and that his regiment was in the vicinity of Karkov. It was then that Mr. Stecker informed them that there had been very heavy fighting in that sector of the eastern front. Later, after the two women had expressed their great concern, he wished he had not mentioned it.

On Sunday when the time arrived for her to return, Maria was almost glad to leave. Although she was very proud of Holzheim, she now belonged to the world of the military and felt her place was with her unit. She was deeply touched, however, when, while friends and relatives were bidding her farewell, she kissed her brother George and saw tears in his eyes.

At Camp Klosterfeld a final check of records, clothing, and equipment was made. Then, early on Tuesday morning, one hundred nurses were loaded aboard camp buses and taken to the Munich depot. There they were joined by a large contingent of physicians, orderlies, clerks, and technicians, who combined to fill a waiting train. Maria was informed by the waiting head nurse, a slender, sharp-nosed captain with wrinkled skin and pale complexion, that she was part of the 66th Evacuation Hospital which was going to set up operations in the east. This made her very happy. Now she would be applying her skill where it counted and in addition, she would be nearer to Erich. But it also aroused curiosity and speculation as to where in the east they were going. It was a secret known to only a few aboard the train.

The 66th Evacuation Hospital was set up in eastern Hungary a few miles outside of Debrecen. It was housed in a number of tents erected on recently poured concrete slabs in a large pasture field. The ward tents, containing forty beds each, were aligned side by side in two long rows. In a far corner of the field stood ten tents that appeared separate and isolated from the rest of the hospital. The nurses speculated these were for contagious diseases or mental cases. Later, they would be surprised and shocked to learn of their actual designated purpose.

• • •

Two days after the capture of Dubovka, a thousand replacements arrived to replenish the losses the Death Head Brigade had suffered in its thrust from Karkov. However, it still failed to bring the unit to more than 80 percent of its full strength. The Black Hawk Regiment received 300 troopers and 40 *Tiger* tanks. Some of the tanks were new, but several were those that had been knocked out of action and abandoned by the regiment, then put back in working order. This brought their total to 147, still short of the full complement of 165.

After Erich's company had been given five of the *Tigers* and twenty-four troopers in neat, black uniforms, he positioned his company in strategic locations in the sector of town he was assigned to defend. Infantrymen with rifles and machine guns were spaced in dugouts along the banks of the river, and his tanks, ready to support the infantry if necessary, were a block inland, hidden in sheds, behind fences, and under trees.

Just as he finished, a messenger walked up to him. "Colonel Stauffer wants all battalion and company commanders to report to his headquarters at seven this evening."

"Thank you, soldier," Erich replied, returning the young man's salute.

The meeting was held in the auditorium of a schoolhouse near the center of town. As the colonel entered, all the men rose to their feet. "Please, be seated," he said in a pleasant voice.

After the men were seated and the room became silent, he continued. "We have two items of interest to you," he said. "First, we will honor five of your brave comrades. Normally we would have a formal ceremony to do this, but these are abnormal times. So, my orderly, Lieutenant Schmidt, will call off the names. As he does so, will these people come forward."

He nodded to his orderly, a tall, slender young man with piercing green eyes, who read off a list of names. Erich and Sergeant Kohlmann were among them.

After placing the Iron Cross First Class around the necks of three men and shaking their hands, he turned to Kohlmann and Erich. "And for bravery and inspiring their company to overcome great odds after it was isolated in a railroad tunnel, I wish to present these two men with the following awards. For you, First Sergeant Albert Kohlmann, the Iron Cross First Class."

He placed the cross about Kohlmann's neck and then turned to Erich. "And for you, Lieutenant Erich Stecker, who already have earned the Iron Cross First Class while serving with the *Afrika Korps*, the Knights Cross of the Iron Cross. Congratulations." He then shook the hands of both men. "One other thing," he added with a smile. "As of now, you are Company Commander, Captain Stecker." He shook Erich's hand. "Congratulations again."

Erich beamed with pride as he walked back to his seat.

Then Colonel Stauffer faced the assembled men. The expression on his face became somber and serious. "And now for the second item." He scanned the young men seated before him. "I know you were promised a period of rest when we reached the Volga. But things have changed." Pointing to a large map on the wall, he said, "Army Group South has sent a spearhead into the Caucasus Mountains to capture the Maikop oil fields and the city of Grozny. Right here." He pointed to a location on the map. "They are well on their way. They plan to go through Palestine and link up with General Rommel in Egypt."

He paused and turned to face the commanders again. "We have been ordered to go south along the Volga and help with the taking of Stalingrad. It won't be easy, but I think we can do it."

A battle-hardened major raised his hand.

"What is it, Major?" Colonel Stauffer asked.

"Why won't it be easy? We've done right well so far."

"It seems Stalin doesn't want his namesake city to fall. The Fuhrer insists on taking it."

The major shrugged and sat down.

"So we'll roll south tomorrow morning." He looked around the room into the faces of the young officers facing him. "Any further questions?" With no other questions, Colonel Stauffer strode off. An aide dismissed the commanders. It was just after dark when Erich and Sergeant Kohlmann returned to the company area to find ordnance trucks servicing the tanks and half-tracks. They climbed a slight rise to the edge of the river to see if the infantry soldiers were properly dug in for the guard duty they had been assigned. Although the sky was overcast, he could see the glossy surface of the river gliding slowly past. To him, it looked little different than the Danube. *Ah yes, the Danube. And Holzheim. And Maria.* Just then he saw twelve flashes of light on the gloomy, distant horizon.

"Looks like Russian artillery is going to fire on us tonight," Kohlmann observed.

They squatted on their haunches to await the whistling scream of incoming shells. Both men had been under fire enough to be able to judge by the sound how far away the shells would land. There would be time to dive for protection if they came in close. When the shells arrived, they dropped harmlessly into the river, creating intense flashes of light and great geysers of water and mud.

"I bet the fish wonder what in hell is happening," Kohlman said, rising to his full height and shaking his head.

"Don't worry. They'll try again in a little while," Erich warned.

Forty-five minutes later there was another dozen flashes on the horizon. This time the shells overshot their mark, landing in vacant fields behind the town.

Later that night, as some of the shells crashed into town, a light rain began to fall. The shells' explosions, lightly muffled by the rain, made the buildings and pavement shine and glow, creating grotesque shadows that flitted about the empty streets. After the whistling scream and explosion of each shell, there was a brief moment of silence. Then pieces of shrapnel that had been blown high into the air, made a patter of noises as they rained down upon the cobblestone streets and tile roofs.

At midnight a *Wehrmacht* infantry division arrived and took up positions in buildings throughout the town.

• • •

A light drizzle was falling the next morning as they awaited the order to get underway. Sergeant Kohlmann turned to Erich. "It sure was a short rest period," he complained wryly.

"Maybe we should be thankful for two days," soothed Erich.

"Maybe," answered Kohlmann. "But our men are still quite tired."

"There's no use complaining," snapped Erich. "It must be done. Just be thankful you're still alive."

"Yes, sir," replied Kohlmann, recognizing that Erich would not tolerate complaining.

When the order came, the regiment began to roll south in two long columns of tanks, half-tracks, personnel carriers, and motorcycles. One, which included Erich's company, followed the macadam road along the river. The other traveled half a mile inland, where it had to traverse a number of ravines running toward the Volga.

As the two columns made their way south, resistance stiffened and rocket and artillery fire from across the river became more intense, resulting in casualties among the infantrymen. Ahead, Erich could see great clouds of smoke rising skyward from a furiously burning city that was being bombed and strafed by large numbers of the *Luftwaffe*. At times, as his column halted to allow the inland armored column to catch up, he could hear the destructive roar of a tremendous battle.

"My God!" exclaimed Sergeant Kohlmann. "I've seen other cities burning, but none had the smoke rising so fast and high as that. Must be one hell of a hot fire."

"That many *Stukas* and *JU-88s* can cause one awful lot of damage," Erich said, squinting as he stared at the distant horizon. "When they get finished, there'll be nothing left." He paused for a moment and then added, "But the smoke and dust keep the Russian antiaircraft batteries from hitting them."

By evening, the Death Head Brigade had slammed into the northern out-skirts of Stalingrad. Since the banks of the Volga were very high at this point, Erich's armored column had to stay back three blocks from the river's edge to avoid exposure to fire from across the river. This also provided a margin of safety from the attacking *Luftwaffe* that was trying to halt Russian supply barges. In addition, because of increasing resistance, the inland column was brought into line so that there were only two blocks of buildings between the columns. Here, where the smoke and stench clinging to the heavy air nause-ated the troops, the brigade paused for the night. Colonel Stauffer ordered his regiment to refuel and regroup. "Tomorrow morning," he told his battalion commanders, "we will drive a spearhead into the center of town. There's only twelve miles to go.

• • •

The next morning Colonel Stauffer's Black Hawk Regiment rolled forward a few blocks under extremely difficult conditions. Infantry casualties were very high for the amount of ground captured. At times it was necessary to level buildings with artillery fire or explosive charges to rid them of snipers and grenadiers who fired heavy caliber rifles at the tanks. As the two columns of tanks pushed forward at a slow pace, Erich's on a broad street, the second along railroad tracks, the Black Hawk infantry cleared the two blocks between them room by room through houses, apartments, and storage build-ings. At first they merely tossed a grenade into a room and went forward. But they discovered that if a Russian was only wounded, he would frequently get to a window or doorway and fire on them from behind.

Some of the enemy filled their pockets with grenades and threw them-selves beneath the treads of Erich's advancing *Tigers*. Lighter tanks could have been damaged, but the heavy *Tigers* merely exploded the grenades and splattered its undersides with flesh and blood. The remainder of the human bomb was flattened into a blood-soaked mass of cloth, soil, and rubble. It was a sickening sight for Erich, but he was grateful to command a company of the heavy *Tigers*.

Early in the afternoon, the *Luftwaffe* began a massive attack on caves the Russians had dug into the riverbank. The caves were being used to protect their artillery pieces as well as the truck-mounted *katyushi* rocket launchers. The trucks, hidden in caves where their racks of launching tubes were loaded for firing, were rolled out, quickly fired, and again driven back into the caves. At night, under cover of darkness, they were especially effective since they did not have to hide from attacking planes. And they were capable of devas-tating attacks on German troops by raining salvo after salvo upon them. For men of the Black Hawk Regiment, regardless of the number of planes the Germans used to attack the river, its banks, and caves, the screaming terror from masses of rockets did not diminish.

As the succession of mild September days passed, progress by the Death Head Brigade was very limited. Again and again it applied maximum power, but the advance was often measured in feet, yards, rooms, or buildings. After a day-long battle, Erich's men dug into the debris for protection during the night. The next morning they found that the Russians had moved in behind them. Then they had to consume several hours ferreting out the tenacious enemy before pushing forward again.

Snipers on both sides were so numerous and so accurate and the rockets so profuse that days often passed before the dead and wounded could be retrieved. At first, the Black Hawk infantry found it distasteful to step over corpses teeming with flies as they pressed their attack, and drivers of the heavy *Tigers* were most reluctant to run over them. As the days wore on, however, these concerns faded and the bodies were considered mere debris to be ignored. After lying in the warm sun for several days they became swollen, bloated, and infested with maggots, often hissing and moving as their skins tightened. In the evening shadows, their movement and noise frequently caused a flurry of rifle and machine gun fire.

• • •

Late in September the harvest moon rose big and yellow, its reflection shimmering on the slow-moving Volga. Thinking the bodies and debris they could see floating past might be charges of explosives designed to sink the supply barges being ferried across the river, the Russians fired machines guns at the flotsam. And when the moon rose high and became blue-white, it flooded the battered, smoking ruins with an eerie light, thus betraying the infiltrating Russians and causing them to be shot or bayoneted by lurking Black Hawk men. The SS troopers also learned that their entrenching shovel was an effective weapon in close fighting. By sharpening its edges, they were able to leap from moon-made shadows and cleave fatal gashes into the necks and chests of the enemy creeping through the rubble.

Erich's company, reinforced with a company of Black Hawk infantry, was ordered to take a grain elevator a block in front of them. It had been badly scarred by shelling and, having been set on fire by the Russians, was pouring forth great quantities of black, acrid smoke. Erich led four *Tigers* up the street to the front of the elevator, their machine guns and eighty-eights spitting out a deadly volume of destruction, but the infantry attempting to follow were halted by crossfire from both sides of the street.

Erich led his *Tigers* up and down the street several times, blasting large holes in the surrounding buildings and riddling them with machine gun bullets. But the return fire was undiminished. Soon large quantities of rocket mortars were raining down upon them.

Erich, sitting in the second tank in line, turned to Sergeant Kohlmann. "Isn't this one hell of a mess," he said, shaking his head. "And Stauffer said we could reach the center of town in a day!"

Kohlmann turned to him. "Never seen anything like it. Don't see why they don't bypass the whole damn place and starve it out."

By nightfall the street was graveled with shrapnel, the buildings were heaps of rubble, and twenty-seven Black Hawk infantrymen had made the supreme sacrifice. The regiment had advanced half a block.

The next day, using flame throwers and hundreds of hand grenades, the Black Hawk troopers cleared the remainder of the buildings on both sides of the street to the very entrance of the smoking elevator. Erich saw a Russian soldier who was hiding behind a pile of rubble raise his arm to throw a lighted gasoline bomb at the leading *Tiger* tank. The machine gunner in Erich's tank shot the bottle from the Russian's hand, showering him with flaming gasoline. The Russian did not fall, however, but picked up another bomb, its wick immediately igniting, and stumbled a few steps to the tank, smashing the bottle against the engine air intake. The *Tiger* was engulfed in flames. The Russian, still burning furiously, fell to the street. The tank driver managed to escape in a hail of sniper bullets, but the remainder of the crew were incinerated within the iron monster.

As they neared the center of the city, they were joined by the *Wehrmacht* 94th Infantry Division. A short distance to the right, the 71st Infantry Division was trying to take the *Mamayev Kurgan*, a rounded, heavily fortified hill 335 feet high that loomed above the surrounding flatland. Its thoroughly churned soil, littered with bodies and equipment, had changed hands several times a day for the past week. The men of the 71st referred to it as the "mushroom of doom." Men and women the Russians had released from the prisons and insane asylums were also dashing about, trying to flee the fighting.

That night, between salvos of rockets and artillery shells, the moans of soldiers buried in the wreckage of the day's fighting mingled with the sweet smell of blood and the putrid odor of burned and decaying flesh. It would etch the memory of this terrible battle into their minds so indelibly it would remain with them forever.

In the morning Erich's tank company began to push forward. The attached infantry company, which had been reduced to less than half strength, was reinforced with another company to begin the final assault on the elevator. The tanks surrounded the large concrete building to isolate it from outside help. Then the infantry began a systematic, foot-by-foot occupation of it. It took two days of strenuous fighting and the lives of thirty Black Hawk men to complete the task. They had taken no prisoners. Forty-two Russian dead were left in the battered hulk of a building when they moved on.

By the end of September, the German army occupied all of the center city except for three blocks along the river's edge. There were some insignificant pockets of resistance and a few unorganized sniper attacks throughout the area. But in occupied territory, that was considered to be merely harassment. Of the half million residents of the city, only 1,500 remained. Nevertheless, try as they might, the German army could not drive the Russians back across the island-studded river.

They had captured the Dzerzhinsky Tractor Plant, the Red Barricade Factory, and the Red October Steel Plant. When the huge oil tanks near the tractor plant caught fire and exploded, a river of fuel, fire, soot, and smoke flowed down the Volga. When they leveled the Barrkady Ordnance Factory with their tank guns, they found pieces of bodies in calico and lace. They had been fighting women workers of the factory. Some of the Black Hawk tank crews leaned against their vehicles and vomited.

After a savage battle, they captured the railroad station. Within three hours, Russians with heavy caliber antitank rifles, supported by multiple deluges of *katyushi* rockets, took it back. An hour later the Black Hawk infantrymen had it in their possession again. Erich, lying on the churned ground a short distance away, gripped the soil as the earth heaved and convulsed with each barrage of rockets and artillery shells. Great geysers dirt and rubble spouted all around him. The air was filled with helmets, machine guns, tank treads, and parts of human bodies. He could hear his men beg God for mercy, plead for forgiveness, and finally, call out to their mothers. After watching the station change hands two more times, he wondered how he could silence the rocket launcher. It was located on a barge in the river, but his men were not in a position to see it.

Cautiously, he looked about the cratered landscape. He could see three blocks in each direction. It was a ghastly scene that reeked of burned and scorched concrete, bricks, and steel. The air was heavy with the putrid odor of decaying flesh. Craters had been made by shells and bombs then filled in again when other craters were made. Some had soldiers, alive and dead, still in them. The entire area was littered with body parts, bones, rags, and wrecked equipment. However, if he could direct the fire of a mortar crew, perhaps he could put the barge out of action. But crawling among the craters would be dangerous. Previously he and his men had come upon Russian snipers who had infiltrated the area and were lying in wait.

Tucking three grenades into his belt, he began making his way back to a signal corps soldier. As he advanced, he crawled to the edge of each crater and peered into the next before going on. His clothing soon acquired the putrid stench of the rubble. In addition to the usual concrete, steel, bricks and glass, there were body parts and tattered remnants of Russian and German uniforms. And each new barrage of shells and bombs created new craters from the old and unearthed more human remains in varying states of decay.

After obtaining two phones and a reel of wire from the signal corps soldier, he made his way back to a mortar crew, who were scanning the area for targets. They were situated in a large crater made by two shell hits in the same location. He gave one of the crew a phone and told him to attach it to the end of the wire hanging from the spool. Then he began crawling across the moonscape toward the river, unreeling the wire as he went.

When he neared the river, he cautiously looked into the next crater. He saw the tops of two Russian helmets. The din of battle kept them from hearing him. After carefully sliding back into his crater, he took a grenade from his belt and pulled the string in its handle. He waited for one second and then tossed it into the crater occupied by the Russians. In two seconds there was a tremendous explosion that tossed a helmet and a segment of quilted coat into the air. He did not want to see what the grenade had done, so he skirted the crater and moved on.

Near the edge of the river, he squeezed between two gutted buildings where he could see the barge. Halting, he connected a phone to his end of the wire and made contact with the mortar crew. By directing their fire, he scored three direct hits on the target. As the barge began sinking and floating slowly down the river, he snapped his head and muttered, "Now, by God, let's see if we can hang on to that railroad station."

• • •

It was early in October when Erich began to feel the stress. The terrible days of fighting had combined into terrible weeks of agony, but the ferocity of the battle never diminished. Since mid-September the weather had become increasingly cold. Still, the Black Hawk men wore summer uniforms, the oil in the tank engines was summer grade, and the hydraulic fluid in the recoil pistons of the howitzers was too thick for winter use. And now small blocks of ice floated down the Volga.

In the distance on the flatland southwest of the smoldering city, the troopers saw a vast field of black soil turning white. As the days wore on, the white covering advanced like a great glacier. It was row upon row of one-hundred thousand neatly lettered white crosses. Each had the name of a German soldier, date of birth, rank, and date of death. It was growing at the rate of two thousand each day.

Initially, each soldier was buried in a complete uniform, including his medals. As military supplies could not keep up with demand, however, the leather boots were salvaged to be reissued to those who needed them. Finally, the warrior dead were merely buried in their woolen underwear. As troop strength dwindled and the fighting continued with an increasing savage ferocity, mass graves were dug. Each was filled with sixteen cubic yards of flesh. Finally, with the ground frozen, the bodies were stacked in ravines and gullies. There they were attacked by crows and rats. The crows became so numerous at the ravines that when disturbed, they rose like giant columns of smoke, some so thoroughly glutted that, unable to fly, they scrambled away in short hops, their wings flailing rapidly at the frozen ground.

• • •

Late in November, a Russian force in the north battered its way across the Don River and swept around in a pincers movement and, with a thin spearhead of armor and troops, linked up with Russian troops in the south. The entire German Sixth Army and its supporting units had been surrounded. Generaloberst Frederick von Paulus promptly requested permission to form a task force using some of the troops within Stalingrad to break through the encircling Russians to reestablish supply lines and communication links with the main German army. Hitler, however, refused to consider such an unthinkable move, assuring the General they would be relieved in due time.

The decoded message read,

The main task of the Sixth Army will be to continue eliminating those few pockets of resistance that still remain within the city of Stalingrad. Everything associated with the name of Stalin is to be destroyed and eliminated. Troops being withdrawn from the Caucasus will soon drive a wedge in from the south and open communication lines with the rest of the German Army. In the meantime, your forces will be adequately supplied by air.

This denial sealed the fate of the general's 334,000 surrounded German soldiers.

When Colonel Stauffer was informed by a headquarters runner that the Russians had broken through and surrounded the troops in Stalingrad, he was stunned. He knew the German troops were under strength and short of supplies, but surrounded? And so far to the rear? How could that be? He immediately ordered his officers to meet at his headquarters located in a roofless concrete garage. Attached to the back of the garage was a coal bin made of concrete blocks where the bodies of a dozen Black Hawk men were waiting for the grave diggers to retrieve them. He quickly had the rear area of the garage cordoned off with yellow plastic tape warning of mines. That way men coming to the meeting would not see the bodies of their comrades killed during the past few days.

While waiting for his men to be seated, he paced the floor in front of them, pausing occasionally to study the map on the wall before him. "Men," he began, "the Russians have pushed a thin spearhead through right here." He pointed to the map. "I'm going to suggest to Generaloberst von Paulus that he let the Black Hawk Brigade cut through them and reestablish our supply lines. Then we'll send those red-ass bastards scurrying back to Moscow!"

The officers smiled and nodded approval.

"I'll ask him to send three battalions of Wehrmacht to take over our positions here in the city. That will free us to go back and do the job." He paused, paced back and forth, and then turned to face them. "In the meantime, check every disabled and wrecked vehicle in the area for gasoline. If you followed my orders, you should have your fuel tanks at least half full. Let's see if we can round up enough to fill them all." Again he paused and surveyed their eager faces. "I have an appointment with General von Paulus this afternoon. I'll meet with you when I get back."

When Colonel Stauffer returned to his headquarters to meet with his officers after a meeting with General von Paulus, he was seething with anger. The assembled men sitting before him could tell by the tension showing in his penetrating gray eyes and the set of his jaw that the meeting at Sixth Army Headquarters had not gone well. In addition, his aide informed him that collecting the gasoline for the Black Hawk vehicles had to be postponed until after nightfall due to heavy shelling and sniper fire.

"Gentlemen," he began, clearing his throat while waiting for explosions of incoming Russian shells to subside. "I have good news and bad news to report to you." He paused to scan the expressions on his anxious officers' faces. "First, the good news. Our winter uniforms, along with heavy, woolen topcoats, have arrived. All armored personnel will be given these. The infantry will, in addition, be issued white capes with hoods. These will furnish camouflage for operations in the snow. That will put us in better shape than some of the units that are still in their summer uniforms. Those poor soldiers have to wear two uniforms, one over the other, to keep warm." He didn't mention that the second uniforms were some that had been stripped from corpses.

"And now, the bad news. At midnight tonight, the Wehrmacht will come in and relieve us. They will bring with them a hundred war dogs, Rottweilers, that they will turn loose tomorrow to ferret out the Russian snipers hiding in the rubble. We are to take up positions back along the Don River on the western approaches of the city." He paused and located the Don on the map with his pointer. "We are to halt a large Russian force on its way from the north. Our primary mission is to protect the airport at Gumrak, which is to be the Sixth Army supply base." He paused again as the officers murmured among themselves. "Marshal Goering has assured General von Paulus that his *Luftwaffe* can supply the six hundred tons of food and supplies needed each day until relief arrives." He raised his eyebrows to indicate disbelief, reflecting the fact that he knew von Paulus was not happy with the decision, but had to follow orders from, higher headquarters at Kalash, town west of Stalingrad where the German High Command Headquarters was located.

Major Helmut Borgman, who had been a supply officer before joining the Black Hawk Brigade, raised his hand.

"A question, Major?" Stauffer said, pointing to the battalion commander.

Borgmann rose to his feet and clicked the hardened leather heels of his boots. "Yes, sir," he replied. "Colonel, do you think we can be supplied by air?"

Stauffer knew the *Luftwaffe* had been stretched thin and doubted it could supply only half of the supplies needed each day. He also knew that many units were on short rations and had been slaughtering two hundred draft horses each day to cover the shortage of the food supply.

• • •

It was shortly before midnight when the first weary soldiers of the *Wehrmacht* replacement battalion began quietly drifting into the craters and improvised defensive positions occupied by the Black Hawk men. A light snow, mixed with the ash of still burning buildings, was falling, muting the sounds the men made and shielding them from the view of the Russian observers stationed along the river. The temperature had dropped to several degrees below freezing, hardening the soil and decreasing the putrid odor of decaying bodies buried in and scattered about the vast area of rubble.

Erich noted that the soldiers, although gaunt and tired with a hollow-eyed look, were well clothed. Clad in warm, woolen uniforms, they also wore long, gray-green greatcoats of heavy material. They had come from Pitomnik, a village to the west where they were guarding an airfield. Although they had a few trucks and self-propelled vehicles, most of their transport being horse drawn, a factor that allowed them to travel with less noise than the motorized units. Erich wondered what would happen when the Black Hawk Brigade started their tanks and half-tracks to leave. When he asked about food rations, one clean-shaven soldier shook his head. "We've been on short rations for over a month."

Since the Black Hawk men carried extra cases of rations in their vehicles, Erich took a case of canned pork and beans from his lead tank and gave it to the soldier for the men of his platoon. He then asked other tank drivers of his company to do the same for the troops who were relieving them.

At precisely five o'clock, shortly before the break of dawn, men of the Black Hawk Brigade started the engines of their vehicles. Along with the noise they created, a pall of exhaust smoke polluted the heavy, snow-filled air, making it difficult for the men to breathe. The Russians, unable to see what was happening, surmised that a relief column was approaching from the west. In a few minutes heavy artillery shells were hissing and sizzling overhead, landing nearly a mile to the rear.

The brigade quickly formed into two columns. With Erich's company designated the lead company of his column, he ordered Sergeant Kohlmann to direct the first tank's driver to slowly maneuver the vehicle around the craters and piles of debris toward a road that would lead out of town. They had gone but a short distance when Sergeant Kohlmann ordered the driver to stop. "What in hell is that?" he exclaimed, pointing to a dark shape bare-ly visible in the distant haze.

Sitting in the tank, Erich looked at a map he held under a dim light. "It's supposed to be the Palace of Culture, according to the map."

"It looks like they've fortified it!"

Erich shouted to the tank's gunners, "Be ready to fire at it if there's resist-ance! Now let's get going!"

The tank lurched forward, its crew straining to make out the form loom-ing ahead.

"My God!" Kohlmann gasped. "It's the bodies of German soldiers! They're stacked like cordwood!"

In the street in front of the Palace of Culture was a row of frozen corpses six feet high and nearly two blocks long. Beyond, was another row of Russian soldiers and civilians.

As their tank rolled past the frozen corpses, Kohlmann stared at the mas-sive pile and shook his head. "I just hope to God I don't get tossed onto a pile like that." He took in a deep breath, again shook his head, and then muttered "Especially not here."

When daylight arrived, the two columns were on the Gumrak road and deep enough within their lines to speed along at a rapid pace. Although the snow had stopped falling, the ground was now covered with a foot of the white fluffy powder that flew about in swirling clouds as the tanks, trucks, and half-tracks sped along the roadway. Erich looked back at the smoking ruins of Stalingrad, its remaining chimneys standing stark and grim as the pale yellow rays of the morning sun illuminated the boiling caldron of struggling men and machines. Great clouds of black smoke billowed skyward and slowly drifted west, covering large areas with ash and giving forth an odor common only to dying cities belching the foul breath of their death throes. He hoped he would never have to witness such a sight on German soil.

Upon reaching the banks of a curve in the frozen Don River, the remaining sixty-seven black *Tiger* tanks fanned out, their guns pointing across it to the west and north. Since the ground was solidly frozen to a considerable depth, the crews began piling quantities of snow around them as a shield from the view of enemy aircraft and artillery spotters.

"I wonder how deep the snow gets here?" a soldier asked as he hauled a pail of snow past Sergeant Kohlmann.

"I don't know," Kohlmann replied wryly. "But if it's anything like Poland, it'll be asshole deep to a tall giraffe."

Some of the men, thinking the gray silt from the edge of the river could be used, tried to gather some, but it was a frozen impossibility. White paint had been ordered several weeks before to paint the vehicles so they would blend with the frozen landscape, but it had never arrived.

The Black Hawk infantry units, wearing white capes, were ordered across the Don. They were deployed over the barren, snow-swept steppe as part of a defense perimeter to halt the onrush of Russian troops that were attacking the scattered and disorganized *Wehrmacht* units reeling before them. During the past days the temperature had dropped from 30 degrees to 25 degrees, then to 16 degrees. And Kohlmann was certain it would soon be down to zero. He ordered the men to conserve every scrap of wood, paper, and cardboard. "You may need it to keep warm," he warned.

A light snow was falling as the infantry soldiers trudged through a fluffy, white blanket squeaking beneath their boots. In addition, it made the ground before them mingle with the sky so no horizon was evident. Erich, searching the area with his binoculars looking for any sign of the Russians, spotted a farm house in the distance across the river. Realizing that farmers used lime to whitewash their buildings and disinfect their hog houses and chicken coops, he decided to find out if he could get some to paint the tanks and half-tracks.

"Kohlmann," he snapped, his breath showing in the crisp air. "Let's see what we can find."

"I'm with you, Captain," answered Sergeant Kohlman as he picked up a machine pistol for each of them.

Since neither Erich nor Kohlmann understood Russian, they asked Corporal Keller to accompany them as interpreter. Erich also slipped two cans of pork and beans into his pockets to use as barter. They quickly sprinted across a bridge and angled for the buildings that were barely discernible before them. Since they did not wear white capes, their black great coats made a decided contrast with the white surroundings. When they passed the last Black Hawk infantrymen, who were busily preparing a shelter in a ravine, they told them where they were going and that they would be returning shortly. Erich, concerned about the infantrymen being able to recognize them through the falling snow, cautioned against firing when they saw the three of them returning.

"We'll be careful," one of the soldiers assured Erich as he continued to dig.

There were two buildings, a house and a small barn, both with white-washed mud walls and thatched roofs. As the three troopers approached, they cocked their machine pistols and crouched low, keeping a greater distance between each other. Peering into a window of the house, Erich saw an elderly man with a bulbous nose sitting in a wooden chair holding an infant. Another small child was asleep on a sagging bed in the corner of the room. He rapped on the door as Kohlmann and the scholarly Keller stood at the ready on either side.

The old man rose wearily to his feet, walked over, and slowly opened the door. He said nothing but merely stared at Erich with a blank, emotionless expression on his face, the infant still clinging to his shoulder. Erich brushed past him, quickly checked the room, and then beckoned his two comrades to enter and close the door.

"Soldiers. Soldiers everywhere," muttered the frail, little man, turning to sit down again. He had light blue eyes and a deeply furrowed face that was covered with a stubble of white beard.

"And are there other soldiers?" asked Keller.

"Oh, yes," replied the man, trying to smooth a shock of white hair with his free hand.

"Where?"

"In the barn. They have my granddaughter—his mother," he stated, nodding at the drooling infant he was holding.

Keller quickly relayed the information to Erich, who immediately asked for a description of the soldiers.

"Russians," answered the old man, shaking his head. "Four Russians."

Kohlmann turned to Erich. "How would Russians get here?" he asked.

"Probably stragglers from Stalingrad," replied Erich, looking out the window toward the barn.

Placing the cans of pork and beans on the table, Erich ordered the man and children to lie on the floor.

"I'll get in the cellar," the old man replied as he lifted the corner of a well-worn rug that exposed a trap door.

When the three Black Hawk men neared the barn, they heard boisterous talking and laughing interspersed with harmonica music being played in a hit-or-miss fashion. Peering through a crack in the door, Erich saw the Russians, dressed in a variety of mismatched uniforms, watching a show they had arranged. In a hog trough on the floor before them was a plump, young woman, naked to the waist and tied hand and foot. Two young pigs were sucking and rooting at her large breasts as she writhed in pain and tugged at her bonds.

When the three German soldiers burst in on them, the unkempt soldiers reached for the machine pistols that were lying on the dirt floor in front of them. Erich cut them down with quick bursts from his machine pistol. While Kohlmann and Keller stood guard a few steps behind him, he kicked the pigs away and cut the ropes that bound the woman. She stared at him in utter terror as he lifted her to her feet. Since she could hardly stand, he kicked a Russian body out of the way and sat her on the bench. Blood still oozed from her nipples.

Certain there was no other Russians in the barn, Keller sat down beside the sobbing woman. "You are safe now," he assured her. Then he and Erich took her by the arms and helped her into the warmth of the house, all the while vapor continuing to rise from her moist breasts.

Kohlmann straightened the bodies of the four dead Russian soldiers and then fired a bullet into the forehead of each. "Beasts," he muttered. "Filthy beasts!"

As the woman went into the bedroom to get some clothes, Erich slid back the rug and opened the trap door. A musty smell of earth filled his nostrils. "You can come out, now," Keller assured the old man.

The man handed the children up to Keller and then climbed the ladder. "Where are the Russian soldiers?" he asked.

"They are dead," Keller said matter-of-factly. "They are in the barn."

"They really aren't Russians, you know," the old man said, taking back the smallest of the children. "They're actually Mongols from Kazakh. They were drafted into the Soviet Army and brought to Moscow to defend it last winter. This winter they were shifted to Stalingrad. They don't want to fight. Don't even want to be in the army. Just want to go back home to their families and their herds of reindeer and goats." He paused for a moment, then, shaking his head, muttered, "The vodka must have turned them into animals."

They learned that the woman's name was Olga, she was twenty-eight years old, and the mother of the two children. Her mother had been dead for several years, and both her husband and father had joined the Russian army. They had received no word from either of them for over a year. She lived on the farm with her grandfather and helped with the work.

After being informed of Erich's medical training, both Olga and the old man became considerably more relaxed and receptive to the Black Hawk troopers. Erich had her lie down on the bed, where he covered her over with

236

a blanket. "You should just rest for a few minutes. When you feel like it, wash your breasts with warm, soapy water and wear as little clothing over them as possible."

After Keller had translated Erich's directions, she asked, "Can I nurse my baby?"

"No," he replied. "Not until all signs of soreness and blood have disappeared."

As Sergeant Kohlmann lifted the sack of lime to his shoulder and headed for the door, the man beckoned Erich to wait for a moment. Then he lifted the trap door and called, "Stella! Stella! Stella! Come up!"

Up from the pale light of the opening stepped a chunky, dark-complexioned girl whose black, piercing eyes reflected the degree of terror she was experiencing. Erich stepped forward, clicked his heels, and bowed slightly from the waist as he shook her cold, clammy hand. She nodded her head and forced a smile. "This is Olga's younger sister, Stella," Keller explained after the old man had told him. With that, the three troopers started back toward the Don through the lightly drifting snow.

Applying whitewash in the extremely low temperature proved a difficult task. Even though warm water was used, it froze and crystallized the instant it came in contact with the cold hull of the tank, causing the brush to freeze to the metal. Sergeant Kohlmann then instructed the men to splash it on with the brush. Soon the rumble of artillery fire in the distance spurred them on to complete the task. In addition, some of the men found lumber from demolished buildings and sheets of metal from wrecked vehicles, which they used to build protective mounds in front of their tanks.

• • •

Early the next day, the first remnants of the fleeing *Wehrmacht* came rolling across the bridge in cars and trucks. They consisted mostly of officers and clerks of headquarters companies. In a few hours the trickle turned into a torrent of wide-eyed, scrambling troops from all branches and of all ranks. Erich saw they were very exhausted and most so hungry they were asking for food from anyone they encountered. He noted a field grade officer trying to halt the troops and get them organized into a unit again so they could turn and fight the approaching enemy. But most continued on their way in spite of his drawn pistol and threat to shoot. Many no longer carried a weapon of any kind as they streamed through the entrenched Black Hawk infantry. Before long, Russian planes appeared overhead but were driven off by antiaircraft fire.

By nightfall bridge traffic was backed up as far as the eye could see with unit commanders shouting and arguing with each other as to which outfit should be given priority and what vehicles should be permitted to cut into the long line at the bridge. Horse-drawn wagons appeared to be the great impediment to speed, but they would not permit the motorized transports to pass or overtake them. A few impatient truck drivers, tired of shouting at the teamsters, bumped and nudged the wagons with their vehicles. One such incident on the bridge resulted in a team of horses bolting, snapping the wooden tongue of the wagon. As the frightened animals lunged forward, the tongue of the careening wagon dropped to the road, spearing an exhausted soldier lying in the snow. The horses raced on for a hundred yards before the harness parted, freeing them and letting the loaded wagon overturn in a ditch. Its splintered tongue was left pointing skyward, holding the skewered soldier aloft, his body quivering as steam rose from his blood-soaked clothing.

That evening the snow stopped falling, and the full moon made the landscape gleam and glisten like a jeweled blanket. Dark blotches of craters made by random enemy shelling marked the otherwise pristine white scene as the weary *Wehrmacht* continued to stumble like ghosts toward the Don River, hoping it would give them protection and rest for their starved, aching bodies. Since the bridge was terribly congested, many walked across the ice. And even motorcycles were crossing in this manner, with one occasionally breaking through a shell hole that hadn't had sufficient time to freeze solidly again.

By morning, what was left of the *Wehrmacht* artillery had crossed the river and the flow of men and machines had dwindled to a trickle again. Heavy guns from the rear were firing overhead at the approaching Russians, while the exhausted, poorly equipped infantry continued to retreat toward the river in a semi-orderly fashion that delayed the Russian offensive. After they had retreated through the Black Hawk infantry outposts, they turned the defense task over to the SS troopers and shuffled on to cross the river. As they struggled through the snow, many fell to the ground, some to be assisted to their feet again and helped on while others remained where they fell, left to the sedation of the cold that would gently ease them into the world beyond.

The first wave of Russian infantry appeared on the frozen horizon at noon and were cut down by Black Hawk machine guns and rifles, only to be replaced by another wave yelling, "Hurrah! Hurrah!" Those in the second wave were pinned down by small arms fire and then decimated by mortar barrages. This stubborn, organized resistance, the first they had encountered in days, confused the Russians, so they raked the area with marching artillery fire and then unleashed another wave of charging, yelling infantrymen. These, too, were stopped, but not before some had reached the outer Black Hawk perimeter, overrunning a few positions. The ensuing hand-to-hand fighting quickly resolved itself, the Russians withdrawing over the bodies of hundreds of their fallen comrades so they could be reinforced and regrouped.

Late in the afternoon, a charge of screaming Cossack cavalry came roaring across the frozen terrain, racing in so fast that artillery fire could not be brought to bear on them. However, the entire line of *Tiger* tanks opened up with their eighty-eights and scattered the formation of horsemen. Much of their effectiveness was then lost in the resulting confusion. Some of the horses were killed outright, but many were so frightened by the exploding shells that they bolted, throwing their riders and then racing wildly about the entrenched Black Hawk infantry. Shrapnel tore gaping holes in their steaming, sweat-covered hides and blood oozed and spurted as they dashed about. One, its belly torn open, trotted on until tripped by the tangle of its own intestines. A Black Hawk trooper in a nearby hole shot it in the head to end its painful thrashing and screaming.

Erich, standing beside his lead tank, lowered his binoculars and let them hang by the leather strap around his neck. He exercised the fingers in his gloved hands to restore blood circulation, gave an audible sigh, and shook his head. It troubled him deeply to see the terrible slaughter of those gentle beasts. He felt sympathy and empathy for the Cossacks, but it was the horses that troubled him most. He recalled stroking the soft, velvety noses of the gentle, accommodating plow horses Mr. Trapp had on his farm in Holzheim, and how faithfully they worked for him. To witness the brutal butchery he had seen on the battlefield with the Cossacks made him feel ill. But then, he rationalized, horses had been brutalized for centuries, both steeds and beasts of burden, whenever they were drawn into the tempests of man's inhumanity to man.

The Cossack soldier, although brave and daring on his mount, became a poor soldier on foot and fell easy prey to the rifles, bayonets, and machine guns of the well- disciplined Black Hawk infantry. Upon retreating, they had left a large number of their unit lying on the already well-littered battlefield. When nightfall came, however, the German troopers, who had suffered numerous casualties, who had been overrun twice during the day, and who were running low on ammunition, were ordered to withdraw back across the Don.

• • •

The bridge was prepared for demolition and the supporting Black Hawk *Tigers* were directed to pull back several hundred yards so they could continue to furnish close-in artillery support for the tired infantry. Most were able to comply, but the engines of two refused to start because of the extreme cold. Using an oil-fired heat gun, the crew was able to get one started, but the other had to be abandoned.

The next day as the onslaught resumed, the bridge was blown to prevent its use by vehicles, but the hordes of Russian infantry continued to charge the

German lines by walking, running, and crawling across the frozen river. They were being supported by massive concentrations of artillery fire and salvo after salvo of *katyushi* rockets. Overhead, Russian planes were becoming numerous, requiring the German tanks to keep well camouflaged and supply trucks to move about with extreme caution.

As pressure from the Russian army continued to mount and their supplies and ammunition continued to run low, the German army began a systematic retreat in an effort to close the breaches that threatened to develop in its sagging lines of exhausted men. As casualties mounted in the Black Hawk Brigade, they were replaced with *Wehrmacht* soldiers, many of whom had not had a full stomach or hot meal for days. As far as the eye could see, the frozen steppe was littered with the wrecked and abandoned machines of war and the bodies of the dead and dying were everywhere. Those of recent demise were covered with a light dusting of snow. Others that had been there longer were sculpted over with two or three feet of drifted snow. Since there was an insufficient number of ambulances to haul the wounded to hospitals, many were loaded into trucks and wagons, which frequently stalled or were wrecked and then abandoned, leaving their cargo of wounded to slowly freeze to death.

On the roads, layers of snow were compressed beneath the wheels of heavy vehicles into layers of ice. At night these icy, windswept highways were crawling with retreating vehicles and men, many of the latter so weak from wounds, hunger, or illnesses that they slipped fell, and were run over before they could rise again. By morning, the bodies had been compressed to a fraction of an inch in thickness, covered with snow and compressed again to form a weird, icy mosaic that stretched for miles on all roads leading to Stalingrad. Grotesque faces as large as barrelheads stared up through the clear, glazed surface, and there were hands as large as hams. Occasionally, where the buttons of a tunic had parted, a hairy chest was exposed.

Each day the retreat continued to the next ravine, the next row of trees, or the next cluster of buildings. Day and night they were pounded with artillery, mortars, and strafing planes. The roaring cannons, the screaming rockets, and the blasts of thousands of tons of explosives dulled their sense of hearing so that even during a brief lull, they would have to shout in order to be heard as they stood beside one another. Great geysers of frozen earth shot skyward everywhere, turning the snow-covered landscape into a gray mixture of frozen soil and snow. The wounded, as they lay helpless in the frozen fields, were covered with this gritty mixture, which would in turn be melted by the heat of their bodies and then frozen into a gray glaze as the severe cold extinguished the last sparks of life and drove the souls from their bodies. The earth shook and trembled beneath them, belching up before them and the sky flamed and roared about them. Everywhere smoke, dust, fumes, and flying shrapnel mowed everything in its path like a mighty scythe. The glowing metal tore at the earth, creating yawning craters that would be reworked by another barrage every few minutes, turning the area into a moonscape littered with rifles, canteens, jackboots, rags, and remnants of human bodies.

The Black Hawk Brigade continued its retreat toward the Pitomnik airfield under the unrelenting, ever intensifying pressure of Russian troops. Colonel Stauffer had been ordered to protect the field at all costs because it was one of the last remaining means of supply. Erich carefully divided what fuel he had left among his remaining *Tiger* tanks and withdrew them the last few hundred yards to set up a perimeter defense. The infantry, using the wreckage of battle, constructed bunkers and parapets, which they camouflaged with snow. One hundred and fifty-five millimeter howitzers were also interspersed with the *Tigers* to furnish the long range shelling to keep the horde of Russian units at a distance.

The airfield was extremely busy during daylight hours. Heavy transports brought in supplies and took out the sick and wounded. But the days were very short, darkness falling a little after three in the afternoon, and the runway was rough, having been repeatedly repaired after being damaged by bombs and shells. Over a hundred planes lined its sides, planes that had been wrecked or damaged or that lacked sufficient fuel for the return trip. The crew of a giant ME 232 *Gigant*, having left its four engines running for fear they would not start in the extreme cold, scavenged enough gasoline from the derelicts to leave. It had brought in a partial load of black bread and canned pork. But it had to take a wide detour to avoid the numerous Russian antiaircraft guns and was low on fuel. As it was refueled, a medical unit loaded it with sick and wounded. The pilot, his eyebrows white with frost, climbed into the cabin and the huge plane roared down the runway, its wheels bouncing over the holes and filled craters. But the load was too great for takeoff, so he returned. The crew unloaded twelve men lying on stretchers and then took off, leaving the bandaged and splinted cases beside the runway. The next morning they were still there, their faces set, frozen specters of a calm, relaxing death by freezing.

• • •

By mid-December, the food shortage was such that each man was allotted half a slice of bread, a dozen peas or beans, and a small piece of meat. When the rations were reduced again a few days later, the slaughter of horses began on a large scale. In early January, all domestic animals were being consumed, including dogs and cats. Medical supplies had also reached a critical stage where bandages were being reclaimed, washed, and reused. Vaccines for tetanus, typhoid, and typhus were exhausted, making control of these dreaded killers impossible. In addition, sanitation conditions were such that lice and fleas were universal. Once infested, it was utterly hopeless to rid oneself of them.

It was an extremely cold Sunday morning, January 10, 1943, when Erich was informed by a runner he was to report to Colonel Stauffer at Brigade Headquarters in thirty minutes. Wanting to be presentable, he decided to shave off three days growth of beard that had been hidden beneath a black, woolen stocking mask he was wearing to ward off frostbite. He had Sergeant Kohlmann start the engine of the lead Tiger tank so he could heat some water in an aluminum cup on the exhaust manifold. Squatting in the lean-to shelter he had constructed beside the tank, he quickly shaved and combed his hair.

After walking the quarter mile path through knee-deep snow that squeaked with each step, he arrived at Colonel Stauffer's tent. It was a small shelter for regimental headquarters, but it had been layered over with several thickness of canvas. Erich knocked on the thin, wooden door and was admitted by an aide.

He walked briskly to the desk in the middle of the tent, saluted smartly, and tried to click the heels of his damp, scuffed jackboots. Noting the black patch covering the colonel's left eye, he assumed it was from the injury he had heard about a week before. He tried not to stare at it. He also saw that Stauffer's uniform was not as neat as it had been on previous visits, and there were food stains down the front of his tunic.

"Have a seat," Stauffer ordered, pointing to the chair in front of his desk. Although there was a small, oil-fired heater behind the desk, his breath still showed in the cold air. "So now you see that I have lost an eye," he said wryly. "A clod of frozen earth hit it during the heavy shelling last week. Afraid of infection, so I had them remove it. It's a good thing man is blessed with two of them."

The Colonel rose to his feet. "Captain Stecker," he began, "as you know, your battalion has been without a commander since Major Borgmann was killed. So I called you here to inform you that you are to replace him."

Erich, overwhelmed by the sudden promotion, merely nodded. He had been fifty yards away when Helmut Borgmann was killed. It was shortly after they began pulling back from the Don. Borgmann had been caught in the open when a salvo of *katyusi* came crashing in, obliterating him in a tumultuous, overwhelming torrent of destruction.

Stauffer looked Erich in the eye. "Do you have any problem with that?" he asked, noting the surprised look on the young captain's face.

"No, sir!" Erich replied, regaining his military composure. Although it could be considered a promotion to be made Battalion Commander, his battalion had been reduced in size so it possessed fewer men than that of a fully staffed company.

Erich, assuming the meeting was concluded, rose to his feet.

Colonel Stauffer stood on the other side of the desk facing him. "Any questions?" he asked in a stern voice.

"Sir, any information on a relief column breaking through the Russian lines?" Erich asked.

Stauffer looked at him soberly. "The *Fuhrer* has directed us to continue on with the capture of Stalingrad. He will direct the operation to see that we are relieved." He paused to give a sigh and then unsmiling, shook his head. "The Russians seem to be getting stronger. They have captured Group Headquarters at Kalash. All we can do is follow orders and hope for the best."

Erich saluted, clicked his heels as best he could, and then started for the open door being held by the aide.

"And, Stecker," the colonel called after him, a grin on his face, "if we get out of this, I'll see that you are promoted to major!"

"Thank you, sir," Erich said, looking back over his shoulder.

As he walked back to his company through the powdery, knee-deep snow, thoughts were chasing themselves through his puzzled mind. He thought of the thousands of young, well-fed Russian troops dressed in warm, quilted uniforms and felt boots who had appeared during the past two months. And they were supplied with a seemingly endless supply of shells and rockets. In addition, they now had an air force that was becoming very strong and nearly unchallenged.

He wondered if he would ever see Holzheim again. *Ah, Holzheim. Safe, serene, pleasant Holzheim.* He remembered window boxes filled with brightly blooming geraniums, the wonderful aroma of ripening fruit hanging on grapevines and apple trees, and the odor of the Trapp barnyard. He recalled the farewell with his parents and time with Maria. Beautiful, loving Maria. How he missed her warm, brown eyes, sweet smile, and soft, white arms. Then he heard several Russian salvos of long-range shells whispering, sizzling, and hissing as they passed high overhead on their way to the distant rear. It suddenly reminded him that he was now surrounded by a fiery ring of explosive force and flying metal.

• • •

Since the Pitomnik airfield was under constant attack, it became extremely dangerous and nearly impossible to be used. With the Russians pressing hard and the defender's food and ammunition running low, orders were received to abandon the defense of the airfield and retreat toward Stalingrad. The

Black Hawk Brigade was to go through the *Wehrmacht* defense positions located behind them and establish a defensive line a mile in front of Gumrak Airfield.

That evening the one hundred-fifty-five millimeter howitzers fired their remaining twenty rounds and then fell silent, abandoned to the freezing desolation that was closing over them. The remaining twenty-one *Tiger* and *Panther* tanks, having used their fuel to keep batteries charged so they could operate the turret guns, expended their few remaining shells before being abandoned by their crews. The temperature was minus 17 degrees Fahrenheit.

Erich and Sergeant Kohlmann checked the infantry outposts and the silent tanks to be certain they had all their men. Then they started walking, leading a long column on the road to Gumrak and the last useable airfield. Progress was slow due to the exhaustion of the men, the encrusted snow in the fields, and the wreckage of battle. In addition, there was danger from trucks with black-out lights that sped along the road, slowing for nothing in their path.

In a snow-covered field a short distance from the road, Erich saw two soldiers in a machine gun emplacement that did not acknowledge him when he waved. He turned to Kohlmann. "Keep the line moving," he ordered, still looking at the machine gun emplacement. "I'll check them out. Can't take any chances."

"Yes, sir!" Kohlmann replied.

When Erich reached the emplacement, he found everything covered with a light dusting of snow. The two men had built a half-circle parapet of frozen corpses to protect themselves from rifle and machine gun fire. But a mortar shell had landed just behind them, killing them as they knelt to man their guns. One had his helmeted head resting on the rear of the barrel, his finger still on the weapon's trigger. The other knelt with head bowed as if in prayer, his two hands supporting an ammunition belt he was guiding from a steel box on the ground into the breech of the machine gun. Both were frozen stiff. Erich, a grim expression on his face, studied them for a full minute. Then, shaking his head as he walked off, muttered, "That monument will be there until the spring thaw."

When he returned to the ice-coated road, he noticed an abnormal clunking sound made by some of his men as they struggled along stiff-legged in an effort to keep up with the column. Their feet and legs had frozen into a solid mass inside their jackboots. "You should go to a clinic," he advised one.

The man shook his head. "Just don't leave me," he pleaded. "If I go to a clinic, I'll never get home."

"We won't leave you," Erich assured him.

The next morning Erich's battalion sought shelter in a ravine containing a few scrubby trees. He asked Kohlmann and Keller to go with him in search of something that could be used to provide foot protection from the biting cold.

"We hadn't better thaw their feet," stated Kohlmann, remembering his experience in Poland the previous winter. "They won't be able to go on if we do."

"I guess you're right," Erich replied. "But maybe we can keep others from freezing."

They found a wrecked truck that had been rolled into a ditch. It contained Christmas decorations and several rolls of burlap and canvas. Each man hoisted a roll of burlap onto his shoulder and they started back, their ears alert to the exploding world about them, their bodies ready to drop to the ground should a shell land too close.

As they approached the ravine, they were challenged by two outpost guards.

"At least they're alert enough," Kohlmann observed with a smile as they were permitted to proceed.

"Sure," responded Keller in a grim tone. "Providing they don't shoot first and challenge second."

The Black Hawk men used the burlap to wrap their legs and feet and to line their overcoats. When they walked, they appeared as stuffed sacks walking on bags of rags. And their sunken eyes, rosy noses, and protruding cheekbones jutted out from a mat of mud and beard. That evening they struggled, trying to stay clear of the dangerous traffic on the heavily traveled road. At midnight, unable to dig protective holes, they took up defensive positions along the raised bed of a rail line. The next morning shells from the advancing Russians were again landing among them.

• • •

Erich's battalion had just dug in across a broad front on the cold, snow-covered approaches to Gumrak when Corporal Keller received a wound in the right foot by a large caliber bullet. Erich valued the young corporal as an excellent soldier and an outstanding translator of the Russian language, so he stopped to see how badly the young trooper was wounded. Kneeling down, he saw no blood around the rip in Keller's leather boot. And Keller did not seem to be in pain. When he removed the boot, he found the foot and ankle frozen solid. The bullet had shattered the crystallized flesh and bone, which was being held loosely together by Keller's sock. Sliding the boot back on, he told the young trooper, "You can't walk on this. There's a hospital just up the road. I'll carry you there."

But short rations and lack of rest had weakened the young officer. He no longer had the stamina to do things that had been routine before. He would seek help. However, when he looked at the hollow cheeks, sunken eyes, and slow response of his men, he decided to do it himself. He had Keller mount his back, and they started up the road. They had traveled a short distance when they came upon a truck that had slid into a depression. The driver and his assistant were using frozen corpses for additional traction, but without success. Erich, his knees ready to buckle from the burden of Keller, trotted across an open space being raked by rifle fire from distant Russian snipers. Nearly exhausted, he lowered Keller to the ground and dropped into a ravine to rest.

Breathing heavily, he realized how truly weak he had become. In addition, he had to breathe through his mouth since the cold air made his nostrils freeze shut. After several minutes of rest, he got Keller to his feet and, by hobbling along with the wounded man's arm around his neck, helped him the half mile to a field hospital.

The hospital was in a large cave dug into the side of the ravine. As they approached, they limped past a stack of several hundred frozen bodies. All around the canvas-covered entrance dozens of sick and wounded sat, stood, and lay on stretchers attempting to gather some warmth from several small, wood fires that were burning in the immediate vicinity. A short distance away, numerous wasted forms were sitting on a long wooden bench, trying to relieve themselves of the terrible torture of white or red dysentery. As Erich watched, two toppled from the bench and curled up on the frozen ground that was covered with vomit and excretion. There, with no one possessing the strength to help them, they writhed and groaned in agony until unconsciousness relieved them of their misery.

Erich pulled the canvas flap aside and dragged Keller in with him. The floor inside was a mass of bodies on stretchers, some waiting for surgery, others recuperating and waiting for transport to evacuate them toward Stalingrad. Along one side, six operating tables with two surgeons each were engaged in the messy business of continuous, rapid-fire surgery. The tables and surgeon's gowns were smeared with blood. And the sawdust-covered floor was saturated with it. A canvas was stretched above the operating area to protect it from dirt that dropped during shelling attacks.

Erich stood for several minutes wondering what to do, his nostrils assaulted by the heavy, humid air filled with odors of rotted flesh, perspiration, and a variety of hospital chemicals.

"At least it's warm in here," muttered Keller, his voice weaker, his face noticeably more ashen.

"He should wait outside," an orderly informed Erich.

Erich looked at him with a determined stare.

The orderly scanned the crowded floor. "There," he said, pointing to an empty stretcher. "Put him there. We'll get to him as soon as we can."

Erich got him to the stretcher amidst the sea of listless, smelly, rag-covered forms. After lowering him as gently as possible, he tucked two slices of dry bread into his tunic and then stood to leave. He had to wait while two orderlies passed carrying a stretcher bearing a rejectee from one of the operating tables. The man, with a temperature from a badly infected chest wound, was considered a waste of time, anesthetic, and bandages. He was being taken outside to make room for more hopeful cases as well as to hasten his death and shorten his suffering.

Erich followed them outside where other cases were lying on the frozen ground. After the orderlies departed, Erich knelt beside the man. A pair of dull gray eyes stared out from recessed sockets. The man swallowed, moved his dry lips, but made no sound and displayed no emotion, his sober, bewhiskered face implying resignation to the fate assigned to him. A sprinkling of snowflakes was falling, melting on those still alive and covering the death stare of those no longer warm.

Erich, ever mindful of the shells from the Russian guns that were blanketing the area as he made his way back to the battalion, doubted he would see Keller again. The young trooper's feet would have to be amputated, he knew that. And he wondered if Keller would be considered worthy of evacuation. Then he questioned if he, himself, would ever get back home again.

Although the battalion still held firm under mounting pressure from the Russians, the enemy's big guns had been moved nearer and their white-clad infantry had crawled to within a few hundred yards of the railroad tracks behind which the Black Hawk men had dug in. Periodically, heavy machine gun fire raked across the steel tracks, loosening the frozen gravel and scattering it about with lethal force, and armor-piercing bullets punched holes through the web of the tracks. Erich knelt and watched as several troopers opened frozen cans of sauerkraut someone had found in an abandoned truck. Others were hacking a slab of ice-encrusted horsemeat into smaller pieces for distribution.

During the night, Erich received a deep laceration to his right forearm from a piece of hot shrapnel that came from one of the many barrages that blanketed the area. Although not life--threatening, he wished to bandage it as protection from the battlefield dirt and filth, but the brigade's supply of bandages and compresses had been exhausted. He would cover it with his handkerchief and make a quick trip to the field hospital in the morning.

Just before dawn, he crawled over to Sergeant Kohlman. "I'll be back in an hour," he said. In a low crouch, he dashed to the ravine and then walked to the hospital.

When he asked an orderly for a bandage in the foul smelling surgical ward, he was handed a length of gauze that had been used and washed. The carrot-topped orderly watched as he looked at it questioningly. "It's all right," he was assured. "It's clean."

"Really?" Erich asked acidly, doubt showing on his shaggy face.

"Yes. There are no others. After we wash them, they are heated in an oven to sterilize them.

"Thank you," Erich responded as he turned to search the floor for Corporal Keller.

The young trooper was still lying on the floor in the same place. He knelt beside the pallid faced soldier and asked, "How are you, Corporal Keller?"

Slowly, Keller opened his eyes. Seeing Erich, his face brightened momentarily, then he said, "My leg hurts."

"Have they helped you?"

"No, my turn has not come yet."

Erich grasped Keller's hand and looked at his dirty, torn uniform and then at the lightly bearded face with its pink cheekbones and dull eyes.

"Captain," Keller responded, his expressionless face gazing upward. He was weak, very weak. "Could you have them take off my boot?"

"Yes. Of course."

The warmth having thawed the foot, Erich expected some skin would peel off when he removed the sock. When he pulled on the boot, however, it came off readily, shucking the flesh from the foot and calf. He quickly flipped the blanket over the hideous sight, then walked abruptly outside to dispose of the foul smelling boot. He inhaled several breaths of fresh air and then returned to the side of the still expressionless Keller.

"It feels better now," Keller murmured through dry lips. "Itches instead of aches."

Erich halted a passing orderly and raised the corner of the blanket to show him the skeletal remains of the foot. Then he stood to observe the medical man's reaction.

"Is he bleeding?" the orderly asked with a shrug.

"No," replied Erich, bewildered at the calmness of the response.

"Good. We'll get to him before long."

"But this man has a very serious problem here," protested Erich.

"At least one-fourth of those lying on this floor have the same problem, my captain," answered the orderly as he turned to walk off.

Erich knelt beside Keller again.

"I must go now, but they will get to you soon."

"Thank you," Keller replied weakly, closing his eyes.

• • •

The remaining men of the Death Head Brigade retreated to Gumrak and set up a defense around a small airstrip, one that could accommodate only light planes used for courier service. Two sacks of mail had arrived for the brigade, the first in more than a month, but most of it was undeliverable because the intended recipients were casualties. Erich received two letters from his mother and one from Maria. He would read them in the order in which they were mailed.

The first, written by his mother in November, stated that she and his father was aware of his plight in Stalingrad but were certain the Russians would soon lay down their arms and surrender. Besides, the news over the radio had stated that two *panzer* divisions were coming up from the south to relieve them. "Keep up your spirits, my son. Maybe you'll get a Christmas leave," she concluded.

Christmas, he thought. *Where was he Christmas? Oh, yes. Retreating toward Pitomnik in the swirling snow.*

The next letter he opened was written by Maria in early December. She voiced concern about the Stalingrad situation but expressed hope that relief would come.

> *"My love for you is so deep and all consuming. It comes from the very depth of my soul. It has been lonely, oh, so very, very lonely since you went away. Each night I pray to God that you will return safely to me. Oh, my God! How I miss you!"*

Tears welled up in his eyes. He hoped he wouldn't disappoint her, but he knew his chance of survival was bleak—very bleak. However, he must put his feelings aside. His sworn duty was to fight the enemy to the last bullet—to the last bit of strength his body possessed.

He swallowed, then slowly opened the second envelope from his mother. His heart sank as he withdrew the letter written on paper with a black border. In a very nervous hand, she had written that his father had been ordered to Nurnberg for a political rally and had been killed in a night bombing raid: "His body is buried in the rubble and hasn't been found yet. They say he will be shipped home when they retrieve it."

Erich sat on the frozen ground, dry-eyed and stunned. He was oblivious to the chatter of machine guns and thunderous explosions of artillery shells crashing around him. Snowflakes falling on the quivering letter caused the ink to run. He was glad. He didn't want to reread it.

Sergeant Kohlmann came scurrying up to him in a low crouch, his eyes dancing in his haggard face. "Captain! Captain!" he half shouted, a broad grin showing through his whiskers. "She's agreed!"

"Really?" responded Erich, not knowing what he was talking about and showing little interest in learning.

"Yes! It's my Roxanne." He thrust a photograph of a beautiful girl at Erich. "She's going to marry me as soon as I get the leave!"

"Wonderful," replied Erich, looking toward the sound of Russian cannon. "Better get back to your parapet so you'll live to get the leave."

"Yes, sir!" the sergeant answered, tucking the letter and photograph into his tunic.

• • •

During the next few days it became increasingly apparent to Erich that the chance of surviving this terrible calamity was very limited. Somehow he hoped a miracle would occur to rescue them, but conditions continued to worsen and all units were retreating toward the center of Stalingrad, a place he considered the very jaws of hell. Food and ammunition were being rapidly depleted, medical supplies were exhausted, and when he shaved at one of the airport buildings, he was shocked to see that he looked like a walking cadaver. He managed to speak optimistically to his troops for purposes of morale, but he suspected their skepticism. Also, he sensed the people of Germany did not believe what they read in the newspapers and heard on the radio.

• • •

It was early on the cold, windy morning of January 22, 1943, that men of the Black Hawk Brigade, along with reinforcements and stragglers they had acquired, retreated to the edge of the airstrip. German artillery fire was keeping the Russians from pressing very close in large numbers. And the machine guns and rifles of Black Hawk men were driving off the more numerous probing patrols the Russians were using to test the German lines. But Erich knew that before long the enemy would organize an assault that would drive them back.

Three neatly dressed, well-fed colonels drove up in a command car, each carrying a briefcase, and dashed into a sandbagged building. A short time later, a single engine plane landed and taxied to a halt not far from where Erich was squatting in a protected emplacement. Leaving the engine running, the pilot opened the cabin door and stepped down. Erich approached him.

The pilot, neatly dressed in a flight suit, was reluctant to shake the hand of such a shabby soldier. He couldn't believe his eyes that the battle of Stalingrad was being waged by troops such as this. And to think, this was a captain in the SS. Unbelievable!

After a few minutes of conversation, however, he began to recognize the terrible fate that had been dealt to these beleaguered troops. Suddenly, sympathy overcame his aloofness. He had been informed that he was piloting the last flight from the last available airfield. Three headquarters officers, carrying important documents, were to go back with him. This would leave radio the only contact remaining with the outside world. Erich asked if he would carry a message back for him.

"Certainly!" replied the pilot.

Since Erich had neither pencil nor paper, the pilot removed a pair of leather gloves and handed him the cardboard back of his log book. Then, pulling a pen from an upper sleeve pocket, held it out to Erich. "Here's something to write with," he said quietly.

A few incoming shells were exploding on the periphery of the airstrip as the colonels emerged from the door of the sandbagged building. Erich quickly wrote Maria's name and address on one side of the cardboard. Then, on the other, he carefully printed a short verse he hoped she would someday fully understand:

> *Stalingrad January 20, 1943*
> *My Dearest Darling:*
> *The candle burns so very low*
> *It may not last the night*
> *But, oh my darling, you must know*
> *How wonderful has been the light.*
> *Eternally yours,*
> *Erich*

He handed it to the pilot as the trim, agile colonels climbed aboard the plane. It taxied to the end of the runway and then roared off. Erich stood and watched as it gained altitude and gradually diminished in size. When it had disappeared in the western sky, Erich shivered. Suddenly, he felt so very, very alone.

• • •

Early the next day, after the few remaining airfield personnel had ridden off, what remained of the once proud Death Head Brigade began the slow, painful shuffle of retreat toward the center of Stalingrad. It was a clear day with the temperature at minus 20 degrees as they followed the two roads leading eastward. Retreating units that preceded them had marked the snow-covered road edges with legs of slaughtered horses, jamming them into the encrusted snow, hoofs skyward, every few hundred yards. The freezing temperature preserved them well, but every morsel of flesh had been gnawed from them.

The two roads had been heavily traveled by men and machines. Many of the men had been run over and trampled into the snow and then compressed by heavy wheels and steel cleats that formed an ice-covered mosaic of heads, faces, and hands over which the Death Head troopers marched. The entire area around them resembled an enormous snow-covered cemetery of men and machines—the flotsam of a gigantic struggle. The fields and ravines were littered with frozen, frost-encrusted corpses, and hundreds of abandoned trucks and railroad cars were stacked high with them.

Although they did not see the Russian soldiers, incessant artillery and rocket barrages rained down upon them from three sides. It blew apart the abandoned equipment and tossed the frozen bodies high into the air as it churned the tormented land. Troopers became more exhausted from dropping to their stomachs at the sound of incoming barrages than from walking.

One shell landed among Erich's men. When they rose again to resume their flight, two did not get up. While others continued on, Erich and Sergeant Kohlmann went over to the two downed men. Their bodies had been punctured in several places by shrapnel. The sergeant stooped to roll one over.

"Don't bother with them," Erich ordered

"Maybe we can help," Kohlmann protested.

"They're dead."

"How can you tell?"

"See all those gray specks in the snow," Erich said, pointing. "They're fleas and lice. They abandon the body immediately after death."

Upon reaching the inner section of the city, Colonel Stauffer assigned a segment of its defense to Erich's battalion—a battalion of eleven men. Although every building was a ruin or a heap of rubble, many of the cellars were in good condition. The walls had collapsed upon them, providing additional safety from bombs, shells, and rockets. While two or three of his men were outside guarding against a surprise attack, those inside huddled and rested, hiding from the enemy and the bitter wind.

The Russians soon learned of the arrangement. "Hurrah! Hurrah!" they yelled as they had been doing on their mass attacks. This brought Germans soldiers up from the cellars into the deadly fire of the sharpshooters. To counter this, Erich and Kohlmann obtained rifles and crawled beneath a sheet of corrugated metal in a nearby crater. There they waited for a sign, a flash, or some movement. In an adjacent crater, Erich observed a German soldier with his little finger on the trigger of his rifle. "Where were you taught to use your little finger?" Erich shouted caustically, trying to be heard above the roar of battle.

The soldier said nothing, but held up his hand showing that three fingers were missing.

"What happened?" Erich asked, feeling somewhat humbled.

"Those three froze and broke off," came the reply. "Works fine with the thumb and little finger."

Erich nodded that he understood.

"But it's all right. My other hand is fine."

One Russian, believing he was unobserved as he hid in the rubble behind a large block of concrete a hundred yards away, decided to eat a slice of bread. The movement betrayed his location. As Erich fired, the sniper's hand flew up, tossing the bread into the air and then the hand dropped back down behind the block of concrete. Although several Russian snipers and sharpshooters were dispatched before the men returned to their cellar, the Black Hawk men continued to retreat.

They came upon the cellar of a ruined library filled with sick, wounded, insane, and dead. It had been used as a collecting point for a hospital dressing station. In the dim light of a single oil lamp, Erich saw hundreds of men lying, pressed together on the dirty floor. More covered the stairways and filled the corridors. Many moaned, some ranted, but most were silent, so weak from dysentery, fever, or hunger that they could neither move nor whimper. Some had been dead for days while others, still alive, were in varying stages of partial decay from gangrene or frostbite. A few were sitting without ears or noses. Lice stung their skin and crawled into open wounds, abandoning them only upon death or high fever. The air was heavy with the stench of decaying flesh, fetid blood, excrement, and sweat.

Erich's battalion, now only six men, moved on to the next building. Within an hour he lost another man, a *Wehrmacht* rifleman replacement, whose head exploded like a ripe melon as a large caliber bullet tore through it. A few minutes before the rifleman was hit, Erich had confided in Kohlmann that he seriously doubted they would get out of Stalingrad without being killed or taken prisoner. "By God," Kohlmann replied in a determined voice, "I'm going to get back to the Fatherland. I have to so I can marry my Roxanne." He paused, then added, "Even if I have to swim the damn Volga and walk all the way across Siberia!"

• • •

It had been two days since Erich had seen Colonel Stauffer, but when he learned that General von Paulus had sent a message to army headquarters in Germany that the final collapse of all resistance in the city could not be delayed more than twenty-four hours, he decided to locate Stauffer's headquarters and confer with him. When he found him, the colonel was very ill and weak, suffering from an initial phase of dysentery. It was wringing the fluids from his tired, fever-ridden body in large quantities. Sitting on a canvas cot in a cellar that was dimly lighted by a single candle, Stauffer's black eye patch made his gaunt, bewhiskered face look as if the eye socket was a large hole in his head. A handful of Black Hawk men occupied the cellars of the buildings around him.

"How many men in your battalion, Captain Stecker?" the colonel asked without looking up.

"Two besides myself, sir."

"That figures," said the colonel. "The Death Head Brigade no longer exists as a unit. The Black Cobra and Black Dragon Regiments have been wiped out. And our Black Hawk Regiment has been reduced to ineffectiveness. We are fighting as individuals."

They were interrupted by the sound of loudspeakers the Russians had mounted on T-34 tanks less than two blocks away: "Every seven seconds a German soldier dies on Russian soil—tick, tock, tick, tock, tick, tock, tick. Surrender! Only death awaits you otherwise!" After a few seconds, the message was monotonously repeated.

"Propaganda!" Erich declared with a shrug.

"Frankly, I don't think so," responded Stauffer, coughing lightly.

"But that's almost fifteen thousand a day."

"I know," said the colonel dejectedly. "We contribute a fourth of them right here in Stalingrad."

Erich was surprised but displayed no sign of it. He recalled complaining to Heinz in Heidelberg about the eleven thousand lost in the Poland campaign.

"How much ammunition do your men have?" asked Colonel Stauffer.

"Two rounds each."

"And you?"

"Two clips for my *Luger*."

After a few moments of silence, broken by several artillery shells landing just outside and another blaring of the loudspeakers, the colonel spoke again. "Tomorrow the Russian infantry will overrun us, so I am ordering the surrender of the regiment at eight o'clock in the morning. I doubt that we have over thirty men left. If any of them wish to try to escape, they should do so tonight. In any case, I do not believe we will live. But I wish to give them a choice—die where they stand, escape, or be taken prisoner. Pass the word to your battalion."

"Yes, sir!" Erich saluted and then stepped forward to shake the colonel's hand.

Without rising from his cot, Stauffer returned the salute weakly, then, in the same motion, shook his young captain's hand. He knew they would not see each other again.

. . .

Later that afternoon as Erich sat in a rubble-filled depression a short distance from Kohlmann, his ears assailed by the horror of horrors, the terrible din of battle, he wondered if the colonel was still alive. Stauffer was one man who would not surrender to the Russians, even if he was so ill he could hardly move, he knew that. The colonel was an elite SS officer who would fight to the death rather than be taken prisoner.

Erich's mind began to wander. *Was God about to call him home? There were so many things yet to do.* Here, so far from the land he loved, and faced with this unexpected turn of events, he felt betrayed by Fate and cheated by Time. He thought of Holzheim and his widowed mother. *How was she going to manage the store without him?* Since his father had been killed in the bombing raid, she was relying on him, her only child, to operate it when the war was over. *If he could just get back to organize things for her, to be sure everything was all right before he left—just for a short time. That's all it would take. If God would grant him an hour or two to tend to things that needed to be done. And there was Maria, lovely Maria. He would marry her like she wanted. At least they would have a bit of time together.*

Kohlmann was squatting in a crouched position behind a short, battered concrete wall four feet ahead of Erich. Erich was staring idly at the sergeant's back, his mind engrossed in the thought of his father's death. Suddenly, at the very point his eyes were focused, there was a small spray of fluid followed by a minute amount of fine lint and then a little puff of vapor. A split second later he heard the crack of the rifle. The sergeant slowly turned his head, his mouth and eyes gaping wide. His body stiffened as his face became a mask of terror and disbelief. His lips pleaded, "Roxanne! Roxanne! Help me!" But no sound came. A surge of blood gushed forth over his tongue and through his nostrils. Erich caught him as he toppled and rolled him into an adjacent crater. Numbed by the intense cold and the terrible agony and destruction he had witnessed during the past four months, he sighed audibly as he looked into the pleading face of his fallen comrade. Kohlmann's body gave a sudden jerk, and Erich knew he was dead. He had been hit by a soft nose bullet squarely in the center of his chest. At that moment, the young captain felt alone, so very much alone, alone in this cauldron of misery, this maelstrom of agony. With tears welling up in his eyes, he straightened the body and placed the dead sergeant's helmet over his contorted face.

Of the thousand men in his battalion, he was the only one he knew existed. There may be others, but they were in cellars or hospitals, most dying or too weak from starvation, typhus, typhoid, or dysentery to really care.

255

• • •

It was the second day of February that the guns fell silent and General Friedrich von Paulus came up the steps from his headquarters in the basement warehouse of the Univermag Department Store to officially surrender. He had been the epitome of German generals, a fifty two year old man of intimidating appearance, slender, ramrod straight, and six feet, four inches tall. His uniform was normally immaculate and neatly pressed, but on this day of surrender, his tired, furrowed face showed the strain he had endured. Although his movements were deliberate, and his eyes cool, steady, and challenging, his thin mouth drooped at the corners as if he had never smiled and the right side of his face twitched from a nervous affliction. He was stooped, and food stains spotted his baggy uniform. He was a man betrayed by his leader.

As the Russians cautiously rose from the rubble, an eerie silence greeted them from the frozen desolation. A white crystalline fog had drifted up from the ravines and the Volga, at first blanketing the area at ground level and then rising fifteen feet to remain as a canopy, a shroud, over this moon city of craters, snow-filled holes, cracked and split asphalt, gutted stone structures, and endless rows of caverns. Every cellar was filled with the living as well as the dead and dying. Many were hopelessly trapped beneath piles of rubble. And when Marshal Semeon Timoshenko returned to reclaim his headquarters bunker at the edge of the Volga, he discovered it had been turned into a German hospital. There was neither lights nor water for the stinking, sweating, moaning two thousand typhus-plagued wounded.

In all of Stalingrad, there was not a domesticated animal, crust of bread, nor roll of gauze left. Many of the streets contained stacks of frozen bodies six feet high and hundreds of feet long. Some had been placed there in November. Hoarfrost covered everything in a strange wrapping of bristling crystals. The defeated army had followed orders from their leader, the Fuhrer. They had fought to the last cartridge, to the last soul.

Of the 334,000 German soldiers surrounded in November, 88,000 were alive to surrender in February. A mere 5,000 would live to return to Germany, and then only many years after the war had ended.

The Road Back

When he returned to his cellar headquarters and informed the two remaining riflemen in his battalion of Colonel Stauffer's decision, they appeared stunned. One stared blankly at a far wall, his whisker-stubbled face reflecting the strain he had endured. Then he turned to face Erich. "Captain, what do you plan to do?" he asked with a sigh.

"I don't really know," Erich replied in a sober voice. "But I don't think I want to be a captive of the Russians."

During the long, dark night, Erich was occupied with many thoughts that raced through his mind. He and one of the riflemen huddled in the entrance to a dark, fire-blackened cellar that emitted the scorched odor common to much of the city. It offered protection from the cold wind and flying shrapnel, but would not permit them to become sealed in a tomb from a direct hit as so many had who had sought protection in the cellars. They each took turns relieving the man on lookout every hour. Even on the hazardous watch, he was engrossed in making the decision he knew he must by morning.

The bombardment had become a mere din in his ears, and he knew that as long as it continued, he would not have to stare into the darkness looking for patrols or infiltrators. But the flying shrapnel would prove very dangerous if he tried to escape through the encircling ring of Russians. He thought of Maria and his home, of Heinz buried on the snow-covered steppe, of food and warm clothing he would have when he reached the main German line, and of the harshness of being a Russian prisoner. Ordinarily there would be no question about taking the risk, but in his weakened state he wavered at the thought of covering one-hundred-fifty miles under such hostile conditions.

• • •

It was five o'clock on the morning of February 2 that he bid farewell to the two riflemen. He looked at their shabby uniforms, the rag-wrapped feet, and the frost on their whiskers and eyebrows. "Are you sure you don't want to come along?" he asked a third time.

"No, Captain," they replied in unison, shaking their heads. "We'd never make it." They paused and then one of them added, "We'll just fire our two remaining rounds at the Russians and then retreat to Colonel Stauffer's head-quarters."

He started toward Gumrak, across the lunar landscape of the once proud industrial city of Stalingrad. Dressed in two overcoats and a white cape, he followed the rubble-strewn streets as much as possible, taking occasional cover from mortar and artillery shells. After reaching an area beyond where the shells were falling, he crouched and moved very cautiously, his eyes straining to pierce the early morning darkness. He was approaching the Russian line.

Suddenly, amid the booming explosions, he detected a faint shuffle of heavy-booted feet. He quickly took shelter in the dark, rubble-filled entrance to a cellar. As the platoon of Russian infantry passed, he became aware of the frozen corpses of two soldiers curled up beside him. Without determining their nationality, he departed as soon as the Russians passed.

Continuing on, he worked his way over the rubble, past numerous trucks, tanks, wagons, and half-tracks. Twice again, he had to allow groups of Russian soldiers who were headed for the center of the city to pass. Then, as he skirted a deep crater that had been made by a large bomb, he detected the faint sounds of several voices. He squatted and slowly turned his head to determine their direction. The heart thundering in his chest and pulse throbbing in his ears seemed so loud. He wondered if they could hear it. He determined there were four or five Russians resting in a nearby crater. Using extreme caution, he sidestepped the area and crawled beneath an abandoned T-34 tank. Several minutes later, they moved on.

As the first light of dawn broke through the surrounding blackness, he discovered he had passed through the scattered clusters of Russian infantry and was in the battlefield vacuum that lay between them and their supporting artillery. Now his concern was for tanks, but their noisy nature would warn him of their approach. However, he would have to discern between the parked ones still in use and those that had been abandoned. And suddenly it was quiet. For the first time in months he could not hear the thunder of belching cannon muzzles and exploding shells. The surrender had occurred.

During the remainder of the day, he made little progress. The streets and roads were swarming with Russian troops moving into Stalingrad. He was forced to hide beneath abandoned vehicles, amid piles of rubble, or among corpses in foul-smelling cellars. When he took refuge in a ravine littered with corpses and equipment, he was nearly run over by a T-34 tank that charged through it. As it sped past where he lay, it tossed chunks of snow and fragments of frozen bodies high into the air.

He found a partially collapsed cave with an inner niche that offered both shelter and protection. Near its entrance in a sitting position was the frozen form of a *Wehrmacht* soldier. His frost-encrusted eyes were sealed shut, and both arms, bandaged and splinted, stuck out before him in a pleading posture. Noting the unit insignia on his uniform, a tall grenadier's hat of the type Frederick the Great's soldiers once wore, he assumed the young soldier had been a member of the 76th Infantry Division. Erich crawled in and, after curling up to conserve body heat, ate the two remaining crusts of bread he had carried in the pocket of his tunic.

When nightfall came, he peered outside cautiously, then crawled out and began walking west. At first he stayed on the heavily used road to Gumrak, but the truck traffic was excessively heavy. Too much time had to be spent hiding in the ditch beside the road. When he tried to walk in an adjacent field, found the sixteen inches of encrusted snow very tiring. Then his eyes detected two faint gray lines that paralleled the road. They were the tracks of a heavy tank that had recently crossed the field. Once in the compressed track, he hurried along as fast as his weakened physical condition permitted, squatting occasionally to hide from troops moving along the road.

After traveling for nearly an hour, he saw a convoy of Russian trucks headed for Stalingrad on the Gumrak road. He dropped down and lay in one of the tank tracks to hide from their view. Breathing heavily, vapor issuing from his mouth, he waited several minutes and then raised up on his elbows to cautiously peer across the frozen landscape. The convoy had passed and was continuing east, leaving a swirling cloud of powdery snow in its wake. Just then, a mouse with a sleek, brown coat emerged from a hole in the snow a few feet from his face. It remained still for nearly a minute, staring at him with its black, beady eyes, its brown nose and white whiskers twitching nervously. Then it darted to a nearby clump of weeds that was tall enough to protrude above the snow and began nibbling on the dried seed pods. Feeling it was safe to continue on, Erich rose to his feet. The tiny creature quickly scampered back and disappeared into its hole, making a trail with its delicate pink feet and shiny black tail in the fluffy dusting of snow that covered the glazed crust.

· · ·

Erich skirted the Gumrak airfield and continued toward the Don River. The traffic had thinned, so he could use a road much of the time. But he was becoming very hungry and tired and had to make frequent stops to rest. After three days he reached the frozen, wind-swept Don. A *Tiger* tank the Black Hawk men had abandoned in their retreat because it wouldn't start still remained where it had been left. He thought of hiding in it to rest, but foot-prints in the snow indicated it was an item of curiosity to the Russians, so he continued on.

Desperately hungry, he scraped food morsels from cans and cartons dis-carded by the Russians, and searched the pockets of the frozen dead. He found that many German casualties had spent their last moments huddled together in small groups in a vain attempt to keep from freezing to death. The clusters, frozen solid and covered by drifting snow, were scattered across the fields. They were especially numerous in ditches and beside the road.

When he struggled to the top of the west bank of the Don River and looked at the seemingly endless horizon, he became so discouraged with the progress he had made that he doubted he could survive long enough to reach the German line. He was terribly exhausted, hungry beyond measure, and so cold he felt drowsy. However, he knew if he stopped to sleep, he would never awake. So he pushed on, looking at the thatched roof of a house in the dis-tance, wondering if he could seek help there. It was the house where he and his comrades had rescued the young mother by killing the Russian renegades. But that was long ago, and conditions had changed. Besides, they were Russians and perhaps, with their army in control, they would turn on him. But now he was desperate, very, very desperate. He surmised there was little else he could do. He thought of hiding in the little barn, but that would be too cold. Then, as he looked more closely, he could see that the barn was gone—it had been destroyed.

Without bothering to peer in the window, he knocked on the weathered door. He saw that shrapnel had splattered across the entire front of the little structure, puncturing it with dozens of small holes. The white-haired grand-father opened the door, but he did not recognize Erich until the bearded trooper clicked his heels and smiled. Then he beckoned him in. Olga and Stella, who had been cowering in a far corner, rose to their feet and, smiling, came over to greet Erich. The grateful family was so pleased to see him again that they hugged him and kissed him on both cheeks. Noting Erich's emaci-ated condition, Olga lowered the child she was holding and beckoned for him to sit at the table. By the time he had removed his white cape and overcoat, Olga had placed a bowl of cabbage and barley soup on the table.

Erich had barely finished the third bowl of soup when the grandfather, who had gone outside for firewood, came dashing in. As he shouted something to the women, Erich noticed a flash of terror show in their faces. The old man quickly lowered the armload of wood to the floor, pulled back the rug, and opened the trapdoor, all the while motioning to Erich to get into the cellar. Erich quickly complied and Olga tossed his cape and overcoat in after him. Then Stella slid in after him.

Erich heard a loud knock on the door followed by the heavy tread of combat boots. He tried to contain his heavy breathing but could not. And the pulse throbbing in his temples combined with the heart thundering in his chest seemed so loud he wondered if they could hear it upstairs. In between his deep, open-mouth breaths in the dank darkness, he heard the irregular breathing of Stella and smelled her musky redolence. There were two Russian soldiers, he knew that. He also knew that if he was caught, they would not spare his life. Besides, they would probably kill the family as well.

After listening to the heavy thump of boots, interspersed with shouts of "vodka! vodka!" and the grandfather's repeated response of "*nyet! nyet!*" for half an hour, Erich heard the two soldiers step out the door, slamming it loudly as they left. Fifteen minutes later, the trap door opened and the grandfather helped him out of the cellar.

Erich stayed with the Russian family three days, eating bowl after bowl of cabbage and barley soup and many boiled potatoes generously covered with thick flour gravy. The women washed his clothes, and he shaved with warm water. For their kindness he would be forever grateful.

On the evening of his departure, they gave him a small sack containing wheat, potatoes, and a loaf of black bread. When he shook their hands, he noted tears welling up in the eyes of the women. He stroked the cheeks of the children and then went out the door to start off across the cold, snow-covered desert. He was, once again, hopeful of reaching the German line.

The clear night sky was a deep shade of purple, glittering with countless blue-white stars that bathed the sparkling vastness before him with a soft, gentle light. The booming of artillery, the staccato of machine guns, and the groaning roar of bombers no longer filled the air. The only discernible sounds came from supply transports, both trucks and horse-drawn wagons, that traveled the roads in small convoys. Fields and ditches were filled with the useless, forgotten litter of war, and snow now covered the wrecked machines and the clusters of bodies abandoned to the indifference of the torn earth and eternal heavens.

As Erich made his way across the glistening landscape, his senses were occasionally brought to full alert by frolicking rabbits or hungry wolves tearing at the frozen carcasses of men and animals. Each time he dropped down and strained to listen and see if there was danger. He had to be certain they were not Russian soldiers for this was no time to be taken prisoner. But in this great expanse of land, Russian troops were no longer very numerous. Hs fear of starvation was also considerably relieved, for the land had not been picked bare like the rubble of Stalingrad. The dead animals still retained great quantities of their flesh. Besides, there was always the possibility of raiding a farmer's barn or granary.

• • •

After ten days of working his way westward, Erich saw a light observation plane flying overhead. It was a German *Stork* with black crosses on its wings. He climbed from the wooded ravine in which he had been hiding and vigorously waved his arms. At first he thought he had not been seen, but the plane returned in a few minutes and circled low. He hurriedly tramped a swastika into the snow. The *Stork* dropped a small package, which landed a short distance away, dipped its wings, and then disappeared to the west. After retrieving the package, he returned to the protection of the ravine to open it. It contained half a loaf of bread and several tins of fish and stew. Fearing he may have been observed, he headed up the ravine at a rapid pace until he came to a road that had been recently traveled. There he hoped his tracks would blend with those already made, and if his luck was good, perhaps, before long, the wind or snow would obliterate all traces of his path.

He saw the plane the next morning but dared not leave the straw pile that sheltered him. It was located near a narrow road that lead to a nearby village that was having a market day. Since there was a continual movement of wagons, carts, animals, and people, he relaxed enough to enjoy the warmth and seclusion afforded by the straw. He also got some much needed sleep.

• • •

When, once again, he heard the distant rumbling of artillery fire, Erich knew he was approaching the front. It signaled the beginning of a very critical time. He saw Russian soldiers more frequently and in greater numbers than he had during the past three weeks, and food had become so difficult to obtain that he resorted to eating raw flesh from dead animals and chipping unharvested potatoes from the frozen ground. His beard had grown long enough to turn white from the frost of his breath, and his tattered clothing was so saturated with perspiration and body oil that it felt cold and clammy. His entire torso itched from the dead layers of skin it was attempting to slough off.

Nearing the Russian artillery units, he found the ravines and roads so choked with moving men and equipment that he had to cautiously continue in the open fields. Fortunately, visibility was hampered by a light snow being driven by a moderate wind. However, the snow hampered his ability to see, and he was suddenly surprised by a noisy group of Russians that passed barely a hundred yards from him. He quickly dove into the snow, flattening himself as much as possible. His heart leaped into his throat. He had come so far and had suffered so much that he must not be captured. His pulse throbbed and thundered in his ears so that in a moment of irrational panic, he feared it would betray his presence. He lay still and quiet for nearly an hour, long after the Russians had passed, while icy granules of wind-driven snow, slithering along at ground level, stung his face and eyes. Finally, rising to his feet, he looked around and then started off again, hoping to find protection from the biting wind. He wanted to wait until darkness to pass between the batteries of firing artillery. And when he found a wrecked wagon in a snow-filled crater, he scooped the snow from beneath it and created the shelter he so desperately needed.

Although the wind made judging distance by sound difficult, through a slow, cautious process he managed to carefully slip between two batteries of well guarded artillery. Once past them he increased his pace, knowing he had a few miles before him that contained little life or activity until he approached the line of Russian infantry. Occasionally, however, he was subjected to periodic shelling from German artillery that fired randomly to prevent movement of troops and supplies. He realized it presented a danger, but the thought of being so near his own army quickened his pulse.

When dawn came, he was a few hundred yards behind a Russian infantry company that was entrenched along a shallow ravine filled with birch trees. He would remain hidden, observe as much as possible during daylight, and then try to pass between their units in the dark. Taking shelter in a deep shell crater, he hoped to remain undetected and warm enough to survive.

By noon the wind had subsided and the sky had cleared, allowing the faint warmth of the sun to enter the crater. This made him feel more comfortable, but also increased the danger of being discovered. Just then a lone Russian soldier left the ravine and wandered to an adjacent crater to relieve himself Erich curled up, pulling his knees beneath his chin to get as much of his body beneath his white cape as possible. Again his heart was pounding like a trip-hammer in his bony breast and his pulse was thundering in his ears. He wondered how long his cardiovascular system could stand the strain. This had been going on for months, every time he faced a life and death situation, and there was no letup in sight. Would his heart burst? Or his aorta rupture? Maybe a blood vessel in his head would give way. Certainly the medical school professors at Heidelberg never knew such stress existed. Fortunately, however, a barrage of incoming shells sent the Russian scurrying back to the ravine with his trousers only partially up. It also discouraged additional roaming by his comrades.

• • •

Erich peered cautiously from the crater. There was a five-hundred yard open space between Russian infantry companies. But there was also considerable foot traffic between them, exchanging messages and delivering food and ammunition. This was a time for extreme care and attention. When the pallid orange ball of the sun settled into the west, starlight from the clear heavens drenched the battered landscape with a cold, blue light. Then the big, yellow disk of the moon glowed like an embarrassed jester as it struggled to clear the horizon. It seemed to halt momentarily to get its bearings and then continued upward. Erich climbed cautiously from the crater and worked his way south a hundred yards to get midway between two infantry units. Then he went west again, crawling the last few feet to the edge of the ravine. Holding his breath as much as possible, he watched and listened, observing an occasional soldier shuffle past. He slipped down the bank, quickly walked among the trees and shrubs to the opposite side, and then climbed out again.

Moving as quietly as possible, he started off again in a low crouch. Then an unexplained moment of intuition brought him to full alert. He dropped to his haunches, held his breath, and slowly rotated his head left and right to ascertain if he could see or hear what he had sensed. Suddenly, he saw it. It was not more than two hundred feet away. Silhouetted against the large, yellow face of a full moon, his eyes focused on the head and shoulders of a Russian sentry. He could see vapor issuing from the well-clothed Russian's nose and mouth as be breathed. Slipping his *Luger* from its holster, he tucked it into his tunic beneath the snow cape to warm it and lessen the chance of a malfunction. Then, as the sentry shuffled his feet nervously to keep warm, Erich slowly crawled away from the area.

Although he had not eaten in over twenty-four hours, he felt no hunger. The excitement within was such that every nerve, every sinew of muscle, every cell of his brains was stretched to a maximum tension. This night was to be the final episode in his attempt to escape from behind the Russian lines, and he was determined to give it a maximum effort to forestall any failure on his part. He knew he was only a few hundred yards from the German line, but the risk in crossing this frozen no-man's-land was very great. He would be subjected to the guns of both sides.

The sector was quiet for the moment, but the thunder of artillery fire in the distance, both left and right, was constant. There were occasional staccato outbursts of rifle and machine gun fire cutting through the din. Cautiously, Erich made his way from crater to crater, a few dozen feet at a time, halting frequently to scan the area around him and to listen for signs of danger. He had a nagging fear of triggering a mine, a weapon of certain death in this tormented wasteland. However, the frozen soil, combined with the churning action of the shelling, had reduced the hazard considerably. Just then an artillery duel developed that made the sky overhead hiss and sizzle as the heavy shells sped on their way. He could see muzzle flashes of guns on both sides as they fired periodic salvos. And each time he breathed a silent prayer of thanks as they continued shelling the rear areas. He knew God was listening because each time he prayed, he heard the lethal missiles continuing overhead in a loud whisper.

As he covered the short distance to another crater, he felt a slight pressure against his knee. Then he heard a sudden swish. He knew he had triggered the trip wire of a magnesium flare, so he dropped where he stood, flattening himself against the snow- covered earth. High overhead the flare blossomed into a brilliant light and began floating slowly down again. The response from both sides was immediate with a tremendous volume of rifle and machine gun fire. Erich breathed in short, heavy gasps as he pressed his face against the snow and watched tracer bullets arch over him from several angles.

The flare seemed to burn for an eternity, but he knew he dared not move as long as it lit the area. However, he also knew that the instant it went out, those watching would have a few seconds of poor vision until their eyes became adjusted to the dark again. That would be the time he could scurry to a nearby shell crater.

No sooner had he slithered into a shell hole when mortars from both sides began firing. For ten minutes the earth heaved, shuddered, and convulsed around him. He wanted to stay low in the hole to avoid flying shrapnel but not low enough to become buried should a shell land on the edge. Once again he thought of Maria, of his mother, and of his father in the rubble of Nurnberg. And there was Heinz beneath the snow along the Volga. Then he thought of the terrible possibility of being buried in this crater without anyone knowing where he was. Perspiration flowed freely over his body as he held on to the pitching soil with both hands and prayed to God he would be spared.

When the shelling stopped, he was so exhausted he remained in the crater for nearly an hour without moving. Then he peered cautiously over its edge to observe the sporadic rifle and machine gun fire. From the origin of the tracer bullets, he determined he must get another hundred yards nearer the German line. Then he would wait until daylight.

• • •

Dawn was breaking when Erich heard orders being shouted among the entrenched soldiers before him. The language was German! Tears filled his eyes as he realized it was the first German voices he had heard in weeks. He knew food, shelter, and warmth awaited him if he could survive the next few hundred feet. Twice he tried shouting to them, but they could not hear. Then he thought of standing with his arms raised, but the danger of being shot from either side was too great. He was so near salvation and life was so precious that he did not wish to risk the slightest chance of losing it now. If he had some means of waving his helmet, perhaps it would suffice. But he had no pole, no stick, and no rifle. He shouted several more times, his voice getting progressively weaker. He thought he heard someone respond, but this, too, passed without establishing contact. Finally, in desperation he removed his snow cape, crawled to the rim of the crater, and waved it in a wide arc over his head.

"Attention! Attention!" he heard in the distance. "Some Russian wants to surrender!"

Several minutes passed and he heard no more. He waved the cape again.

"Hello! Hello!" came a response. It was followed by a statement in Russian. "Hello! Hello!" he replied in German.

Hello! Hello!" This time it was in German

"I am German!" shouted Erich.

"Come forward with your hands up!"

Slowly, Erich got to his feet with both hands overhead, one holding the tattered and soiled snow cape. Since the area had been shelled heavily, the mixed soil and snow did not contrast sharply with his black overcoat and helmet. He stumbled ahead as fast as he could, noting several *Wehrmacht* soldiers in foxholes with rifles aimed at him. As he approached the first entrenched soldier, he slowly moved his head from side to side. "My comrades, my comrades. How pleased I am to see you.

"Keep on moving to the rear with your hands up!" came the stern reply by two other soldiers who had gotten out of a hole to follow him.

A hundred yards beyond, he was searched, relieved of his *Luger*, and told to put his arms down and cape on. Escorted to a company headquarters in an underground bunker, he was fed and interrogated for an hour before the amazed commander, a *Wehrmacht* captain, returned his *Luger*. But he wondered if the commander really believed him. Then he was loaded aboard a returning supply wagon and ordered to the nearest field hospital.

• • •

During the next three weeks, he was evacuated through a series of medical facilities, each successive one becoming larger, better equipped, and more complete. He had shaved and bathed, was being well fed, and his clothing was washed and sterilized. In addition, he was issued new boots, socks, and underclothing.

"I don't have any SS uniforms here, Captain," the supply sergeant informed him, "or I'd give you a new one."

"This one will do just fine," Erich replied, feeling extremely grateful to be alive, warm, and away from the roar of battle.

He had written Maria and his mother informing them he was well and safe but did not expect a reply since he was still unassigned and changing locations. He knew, however, he would soon be reassigned and sent back to the front. Perhaps he could see the two women in his life before then. He hoped and prayed he would.

• • •

In the large, well equipped General Hospital in Cracow, it was determined Erich had regained more than half of the thirty-two pounds he had lost during his terrible ordeal. A new uniform of the same size he used to wear was issued to him. It made him feel like the trooper he once was. It was then he was ordered to report to the commanding officer of the hospital for an interview.

"Somewhat different than Stalingrad, don't you think, Captain Stecker?" began the chubby colonel from behind a large, walnut desk. He motioned for Erich to sit in an overstuffed chair across from him.

"Much different," replied Erich as he sat down.

"That must have been a terrible battle."

"Yes, it was quite bad," Erich agreed, hoping the colonel would change the subject since in previous interrogations he sensed that officers doing the questioning were doubtful of many things he told them.

"Well, I have good news for you," smiled the colonel, jamming a short cigar between the pursed lips protruding from his round face. "We're going to give you thirty days leave."

"Wonderful!" exclaimed Erich, trying to minimize the show of enthusiasm that effervesced within him.

"Here are your papers," the colonel stated, handing him a brown envelope. "You will report back here for another checkup and then be reassigned."

"Thank you, sir," replied Erich, beaming pleasantly.

• • •

Shortly after the medical staff arrived at the 66th Evacuation Hospital, the first patients began arriving from the eastern front. Within three days, it was filled to capacity. Its assignment was one of administering the final medical and surgical care to seriously ill or wounded soldiers before they were evacuated to general hospitals inside Germany. One task distasteful to many on the staff, especially Maria, was judging who was expected to live and who was expected to die. The patients were to remain at the 66th for seven days. On the eighth day, those who were expected to live were put aboard trains and planes for the trip west. The remainder were transferred to the ten tents at the far end of the hospital compound. There, for their remaining hours, they would wait until all life had oozed from their battered and torn bodies. Then the bodies were slid into a muslin shroud and buried in an adjacent field. "It is merely a matter of logistics," the commanding officer explained to his staff. "Transportation is so overburdened that precious cargo space cannot be spared for such unavailing cases."

Maria's task at the 66th Evacuation Hospital was that of serving a twelve-hour shift each day, seven days a week, as a ward nurse in one of the forty-bed tents. She bathed and shaved her charges and checked their body processes. She took temperatures, gave injections, changed bandages, and maintained charts. Tirelessly and without complaint, she did her job. It was not so much a labor of love but because she was serving the cause of her country. And it was a way of bringing the time nearer when she and Erich could be together.

Frequently when she returned to her quarters, a tent she shared with three other nurses, she opened her wooden footlocker and reexamined the notes, cards, and letters she had received from Erich. On occasion, she peeked at the carefully packed bridal gown buried beneath her other belongings. After going to bed on her canvas cot, she sometimes laid awake with her eyes closed and mentally went through the wedding ceremony with Erich at her side in the great cathedral at Ulm. Sleep came easily afterwards.

As the war continued on the eastern front, she watched its progress on a map that hung on the wall of the recreation room. Through letters from Erich and information gleaned from Black Hawk casualties who passed through the hospital, she learned of action involving Erich's unit. She was pleased when they reached the Volga, for she was told they had been promised a rest. However, when the Death Head Brigade was ordered to attack Stalingrad, reports became sketchy and letters from Erich arrived less frequently. Based on his letter writing when he was with the *Afrika Korps*, she assumed fighting was intense.

Battle casualties confirmed her suspicions, and when the front began collapsing in the Caucasus and Stalingrad became encircled, a wave of concern enveloped her. Although Erich's letters continued to express optimism, she knew him well enough to believe that it was a reflection of his positive outlook on life as well as an attempt to avoid worry on the part of those he loved.

One night in late January she awoke, frightened and covered with nervous perspiration. She felt exhausted—overwhelmed by a terrible premonition. Erich's death was imminent. She sat on the edge of her cot and wrapped a blanket around her shoulders. She could not sleep again that night.

For several days she was tormented, her stomach so upset from the resulting anxiety that work was difficult. Her friends attempted to console her by telling her it was only a bad dream. She tried with utmost sincerity to believe them, but she knew her inner self. She remembered how, as long as she had known Erich, their thought waves had alerted each other.

A week later she returned to her quarters after a long twelve hours at the ward tent to find Erich's tersely written little poem shakily written on the piece of cardboard. She fell upon her cot with tears flowing so profusely her pillow was soon saturated with moisture. She cried until tears would no longer come and her chest ached from the convulsing sobs that racked her body. Although her tent-mate, Anna, had told her the chance of Erich's unit breaking out of the Stalingrad encirclement was good, she simply could not believe it until she heard from Erich.

Later in the day when two friends came into the tent and asked what was wrong, she was so distraught and weak she could not answer. One of them picked up the card and silently read it and then passed it to the other. "Maybe he's a prisoner," stated one, trying to ease Maria's pain.

"Yes. And now he sleeps warm and eats well," quietly soothed the other.

Maria continued to lie on her stomach, convulsions of violent sobs tearing at her body as she shook her head in a negative manner. She knew the Russians would never take him prisoner.

Then in March, just as winter was releasing its icy grip, she returned to her quarters to find an envelope addressed in Erich's hand on her cot. At first she suspected someone had gotten one of his old letters from her footlocker and left it there. But when she picked it up and found it unopened, her heart leaped to her throat. Her hopes sagged again when, as she tore it open, she noted the return address of a hospital. In the first sentence he stated he was alive and well. The tears flooded her eyes, blurring her vision so she could not read on for several minutes. A short time later, her two friends came in and asked why she was crying.

"I'm happy," she blubbered, handing them the letter.

When they learned what the letter said, each embraced her with an affectionate hug and whispered, "We are happy, too."

All three of them went to the chapel to offer a prayer of gratitude.

• • •

When Erich received his leave papers, he went directly to the Cracow Railroad station and boarded the westbound passenger train that passed through Prague. Days had become noticeably longer and warmer, giving rise to the hope that a new awakening of the countryside was not far away. As the train made its way swiftly across the land, Erich noticed that much of the snow on the plowed flat-land had disappeared but the evergreen topped hills still wore a white mantel causing the stands of pine and spruce to look almost black. And children still trudged home from school wearing heavy woolen clothing and cumbersome overshoes, which they tested by wading through muddy puddles. Erich smiled. He was back in his element, and it made him feel good.

His arrival home was a cause for celebration. His mother closed the store and nearly dissolved in tears as she sobbingly held and caressed him. The black clothing she wore made her look more slender, but Erich was certain she also had lost some weight.

"My boy! My boy!" she wailed as she clung to him. "I thought I had lost you, too."

"Oh, Mother!" Erich said, trying to comfort her. "I'm all right. I'm well and alive!"

"But you are so thin!" she muttered, tugging at the looseness of his uniform.

"Yes, I've lost some weight. But there's nothing wrong with me."

She backed away and dabbed her eyes. "You must be hungry. Such a long trip." She turned around and went to the kitchen.

He let her go, knowing she was going through the same routine she had gone through each time he returned. This would give her something to do to take her mind off the sorrow she had felt during the past months. He went upstairs and changed into his civilian clothes. When he returned to the living room, he sat down, relaxed, and enjoyed the aroma drifting in from the kitchen. The clang and clatter of pots, pans, forks, and spoons reminded him of the good life he had been away from for so long.

For nearly two weeks he lounged about, enjoying the quiet solitude and pleasant tranquility of his little village sanctuary. At the post office he spoke at length with Mrs. Juergens, mostly about Maria. "Maria was very distraught when she thought you had been killed in Stalingrad," she said matter-of-fact-ly as she continued to sort the mail. "And elated beyond words afterwards when she received a letter from you." She smiled as she looked up at him. "We are so glad you are all right."

"And how is George?" Erich asked.

"He's fine. Going to trade school in Bayreuth. He wants to be a truck mechanic." She paused, sighed audibly, then added, "But he wants to join the army. He'll be old enough before long."

Friends of the family came by the store to see him, only to confide to his mother that he looked as if he had lost weight. He went to his father's grave and knelt at the black marble headstone to offer a prayer for the repose of the departed soul. Afterwards, he wandered about the paths, observing new graves and markers. It was at the Feldmann plot that he noted four black slabs standing side by side, indicating all four of the boys had been killed in the war. The latest had fallen in December in the Caucasus Mountains. He knew none was buried in the plot.

When he stepped into the Holzheim Tavern, he was greeted by several farmers who were waiting for the land to thaw so they could work the fields. They plied him with beer as they sought his assessment of the war. When he offered limited answers, they told him of their exploits in the First World War.

Mr. Trapp came to the store and asked if Erich would look at a horse that had been ill for a few days. Erich, eager for something to do, went directly to the Trapp barn. The horse was lying down, unable to rise to its feet. They slid a canvas sling beneath the ailing animal and then hoisted it to its feet with a rope and pulley.

"I think it's got locked bowels, Mr. Trapp," Erich stated after a brief examination. "Let's give it an enema."

Mr. Trapp located a large syringe used for the purpose and Erich filled it with a solution of Epsom Salts. While Mr. Trapp held the horse's tail high, Erich, standing clear of the animal's flailing hoofs, administered the large quantity of the solution. The horse bellowed twice and then forcefully discharged a tremendous volume, splattering the harness that was hanging on the wall eight feet to the rear. Although the horse appeared able to stand, the sling was left in place as a precautionary measure.

"Let's go to the house and wash our hands," suggested Mr. Trapp.

As Erich bent down over the wash basin, he heard a loud voice from the kitchen. "Hello, Erich!" Without looking up, he knew it was Inge.

"Hello, Inge. How are you?" he responded politely.

She held a nude baby boy on her hip as she walked up to Erich, who was drying his hands on a soiled roller towel.

"Yours?" he asked, looking at the boy he assumed to be a year old.

"No. My sister's."

"How's Max?" he inquired.

"Fine. Still in Russia."

"Well, I must be going," said Erich as he nodded.

"I've got dinner all ready," Inge stated with a disappointed smile. "Won't you eat with us?"

"I really should be going," he answered hesitantly.

"Oh, come," begged Mr. Trapp. "We'd like to have you."

"All right," Erich agreed, not wanting to hurt their feelings.

They gathered around a bare, rectangular, plank table that had several large bowls of steaming food on it that Inge had prepared. When seated, Mr. Trapp held a round loaf of black bread against the soiled bib of his overalls. With a large, steel knife, he cut thick slices from the loaf and stacked them onto the table as Inge filled their plates from the bowls. The baby boy, still without clothing, sat in a high chair next to Inge. Wanting food, he crawled onto the table, grabbed a boiled potato or slice of bread, and then crawled back into his chair. After several such trips, Mr. Trapp turned to Inge. "For God's sake, feed that boy! He's dragged his tool through the gravy three times already!"

"Oh, Father!" she replied indignantly, filling the boy's plate.

When the meal was finished, the men looked at the horse. Believing it was on the road to recovery, they removed the sling.

• • •

Erich received a letter from Maria that ignited a burning desire to see her. When he got to Regensburg, however, the agent refused to sell him a ticket. A military policeman informed him that due to bombing disruptions and heavy traffic, only persons on authorized business were permitted to travel.

"But I am on leave and have my orders!" protested Erich, reaching into his tunic pocket for his travel orders.

"But your orders state you are to travel between Regensburg and Cracow," the blocky policeman informed him in a firm voice.

Disappointed, he started back to Holzheim. At the Danube River Bridge, a truck driver, noting the neat, black officer uniform, gave him a ride to the Holzheim turnoff. As he walked the final distance on the narrow, winding road he knew so well, he stopped a few minutes to watch the small, bubbling stream running alongside in the shadows of flourishing, verdant pines. Topping the last rise before entering town, he paused again and took in a deep breath. His nostrils filled with a refreshing scent of pine needles, lightly tinged with an odor of Mr. Trapp's barnyard and some wood smoke. He looked down at his uniform, the dress of a battle-tested warrior who was trained and experienced in death and destruction, and then gazed at the serene, peaceful little village that knew war only from the absence of its sons and the nightly drone of bomber squadrons passing high overhead on their way to distant targets. Suddenly, he felt out of place. Emitting an audible sigh, he began the slow walk into town.

Bored and restless, he walked the streets, stopping to chat with the people he had known all his life. He drank more beer at the Holzheim Tavern and climbed the soggy hill behind the town. Having regained most of his lost weight and stamina, he felt he should return to the front, to a life he had become accustomed to, to a place where he was needed. In his room he played the piano, finding it more difficult and laborious since he had not practiced for so long. And he lay on his bed and stared at the ceiling, attempting to sort out the many confusing thoughts that passed through his mind.

He dozed off and dreamed of Stalingrad—that city of moon craters with its snow-filled holes, cracked and split asphalt, gutted stone structures, groaning human-filled cellars, and endless rows of caverns. Vividly, he saw frozen feet, the missing ears and noses, the dangling strips of skin, the red spots of typhus, and the insane minds and frothing mouths of tetanus.

When he awoke in a nervous sweat, he realized he had been witness to the greatest battle ever fought in the history of warfare. And he had seen the ultimate in patience, adaptability, tenacity, capacity for suffering, perseverance, silent endurance, dutifulness, sheer agony, and ability to fight to the very last. He also realized he did not belong in this little town of old men, women, and children. His place was with his comrades at the front. He also knew, however, that once there, he would wish to be back in Holzheim.

• • •

When Erich returned to the hospital in Cracow, he was declared fit for combat and sent to a replacement depot in Kiev. The army was assembling all the unassigned *panzer* soldiers in preparation for a summer offensive. He was designated a company commander in the *Panther Brigade* that had been attached to *Das Deutschland Division*. It was located in a holding position on a protruding bulge in the Russian line near the city of Kursk. The commanding generals had been waiting since the spring thaw for replacements to fill their depleted ranks and for the moist, black soil to become firm enough for the heavy *Tiger* and *Panther* tanks to maneuver. Then they would begin the offensive by cutting off the bulge in a drive north that would link up with the attacking Ninth Army.

The fifth of July, a hot, humid day under a blazing sun, began with a tremendous air and artillery bombardment. The roar of heavy bombers made the air above throb and shudder as they lumbered to their targets in the Russian defense lines. Penetrating screams made by holes in the tail fins of bombs they dropped were matched by the shrill shriek of *Stukas* as they dove on select fortifications. Massive salvos of artillery shells hissed and sizzled overhead before making their diving howl into Russian bunkers and hidden T-34 tanks. And great geysers of black earth from the grass-covered steppe erupted into the air—air that became filled with broken tank treads, machine guns, and helmets.

Twenty-five hundred German tanks along with several hundred self-propelled guns and armored personnel carriers were waiting along a hundred mile front. Companies of tanks were lined up in a series of vee formations, the heavy *Tigers* located at the point and leading edges. The *Panthers* formed the rest of the trailing edges of each unit. Large numbers of half-tracks and armored personnel carriers filled in behind the flying wedges.

Erich, standing in the open hatch of a leading *Tiger,* watched through binoculars as the heavy bombardment tore up the Russian lines. Feeling a certain empathy for them, he lowered the binoculars, shook his head, and smiled. Although he sensed a certain empathy for those suffering the terrible destruction raining down upon them, it would feel good to be on the offensive again. With the massive array of tanks and fire power, the *panzers* should easily break through the Russian line. Then they could drive a spearhead deep into their territory and recapture land that had been lost during the winter. Perhaps they could recapture Stalingrad.

He did not know, however, that the *Lucy Spy Ring* in Switzerland, in concert with a Czechoslovakian spy who had defected several weeks before from German Army Headquarters, had presented the Russian generals with a copy of the entire plan of attack, including the most minute details that had been designed by the German generals. The Russians then assembled three thousand tanks, planted huge quantities of mines, mounted numerous artillery pieces, and entrenched enormous numbers of soldiers along every designated route the *panzer* columns were to take.

An hour after it began, the shelling and bombing stopped. An order came over the radio headphones for all vehicles to start their engines. In unison, twenty-five hundred tanks, with several hundred self-propelled guns and armored personnel carriers, sprung to life. The huge cloud of exhaust smoke created a pall over the land so dense it hid the sun and darkened the sky. The advance was postponed for thirty minutes until a gentle west wind floated it forward beyond the Russian lines.

Just as the *panzers* lurched forward, the Russians started their vehicles, creating another huge cloud of exhaust smoke. Since it was over the Russian lines and blowing in an easterly direction, it did not deter the German charge. As the attack rolled forward, vast open spaces before the advancing German formations spouted with great black geysers of soil. And the air filled with bullets from machine guns and rifles. Great numbers of entrenched Russian infantry were overrun and machine gunned to death in their holes or crushed beneath the heavy treads of the *Tigers* and *Panthers*. Russian tanks, no match for the heavy *Tigers*, were blown apart or driven off. The first day they advanced five miles, but on the second day they encountered the heavily mined areas and large antitank guns. Casualties increased at a very high rate, slowing the charge. At the end of seven days after penetrating the fourth successive Russian defense line, they had driven only twenty-five miles instead of the hundred that had been planned. In addition they had lost nearly half of their *panzers* and suffered heavy casualties among the infantry and engineers.

It was on the eighth day of the attack while leading his company of *Tigers* and *Panthers* across an endlessly undulating, shell-hole scarred wheat field that Erich was wounded. He was standing in the point *Tiger*, directing the formation as it churned and ground its way forward while blasting Russian tanks, guns, and soldiers, when a machine gun raked across him. Four bullets made stinging hot spots in his flesh. He continued to guide the action for several hundred yards until all resistance in the immediate area was suppressed. Halting the tank, he removed his headphones and placed them on the sun-heated deck and then climbed out of the hatch. Standing above the driver seated in the other hatch, he yelled to him, "Sergeant, you're in charge now!" He hoped the driver could hear above the roar of engines and din of battle. When he saw the driver look up and nod, be walked to the rear of the tank and jumped down into one of the tracks the huge machine had made in the soft earth.

Three of the four wounds were minor flesh punctures—one on the left side of the neck midway between the shoulder and jaw; a second on the right side of the neck; and a third through muscle tissue high on the right shoulder. The fourth, however, had penetrated lower on the right shoulder, coming out through the shoulder blade. It carried with it a quantity of bone and flesh, leaving a sizeable opening.

Being careful to stay in the track to avoid mines, he followed it for a hundred yards until he came to a medic dressing a leg wound of an infantryman. The medic, facing the sun, looked up.

"I need some assistance," Erich said without emotion.

The medic squinted, and said, "I'll be with you in a moment."

When he rose to his feet, he saw the blood oozing from Erich's neck wounds. "Sit down!" he ordered, pointing to the ground.

After the medical aid man had finished wrapping the oozing neck wounds, he could see that a mild state of shock had set in. "Lie down!" he ordered, motioning with his hand.

He cut away a portion of Erich's tunic and then applied compresses to both the point of entry and the larger exit opening. "No air passing through," he said with a nod of the head. "You're lucky. It didn't hit the lung."

"Good!" Erich responded, perspiration running from his face and hair.

As the armored column again moved forward, Erich could hear shells bursting nearby. The aid man tied a length of gauze to the stock of a Russian rifle and then jammed the attached bayonet of the weapon into the ground.

"We radioed for stretcher bearers. This rifle will let them know where you are." He stood and looked down into Erich's face. "Also, it will keep other vehicles from running over you."

"Thanks," Erich replied with a weak smile.

While the tide of battle moved on, two litter bearers arrived and helped him onto a stretcher. After fastening the security straps, they trotted off in a low crouch as incoming Russian artillery shells exploded around them. When he arrived at a nearby casualty dressing station, his wounds were quickly examined. In a few minutes he was loaded with five others aboard a white ambulance for a bouncing ride to a field hospital.

• • •

Five days later, after he had been evacuated through a series of medical units, he was permitted to walk. Then he was put aboard a hospital train that was going to the 66ᵗʰ Evacuation Hospital.

A fleet of white ambulances with large red crosses painted on them was waiting at the station in Debrecen. Since he was one of the walking wounded, he squatted on an ambulance floor between two tiers of stretchers for the short ride to the hospital. The thought of being near Maria made his heart beat with sufficient vigor to create a noticeable throb in the shoulder that had been immobilized with an arm sling. He tried to peer out the small window in the rear door to glimpse at the countryside, but the pain it created made him sit on the floor again.

Several ambulances halted on a graveled path between two rows of ward tents. The door of the ambulance opened, and Erich stepped outside. As hospital staff soldiers began the task of carrying patients to their assigned tents, he was directed to one of two tents at the end of the line that were reserved for officers.

After he had been processed and assigned a bed, he walked up to one of the two ward nurses. "Do you know a Maria Juergens?" he asked quietly.

The nurse surveyed his face before answering. "Yes," she replied. "She's four tents down. It's an enlisted ward."

"Do you think I can visit her?"

"Not until the doctor has examined you," came the curt reply.

"Where is he?"

"That's him at that bed there," she stated, pointing as she moved to the next bed. "He's coming in this direction."

"Thank you," Erich said, nodding and smiling.

The physician searched through the packet of papers the nurse had tied to the footrail of Erich's bed and then checked the cardboard tag wired to the buttonhole in of his tunic. Carefully, he examined the wrap-around bandage covering the neck wounds. "This all looks good," he said with a smile. "Now, let's look at the shoulder."

Since Erich's right arm was in a sling, his tunic was fastened only by the top button. The doctor unfastened the button, withdrew the coat from the shoulder, and removed the bandage. Erich winced as the stuck gauze was pulled from the oozing hole in the shoulder blade.

"That'll take a few more days to close," the physician stated as he finished applying a new bandage. When he had finished, he stepped back and asked, "Now, how do you feel, Captain?"

"Just fine, except for a little soreness in the neck and shoulder."

"Fine, fine," the doctor said as he walked off.

Erich walked over to the ward nurse. "May I see Nurse Juergens now?"

"Yes. She's in the fourth ward on this same side of the street."

Erich hurried past the unloading ambulances and peeked into the fourth tent. Maria was busily helping the stretcher bearers as they lifted patients onto their beds. Realizing his appearance would cause a disruption, he slowly walked on down the length of the graveled path. At its end, he sat on a wooden crate and looked over the tranquil countryside. He observed a small herd of contented cattle grazing and heard a meadow lark trill its song. While the warm rays of the sun soaked into his body, he wondered how to approach Maria.

When the ambulances no longer stopped at Maria's ward tent, he assumed it was full. He walked back and stood in the open doorway. From far down the center aisle, she looked toward him. Not certain she was seeing correctly, she walked hurriedly in his direction. Certain she had recognized him, he stepped outside and waited. Since she was already crying when she reached him, he drew her close with his free arm and held her until she regained her composure.

"Oh, Erich," she sighed between sniffles. "What happened?"

"Just a couple superficial wounds," he assured her.

"Are you sure?"

"Certainly!" he said, standing back. "Look at me! I'm in good shape!"

They talked for a few minutes and then a call came from within the tent.

"When are you off?" he asked, wiping a tear from her cheek.

"At six."

"See you here then."

"Good."

At six o'clock they walked arm-in-arm to the section of pyramidal tents that comprised the nurses quarters. Sentries with orders to prevent unauthorized males from entering the area -patrolled a gravel path that marked its boundaries. Maria walked up to the nearest one, a tall, slender *Wehrmacht* trooper. "Guard," she began. "Captain Stecker is going to help me for a few minutes at my quarters."

"Yes, sister," came the agreeable response.

At her tent, she handed Erich a magazine and told him to sit on her cot and read it. She scooped up some clothing and toilet-articles. "I'll be back in a few minutes," she said, kissing his forehead.

A short time later, two nurses, dressed in the same pin-striped poplin uniforms as Maria, pranced into the tent. They looked up, mouths agape with surprise, when they saw Erich.

"Good evening, ladies," he stated pleasantly as he rose to his feet and bowed.

"Good evening," one of them stammered.

"You must be Captain Stecker," the other added, trying to appear calm.

"Yes," he answered. "Maria asked me to sit here for a few minutes until she returns."

"Of course," the shorter of the two replied. "Please, sit down. Your shoulder must pain you." Her chalk-white skin emphasized the color of her auburn hair.

"Thank you."

"I'm Salli Rotke," she continued. "And this is Pauline Pranka."

Erich rose to his feet and again bowed.

"Oh, please sit, Captain."

"Maria was very worried about you," Pauline, a slender, blue-eyed blonde began as she walked toward him.

"She has a tendency to worry too much," Erich countered.

At that moment, Maria entered. She was neatly dressed in her brown dress uniform.

"You look lovely," Salli stated with a smile, scrutinizing the trim uniform.

"Going to dinner?" asked Pauline. She had a devilish twinkle in her eyes.

"Yes," came Maria's quick reply. "To the *Restaurant de Messhall*."

She took Erich by the arm and escorted him from the tent.

After eating at the hospital mess tent, they strolled down a narrow lane that led to a nearby vineyard. At the growth-covered entrance, they embraced passionately.

"Oh, Erich," she said with a deep sigh. "I love you beyond comprehension."

"I love you too. More than words can tell." He caressed her back and kissed her neck and cheek. "It's you. Just you. Forever you."

"Oh," she whispered, "I wish we could get married right away. It's so hard trying to live and carry on with this tremendous love throbbing inside. It gets so hard trying to live only for your letters. When they arrive, they set me on fire. When they don't come for a long time, I nearly go insane."

They walked slowly back to the hospital area and entered a large tent used for recreational purposes. Several soldiers were in the facility playing cards, throwing darts, and writing letters. They sat down at a small table in one corner.

He looked into her face. What he saw troubled him. She looked tired and drawn, and she appeared older than her twenty years.

Looking into his eyes, she sensed his concern. Ever since she was a little girl, she had been able to read his thoughts. "This is not a pleasant job," she began. "I'm constantly fighting death for these young men, the flower of our country. They have been severely wounded. The scars will remain with them for the rest of their lives. Fingers and arms have been blown off. Some have high fevers from infections caused by filthy soil. Some have lain on the battlefield long enough to be infested with maggots."

Erich caressed her hand. "I know," he said, trying to ease her discomfort. "I took part in the most gigantic tank battle in modern warfare as well as the monster of all agony in military history, Stalingrad. And we lost them both." He shook his head. "War is evil. But there is no way out until someone above us decides to stop it." He paused, wiped a tear from her cheek, and said, "Let's talk about us. How long will I be here with you?"

"Only seven days," she replied, inhaling a deep breath.

"Then what?"

"Back to the front or to a hospital in Germany. Some will go to one of the mortality wards in the other field."

She then explained that the hopeless cases were moved to the mortality wards to die. "Some will go back to the front, but the majority will be put aboard planes or a train for transport back to Germany. Planes haven't been used lately. Every seven days a hospital train comes from the west and clears them out. The next day another train arrives from the eastern front to fill it up again.

"Where will I go?" he asked with a smile.

"To Germany, of course," she assured him.

Maria withdrew a gray piece of cardboard from her pocket and handed it to him. It was the last communication he had sent from Stalingrad.

"You saved it!" he acknowledged, looking surprised.

"Of course. I save all of your letters. But this one has special significance."

"Really?"

"When I received it, I realized how much I actually cared for you." She paused and then placed her hand over his. "Afterwards, life lost its meaning and purpose."

He rubbed her hand and looked deeply into her clear, brown eyes. "I should not have sent it."

"I'm glad you did. I want to share everything with you."

"I did not think I would survive," he confessed. "I just wanted you to know I was thinking of you until the very end."

Tears reappeared in her eyes.

• • •

The next day Erich arranged to be transferred to Maria's ward. She was thrilled to be able to care for him. On the fifth day, the sling was removed, and the only bandage he needed was the one to cover the sunken, slightly oozing depression on his shoulder blade. On the seventh day they watched soulfully as eight patients were transferred to the mortality wards at the distant end of the compound. The remainder, including Erich, were alerted to be prepared for the order that was to direct them back to the front or to board a hospital train for Germany. Then word came that the train had been delayed by bomb damage to the track.

Shortly after midnight, Erich awoke to a muted commotion. He raised up on his elbows and looked at the entrance of the dimly lighted tent. There, at the entrance, the night nurse counted as a new load of casualties arrived from the eastern front. The hospital train had to be unloaded to maintain its schedule, so the wounded were being left on stretchers and placed on the concrete floor between the beds and along the center aisle. In a few minutes, forty new arrivals were in place, and the directors, two men carrying lanterns, moved on to the next ward.

Maria, along with other day nurses, had been awakened and directed to assist. With a tender feeling of pride, Erich sat cross-legged in his bed and watched as she, flashlight in hand, knelt beside the stretchers to examine the patients. Remaining silent, he observed her make her way down the aisle, unbuckling the straps and lifting the blankets so she could read the waxy cloth tag wired to the soldier's tunic or blouse. She quickly read each tag to ascertain the degree of wounds and determine if medication had to be administered. He heard her speaking assurances in a low voice as she worked. "How is it, soldier?" "Where does it hurt?" "Does that feel better?" "Warm enough?" He surmised she had done this many times before. As he watched her silhouette against the soft, yellow glow of her flashlight, a deep emotional feeling swelled within. He began breathing more heavily and swallowing more frequently.

He was still watching as she knelt beside a stretcher a short distance from his bed. She unfastened the holding straps and then shined the flashlight on the tag. Quickly, she directed the light into the patient's face and then fell upon him sobbing. "George! Oh, George!" she cried.

"It's all right, sis. I'm all right," came a tired reply.

Erich bounded from his bed, clothed only in his underwear, and squatted beside her. Taking the flashlight, he read the card.

Private George Juergens
309th Grenadier Regiment
HE puncture right forearm
Fracture right ulna

"Hello, Erich," said George, managing a smile.

"Hello, George," Erich replied. He put his arm around Maria and held the light so its reflection clearly lighted George's face. "How do you feel?"

"Fine. Just fine. Rather tired though."

"Did they operate on your arm?"

"Yes. It's all right now."

"Good!"

George had been wounded by a piece of shrapnel from an high explosive artillery shell that had fractured a bone. The shrapnel had been removed and the bone set. In a few weeks it would be healed and well again. He had been at the front only two days, in the army a mere six weeks.

The shock and surprise was very great to Maria. She did not know he was in the army let alone at the front. Erich dressed and took her outside. As they walked about the area, he tried to calm her. She conceded that her mother had not been well the past few months and that letters had been infrequent and sketchy. Perhaps Mrs. Juergens had omitted information about George to alleviate concern.

"She appeared well when I was home last spring," Erich told her.

"She wouldn't let on," Maria replied. "And during the last two months she apparently has been having fainting spells."

After nearly an hour, he walked her back to the area of the nurse's quarters. "Go to bed and try to sleep. Six o'clock is not too far away," he cautioned.

"I'll try."

He kissed her and tasted the salt from her lips. Then he watched her disappear down the path to her tent.

Mid-morning the next day, the hospital train from the west arrived to take patients back to Germany for further treatment and rehabilitation. Erich, however, much to the surprise of Maria, was directed to the quartermaster supply tent. There he was issued new clothing and then ordered to board a truck in a convoy that was headed for the front. Maria broke into tears.

"But you're still bandaged!" she protested as he kissed her goodbye.

"I'll be all healed by the time I arrive at my unit," he stated, trying to soothe her.

• • •

It was late in September and Erich was assigned to a *Wehrmacht* infantry regiment as the commanding officer of a rifle and machine gun company. They were entrenched on a flat wheat field a short distance west of Karkov, not far from the staging area used by the Death Head Brigade the year before. However, conditions were considerably different. The infantry regiment had been forced to evacuate Karkov by a Russian pincer movement that nearly surrounded it. Casualties had been light, and the company was at full strength, but most of the soldiers appeared very young to the veteran Erich. Besides, it had been five years since he had entered the service, and he was getting weary of warfare. Initially he thought it would be over in a few months and he could return to medical school. Now, the army was retreating on all fronts and his proud homeland was being destroyed by British and American massive bombing raids.

The men had dug deep foxholes in the soft, black Ukrainian soil where they were awaiting the next enemy attack. The weather was excellent—warm, balmy days, cool, crisp nights. Every morning, the frost-coated wheat stubble glistened in the morning sun, but within hours, all traces of the frozen moisture had disappeared. Erich was pleased that his men were adequately clothed in the green uniforms they wore beneath brown and green mottled capes. Although he still retained his black uniform, he covered it with a lightweight coverall of camouflage material.

As fall turned to winter, the ground became frozen. Initially, there was merely a light crust that melted each day, but later in the year it solidified to a considerable depth. Then the snow came, a dusting at first and then a heavy coating that covered everything with a deep, sparkling mantel. The troopers had to don white capes.

Except for one massive thrust by the Russians that forced them to retreat five miles, military action was limited to probing combat patrols and artillery duels. Each side was stock-piling equipment and supplies for an anticipated spring offensive. Although the cold and snow was much milder than at Stalingrad, the men of his company still suffered from respiratory infections, frostbite, and trench foot. During shelling lulls on moonlit nights, however, they were amused by frolicking rabbits being pursued by marauding wolves, and occasionally, a lone fox came into view as it searched for field mice that had bored a vast network of tunnels beneath the snow in their quest for weed seeds.

• • •

When the spring thaw came and the frost left the ground, the terrain firmed. Heavy equipment could operate without becoming mired in mud. It was then that the Russians launched a tremendous offensive. Initially, the German lines held, but with thirty days of round-the-clock shelling, countless numbers of tanks, and hordes of Russian infantry pressing them, they were forced to retreat. The Russians, however, paid a very heavy price. In some places the ground was littered with so many casualties the advancing troops had to pick their way through the piles of dead and dying. Erich's riflemen and machine gunners, under his calm, knowledgeable leadership, laid down deadly volleys of crossfire that, time and again, destroyed entire attacking units.

By the time the offensive had lost its momentum, the German troops had consumed the meager stockpile they had accumulated for the spring offensive. They were unable to launch a counterattack. Artillery shells had become rationed and tanks broke down, but promised repair parts did not arrive. And the *Luftwaffe* showed less often and in fewer numbers when called upon for help. Erich realized that the bombing of Germany's industrial complex by the American and British heavy bombers had created a drastic problem for equipment and supplies for the front.

The replacements he was receiving to fill the gaps in the ranks were so very young and inexperienced, just boys of seventeen and eighteen. They wore uniforms their immature bodies could not fill, reminding him of Maria's brother, George. He took extra care to give them as much advice and information as he could before sending them into direct enemy action. By personally leading small numbers on patrols, something he would not normally do, he demonstrated how to string concertina wire, plant mines, and establish night listening posts in no-man's-land. His aim was to create a confidence in themselves and a respect for him so they would not break and run when the multitudes of Russians launched one of their furious charges.

• • •

As the summer progressed, they continued to be rolled back across the flat, fertile plains in a series of thrusts by massive concentrations of Russian troops and artillery. When they attempted a counterattack, they were overwhelmed by an enemy that grew in strength as they grew progressively weaker. And now, the decimated *Luftwaffe* gave only token support. The barrels of their supporting howitzers were so badly worn that their accuracy was no longer reliable, occasionally dropping shells so short they landed among Erich's hard-pressed troops. Within his company, replacement barrels for machine guns had not arrived for several weeks. The ones in use no longer had the range or accuracy needed for effective operation. The situation was such that Erich felt hopelessly frustrated in any attempt to rally the morale and enthusiasm of his company.

• • •

It was late in September 1944, with a cold drizzle falling from a overcast sky, that Erich had his company dig their foxholes in another defensive position. This time, however, they had withdrawn to the foothills of the Carpathian Mountains. In consultation with other company commanders of his battalion, the position selected was along the crests of a series of small, tree-covered elevations. The land behind them rose in a progressive sequence of rises and ridges to a considerable height. Before them they could see for miles across the flat wheat fields. They were entrenched in a stand of slender birch and aspen interspersed with a sprinkling of oak. The trees had retained most of their leaves, but were taking on the gold and red of fall.

"Well, Guenther, at least here you've got more than a blade of grass to hide behind," Erich observed as he looked down at a perspiring lad digging in the yellow soil.

"Yes, sir," replied the youth, pausing to wipe his brow. "But the roots and rocks make it a lot harder to dig."

Guenther Weigel was one of two sons of a cobbler in Rostock. Since the oldest son, Sergeant Albert, had been killed in the far-off Caucasus Mountains near Grozny, Guenther began learning his father's trade as a cobbler. A tall, slender, wiry young man, he was expected to take over the small business establishment when his father retired. Upon becoming seventeen, however, he was conscripted into the army, given six weeks training at Hofgeismar, and then shipped to the front. He had come in as a replacement shortly after Erich had taken over as company commander. Almost immediately, Erich noticed that Guenther had a keen sense of distance and direction in locating groups of Russian troops. This made him very adept at leading night patrols into enemy territory.

Initially Erich led the two and three man patrols, always taking Guenther along. They probed behind enemy lines to gather information about amounts and locations of men and equipment. On occasion they set explosives to destroy a gun or bunker. And sometimes they captured a prisoner to take back to battalion headquarters for interrogation. When leading these forays, Erich noted that Guenther moved with the quietness and cunningness of a cat, frequently slipping up behind an enemy sentry to place a loop of piano wire around the enemy soldier's neck and drawing it tight. This did away with the sentry in a very efficient, noiseless manner. After two weeks, Erich placed young Private Weigel in charge of patrols.

To Erich it was a pleasant respite to be snugly entrenched, knowing they were well protected by the mountains behind and could see every movement of the enemy for miles before them. If only they had ample shells for the howitzers and the *Luftwaffe* was available in strength to assist. Then they could defend this position with a minimum effort.

• • •

Maria continued the dismal task of serving her daily shifts, aiding and comforting the young men of her generation. As the steady flow of thousands passed through the 66th Evacuation Hospital without end, her enthusiasm waned, but she continued to give a maximum effort to the task. And now that German troops were retreating on all fronts, she questioned the wisdom of continuing the useless slaughter. But she realized her opinions were of no consequence to those in control, so she continued to do her best in a silent, solemn way. Her friends, Salli and Pauline, were considerably more lighthearted about the situation. Of course, they had no immediate family old enough to serve on the battlefront, so they did their best to raise her spirits between letters from her mother, Erich, and George.

During the summer of 1944, she had a leave of two weeks to visit home and to rest. As she traveled, she was appalled at the damage she observed in Munich. The rail depot was in a complete state of ruin, so she had to disembark and walk several hundred yards to catch another train. Several fires were burning in nearby areas of the city, and there was the constant braying of emergency vehicles as they attempted to find their way through the rubble-filled streets. Some people carrying all their possessions in carts or on their backs were trying to leave. Others probed the ruins in search of loved ones. In some places, a wreath or flowers had been placed on a heap of rubble, giving mute testimony about the fate of its occupants.

After seeing the damage in Munich and Regensburg, she realized how fortunate she was that her mother lived in little, out-of-the-way, inconsequential Holzheim. Once there, however, she saw that her mother's health had slipped considerably. Although Ilsa Juergens continued to work diligently at the post office, her puffiness, pallid color, and difficulty breathing disturbed Maria.

Maria walked the streets slowly, inhaling the clean, fresh air filled with the sweet scent of lilac blooms, the fruity aroma of wine grapes, and the pleasant smell of ripe apples. Stoically apprehensive about the war, she had to force a smile when she met someone. All the young men had gone to war, and older men were being conscripted. And now the Americans were at the western border. When she entered the Stecker store for another visit, Mrs. Stecker was sitting on a chair behind the counter. Upon seeing Maria, she rose to her feet and said, "Let's go to the cemetery."

After locking the store, they strolled up the street past the church entrance. As they passed, Maria studied the heavy, carved, wooden doors, remembering the many times she and Erich had entered them to attend Mass. Behind the church they stood, side by side, silently looking down at the gold lettering on the shiny, black marble tombstone:

August Stecker
1894-1944
Rest in Peace

After standing quietly for a full minute, Mrs. Stecker mumbled, "Murdered. Murdered by the Nazis." She opened her purse, took out a white handkerchief with a black border, and dabbed at her eyes. "He had no business in Munich, but they ordered him to go." Tears dropped to the ground as she wiped her eyes and nose.

Maria placed an arm around her shoulders and led her away. They took a few steps and then Mrs. Stecker stopped. She carefully folded the handkerchief and put it back into her purse. After taking a few more steps, she stopped again and looked up into Maria's face. "And they continue murdering our sons and brothers. We don't need more land or more slaves. The people of Holzheim were just fine before the war."

They sauntered along the tree-lined path that ran beside the little stream and past the town park. Maria looked at the shrubs along the stream bank and the verdant grass that covered the area. It was here, when she and Erich were children, that they had discovered the strange bond of mental telepathy that existed between them. When she thought of something and was about to tell him about it, he would suddenly speak about it. And later, he told her he had often experienced the same thing with her.

When she came to a fallen chestnut leaf, she pushed it aside with her shoe to reveal a shiny, brown chestnut it had covered. She smiled as she recalled her father telling a friend to always carry one in his pants pocket. He called it a buckeye. "Keeps you from getting rheumatism," he advised.

Mrs. Stecker broke the silence. "What do you do in the hospital?" she asked.

"I'm a surgical ward nurse," Maria answered. "I tend soldiers who have been wounded or injured."

"Are there other kinds of nurses?"

"Yes. There are some medical ward nurses. They tend those who are sick."

"And do some work in the operating room?" Mrs. Stecker asked, stopping to look at her.

"Not in our hospital," Maria replied. "That is done with highly trained male surgical technicians." She was grateful for that.

Their conversation was interrupted by noisy youngsters intently playing a variety of games, including the game of war. *Oh*, shuddered Maria, *if they knew what war was really like they would not show such enthusiasm.*

• • •

It was mid-October when the commandant of the 66th Evacuation Hospital received orders to evacuate all patients to the interior of Germany and prepare the hospital, including equipment and staff, for withdrawal. Within a week all patients had been removed, including those in the ten wards at the far end of the compound. And the staff packed and crated the ward tents. Tents used for staff quarters and the kitchen would be left intact until transportation arrived.

It was then that Maria received a letter from her mother. In a brief, simple sentence it stated that George had been killed in Poland. Accompanying the note was a letter she had received from the division chaplain. George had been wounded in the stomach with a machine gun burst near the city of Bialystok. He died eight days later in a field hospital and was buried in a military cemetery by the village of Zambro.

After reading the letter, she sat on her cot in dry-eyed sorrow and examined the accompanying photograph. It showed a row of white wooden crosses, the one in the foreground being that of her brother. On its face, in carefully lettered black, was an inscription:

Corporal George Juergens
309th Infantry Grenadier Regiment
27-5-26   14-8-44

She was staring blankly across the tent, still fingering the picture, when Salli and Pauline entered. They sensed her grief and scanned the photograph, which she readily handed to them. Realizing that tragedy had indeed struck, they sat on either side and placed their arms about her in a sympathetic gesture. A flood of tears suddenly poured from Maria's eyes as she sobbed uncontrollably.

After several minutes, she stopped crying. "I think I would like to go for a walk alone," she said softly.

They helped her into her coat, and she walked slowly out of the tent and down the narrow, gravel path.

The hospital was reestablished near a small village just inside the border of Germany. This time, however, much to Maria's satisfaction, it did not have the ten isolated wards for the hopeless cases. It served as an intermediate resting place for the sick and wounded who were to be distributed to hospitals near their homes. Although she worked the same long hours as before, she worked with renewed vigor. She was back in Germany, the isolation wards had been eliminated, and the war was approaching an end. Although Germany was losing, she felt a burning desire to end the conflict, to halt the killing, maiming, and suffering, and to bring her Erich back safely to her. Regardless of the outcome of the war, she felt certain the two of them could settle somewhere and begin a wonderful life that would be the epitome of love and happiness.

• • •

Late in February 1945, Maria returned to her tent to find a letter from the mayor of Holzheim. It stated her mother had quietly passed away in her sleep a month before and, after a funeral Mass, was buried in the church cemetery beside her father. Her neighbors had covered the doors and windows of her home with boards, and the people of Holzheim would take care of it until she returned.

She sat down on her cot, folded her arms, and placed her elbows on her knees. She stared at the duckboard floor and tried to cry, but tears would not come. Once again, she felt betrayed by Fate, damnable Fate. Fate had provided her with parents who grew up in an orphanage, depriving her of aunts, uncles, cousins, and grandparents. Fate had taken her young brother, George, into the army where he was killed in Poland. And now, Fate had taken her mother.

Although saddened, she received the news without showing passion or feeling, having become accustomed to death and sorrow in her work. Yes, she loved her mother dearly and appreciated everything Mrs. Juergens had done for her and George. But, she rationalized, the ailing woman was better off, relieved of the pain and suffering she had endured for the past few years. She regretted not being notified in time to attend the funeral, but she realized, of course, that all communication and transportation had been badly disrupted.

Feeling so terribly alone in her solitude, she decided to turn to God. Kneeling on the rough duckboard floor, she placed her elbows on the cot, crossed herself, clasped her hands tightly, and then silently prayed for the repose of the souls of her mother, father, and brother George. Then she prayed for the others she knew who had passed on. She reviewed her life in Holzheim and prayed forgiveness for any offense she might have committed. When she thought of Erich, she shuddered and prayed for an end to the war and his safe return. He was all she had left in this violent, turbulent world.

Speaking softly, she pleaded, "Oh, Lord. Please hear my prayers. I feel so help-less and alone." After a full minute of silent meditation, she crossed herself and rose to her feet.

When she got into bed, she clasped her pillow and pulled it against her face and chest. When she closed her eyes, the tears came, a few drops at first, and then a flood.

• • •

In the Carpathian Mountains, Erich's company of young warriors felt secure in the defensive positions to which they had retreated. Observation of enemy movements was hindered only by the haze of distance. Each time a concen-tration of enemy action was spotted, artillery and mortar fire was called to rake the area. On two separate occasions, the Russians had attempted assaults using masses of infantry and tanks. When the German artillery spot-ters saw the long lines approaching like osmosis in a giant tree trunk, they blanketed it with fire. With the Russians weakened effectiveness, Erich's company of riflemen and machine gunners found it easy to repel them.

But tree bursts were serious threats to his troops. On the flat steppe, artillery fire had to land very near an entrenched soldier to harm him since shrapnel flies upward and outward. When shells hit the tree branches, how-ever, they rained the deadly pieces of flying, hot steel down upon soldiers who were not protected. As a counter measure, Erich had his men cover their holes with a layer of logs cut from nearby trees.

The division commanders, snug in their bunkers, thought they could spend the winter in this location. They were certain they could repel any Russian attacks since food and equipment, now coming over shorter supply lines, was arriving in nearly adequate quantity. The first frosts arrived, killing bothersome gnats and mosquitoes, and sweaters donated by German civilians were distributed. Leaves on the trees turned to bright gold and flaming red and then began to fall, initially a few each day and then in great numbers. As the leaves flipped and tumbled on their way to the ground, an occasional bee or butterfly passed on its final search for food before winter's snow came. In the meantime, most birds and animals had fled to higher elevations and hid among the dense evergreens to escape the thunder of battle.

Shortly after the first snowfall, an urgent message crackled over the divi-sion headquarters radio. The Russians had penetrated German lines with an armored spearhead some distance to the south. The order was given for the division to abandon its position and withdraw to the other side of the moun-tains. Since gasoline was very scarce, horses, mules, and donkeys were used to move everything from the division's records to heavy howitzers. As the long columns wound their way up and down the narrow, crooked, snow-covered roads, Erich looked at the company of fuzzy-faced youngsters behind him and wondered how the Russians could possibly be stopped. Since he was certain the war could not be won, he hoped a negotiated peace could be arranged.

The Russians must not be allowed to enter Germany. His countrymen, especially Maria, must be spared the vicious abuses that had been committed against the citizens of Poland when they took the eastern half of the country in 1939. The Poles had reported that the Russians had gang-raped every female from the age of eight to eighty.

When they dug in along the rich valleys before Budapest, the division's strength was considerably diminished. It had lost great quantities of equipment and supplies. Some could not be carried because of lack of transport, but many of the wagons and heavy guns had slipped off the icy mountain roads, tumbling from great heights carrying their attached beasts of burden with them. The hope of obtaining more was dashed when higher headquarters informed the commander that none was available.

The Russians, sensing victory, attacked in waves, forcing Erich's company to begrudgingly give ground. Twice he led his men against an approaching tank. They killed the accompanying infantry and then jammed a short log in the tread. He climbed upon the stalled vehicle, pried open the hatch, and then tossed a grenade into it. However, the Russian superiority in numbers and the devastating artillery fire that pulverized the frozen earth gradually forced a retreat across the Danube and beyond Budapest.

In the early morning hours of Friday, March 9, 1945, an order to counterattack was issued by the commanding general. Erich's company, recently reinforced and entrenched in a grove of barren hardwood trees, checked their weapons. Then they waited for the preliminary artillery bombardment to begin. One third of the young soldiers had not engaged in an attack. And most had a totally blank page twenty-three in their paybook under the heading of "Previous Actions." There was to be no support from tanks, so the infantry would have to bear the burden of the attack.

The temperature was slightly above freezing. Most of the snow had melted, but a mere fraction of an inch of ground had thawed. Erich was huddled in a foxhole with Guenther as the final rounds of the artillery barrage hissed, sizzled, and screamed overhead, landing in a crescendo of explosive crashes a short distance ahead. He squinted at the luminous dial of his wristwatch and noted there were two minutes before he would order his company to charge across an open field and into a grove of evergreens that hid the entrenched Russians.

When the artillery fire halted, he slapped Guenther on the back. "Ready to go?"

"I'm with you, Captain," came the determined reply.

"All right! Let's go!" Erich shouted as he left the foxhole, waving his arm for others to follow.

Looking ahead, he could barely discern the black outline of the ever-greens that loomed in the misty distance. Others to his left and right were rushing forward in a low crouch. When they were within a few yards of the moisture-laden pines and spruces, the Russians began firing. But the momentum of the charge carried the leading wave into the trees, where they shot and bayoneted the confused defenders.

By the time Erich got his men regrouped, it was light enough to see that the Russians had merely retreated to the other side of the grove and were digging in again. Then mortar shells began to rain down, most detonated by hitting upper branches of the trees above the fuzzy-faced German troopers. In addition to showering them with shrapnel, the shells caused large quantities of tree limbs and foliage to fall, eliminating visual contact with each other. In a few minutes the ground was covered with several feet of dense debris.

As quickly as it began, the barrage stopped. Then the Russians counterattacked. For several minutes a nightmare of stalking and killing ensued. Erich, seeing his company being consumed in this quagmire, ordered them forward out of the blinding confusion.

"Forward! Forward!" he bellowed, waving his arms. "Advance! Advance!"

He ran forth, fighting his way through the tangle of branches, shooting two Russians as he went. When he emerged from the defoliated area, he continued to yell. Then he saw two of his sergeants emerge, yelling to the troopers of their command. Quickly, they charged on, halting to take defensive positions facing front and rear. When all had emerged into the next clearing, the overrun enemy laid down their arms and surrendered.

It was then that they discovered a second line of enemy entrenched a hundred yards ahead in line of deciduous hardwoods. After firing several rifle grenades, Erich ordered his men forward across the field. Halfway across, enemy fire became intense. He ordered them to drop to the prone position. The field, wet and muddy, was covered with a crop of unharvested cabbage that was had been reduced to rows of rotted mush. As they inched their way forward, their clothing became impregnated with an odor most foul.

Guenther was near Erich, so the two of them lobbed hand grenades as they crawled forward. A few of the enemy retreated. As the two men continued to crawl forward, however, the retreat gained impetus. Soon Erich's company was into the grove of barren trees. Guenther's actions reminded him of his days with the *Afrika Korps* when he and Heinz had used the same tactic.

After making certain the wounded were being tended by a medic, Erich decided to scout the forward terrain. Noting many of his men were lying prone using grass and leaves to wipe away the mud and cabbage, he turned to Guenther. "Keep me covered," he ordered.

Guenther nodded.

Walking in a low crouch, he moved forward to the crest of a rise and then dropped down to observe. *This place*, he thought, *was little different from Holzheim.* Here, no man needed to be lonely if trees were his friends. The towering oaks and beeches stood like guardians above the younger trees. For a few moments he simply wished the war would go away. A few months ago the ground was shaded and the interlocking branches above met to form arched cathedral aisles, but now all was open. When the winter sun shone, it formed blue-gray shadows, warmed the bark, and revealed delicate textures and patterns.

A sudden movement a hundred yards ahead brought him back to the reality of war. Squinting for a better view, he felt the breath of a bullet as it hissed past his cheek. An instant later, he heard the report of the shot. He saw fallen leaves jumping about, and twigs were dropping from low-hanging limbs, followed by the sound of ripping canvas. Bark was flying from the tree trunks just a few inches above ground level. He knew a machine gunner had located him and was raking the area.

Unable to move, he flattened himself against the ground, pressing his cheek against the soft cushion of leaves. When he heard a quick sequence of popping sounds followed by the hum of the machine gun, he knew that bullets were passing a few inches above his head. There was nothing he could do but wait for help. A play of wind cooled the wetness on his face as he hugged the ground and breathed through his mouth.

A few minutes later, he heard the sharp crack of a Mauser rifle. Help had come. Then came the explosion of a grenade followed by two more rifle shots.

"I got him, Captain. You can move.

It was Guenther. He had maneuvered into a position so he could knock out the machine gun.

• • •

The next day the company worked its way through a small, wooded plot. A short distance beyond, they saw a small group of farm buildings. Erich halted his men and ordered them to spread out and conceal themselves behind a vine-covered stone fence. He then told Guenther to lead a three-man patrol to see if any Russians were there. Under leaden skies, with Guenther in the lead, the patrol trotted off across a small pasture field, hoping the buildings had been abandoned.

After covering barely a hundred yards, the three men were cut down by a machine gun hidden in an upper loft of a small barn. Although the three men dropped to the ground wounded, the machine continued to fire, concentrating on one of them. The young trooper gripped the frozen sod and, yelling as his body curled and quivered, cried out. He begged for mercy and, whimpering, asked God for forgiveness.

Erich ordered the rest of the company to riddle the buildings with rifle and machine gun fire. In a few minutes, tracer bullets had set them on fire. Erich vaulted the stone fence and dashed to where the patrol lay. Lying beside Guenther, he looked at the lightly bearded face and saw the eyes were closed. A bloody froth bubbled from the young trooper's parted lips as he gasped for breath. Erich removed his helmet and brushed his hand across Guenther's face. "Hang in there," he said, yelling to be heard above the din of battle as the rest of the company rushed past. "The medic is coming."

Guenther opened his eyes. "What will Mother and Father do now?" he asked. When the medic arrived, Erich noticed his face had paled and his eyes were beginning to glaze over.

Suddenly, a concentrated salvo of mortar shells dropped around them. Tremendous explosions creating bright orange flashes drove stinging soil and small particles of shrapnel beneath their skin surface. The larger pieces of hot metal mixed with frozen clods of earth flew upward and outward, and great pressures from the explosions pummeled the men's bodies. Initially, their bodies were severely compressed and then the partial vacuum that followed caused them to expand. This action broke their belts and split the seams of their boots and clothing. Twice, in an attempt to get up, Erich rose to his feet. Each time, however, he fell back onto the ground. In a few minutes unconsciousness overcame him, and he remained motionless on the torn pasture field with members of the patrol.

• • •

When Erich opened his eyes, he realized he was in a bed. He suddenly remembered the words of Corporal Strausmann during basic training at Camp Schwartzenborn. "Every time you wake up, you don't move a muscle until you verify your surroundings! Every time! Do you understand that, Stecker?" He could almost hear the echo in his ears.

His tongue and throat were dry. He must have been breathing through his mouth. He closed his mouth, generated some saliva, and swallowed. Without moving his head, he rolled his eyes to their maximum extent in every direction. He was in a small ward filled with battle casualties, some groaning in pain, others babbling incoherently. All appeared to be German soldiers, but he continued to watch for additional signs. A young man wearing a short white coat over his *Wehrmacht* uniforms came down the aisle.

Erich raised his hand. The hurrying young man halted and looked down at him questioningly.

"Where are we?" Erich asked.

"In a hospital," the orderly replied with a sigh.

"German?"

"Yes, of course."

"Thank you."

The orderly shrugged and then moved on.

Although his entire body was very sore, he found he could move, so Erich sat up in his cot. He located a heavy bandage on his right thigh and found a large portion of his body was covered with a measles-like eruption. A foul taste filled his mouth and his chest gurgled as he breathed.

A nurse dressed in green jacket and trousers came over to him. "Good afternoon," she said, forcing a smile.

"Hello, nurse," he replied, looking up at her.

"You should not be sitting up."

"I feel fine." There was a noticeable gurgle.

"Just lie down. The doctor is coming."

A few minutes later a medical officer came by and sat on the edge of his cot. He was an older man with a shock of steel gray hair that matched the color of his neatly trimmed mustache. There was a touch of rose color in his shiny, pouched cheeks. "Nice to see you awake," he began. "You had a long sleep."

"Oh?" Erich replied, surprise showing on his face. "What day is this?"

"Monday. The twelfth."

Erich looked puzzled, but said nothing. He had been unconscious for two days.

"How do you feel?" asked the doctor.

"A bit sore."

"You apparently were very near an explosion," explained the doctor. "Your back and arms have a lot of fine particles of metal just beneath the skin. They'll probably all work out in a week or two."

"What about my leg?" Erich pointed to his thigh.

"There was a large piece of shrapnel in it, so we removed it." He paused briefly, feeling Erich's pulse and forehead. "You obviously inhaled some of the gas from the explosion. Your lungs have a bit of fluid in them." He stood and smiled. "You'll be all right; though." Then he walked off

• • •

Late in March, Erich arrived at the 66th Evacuation Hospital. After a brief discussion with the hospital commandant, he was assigned to Maria's ward. In addition, he would stay at the hospital until he was well enough to go back to the front. The way the war was going, both he and Maria felt the war would be over before he had to return to action.

As the days passed, the rough skin condition disappeared and the lung congestion subsided. Although his thigh was still bandaged, he knew it was but a matter of time before it would be healed. And when he was issued a new uniform, he took it to a tailor in the nearby village of Freikirchen to be altered for a better fit. Life was good. He was pleased.

The weather had become mild—spring had arrived and summer was not far away. The snow was gone and signs of new life were everywhere. Maria, depressed during the past few months, was feeling more contented as she and Erich, during the early evening hours, strolled in a nearby woodland. She had even discussed marriage with him, and he agreed. The war certainly would be over soon, and there was a good possibility he would not have to return to the front.

One evening as they left the ward tent, she took him by the hand. "Come with me," she said. "I want to show you something."

When they arrived at her quarters, she stopped in front of the footlocker at the lower end of her bed. Lifting the lid, she carefully removed the wedding dress and held it up in front of her.

Erich stared in disbelief "When did you get that?" he asked, reaching out to touch it.

"A couple weeks after you left Camp Reichstein." Then she added, "It'll need a little pressing, but I can take care of that."

"Good God!" He exclaimed in utter astonishment.

"Do you like it?" She asked, a wrinkle forming across her brow.

"Certainly! It's the ultimate!" he assured her. "How about July in the Ulm Cathedral? It has the tallest church spire in the world." He remembered what she had told him.

She placed the dress on her cot and they embraced.

"'Mrs. Erich Stecker,'" she whispered. "It sounds so naturally perfect."

• • •

As they strolled along a country lane admiring the budding trees and singing birds, a gust of wind warned them of a rapidly approaching thunder storm. They ran to a small barn, located a few hundred yards beyond a local farmhouse just as the first large drops of rain began to splat against the clapboard siding of the little building The barn had been used for storage of hay and straw, but after the long winter, only a small amount remained in the a loft.

"Let's go up and watch the rain from the open door up there," Erich suggested, pointing to the loft.

Maria made a dash for the ladder. Erich, standing at the base of the ladder, discreetly turned away until she reached the top. Then she turned and urged him to hurry.

They lay for some time near the open door, watching the rain come down. Then Erich rolled her over on her back and kissed her. A few minutes later, Erich slipped his hand beneath her skirt and caressed first her thighs and then her stomach. In a sudden move that surprised him, she reached down and removed her panties.

"Better?" she asked in a whisper.

"Yes," he replied.

The rain was falling softly on the shingled roof overhead with the sound of a hundred purring kittens as he felt the softness of her abdomen, the tenderness of her thighs, and the silkiness of her fine, curly hair. As her breathing became more rapid, he kissed her neck and ears. Then his finger located the fibrous button and began a circular massage that made her sigh audibly. She stiffened and grasped his head, forcing him to look into her the eyes.

"I want you," she whispered forcibly. "Not your finger. You."

"Are you sure?" he questioned.

"Yes," she replied, nodding her head emphatically.

He removed his tunic and slipped it beneath her hips. When he positioned himself, he could feel resistance from the small, elastic opening.

"It will hurt," he warned in a tone of uncertainty.

"I don't mind," she assured him.

The image of her white wedding dress flashed across his mind. He quickly raised himself from her and pulled her skirt down. Then he fell upon her, hugging and kissing her about the face. "I just can't bring myself to do it, my darling," he stated.

"Please. Erich," she begged.   "I want it."

"We must wait."

After the shower had passed, they slowly walked arm-in-arm back to the hospital.

• • •

Dawn broke early with the sun rising clear and bright, giving promise to a beautiful spring day. Showers two days before had bathed the land, rinsing the tender new leaves and grass to a shiny green and washing away the countryside's leftover winter grime. Maria had started her shift as usual at six o'clock, taking care of the routine chore of completing the charts on temperatures, pulse rates, and bowel movements. Since it was Sunday, she finished items requiring her attention and then placed the ward on a self-help basis so she could attend ten o'clock services in Freikirchen. She and Erich, in their dress uniforms, ate a leisurely breakfast. Then, after checking her ward, they walked a short mile to the village church. Several dozen others, staff and patients, joined them at the solidly built stone structure. Together with the villagers, Mass was heard by a full-capacity crowd.

Emerging from the church, they stepped out into the warm sun and sweet spring air that was much like that in Holzheim. Erich took Maria by the hand, and they slowly walked around the square in front of the church, looking at meager displays in the store windows. They then started back along the narrow macadam road, leaving many from the hospital chatting with the priest and villagers in front of the church. Maria felt extremely contented as she strolled along holding Erich's arm, sometimes talking, other times looking at the grazing cattle, flitting birds, and puffs of fluffy clouds in the azure sky. Although there were vapor trails from a flight of high-flying bombers to the north, the war seemed remote to Maria. A faint smile graced her lips, something that had not been present for many months. She hugged Erich's arm, closed her eyes and sighed, "Oh, I love you so."

"I love you too, my darling," he replied, turning her head with his hand so he could look into her eyes.

"You're all I have, you know."

"I hope I'm worthy."

With the suddenness of an earthquake, they heard the tremendous roar of a powerful engine from behind mixed with the staccato of a machine gun. Pieces of asphalt spewed up all around them. Instinctively, Erich gave Maria a hard shove to the earth before dropping down beside her. Looking up, he saw a big, red star on the underside of the plane as it climbed skyward before them. Then he noticed a row of small, white parachutes a few feet off the ground stretched out behind them. One was directly overhead. He moved in an attempt to shield her, but before he could, the small bomb beneath it touched down and exploded. The Russian pilot, seeing the line of people along the little road, had made a practice run, using his machine guns and tiny antipersonnel bombs.

Erich opened his eyes to find he had been tossed into a ditch and was entangled in some wire. Although dazed, he looked over to see the still form of Maria lying on the road. As quickly as possible, he undid the restraining wire and rushed to her side. Her left leg had been severed high on the hip and a torrent of blood was gushing forth. Digging beneath the collar of his tunic, he located his identification disk cord, tore it free from his neck, and quickly fashioned a tourniquet. Time and again he tried to apply it, but it merely slid off the slippery, jagged flesh.

In a desperate state of hopeless frustration, he seized the end of the femoral artery, then cradled her head in the crook of his arm. Although her eyes opened once momentarily, she uttered no sound. In a few minutes, it was over.

He looked down at her parted lips and partially opened eyes and then, ignoring her severed leg, gathered her into his arms. He placed his cheek against her yet warm face and, oblivious to the cries and moans of those about him, began trotting toward the hospital. Although he said nothing, tears streaming profusely from his eyes, ran down his cheeks, across her face, and onto the ground.

• • •

Maria's friends, Salli and Pauline, clothed her in a dress uniform and enhanced her pale cheeks and lips with a touch of color before placing her in a plain, knotty-pine coffin. Then Erich looked at her one last time before the lid was fastened down. The next day the coffin was loaded aboard an ambulance and a short cortege of canvas-covered trucks, filled with friends from the hospital, wound its way along a narrow, macadam road to Traunstein. With sad eyes and a drawn face, Erich rode beside the ambulance driver.

The column of vehicles entered the walled section of the ancient city, rolled past the busy market square, and exited through another medieval gate. It descended into the newer section of homes, crossed an old iron bridge that spanned a meandering river, and then climbed a crooked trail to the crest of a bill. There, in a newly established military cemetery, Maria was carried to a plot and placed on support straps over a freshly dug hole located among other fallen brothers-in-arms.

The hospital chaplain offered a brief prayer, and then the coffin was lowered into the hole. As it descended, a sudden message surged into Erich's mind. He could hear it. "We were betrayed by Fate, and Time has cheated us, my eternal love." He knew it was from Maria. She was communicating with the extrasensory telepathy that existed between them since they were children.

As the hollow thud of shovelfuls of soil echoed in his ears, Erich walked slowly back to the ambulance. He stood for a long moment, his hand on the door latch, and looked at the walled city situated on high ground across the slow-moving river. Then he climbed into the vehicle for the sad return ride to the hospital.

He spent a second sleepless night searching the far reaches of his mind for answers to questions about reasons for the turn of events. He had neither the stamina nor the spirit to continue fighting the war. But memories of Maria would not permit him to remain at the hospital, and his conscience would not permit him to return to Holzheim. Since he did not care to eat breakfast, he dressed carefully and went to the office of Colonel Heinrich

Grosskopf, hospital commandant. The sympathetic colonel listened as he explained why he would like to return to active duty.

"We can send you to another hospital, Captain," the colonel offered.

"No. I wish to go back to the front," Erich replied solemnly.

"I'll arrange for it right away," Grosskopf replied, shaking his head. He reached into the top drawer of his desk and withdrew a photograph. Handing it to Erich, he continued, "I thought you might want this."

It was a photograph of Maria's grave. Erich slowly read the inscription on the white cross.

Nurse Maria C. Juergens
66th Evacuation Hospital
5-11-23   8-4-45

That afternoon, Erich climbed into the back of a truck with several other soldiers. They were taken to Vienna. He was placed in charge of a small contingent of troopers who were being organized as part of the defense of the city. Most were either very young or very old. The remainder were returning wounded veterans, some still heavily bandaged.

A few days later they were surrounded, overwhelmed, and disarmed by hordes of Russians, many with almond eyes and high cheek bones. The conquerors swarmed over the city in an orgy of pillaging. As he walked through the city in a long line of prisoners, he saw the civilian population being pushed, beaten, and bullied by the rampaging armed soldiers and could hear the screams and cries for help from women being gang-raped by the barbaric victors. He was glad Maria would not have to be subjected to such cruelty.

•   •   •

Late in May, he was released. Since all civilian transport was down and the victorious military were forbidden to give German soldiers a ride, he began the long trek home. A pathetic sight, indeed, for the once proud, dynamic officer of the elite Death Head Brigade, a unit considered invincible—a unit consumed completely in the battle of Stalingrad. He was forced to beg for food from peasant farmers in villages through which he passed. Frequently, he was stopped by a mother whose son was missing on the eastern front. She would describe him and his unit and then show a photograph of the young man in uniform. Such pitiful sights gnawed at his heart, but he could only shake his head and state that he was sorry he could not help.

He hurried through cities and towns of larger size, for they were islands of ruin and destruction. And there was much starvation, death, and disease.

Often he was looked upon with scorn, blamed for losing the war and creating the horrible catastrophe of a proud country. At the last checkpoint in Regensburg, he learned that Holzheim was in the American sector. He was grateful for that. "Any troops stationed there?" he asked the American sentry standing guard on the bridge.

"No," the American replied as he motioned for the next person to show identification.

The last mile was the most difficult. It brought to mind the many things that meant so much to him. He remembered the many happy times when he had traveled it before—how anxious he was to get home and see his family and loved ones, or so proud when he and Maria walked it together in their trim uniforms. There were also the times he rode with Max Dorten and Mr. Trapp and the many times he strode it alone, observing the marvels of nature, hearing the sounds of the forests, and smelling the refreshing odors of the countryside.

Reflecting, he stopped and looked down at himself, a battered hulk, confused and restless. His uniform was torn and threadbare and he wore no socks, so straw stuffed in his jackboots kept the abrasive surface of the road from scuffing the balls of his feet raw. His main concern, however, was how he would be received in Holzheim.

As he entered town, a small, barking dog came at him and then ran along behind, nipping at his heels. Some children playing nearby, most not old enough to remember him, looked up at the noise and then continued with their game.

He went directly to the church, pulled open the heavy oak door, and walked to the foremost pew. There he knelt, alternately praying and meditating, for half an hour before feeling satisfied to leave. When he approached the rear of the dimly lighted house of worship, Father Kurz, who had been kneeling at the last pew, rose to meet him.

"Welcome home, my son," he said, extending his right hand to Erich while placing his left hand on the soldier's shoulder.

"Thank you, Father Kurz. It's nice to be back."

"I saw you enter the church, so I came to pray with you."

"Thank you," Erich replied humbly. "I appreciate that."

"I suppose you are anxious to go," the priest concluded. "Drop by again sometime when we can talk."

"I will."

He made his way past the little post office building, now operated by a stranger, and on to the Juergen's house. Standing before it, he looked at the weathered porch and the boarded windows and door. The lawn and garden, once carefully tended, grew a profusion of weeds. He mounted the porch, by habit carefully avoiding the squeaky middle step, and peered through a space between two boards nailed across the front door. Inside, everything was as he had last remembered it—the couch, the rug, and the little vase on an end table that Maria had kept filled with flowers that George had grown in the garden. On top of the piano were three framed photographs. The center one was of Mr. and Mrs. Juergens. The two flanking it were pictures of their children dressed in military uniforms.

As he turned to leave, he looked down at the wooden steps and hesitated. Bending down, he sat on the top step as he had done so many times with Maria. Looking about, he realized everything had changed, and nothing would ever be the same again. Then he saw his mother rushing toward him. He rose and hurried to meet her.

Two days later, dressed in civilian clothing, he left Holzheim on a mission to Dinkelsbuhl. He had to fulfill a vow he had made to Heinz on the bank of the Volga. He must tell Irma how proud and happy Heinz was when he learned she was going to have his baby.

The Legacy—1971

The village of Holzheim has nearly returned to its former state of isolation where people still till the soil, cut wood, and tend cattle. The quiet tranquility that once prevailed, however, has been superceded by noise from tractors that have replaced horses and machines that have eliminated much of the back-breaking labor. But now one has to listen intently to hear the cackling of hens and the cooing of pigeons above the din and roar of mechanization. And the tantalizing scent of blossoms and ripening fruit has been tainted with exhaust fumes of internal combustion engines.

The barber, the blacksmith, the shoe repairman, and the butcher, all killed in the war, have been replaced by newcomers who were uprooted and evicted from the east. In addition to Erich Stecker, only Max Dorten returned from the war, and he has a shriveled right arm from a serious bayonet wound sustained in his biceps. He and his wife, Inge, along with their three sons, operate the Trapp farm. Mr. Trapp still lives there with them but does only light work such as feeding chickens and geese and picking a few grapes. Mostly he sits on a bench in front of the Stecker store, basking in the sun with a few of his friends, reminiscing about the war and complaining about the automobile traffic. And the elderly, arthritic Father Kurz is disappointed that many of the younger people do not attend Sunday Mass.

The Stecker store has changed little since Mrs. Stecker passed away in 1947. However, another general store has opened nearby, creating significant competition for the limping, aging Erich. Down the street, the Juergen's home has been occupied by a displaced family from East Prussia. The old, weathered porch was replaced by a new one, eliminating the squeaking middle step. Beyond the Trapp farm, six new houses have been constructed for German refugees ousted from the *Sudetenland*. On the far side of town a razor blade factory and brandy distillery have been built.

Each year on April 3, the Stecker store is closed while Erich makes his annual pilgrimage to Traunstein. Although he does not mention it, his customers have learned to expect it. The older ones have been aware of it since the end of the war, the newer inhabitants having been informed by whispered word of mouth. After closing the shutters and turning the key in the lock, he climbs aboard a bus for Regensburg. There he catches the train to Munich and then transfers to the Salzburg Express. When it stops at Siegdorf, he gets off and walks several miles over the narrow macadam road to Traunstein. By the time the sun has set, he has checked into the Hotel Bavaria. Then he strolls down to the empty market square, where he eats a leisurely meal in the small *Golden Eiche Speisehaus*. On his way out, he buys a newspaper and then slowly makes his way back to the hotel along the narrow, winding cobblestone streets.

The next morning, after a continental breakfast in his room, he returns to the ancient market square. It is congested with wagons, carts, and booths of local vendors selling a variety of wares and produce. Seeking out a seller of flowers, he carefully selects a potted, profusely blooming white begonia.

Upon leaving the square, he passes through a tower gate in the old wall and descends the few blocks among the more modern houses. There he crosses the rusting iron bridge that spans the black water of the meandering Traun River. After ascending the asphalt path that winds its way around the hill to the neatly groomed cemetery, he stops at a small, covered stone monument to sign the register. Then he proceeds to the carefully arranged sections, each containing the graves of five hundred fallen dead. Quickly, he walks to the appropriate section and turns down one of its rows. Standing, he looks down momentarily at the flat, gray headstone before dropping to his knees. After gently nesting the potted begonia against the top of the headstone, he clasps his hands to pray.

The reverently tended cemetery is laid out in square sections separated by paths of rose-colored gravel. The thousands of graves, their white wooden crosses long since replaced by flush, rectangular stone markers and seeded with a lush coat of close-cropped grass, represents but a small portion of the eight million German servicemen killed in the war. A scattering of chestnut trees grows along the waist-high stone fence that encompasses the area and separates it from the surrounding fields. Each day visitors come, some to place flowers and wreaths on the graves of friends or relatives, others to merely wander up and down the rows of markers and read the inscriptions. All wear somber faces, tread lightly, and speak softly.

After Erich, silent but with lips moving, has offered his prayers for Maria, he listens for a message from her. But he hears nothing. Then he rises to his feet, hands clasped, and stands for a long while looking down at her grave. He reads the inscription aloud "Nurse Maria C. Juergens, 66th Evacuation Hospital, 5-11-23, 8-4-45." Tears run down his cheeks and drop onto her grave as he thinks of the many wonderful things they shared together and the plans and promises they had made. He has so many, many things he would like to tell her. He knows she is only six feet away, but he cannot communicate with her. Oh, how he would like to trade a thousand tomorrows for but one yesterday. Again, he is overcome by the finality of death.

Most of the day he spends at the cemetery, sometimes wandering about, looking at headstones and recalling various military units represented, but mostly sitting on a concrete bench in the warm sunshine looking over the area and reliving memories of the past. Twice during the day, he returns to the center of the city to eat, and then in the evening, he comes back to the cemetery.

He offers another prayer at Maria's grave, afterwards sitting on a bench at the head of one of the graveled paths. As the sun drops below the horizon and the stars begin lighting the landscape, dew moistens the surroundings, making them glisten in the soft, blue-white light. It is at this time that Erich sometimes sees her, coming down the path toward him, wearing her wedding dress. Although he likes to believe it is real, he knows it cannot be. The yellowing bridal gown, along with Maria's other personal possessions, remains in her gray footlocker in the large Office of Military Cemeteries warehouse in Kassel. And there it shall remain, for no living relative exists to claim it.

Numerous unclaimed heavy brown envelopes, canvas bags, and footlockers, some unidentified, have been stored on tiers of shelves. Stapled to the front of the shelf beneath Maria's footlocker is a yellowing identification strip of white cardboard. The stenciled black lettering merely states, "Maria C. Juergens, Krankenschwester, 66th Evacuation Hospital."

• • •

Gentle summer zephyrs make vast golden fields of ripening grain nod, bow, and dance on the undulating plains before Stalingrad. Taller, lush strips stand out to clearly identify filled ravines that once knifed across the area. Meadowlarks sing their enchanting song, mourning doves coo soulfully, and magpies scavenge the land. A few crows still haunt the area, but most have retreated to the fenced and forested places so they can perch and preen themselves while keeping a watchful eye on the surrounding countryside.

The city of Stalingrad, its name changed to Volgograd after the death of the despot dictator, Josef Stalin, has been cleared of the mountains of rubble that was the sole remaining heritage of a gigantic struggle, a fierce and savage battle unmatched in the history of warfare. It has been reconstructed in the modern form of concrete, steel, brick, and glass. Its streets have been resurfaced and the utility systems modernized and restored to satisfy the expanding needs for generations to come. Also covered are the ugly scars from incessant artillery and rocket barrages that once rained so freely from the skies. And the final two blocks on the downtown riverbank the Germans could not capture have become a museum, the battered remains of two concrete warehouses left as stark reminders of the ferocity of the struggle.

Children in blue and white uniforms stand shifts of perpetual guard before a small monument dedicated to Soviet military casualties suffered in the defense of the city. At the far end of the grassy plot, the only tree in the city to survive the battle struggles to have its small, battered trunk heal.

A short distance from the center of town looms the *Mamayev Kurgan*, the 335-foot domed hill that dominates the area. Soldiers of the German 71ˢᵗ and 94ᵗʰ Infantry Divisions knew it as "the mushroom of doom." For weeks it was a contested battleground that changed hands several times each day, its few acres littered with mutilated bodies and broken weapons of war and its soil so saturated with coagulated blood that it formed a putrid, ankle-deep paste. Upon its crest the Russian people have built a huge, white statue of Mother Russia. Beside it is an enclosed, marble-lined building with an eternal flame and walls inscribed with the names of thousands of Soviet soldiers, part of the million casualties who were sacrificed in the defense of Stalingrad.

Early autumn brings chilly winds, forewarning of the bitter, relentless cold that will descend upon the land and remain until late spring, halting all but the most necessary tasks. In winter, miles of open plains shorn of their harvest lie beneath a deep covering of fluffy snow. At night rabbits romp, play, and hunt for food in the ghostly blue-gray light of the moon as foxes and wolves stalk them. At times hoarfrost makes the heavy blanket sparkle and glimmer in a silent solitude that is absolute. Starlight from a brilliantly bejeweled purple canopy floods the fields in an eerie, iridescent luminescence.

Scattered throughout this flat, seemingly endless, barren land are the cemeteries, ravines, and ditches long since covered over and forgotten, wherein repose the remains of hundreds of thousands of brave warriors who rest in an everlasting sleep. Their exact locations are known but to God. And they have been forgotten by all but those who knew and loved them. They are the young men and women of yesterday denied the opportunity to leave a legacy in the generations of tomorrow. It is a legacy of descendants who will never be born, for they were never conceived in love-beds never lain in, because these warriors sleep forever beneath the cold, eternal, starlit skies of Stalingrad.